A Special Type of Torture

Andrew Robert Stoikes

A Special Type of Torture Publishing—Madison, WI
ISBN: 978-0-578-98370-7
Library of Congress Control Number: pending
Title: A Special Type of Torture
Author: Andrew Robert Stoikes
Digital distribution | 2021
Paperback | 2021

This is a work of fiction. The characters, names, incidents, places, and dialogue are products of the author's imagination, and are not to be construed as real.

Dedication

For my mother, I wish you could see the end of my story.

Chapter 1

It's a special type of torture, looking on, as someone you have loved and cared for fights a battle that cannot and will not be won. You sit up close and watch from afar as they breathe loudly, struggling for air. Over-hearing the oxygen machine release the building pressure as it beeps to a rhythm. You glance at the nurses and social workers coming in and out of your living room checking the machines, trying to give off consoling and polite vibes. Gazing down in a covered shock, you wonder what life will be like without them, and it scares the hell out of you.

Patrick sat on the edge of a high wooden chair, hunching over with elbows on his knees. He looked intensely over to his mother, who was lying in the bed he knew she would die in. He stared with a mix of anger, sorrow, and hazy shock that had taken months to manifest. The feelings constantly swirled and folded into each other, making Patrick feel a familiar floating sensation. He stared over to his mother, who was holding the stuffed horse she's been hugging for months. She always loved horses, and that tiny stuffed horse brought her a comfort that nothing else, not even Patrick could. She had glioblastoma, or brain cancer in non-doctorate terms. When diagnosed, the doctors told them eighteen months is the average time left to live for those with this type of cancer. There was no cure or solution. All there was to do was try and delay the disease and the inevitable as long as possible. And she had. She and Patrick battled and lived as hard and as fun as possible. But as fate and cancer would have it, her death was right on time. Eighteen months later, there they were, living their last day together.

Patrick sat and stared, no thoughts in his head, no tears in his eyes, no words spoken. He sat, and he stared. She's all Patrick has had since birth. He has extended family, but this will drive him into a mindset of grief and loneliness. Patrick has known that for a while, and oddly enough, Patrick felt it somewhat calming. There is a comfort in loneliness, simultaneously neither positive nor negative. Always there for you even when you wish it not. Just there, and you certainly cannot say that about everything.

Patrick stared over, scanning her face for any sign of pain or heavenly relief. He wanted to talk to her, to say everything will be okay and that he will be too. He hoped to tell her how amazing she has been, and that he's going to make her proud. But he didn't. He knows those regrets will follow for the rest of his life, but it's too hard at the moment. He hoped she knew.

Patrick felt someone walking up from behind him, feeling the pressure building as they approached. Keeping his eyes on his mother, he felt their presence reach closer and closer behind him. The soothing voice of a woman spoke up from close behind.

"Excuse me? Patrick, we need to confirm the spelling of your last name." The nurse asked.

Patrick recognized the voice, knowing they had met before, he remembered meeting her, but had forgotten her name, which made him feel bad. Without looking, Patrick answered her request. "It's Thempa, T-H-E-M-P-A"

"Thempa?" she confirmed, sounding it out.

"Yeah, that's right," Patrick responded, sounding deflated.

A nurse quickly stepped into his vision to check the machines. Patrick forgot her name too. She finished her check but stayed to look at his mom. She bent and fixed the sheets that were coming undone and slid another pillow behind her head. Although the nurse was silent, Patrick could feel that she wanted to say something. After a moment, Patrick sat back up and adjusted his position on the chair. Before he could get back into a comfortable position for staring, the nurse glanced at him and smiled. She took one last look at the oxygen machine and walked off.

Maybe I was wrong? Patrick thought.

He looked back to her and tried to replay all the great memories they had together in his head. At first, it was tough to recall, but then he started thinking about all of her weird phrases and sayings she had. The way she smiled at him when she was proud. He even remembered her almost burning the house down when she tried burning the brush by the front door. That was a hectic moment, but one Patrick has already looked back on with fondness. His mind hazily returned to the situation, and he could feel it. He was alone now.

Patrick sat outside on the lawn of his house, trying to contemplate the moment he had just lived. The moment seemed to take a lifetime, yet, it was already over. He was there with her the whole time. No way he could leave. She would have appreciated that. His Aunt Judy arrived from out of state shortly after. She offered to take care of the business with the funeral director, social workers, and the curious neighbors. Patrick was appreciative of that and chose to head into the backyard where he sat, ripping out the grass and letting it slide through his fingers, blowing away in the wind.

After watching his mom wheeled out the front door, and the black hearse pulling out the driveway, everyone but Patrick and his Aunt had left. She loved her older sister. Judy was an ever-energetic woman who could tell a great story, many of those stories included his mom, but today the energy was understandably dim. Patrick wondered how Judy was going to handle this.

Better than me? Patrick speculated.

Judy lived two states away and was very preoccupied with her own family and her clothing business, but she always made time to visit and attend vacations with them. Judy walked out to the backyard to Patrick and sat beside him.

"Everyone left, and I had to tell the neighbors what happened," Judy said.

"That's okay. They can spread the word" Patrick said, staring into the thick green grass.

"I wish I would have been here for you guys, I should have. Thanks for calling this morning"

Patrick nods his head slowly.

"I was thinking of ordering some pizza. You look like you could use some food," she said.

Staring into the grass, Patrick shook his head slightly. "Eating doesn't seem important right now," he said before exhaling, almost sighing. "I'm not hungry anyway...and I think I might leave soon too."

"You sure? "Judy asked.

"I can't be here tonight, but I'll call soon, about... all this" Patrick said and gestured toward the house.

They sat together for another twenty minutes in silence, taking in the sunny, care-free day. Patrick has always been comfortable with silence, never getting stressed about the dead air. Judy, on the other hand, has mentioned many times how she is the opposite. She actively tried to avoid silence, But now she lies in the grass with Patrick, living through the moment. Patrick was surprised, but he understood her pain too. They spent years together as best friends. *This has to be really hard for her too*, Patrick thought.

Patrick collected his things together and said goodbye to his Aunt Judy, leaving her to lock up. Driving away from his old family home, Patrick refused to look back. He made the thoughtful drive to his apartment in silence, thinking more about the day that changed his life completely. Unbeknownst to him, Patrick will be waking up tomorrow morning to another life-changing day.

She died today, remember?

Chapter 2

Patrick woke up and immediately replaced the events from yesterday, frame by frame as if it were a movie. Patrick could feel the hollowness in his chest, knowing that it would be a weird morning. Having been so used to waking up every morning knowing his mom is sick and that he has to see her, he isn't sure how he'd spend that time now. It does not feel real to him. She's dead, but it didn't feel real. Between showering, drinking coffee, and driving to work, life has lost a lot of color. Life is bleaker now. Patrick is used to sad days. That constant comfort in his life. It will never leave, and it will never die out.

Preparing for work this Monday morning went as usual for him. He moped around his apartment, getting dressed, and thinking over the coming day's events. Normally having a seat on the floor, he would imagine what he'd expect to happen during the day. Patrick would close his eyes and walk through it, wondering what he'd see, who he'd be interacting with, and what could potentially go wrong. The morning walkthrough, he called it. It helps the anxiety Patrick has felt every day for the last two years. Whatever the upcoming day had in store for him, he knew it couldn't be worse than yesterday.

Patrick worked at the local University in the Media Relations Department, replying to emails, making calls, and walking around the campus, like the other functioning adults. Patrick does get in free to all sporting events, which he loved. His job granted him that happiness and also paid his bills. But that is not the job Patrick is proudest of. His pride is with an orphanage downtown called Building Blocks. He had been helping there for about two months, trying to ease his mind about his own sliding life. Patrick has grown to feel comfortable there. He wanted to get a job close to his mom, and-also one that was a worthwhile cause. Patrick knew Building Blocks would be a hard place to do good but wanted to help people and the community somehow. He does not have a formal title there but does not care. He likes to hang out with the kids and hopefully be a good role model.

Working at an orphanage is a hard job, for obvious reasons. Orphanage workers help these kids through a dire time of uncertainty and fear. They have the potential to be that small light in an ocean of darkness. That is what the Director of Building Blocks, Mrs. Amanda Pierce, told Patrick during his interview. He remembers that interview vividly. He arrived early and waited in her office. She was a couple of minutes late, but Patrick was willing to wait. She came into the office and introduced herself immediately. She was wearing similar clothes to what Patrick remembered his mom wearing when she would leave for work. A long grey skirt and a white button-up shirt. A very professional look, Patrick thought. She was distraught during their first meeting but was hiding it well. Ever since his mom's diagnosis, Patrick's ability to empathize and relate with people has changed. Patrick could experience and read their emotions, similar to an empath yet, more rooted in emotion. Now their emotion seeps out through their eyes, their bodies, and their words. The emotions like colors, some dark, and some bright. Mrs. Pierce's colors were dull and cold back then. During their interview, Patrick learned a lot about Mrs. Pierce. She was a strong woman who projected toughness and grit, a quality surely desired in her chosen profession. Mrs. Pierce spoke with passion and a sense of care for Building Blocks. She understood what family and care truly meant.

Mrs. Pierce liked Patrick from the moment they shook hands. She thought he was polite and mature, a little strange, but charming. Mrs. Pierce interviewed many candidates in the past, but never got the same feeling when meeting Patrick. Good help is hard to find at an Orphanage, so she has to be picky when hiring. Mrs. Pierce liked to test them, make them nervous and uncomfortable to see if they could handle tense situations. Patrick passed all the tests. The moment Patrick remembered most vividly was when Mrs. Pierce asked him when he would be leaving.

"Patrick, you seem nice, and we could use some nice around here. But that's not going to be good enough to work here. You need to be committed to these kids. So many workers and volunteers come here to cleanse their minds and beat their demons. But when they do, if they do, they leave and never come back. Some of these kids will be here for years, and to see people come and go in their lives so quickly will only make things worse." Mrs. Pierce said, placing her hand over her heart to slow its beating. Mrs. Pierce spoke with such energy and passion, but with also a hint of frustration. It was clear to Patrick she was upset, and this interview right now might not be at the best time.

"I'm guessing you got some bad news before our interview?" Patrick asked, cutting to the chase.

"Yeah, yeah I did" Mrs. Pierce exhaled heavily before continuing. "I just got off the phone with the Head Director. Building Blocks funding is decreasing. I'm not even sure I can afford to hire you, or anyone." She paused while staring at the ground, then back to Patrick, realizing her poor choice of phrasing.

"That's probably not what you expected to hear. This place needs so much help...these kids need help" She looked away from Patrick. "I'm sorry, this interview has gotten a little sloppy. It's a hard time right now."

Patrick nodded in empathy.

"I can feel that. Life is hard, and you have a hard part to play in it." Patrick paused for a moment and looked down at the floor. He felt an intense sorrow for these kids and for Mrs. Pierce. He looked back up at her, seeing that she was noticeably calmer.

"And I want to help Mrs. Pierce. I want to help these kids anyway I can, I don't know how or even if I can, but I know that I will be here. I didn't want to work here for the money anyway.`` Patrick said with a smile.

"You want to volunteer?" Mrs. Pierce asked.

"Yes I do, anything you need".

Mrs. Pierce takes a breath and smiles. "You really want to help huh?"

"Yep," Patrick says enthusiastically, trying to hide the pain Mrs. Pierce assumed he had.

"Okay," She said, smiling, and loosening her shoulders. "First thing though. Do not call me Mrs. Pierce... It's Amanda."

Patrick called into his university job, letting them know he will be out for the day, but headed over to Building Blocks to be with the kids. He arrived and walked through the front door. To his surprise, he found it to be silent. Normally, on a typical day at Building Blocks, at least three phones are ringing somewhere or some staff-member yelling for a kid. But, there was only silence. He walked around for a while, still unable to find anyone. He walked up the central wooden staircase and checked Amanda's office. Patrick checked the kids' rooms, but still, no one was around. He was about to call Amanda when he heard a loud crash of pans in the kitchen. He descended back down the stairs and quietly peaked around the door to the kitchen. He saw the trays on the floor but no suspect. He prowled around the island table, where he saw a girl trying to hide behind the table. Patrick made eye contact with the girl who stayed as still as possible.

"You're doing a horrible job of hiding," Patrick says. "Where is everyone? I'm a little worried."

"Who are you talking to?" The girl asked, still hiding behind the table.

Patrick rolls his head back. "You Anna"

Anna stood up and looked down at the trays." Are you going to pick those up?" she asked playfully.

"No. But, I'll help you" Patrick answered.

Anna is a fourteen-year-old Latina girl. She always has a feisty and defensive attitude. She and Patrick get along well because they both like to playfully tease people. Anna, just like Amanda, would put on that exterior mask of strength to hide her feelings. Although she is an orphan and has things to be understandably upset about, Patrick always saw more bright colors than dark.

"So, where is everyone?" Patrick asked, bending down to grab some pans.

Anna circled the island. "Amanda took a lot of the kids and the staff to a park for some bonding thing"

"Why didn't you go?"

Anna looked at Patrick like she expected him to know why already, which he did.

"Uh because it sounds horrible and boring" Anna remarked anyway.

"Right, you don't want to bond with everyone?"

"We bond every day. This place is like a prison, there's only fifteen of us here, but it feels so cramped all the time."

"You think this place is a prison?" Patrick asked for confirmation.

"Well I mean no, but like theirs not a lot of space, you know. And I can't leave, or you guys freak out"

"That's why they take bonding adventures to the park, so you guys can get out of this prison" Patrick answered.

"Yeah whatever," Anna remarked quickly.

"I know what you mean though. There are a lot of restrictions that come with an Orphanage." Patrick said, trying to relate with her.

8

"I know, I've lived in three of them." Anna said.

Patrick contorts his expression to one of pain to show he is empathizing. He's reminded everyday of how tough life has been for these kids. *That's why I'm here*, Patrick thought. He nods lightly before changing the subject.

"So you are just getting a snack or something?" Patrick asked.

"Yeah, not for me though"

Patrick's head tilts in confusion, "For who then?"

"There's a new girl here today. Her name is Laney, she's like eight"

"What? Well, where is she?" Patrick asked in a worried tone, as he scrambled the pans together.

"I don't know, somewhere. I'm supposed to watch her, that's why I stayed here" Anna mentioned.

"Well she can't be alone, that's one of those restrictions I was talking about, Anna"

"Well go find her. And take her this" Anna reached out and handed Patrick some goldfish in a Ziploc bag, "You can watch her now."

Patrick grabs the bag, giving Anna a playful and stern look and walked away to find Laney. He found her in the backyard playing with the chalk. He walked over to her with goldfish in hand. "Hi Laney," he said.

Laney turned to look at him then back over to her work. "Hi," she returns quietly.

"My name is Patrick, are you hungry?" Patrick showed Laney the bag of goldfish, presenting it as if it were a bag of diamonds.

Laney looked at the bag and reached out for it. Her eyes got covered by her curly brown hair as she reached, she wiped it away and grabbed the bag. Her look lingered over Patrick before she broke it and looked back to her drawing on the sidewalk.

Patrick looked over her shoulder down at her drawing, seeing a woman dressed in grey. Patrick knows that he can be silly and light with kids because they truly don't know any better. They just think he's weird. So he had the freedom to be weird.

"I like your elephant," Patrick said, expecting her to scold him.

"It's not an elephant, she's a princess superhero, her name is Silver Princess."

"A princess superhero?" Patrick said in a very impressed tone.

"Yeah she fights bad guys and saves her friends, then they all have tea parties together"

Patrick chuckled. "Even the bad guys go to the tea party?"

"Yeah they hate it, that's why they never do bad things after"

Patrick chuckled again. "She sounds like an amazing hero, and what's so bad about tea? I drink it...sometimes." Laney looks up and smiles. "You must like superheroes then...and tea?" Patrick asked.

"Yeah, my dad was a superhero who could fly and jump high, I haven't seen him in a long time," Laney said, opening up to him already.

Patrick got that feeling again, that sadness for these kids. *She probably won't ever see him again*, he thought.

"The Silver Princess is always here for me though, I want to be a hero someday just like her and my daddy" Laney said, looking down fondly at her art.

"Why do you want to be a hero, Laney?" Patrick asked, leaning forward, awaiting her youthful answer.

"Because my daddy was, my daddy said that he was a hero so he could be good and do good things, he was brave for them, and for me," Laney said.

Patrick soaks up those words for a moment. *Maybe that is what I need to hear*, he thought, before speaking back to Laney.

"So Laney, what if your dad...or the Silver Princess didn't want to be a superhero? You think that's okay?" Patrick asked, then looked to Laney for her reaction. Her head tilts down, but Patrick can feel she is confused by the question, almost like she never expected to hear that. Patrick thought he may have gone too far. She looked down at the warm cement and answered.

"They wouldn't do that, their heroes, they only care about the people that need help"

Patrick took a deep breath and looked at the sky, knowing that struck a chord inside him, sending him into a guilty sadness. He woke himself out of it and smiled down at Laney. "Your dad sounds like a very smart person...and so are you, Laney."

Amanda, the staff, and the kids all arrive back at Building Blocks. Patrick met everyone in the dining hall, knowing that it was lunch time. He sat down and ate with the kids and staff, trying his best to enjoy the kid's company. But it's hard. He hasn't told anyone about his mom dying, or what's going on in his life.

They have it hard enough already. She's dead, remember?

They finished their meal and all headed to their rooms. Patrick stayed back to help clean the kitchen and tie up some other loose ends. He stopped by Amanda's office, knowing she will be there this time. Patrick found her in her office with a book, drinking tea. She thanked Patrick for his work and wished him a good day. Patrick got in his car and drove back to his apartment, heading downtown into the dark city. He could walk home, but he knew walking and thinking are synonymous, and he'd rather not be alone with his thoughts.

He stepped inside his one-bedroom apartment, finding just that, a place dark and quiet. He dropped his keys to the side door table and flipped the light on. He was hit with a self-reflecting moment and sat on his island stool, leaning over the counter table, digging his elbows into the hard ceramic sheet. *She's dead, remember?*

He snapped himself out of the reflection and checked his phone, seeing no messages or voicemails. Many of his friends went on to make something of their own lives. Patrick doesn't blame them for never checking in or calling, it's not like he ever did either. He wished his life was different, that he went on a different path and that things worked out differently, but it's meaningless. Patrick knows that will only make his feelings worse. His life fell apart, and all he did was watch. He thought of the new girl Laney. What she is going through, what she has already been through at such a young age. *She has it harder than you. Stop complaining,* he thought.

He jumped off the stool and walked through the dark shadows into his bedroom. Seeing the window open, knowing he left it open before he left, sounds of the city enter into his room. He heard the city outside bustling with life and emotion. He stood by the window looking out, brooding with negativity and despair. He repeats softly what Laney said earlier about heroes.

"They wouldn't do that, their heroes, they only care about the people that need help."

He closed his eyes to trap himself with his thoughts. After a moment he shook his head and opened his eyes. Turning to his closet, he walked over, and opened the door. He grabbed out a pair of black pants and boots and put them on. He grabbed a black hoodie and threw it on quickly. He reached down to the pile of clothes on his floor and rifled through them, looking for a finishing touch. He finally grabbed out a black cloth and searched around for eye holes. He inspected the mask and realized there were too many rips in it to wear again. *That*

11

won't work, he thought as he searched the pile once more. He came back up with nothing but remembered a dark colored University bandana sitting at his desk. He tied that around the back of his head and flips up his hood, leaving only his eyes shining from the shadows.

Patrick stood by the window and closed his eyes. *She's dead, remember?* The voice in his head repeats. He clenched his right fist tightly as his face grew hotter. He clenched his fist tighter and tighter, putting all of his anger and energy into it. Patrick felt the power rising into his hand, building, becoming warmer and warmer. He brought his fist up to his face, staring, waiting for something to happen. Patrick willed himself harder when suddenly a warm blue light appeared out of his knuckles, almost like flames. He urged his clenched fist more and more until it felt like it was going to burn his entire arm. An abrupt yellow light sparks bright for a split second from his hand, then retreated into his palm. Patrick opened his hand, letting a long glowing yellow rope fall and unravel to the floor, materializing from the blue flames. Patrick stood stall, unsurprised, feeling a surge of warm power soar into and over his body. He tightened his grip on the rope as the feeling of warm aura seeps fully into his hand. Patrick jumps out of the window and climbs to the roof. Holding the warm yellow rope, Patrick looked out over the city and repeated Laney's words.

"They only care about the people that need help,"

Chapter 3

Located on the corner of Eighth and Frazier, a woman being held at knifepoint at a local gas station ATM pleaded for help. At one forty-five in the morning and alone in the dark city, she may be out of luck. She just needed a few bucks to buy a cab, but two men were waiting there all night for unsuspecting victims to take the bait and use the ATM. They've been lucky all night, she was their third victim, quite the gig. She's a long way from home and terrified.

"Listen lady, you're going to be fine as long as you do what we say, now punch in your code and give us what we want " The thug told the woman. He wasn't holding the knife or the or holding the woman up, but he definitely is the alpha between the two. The man holding the knife pushes the woman toward the machine. She stumbled and grabbed the machine for balance. She is frozen in terror showing nothing but life threatening emotions over her face, she was just trying to get through the moment.

"Hurry up!" The man holding the knife screamed as he shoved her again into the wall. She cried out and started typing in her code.

"How much do you want?" The woman asked.

"Uh, all of it" remarked the man keeping watch. "Now hurry up"

The woman grasped tightly onto the machine. "All of it? No, that's everything I've got, everything I've worked for. I'll be homeless without it."

"Not our problem, now hurry up!"

The woman stopped typing her code and realized there would be major ramifications of her actions, of their actions. These two men are going to take everything she's earned in one heinous act. The man holding the knife sees she stopped and pinned her against the wall in anger. Just as he does a bottle flew from the alley behind the gas station hitting the ground by their feet. The bottle rolled away unbroken as both men froze and contorted their heads over to the alley. They look into the shadows and see nothing but more bottles.

"Evenin"

The men swing around behind themselves and there stands Patrick fifteen feet away dressed in his black outfit, holding the glowing yellow rope behind his back, hidden from sight. They stare open mouthed at Patrick in a stunned silence. Patrick spoke up again.

"You know I gotta say, you criminals are hard to find, I've been looking for something all night. They say crime is rampant in this city but you guys...." Patrick wagged his finger at the men. "You guys are good at staying secretive, that's why you're the pros I guess huh?"

The man holding the knife let the woman loose but kept her still at the ATM, he then stepped forward. "What do you want? Are you here to rob her cuz we were here first."

"No, I'm not here to rob her, I'm here t—."

"Are you here to save her?" the man who was keeping watch asked playfully.

"Well yeah I was about to— "

"You were about to say that?" Went the knife wielding thug.

Patrick shook his head. "Yes, what is happening? Just let her go or—". Patrick jumped up and down like a boxer, prepping for the fight, he bobbed while he kept his yellow glowing rope hidden. "Or I'm gonna get physical."

He stopped jumping to wait for their answer.

The man holding the knife stepped away from the woman by the ATM and walked over to Patrick and pointed the knife right at him, cutting end first.

"Kid I didn't want to stab anyone tonight, I really didn't. But this score is too good for you to mess up... so I'm gonna stab you, whether you die or not is on you."

The man leaned forward and grabbed at Patrick's chest, as he did Patrick sidestepped smoothly away. Patrick watched the man's hand go by in what seemed to him like slow motion. Patrick grabbed the man's wrist and thrust his elbow into the man's shoulder with such force the man's legs buckled. Patrick held the thugs wrist up in the air as his weight collapsed to the ground. Patrick twisted his wrist and threw him fully onto the ground. The man keeping watch reached into his pocket and pulled out a knife of his own. He grabbed the woman by the shirt to bring her closer,, while he did, Patrick whipped out the glowing rope and thrust it at the man. The glowing rope extended toward the danger, getting longer to reach its target. It wrapped it around the man's wrist holding, which was holding the woman's shirt. The rope

14

was apparently hot to the touch for the man as he screamed in burning pain. Patrick tugged the man off balance and leapt toward him and connected with a leaping kick to the man's head, sending him backward to the ground unconscious. The other man stood up holding his shoulder and began running away into the alley. Patrick cracked the glowing yellow rope across the man's back leg from twenty-five feet away. The man fell then began crawling. Patrick gracefully walked over to the man clawing at the alley's dirt. Patrick grabbed him by the collar and looked him straight in the eye.

"Sorry about not getting that big score... but like I said I'm here to—"

The man on the ground interrupted again. "You're here to—" Patrick cut in and jabbed the man in the nose which knocked him out.

"That guy sucked," Patrick said aloud as he stood up and walked back over to the woman. Patrick saw the shock in her eyes as she stared at him, seemingly to have forgotten about being mugged.. Patrick noticed the colors change around her, shifting from dark to light slowly above her.

"What is that thing?" The woman asked, amazed by what she just witnessed from the glowing yellow rope.

She pointed at it and asked again.

"How did it do that?"

Patrick looked at it wondering what he could tell her, or even if he should at all. He pondered for a moment then chose to look back fondly to the brightly shining rope.

"It's pretty special isn't it….it came into my life a while ago, other things too. I don't exactly know either"

Patrick felt the woman's confusion all around him in the air, he could practically touch it. "But that thing seemed to grow and get longer when you threw it….and it burned that guy's hand when it touched him…. Does it burn you?" The woman asked, still looking lost.

"No it doesn't"

"Why?" the woman asked.

"Not sure, I really don't know anything about this thing. It appeared one day after I heard a voice in my dreams, and its came back every day since"

The woman wanted to ask more of Patrick, but was too tired and anxious to inquire any further about her saviour. She looked absentmindedly over to the ground where her purse lay, "I'd like to go home now." She said, picking it up, clutching in her chest.

"Okay, I'll call these guys in and wait for the police. You'll have to go into the precinct tomorrow morning and identify them, otherwise they'll be out doing this again to someone else" Patrick took a deep breath, then continued.

"There's a hospital a few blocks that way, wait there for a cab." Patrick gestured with his hands as the woman walked off.

She turned back around to say thank you, before jogging off back into the city. Patrick dialed the police and waited on a nearby rooftop until they got there, making sure he got his one and only win for the night.He trekked back to his apartment and climbed inside through the alleyway window. Lucky for him, the fire escape is always available to climb, so no one would ever notice him and his dark and pajama style outfit. He changed out of his gear and threw it into the closet on top of the glowing yellow rope and fell onto his bed.

Only one crime tonight, he thought to himself. *What difference is that going to make? Should I be a hero? Am I?* He argued within.

Laying down staring at the ceiling, he noticed how quiet it is in his room, it's quiet in his apartment and now it's quiet in his life. *She's dead, remember?* He pictured his mom, trying to conjure up an image of her smiling, he knew it's been a long time since he's seen that smile. He knew he wouldn't ever again. His emotions welled up inside as he realized he was about to cry. Tears started to build, yet he tried to think his tears back inside. The emotions were too strong in the moment for him to conceal. He broke down and fell off the bed onto the floor. Tears and painful emotions sept out his mind and body. He could feel the dark colors draining out from him, leaving his body like steamed water vapor. The most heartbroken he's ever felt, and it's the most alone he ever felt. He thought about the long lonely life ahead of him. He missed her. He wished he could still save her. He hoped that she was out there somewhere, missing him as much as he does her. But those are all just thoughts, the only thing for certain is that she is gone, she is dead. Patrick calmed himself down and sat at his bedside for a while. He sat and thought, trying to gather answers and peace within his mind. That is part of the special torture. The mindless time spent on grieving and coping with the new reality. But it's only one part of it. *This is normal,* he thought.

Patrick crawled up onto the bed and slid under his blankets and searched for comfort. He stared over to the side of his bed where the blankets look like rolling hills. Thoughts of his life float back into his mind. He doesn't remember when but he did fall asleep, ready to live out another day.

Patrick awoke the next morning in a calm state. A good cry will allow for that. He knew the science of it. He stumbled through his morning routine of starting the coffee machine, walking to the shower, turning it on and heading back to his room for whatever he chooses to wear. He started the coffee and the shower and paced into his room. He opened his closet door and flipped the light on. His attention was immediately grabbed by something odd. Something that he has never seen there before. The glowing yellow rope.

"What are you doing here?" Patrick asked the rope, half expecting it to answer.

It's weird for the rope to be there because every time Patrick has used it before, and then left it out, it's gone by morning. He's always needed to bring it back out through his fist. Patrick reached down by his boots to pick up the glowing yellow rope. Grabbing the rope, he lifted it up and brought it to his face. *The rope feels even warmer than it did last night*, he thought. Patrick whipped the rope at his wall just for fun narrowly missing his lamp and table. He cocked his arm back, about to toss the rope back onto the ground when something even stranger happened. The rope did speak.

Chapter 4

"What the f—!" Patrick yelled, stopping himself from swearing and stumbled backward.

He tossed the rope to the ground like an invasive spider crawling on him. Unsure if what he just heard was real or not, he stood incredibly still. He looked down at the rope.

"Did you just talk?" he asked loud enough for the rope and outside birds to hear him.

His room stays violently silent; Patrick could hear the slight humming of the rope, but got no answer, the rope laid on the ground, eerily still. Patrick walked over, keeping a close watch. Patrick kicked the rope and jumped back before it could bite him, but to his surprise, it remained still.

He went back to his morning routine, keeping a close eye on the rope. At first, the glowing rope was cool. It was this magical glowing entity that appeared from out of his hand. *How insane?* Patrick wondered. But it scared him now. For some reason, Patrick has proven special enough to be gifted magic. He has never told anyone and chose to keep it a secret. He did tell his mom once, but she wasn't able to, or could not even remember he did.

Patrick finished getting dressed and checked himself in the mirror, avoiding eye contact with himself. *She's dead, remember?*

He walked back to his room to see the rope still lying on the clothes. He has not forgotten the moment earlier, but that feeling of unease subsided.

"Probably shouldn't have you sitting out," he said as he walked over. He crouched down and grabbed the warm glowing rope confidently. "What are you?" He asked as it dripped off his fingers. As he looked at it, getting lost in its luminescence, it got warmer and warmer, brighter and brighter.

"Hi!"

"Oh my god!" Patrick yelped as he threw it again, this time smacking the door frame. "You just talked! I heard that one, what the hell!"

Patrick felt the anxiety flood back into his mind. He waited for a moment before he walked back over to inspect it. Patrick picked it up and looked at it.

"Are you talking?" he asked the rope, definitely expecting an answer this time.

"Yes! Hello!" the glowing rope replied.

Patrick stays brave and unflinched. His mind went blank as the confusion took hold of him. He stared at the rope as questions floated into his head.

" Why can you talk? What are you?" Patrick asked rapidly.

"I am your guide," the glowing yellow rope replied. "I'm here to help you learn."

"Learn what? Guide what?" Patrick asked, gazing at the rope before abruptly remembering that he has to be at work soon. "Uh, actually I have to go, I'm late" Patrick looked at the rope harder and gave it a confused look "Will you still be here when I come back?"

"I will! Unless you put me back" the rope said.

Patrick looked around his room and to his closet. "Like onto the clothes or?" Patrick asked, letting the question trail off.

"No back into your fist" the rope states.

Patrick looked at his fist, wondering if he knew how, fairly confident that he did not. He looked back to the rope.

"Well uh, yeah I mean, you've always just disappeared when I sleep and well, I can't go back to sleep now I have work. Could you do it this time?" Patrick pleaded with the glowing rope as he started hustling around his apartment. Still holding the rope, he got to his front door.

"I can do it this time, but you owe me" the rope stated from back in his room.

Patrick leaned his head back in surprise and squinted at the rope. "What would I owe you?" Patrick asked.

"That's just something you humans say, right?" the rope asked. "A joke" the rope stated.

Patrick doesn't get it but found it amusing. He let out a crack of a smile.

"Yeah, that's fun… I got to go"

Patrick walked back over to the closet where the rope lay on his pile of dirty clothes. "See ya," he said skeptical as he walked to his door and out the apartment. He shut the door behind him and stood for a moment in thought. *Did I just live that?*

Chapter 5

Why am I going to work?... She's dead, remember?

Patrick's mind has been in a hurricane of negative, life-wasting thoughts as of late. Life has gotten more and very less complicated this past month, not to mention the past few days. He has been quietly and heartbreakingly grieving about his mother dying, unknowing what he should do next. He has considered therapy for that soon but is not sure it can help him. He finished his morning walkthrough quickly in the morning and headed out. No coworker noticed or asked about the heavy dark clouds that were hovering over his head all day. It takes an empathetic and special type of person to see those, let alone ask.

Liking to stay busy but enjoying his free evenings where no one counts on him for anything, his life schedule is very open. He enjoyed exercising and the arts. Any sport in the past, he has been willing to try. He has been a natural at them all. These days he'll have a lot more free time. *She's dead, remember?*

Today there is only one thing he has been thinking about doing after work. *Well, there are two,* he thought. Patrick has had a crush on this girl he sort of worked alongside. Her name was Summer, and he saw her now and then around the building, and sometimes on game days. He got the feeling she liked him too from the times he had spoken with her. But the only way for them to be together is if she got down on one knee and proposed to him. Even then, he might freeze up and add that to the list of his regrets. Today is all about that glowing yellow rope. *She's dead, remember?*

He forgot just then. *How could I forget?*

His thoughts are ever conflicting. For in that moment in his head, he had peace, no depressing thoughts, no aggressive reminders. Today what he wanted was to go back and speak with the rope, or to see if he was crazy. He rushed back to his apartment and settled in. Still conflicted on what he should do, he stepped into his kitchen and stood by the table and pressed his hands into it. He exhaled slightly before bringing his right hand to his face, inspecting it to be normal, no discolorations or scars, just a normal hand. He focused his energy on his fist. He could feel it building again. Simply by imagining the glowing yellow rope, he could believe it to become true. His hand burned up quickly, and out of his palm appeared the blue flame. A little more focus and energy, and then boom, the flash of light turns the blue flames into the glowing yellow rope. Part of the rope fell out of his hand and dangled to the side, almost touching the floor. He stared at it for a moment before engaging.

"Hello," he said, then waited for an answer like he just rang its doorbell.

"Hello, Patrick," said the voice.

"Oh, so you know my name too?" Patrick asked.

"Of course, I have learned a lot about you these past months, more than your name"

"So what do I call you? Do *you* have a name?"

" Names mean nothing, call me what you please" the rope stated.

"Right, you're just my guide," Patrick nodded. "I've always thought you looked sort of like a halo, from angels, just a longer version of one. I'll call you Halo." Patrick told it.

"Halo sounds right," The newly christened Halo said.

"Okay great, well you said you were going to help me learn?" Patrick questioned Halo.

"I know right where we should start," the rope told Patrick.

Patrick's eyes widened as his energy sparked. "Oh yeah?" he asked.

"With learning to put me back into your fist," the rope said in its soft angelic voice.

It could be a human man's voice, hard to tell, but the voice seemed distant, as if it were hiding behind something. Patrick still heard the hint of sarcasm in Halo's words however.

Disappointed, Patrick dropped his head. He was hoping for a far cooler practice session than that.

"But that can wait until we're done with our *real* training," Halo said. .

Patrick got excited once more, then furrowed his brow in speculation. "That was weird," Patrick stated.

"What was?" Halo asked.

Patrick paused for a moment to choose his words carefully. "In my mind...as soon as I hoped for something, it was like you understood my thought. Or heard it."

"I did understand you, "I am in your mind, I hear your thoughts" Halo answered.

"Like all my thoughts? That's...crazy" Patrick replied, feeling unease.

Halo didn't respond, so Patrick spoke up again. "So yeah, training. I think I know a spot"

"The woods," Halo answered.

Patrick smirked as he stepped to the door . He knew they should be alone out there so he can train without being seen. After he pulled into the empty lot, Patrick quietly walked into the woods and off the trails. He crossed a small river and over a hill, completely out of sight, ready to train. Finally having arrived at the spot, Patrick saw his familiar surroundings. An open area with a canopy of trees overhead, shrouding the light, leaving only slivers of sun reaching the ground he walked on. Patrick has come here in the past. Whenever he wanted to be alone, he'd make the drive to be in the woods. He has never seen anyone out here before, especially as late as it were, so Patrick was confident he'd be alone.

"Okay so let's start," Patrick said as he rubbed his hands together in excitement.

"Wait, hold on," Patrick interjected. "I don't know how this hasn't come up yet...what are you? What am I?" Patrick asked and stopped moving, then pulled Halo out from his sweater.

"I'm your guide, I'm here to help you learn...and my name is Halo"

"Yeah, I know that last one...and the first two, but, where are you from? Why can I hear you in my head" Patrick pleaded with Halo.

"You needed me," Halo said to Patrick.

"I needed you?" Patrick said then looked down at the ground. "Because of my mom?"

"Possibly, I do not know," Halo said, which sounded honest.

Patrick looked at Halo, and held it up to his face. "Where are you from, who sent you to me?."

"We can't tell you that, we're just here to guide," Halo said through Patrick's head.

"Oh, now it's *we*? I'm sure there's a lot you can't tell me" Patrick said knowing the answer.

"Yes"

Patrick took a deep breath and thought of his mom. *She's dead, remember?*

Patrick looked at Halo and smirked. "Well, that is a little fishy.... but you'll tell me things as we go right?"

"Of course, the more you learn, the more knowledge will be shared," Halo said to Patrick, giving him goosebumps.

"Easy," Patrick said confidently to Halo.

"Okay, the rope has many incredible talents," Halo said, starting off the practice session.

"Yeah, it gets longer or shorter when I need it too," Patrick answered.

"Yes, the material can expand to many different forms. To put it back into your fist, all you need to do is force it back in." Halo said.

"Sounds weird," Patrick replied. "So just like... squish it back in?" Patrick asked for confirmation.

Halo didn't respond, so Patrick went for it. Patrick put the rope between his hands the best he could and squeezed. He pressed it tight into his hands, and suddenly, it vanished.

Patrick looks at his hand. "I did it!" He said and waited for an exciting reply but realized that Halo is back in his hand. "Can you still hear me Halo?" Patrick said then listened, getting nothing in response. He looked at his fist and started to bring Halo back out. The flash of light makes Halo appear in hand once more.

"Good work, first try!" Halo said in encouragement.

"Nice, what's next?" Patrick asked, lifting Halo.

"Learn more about the different forms you can make, mold the material.".

Patrick stretched the rope outward like a piece of slime between his hands. "Forms like a shield or disc?" Patrick said quietly to himself.

"Yes, both those and more," Halo answered.

Patrick stretched the glowing mold into a shield large enough to cover his body and thrust it into the ground by his feet. "Whoa, this thing is way crazier than I thought, I'll try a disc now."

Patrick smushed Halo down into a sharp flat disc then looked on to his creation. "Oh, I'm going to use this someday" He took a couple of form practice throws and looked at Halo. "I'm going to throw you...at that tree, cool?"

"Ready!" Halo responded.

"And you'll come back? Just like a Frisbee" Patrick's asked, a little unsure.

"That's a boomerang. But yes, I will if you want me to" Halo answered.

"Oh, I knew that…okay here we go," he said in anticipation.

Patrick took two shuffle steps forward and whipped the disc forehand at the tree from thirty or so yards away. The disc flew through the air, buzzing as it went. It connected with the tree lower by its trunk. Patrick watched on and expected something to blow up, he wanted something to blow up, but nothing happened, then from behind the tree came Halo cutting back toward him. The disc was moving fast. Patrick for a split second regretted having thrown it so hard, he may have gotten carried away. As the disc got closer and closer, he put his hand up in preparation to catch it, or lose a finger. He watched carefully as the disc flew toward him and squinted his eyes as the disc flew to his hand. The disc collided with and then disappeared into his palm on contact automatically.

"Wahoo, wow" Patrick exclaimed, "That was awesome"

He took a deep breath to calm down before he brought Halo back out and walked over to the tree he was sure he had hit. He approached the tree to see that the disc went straight through as if the tree was warm butter.

"Nicely done, now for something else I think you'll like," Halo said, grabbing Patrick's attention.

"Let's hear it then," Patrick told Halo.

"It's a hand cannon, it makes things blow up"

"It makes things blow up? I do like that...wait, you knew I would like that because you're in my head, right?" Patrick asked Halo, fully knowing it was true. Halo, understanding that was a rhetorical task, kept silent.

Patrick took a few steps toward the center of the cave hidden away under a large mound of dirt and trees.

"Okay, I'm ready, guide me Oh-chosen-one," Patrick said sarcastically, as he stuck his hand out, holding Halo in its rope form.

"Okay, first thing...put me down, you don't use the rope for this."

"Really? So this is all me then? Okay," Patrick said confidently.

"No, this is still us, we have given you all your gifts," Halo told Patrick.

Patrick held Halo in the air in front of his face. "Right. What other gifts?"

"Increased agility, increased fighting prowess, increased body durability, increased emotional awareness."

Patrick dropped Halo to his side and sighs. "Oh," he mumbled.

"Did you think you were just able to do all of those things before?" Halo asked.

"Well no but I— I have been doing planks," He said playfully while he dropped Halo back to his side. "Okay, hand cannon time."

Patrick put Halo on the ground by his feet.

"Now bring the blue flames back and build the energy up until it feels it is going to burst," Halo said.

"Okay, easy enough"

Patrick took a breath and started building up energy into his hand. He focused as hard as he could until he saw the flames beginning to appear. He pushed himself even harder and pointed his open palm into the mouth of the cave. The blue flames and his energy turned into a bright yellow burst of energy and quickly shot into the cave. The light of the yellow beam shined brightly in the dark cave before making contact. It exploded on impact. The blast pushed a gust of wind into Patrick as he fell backward, watching from the ground. The blast was loud and aggressive and blew the small cave inside out. Large chunks of rock flew out of the cave, and more now filled the area where the cave was. He got the explosion he wanted. Patrick stood up to look at the wreckage and scanned the area for any other watching eyes. *Someone may have heard that though,* Patrick thought without seeing anyone. He looked at his hand in shocked silence as thoughts of his mother flooded into his mind, filling him with sadness. *She's dead, remember?*

"I think that should be enough for today, your energy is running low." Halo spoke up then mentioned.

Patrick quickly remembered that Halo can feel him. Halo would know If he was tired, or hungry, or sad, or guilty.

"Yeah, I am hungry," Patrick said as he rubbed his stomach.

Patrick molded Halo back into his hand and headed back to his car. He walked past what was once a cave and kicked some rocks out of the way. Patrick couldn't help but smirk happily at the pile of destruction he caused and even drove back home thinking of his new explosive powers. He arrived back at his apartment and opened the door. As he does, he got a surprising phone call. He checked the name, seeing Aunt Judy, Patrick knew he should answer.

"Hello," he said as he put the phone to his ear.

"Hey kiddo it's your Aunt Judy"

"Hey"

After a moment of dead air, Judy brought the call back to life. "How are you doing"? She asked.

Good question, Patrick thought, *so many layers*. "Uhhh I don't know, it's been a weird week" he said.

"Yeah, it has" Aunt Judy agreed.

They both go silent for a moment before she chimed back in." I spoke with the Funeral Director and the church. The wake is Wednesday at six and the funeral on Saturday"

"Thanks for doing that," Patrick said, through an exhale.

"Your welcome sweetie, your mom would be pissed if I let you do everything on your own"

Patrick almost laughed because he knew it's the truth. He managed to chuckle. "Yeah she would," he said.

There's more dead air before Judy spoke up "Well I'll let you go. I know you don't like phone calls, and I'm sure you're up to something. I just wanted to tell you. I'll see you and talk with you in person on Wednesday, okay?"

"Okay Aunt Judy, thank you"

"Bye Patrick"

Patrick put his phone down on the table. The room suddenly became deafeningly quiet. A cold breeze rolled over his shoulders.

She's dead, remember?

Chapter 6

The day of the funeral came and went. Patrick found himself alone at his mother's house, the house he grew up happy in. He sat in the grass just as he did after she died.. This time he thought about her being lowered into the ground. That hurt him as much as watching her take her last deep breath.

He met so many new people who knew his mother. They were all so sorry for his loss, he'd been told that multiple times. For the most part, most of the people were strangers. He knew his close family, of course, his cousins and his aunts and uncles, but many people were new to him. When they would walk over to him sitting at the front pew or in the dining area, he didn't think he could trust them. He felt guilty that way, but they were strangers to him, they wished him well and were friendly, but they weren't in his life, they didnt know him, nobody knew him. Patrick didn't cry at the funeral or the wake, he knew he wouldn't. During the burial, things changed. He sat in the front row with his aunt and some other family. He remembered the pallbearers bringing her coffin through the cemetery and placing the box onto the lift. He watched stone-faced as they lowered her into the ground. That was when he broke. He stood up, grabbed a rose from her bouquet, and raced to the car with tears begging to be released. He just wanted to be alone. Patrick was alone for a couple of minutes before his Aunt Judy opened the back door. She got in and sat with Patrick in total silence. Patrick could feel her hurting too. The pressure of her emotions added into his. She placed a hand on his shoulder, letting him know she's there with him.

"I'm so sorry, sweetie," Judy said, finishing the last word before she started crying too.

Sitting in the grass he would remember that being a moment he'll remember for life. The rest of the services were a blur. They ended as quickly as they began as the close family met back at the house to celebrate Maria's life. They laughed and told stories about her, some new stories and some very old to Patrick. He has heard so many of them and knew that his mother had quite the sense of humor. It was dry but smart and witty. Aunt Judy was the fun, carefree sister, Maria was the studious one who was always reading and learning. Most of the stories involved Judy doing something reckless, and Maria would be there to save the day. She was that kind of sister and that kind of woman. She made a great mother.

He remembered something else happening during the burial. After the Pastor's closing words, the weather changed dramatically. It went from cloudy and dreary one moment, to warm heat and sunshine the next. He was not the only one who noticed either. It was a big talking point afterward. It was almost as if his mother had finally reached heaven and wanted to brighten up the day. Patrick noticed at the moment but was too sad to care. Looking back, that's another moment he would remember and hopefully feel good about. This is when it gets hard, Patrick once heard. You do your best to move on and cherish your families, a funeral is an abrupt wake-up call that way. People move on, but not him, not the ones who have lost their everything, they will always remember.

Patrick sat up, unwilling to think anymore. He wanted to do something, and he knew it was getting late. He's been training in the woods with Halo for some days now and feels he's getting good. He loved the energy and warm feeling he got holding Halo and practicing his moves, it was almost an addiction. Patrick walked back inside the house. It's quiet. He checked the driveway to make sure nobody had stuck around. He shut and locked the door before stepping into the kitchen. He took one more good scan around before summoning out Halo.

"Hey Halo, how about we hit the *actual* streets and get some practice that way?" Patrick asked quietly.

"I think that is a great idea!" Halo responded in an unusually energetic tone for him as if he hoped for Patrick to say that.

"Okay nice, I'll drive back to the city, change clothes and go find some crime," Patrick said, planning their next move.

"Crime like robberies, drug dealing, kidnapping, and murder?" Halo asked.

"Yes, exactly those, the basics. Let's go find those" Patrick stated.

"Would you like me to show you where to go?" Halo asked.

"You can do that?"

"Yes, of course, I don't just feel your emotions, I feel everything. The colors of the city, wherever it's darkest are where…what you call crime happens" Halo answered ominously.

Patrick held Halo up to his face and stared inquisitively, half smiling. "So, you're like a crime finding GPS?."

"Yes," Halo said quickly.

"Yeah awesome, now I don't have to run all over the city just trying to help one person," Patrick said while stretching his shoulders. "Okay let's get going."

Patrick arrived back in the city and changed as quickly as he could into his black outfit. He looked down at his apparel, wondering if he should spice it up a bit. He knew he wanted to stay black, so he'd be harder to see, *vigilante one-o-one*, he thought. He checked his look in the mirror, sprinting around his apartment after each failed attempt at style. He tried sunglasses, headbands, bandanas, even a blue scarf he had in his closet. Everything looked stupid and he was getting too frustrated, so he thought he'd try another time. He climbed to the roof of his building, ready to go and summoned Halo.

"Okay, where to? "He asked.

"The dark-colored areas," Halo replied.

"I don't see—" Patrick said as he looked up to see a dark sky with so many colors in it. *That's a very strange-looking painting*, he thought. But amazing at the same time. The sky is dark, but he could see the colors well. *No bright colors anywhere. That can't be good*, he thought. Only purples, blues, greys, some dark greens, but no bright colors. Some light was shining through each, which was encouraging. Yet deep down Patrick knew the city was worse than he ever imagined. He spotted a dark purple area in the distant horizon.

"That area is dark, over there?" Patrick said, then pointed.

"Good pick," Halo says.

Patrick nodded and started running off. He jumped from rooftop to rooftop with ease, climbing walls and gliding through alleys. He arrived in the purple area when he started to feel the emotions from around him. He's in one of the rougher parts of the city, Patrick knew. He looked around to see a few larger buildings on one side and then some small run-down houses on the other. The emotions are strong and damaging, eating away at his own thoughts. *This must be the right area*, he thought, as he stood up on a high roof looking for signs of foul play.

"There, that building," Halo said.

Patrick understood exactly which house Halo was referring to. He ran to a better spot so he could get a better view, but still couldn't see anyone. He climbed down the roof and ran to the building's alley to hide in the shadows.

"The crime is inside, you'll be okay going through there," Halo said, referring to the door next to Patrick.

Patrick got ready to open the door and go in but stopped suddenly. "So what kind of crime is it? Can you tell? *Can* you tell me?" Patrick asked anxiously.

"It's what you would call a kidnapping and human trafficking" Halo responded with a sense of coldness.

"Oh, that's not good," Patrick said quickly, "How many guys are in there?" He asked, hoping for a low number.

"Six "Halo answered.

"Six!" Patrick said in a surprised nervous way. "That's a lot, do they have guns?"

"Two of them do. The lookouts, I suggest starting with them." Halo instructed Patrick.

"Yeah, smart"

Patrick got ready to go in but stopped once again. "Man, am I ready for this?" He looked to Halo in his hand for support. "No, no I'm ready. I can do this" Patrick said before Halo could answer.

Patrick entered the large warehouse through the alley door. It's a decent-sized building. Patrick imagined it being used to store school buses or airplanes. He looked quickly over the warehouse floor to see an actual old white bus located a few yards close by, one of the smaller sized ones. He quickly rushed over behind a few barrels filled with some strange liquid and crouched down. He could see the bad guys now, dressed in their typical black attire. W

Wait, I wear black, Patrick thought.

"They look mean *and* professional," Patrick said in a whisper to Halo and himself before noticing something else about the criminals.

They are all wearing different colored hats though" He said, looking at each man.

"Red, green, blue, violet. What are they, the power rangers?" Patrick asked Halo.

Patrick scoped out the area, looking for the two men keeping watch. He saw them on the other side of the bus, spread out. *Blue and green*, he thought.

The four others were close by, speaking in a huddle. Behind them are three people sitting in the dirt unmoving. Their heads covered in bags and their hands tied behind their backs. Patrick knew he must take out the green and blue hat guards first, or they may go for the hostages. He crouched and quietly moved around to the bus, staying out of sight. Both men, luckily, were facing toward the other group now, only taking peaks at their prisoners. Patrick watched the blue and green hat guards as they acknowledged each other. The blue hat guard spoke up.

"Last time, the boss seemed pissed. Knocked three teeth out" The man said as Patrick watched him rub his cheek.

Patrick prepared himself to strike, knowing he needed to help these people. He needed to be brave for them. In his head, he started a mental countdown. *3...2...1...GO!*

Patrick stepped into the open and ran to the lookouts. He whipped Halo around the blue hat lookout's neck and yanked the man down with incredible force head-first into the bus's engine. The green hat lookout turned around after hearing his partner fall. He checked his partner, then turned behind him seeing Patrick. Before he could register what was happening, Patrick whipped Halo around the man's wrist and pulled, trying to knock the gun loose. The man squeezed a shot off before dropping the gun, screaming in agony. Patrick yanked the man down and pulled him behind the bus.

The other group of men turned to check on their lookouts. They stared in silence for a few moments before they shuffled forward. Patrick walked out from behind the bus in clear sight, holding Halo in his left palm. He stepped forward and turned slowly to look at the two men he knocked out and nodded proudly to himself. *It was a little loud*, Patrick thought, critiquing himself.

The four men all stepped forward, ready to fight. Patrick raised his hands for them to pause.

"Hold up, four is a lot," Patrick said, as he paused for a moment. From left to right, Patrick scanned the men. *Red, yellow, violet and orange.*

He can't see their faces, but he waited in the tension until he thought they were off guard. Patrick quickly swung Halo around the man in the orange hat, lassoing him around the feet. He yanked the man down, pulling him inward before retracting Halo and flinging the man violently and effortlessly behind him. The man crashed hard into the ground behind and rolled over the ground. Patrick looked at the man in shock.

"I may have over-done that guy," he said to the others. "*But,* three *is* better," He said as he quickly rushed towards the others ready to fight.

He dodged the first swing from the black hat, gliding by him, focusing on the two behind. Red hat tried a jab from the side, but Patrick evaded and grabbed his arm. He slid under his shoulder and tossed him a few yards into the dirt. The other man reached for his shoulders, but Patrick slithered right off and side stepped, then countered with a swift punch to the throat. The man stumbled back, clutching his throat. The man in the black hat man swung for the back of Patrick's head but missed. Patrick could feel it coming and ducked. The man fell off-balance after punching, and Patrick took advantage, he grabbed his back and elbowed him in the head, knocking him out. The man holding his throat comes back for more. He dug through his pockets and located a knife. He stumbled over to Patrick, ready to attack. Patrick put his hands up like a boxer, ready to defend himself. The man swung weakly, leaving his arm and wrist exposed. Patrick grabbed his wrist and twisted violently, which caused the man to almost flip. The man screamed out in pain right before Patrick knocked him out.

Patrick remembered there was one more still conscious somewhere. He turned to see the red hat-wearing man walking over to the hostages. The man turned to look at Patrick before pulling out a knife.

Another knife? Patrick thought. *Better than guns, I guess.*

The man turned back to the hostages and stumbled behind them, looking for one to grab. Patrick knew what this man was feeling and what his intentions were.

I have to hurry, he thought.

Patrick slid Halo behind his back and molded a disc. He'd rather not kill this man, but he had to do something drastic to save these innocent people. Patrick gracefully dove to the side, getting a better angle to the man and whipped the disc and watched as it flew through the air swiftly. The man reached for a hostage, but before he could lay a hand on one, Halo appeared and sliced right through his arm. The man screamed out as his arm and knife hit the floor. The man fell to the ground and rolled around in agony. Patrick caught the disc as he approached the man, seeing the arm lying next to him.

"Yeesh, I didn't want to do that," Patrick said. "I was only going for a finger or two".

The man in the red hat's eyes turned to anger, and it was clear to Patrick he was about to yell something. Patrick crouched by the man and knocked him out before he could say whatever mean thing he was about to. He tied Halo around the man's arm to cauterize the wound, saving his life. Patrick walked around the warehouse, collecting each man to tie them up before he released the hostages. He took their bags off and untied them carefully, trying not to scare them. They are all young, in their twenties like Patrick. A man, and two women, who are visibly shaken and scared. Patrick assured them that they are safe and they can go home if they have one. He isn't sure they understood but wanted to be kind regardless. Patrick called the police and waited in the warehouse with them. When the police arrived on the scene, he climbed up high and watched as the people he just saved got the help they needed.

The rest of the night, Patrick stopped a few pettier thefts that night. Halo wasn't able to find any more major crimes. Nothing compared to how he started the night off. Any uncertainty Patrick had with himself was washed away with freeing those hostages. He ended the night and snuck home. Patrick showered, changed clothes, and made something to eat. It was late, and he was tired. He laid down in his bed and stared at the ceiling, thinking about all of the people he's going to save in the future. He smiled a little and closed his eyes, ready for sleep. Just as he did, his hand started getting warmer. He opened his eyes and shot up, seeing the blue flames appear from his hand.

"Hey, quite the Saturday night, huh?" Patrick told Halo.

"Yes, good work today. You're getting good at this"

Patrick smiled. "Yeah thanks, helps to have you guide me"

"You need to learn more and very fast," Halo said in a serious tone.

"Why the rush?" Patrick asked.

"There's different kinds of evil out there, Patrick. And one kind has just arrived," Halo remarked.

"More bad guys?" Patrick asked.

"No, not criminals. Something different, something...hateful,"

Patrick stared at Halo, waiting for more information, beginning to feel a little uncertain now.

"You'll be needing an upgrade," Halo cut in.

"An upgrade?" Patrick asked, looking at Halo.

Halo vanished into his fist, without prompt, providing no more information.

"That's a bit ominous," Patrick said aloud.

He looked out his open window, feeling the gust of wind blow over his forehead. He took one last look at his hand before he turned out the lights.

Chapter 7

Patrick shot up from his sleep before his eyes were even open. Not from a nightmare, and certainly not from a good dream, his body naturally awoke early in the morning, as well as his thoughts. Patrick's brain has been re-wired since his mother's diagnosis. He woke up feeling the weight of hopelessness and little motivation weigh him down. Back then every day was a challenge. From driving back home to see her, to the agonizing choice of staying the night or not, having to say goodbye. *Was I there enough?* Patrick wondered.

These days are still the same, yet painfully different. The guilt of her death stabbed Patrick in two ways. The first stab was the pain of losing her, watching her suffer, and to see the fear of death in her eyes. The second. The known relief of her dying.

Patrick peered out his third-story window as he cracked it open. Patrick leaned over the window, hearing the buzz of the city, feeling the warm breeze run over his face. He thought of the night before. Halo said some pretty weird things before he fell asleep.

I can ask questions, but Halo probably won't answer. So what's the point? He thought.

He went about his day, doing his regular hobbies, living a normal, mundane day. He wanted a quiet day, and he got it. The job there might be the most normal thing about his life, besides the lack of relationships. Nothing was ever weird or magical there, and he appreciated that about it. He found comfort in its familiarity. He liked working with his co-workers, and sometimes his boss, who could be un-supporting in major ways. But most of all, he enjoyed working in the same building as Summer.

I'm sure a lot of these guys do too, he thought to himself as he looked around his building at all of the other men.

Patrick finished his day and arrived at Building Blocks. He opened the door and walked in, finding it a madhouse as usual. Kids were running around as fast as possible, either chasing each other or running away from the staff. Other staff members were shouting directions, and he knew somewhere a phone was ringing. He paused for a moment to listen and heard it, *ring ring ring. There it is,* he thought.

Suddenly a rush of blood swirled through his head. Patrick felt his eyes twist and his brain go numb. With a sudden jolt, his mind brightened back up, causing him to steady himself against the wall. He regained his head and continued through the living room. A little boy ran across his path, causing him to stumble.

"Hi, Patrick," said the impeding boy before he ran off.

Patrick sighed a happy sigh and smiled. *This place can be normal too*, he thought.

"Mr. Patrick!" screamed another little boy named Connor. Connor and another kid named Zane rushed over to Patrick's legs and hugged them tightly.

"Whoa," Patrick said as he balanced himself out. "Hey, guys...I might need my legs back."

Both kids let go and look up at him. "Mr. Patrick, do you want to see the fort we built? We made it out of blankets and paper" Conner asked

Paper? Patrick wondered.

"You guys made a fort? That's awesome! Of course, I want to see it!" Patrick replied. "I have to go see Ms. Amanda first, but I'll be right back down, okay?"

"Okay but hurry! Christopher has been destroying it, he won't stop!" Connor said in a very animated way, using his hands and shoulders.

"Okay, okay. I'll be right back" Patrick said quickly before he turned and ran upstairs. Saying hello to the kids and staff that he passed by, Patrick turned the corner and walked to Amanda's door. He knocked and entered to see Amanda and Anna speaking.

"Patrick hey, come in," Amanda said looking genuinely happy to be seeing him.

"Hey sorry, I didn't know you guys were talking." Patrick apologized then looked at Anna. "Hey, Anna."

Anna smiled back politely.

"It's fine, come on in," Amanda said, as Patrick walked further in.

"Yeah, so I just wanted to see if there were any special things you wanted me to do tonight" Patrick said then clapped his hands together.

"Otherwise Conner and Zane built a fort, so I was going to check that out, it sounds cool."

Amanda looked down at her desk as if she had a list. "Nothing much tonight. If you wouldn't mind helping in the kitchen again for dinner. That would be great."

"Yes for sure, I'll be there!" Patrick exclaimed while turning for the door.

Amanda spoke back up. "Hey Patrick, so we were just wondering... what do you do when you're not here, being amazing"

Anna slowly turned around to look at Patrick, awaiting his answer.

"Why, what have you heard?" Patrick asked in a coy, joking way.

"Nothing, that's why we were wondering," Anna said.

"Oh, WE? We were wondering? Patrick asked, looking directly at Anna.

Patrick smiled and turned back to Amanda before answering.

"I like to work out and play video games. Uh, I play the piano, and I've gotten pretty good at that. You know normal stuff," he said.

"Do you have a girlfriend?" Anna asked.

"Yeah there it is...I thought so... but no, I don't" Patrick answered.

"Well you're a very handsome man, I'm sure there's someone out there interested," Amanda said, sounding like a supportive mother.

"Anyone, you're interested in?" she asked.

Patrick froze for a moment. Unsure if he wanted to share that information, he looked at Amanda and Anna, who stared back, waiting for an answer. Patrick caved from their pressure and eye contact. "Yeah, there is this one girl," he relented.

"Oh, what's her name?" Amanda asked.

"Uh, her name is Summer, and we work together,"

"What's she like?

"Do you have her number?" Anna followed up.

I want out of this moment so badly, Patrick thought. *That blanket fort sounds awesome.*

"She...is...nice, yeah she's nice," Patrick said, getting his point across hopefully.

"Do you have her number?" Anna asked again.

Patrick shot a glance at Anna who seemed to be enjoying the moment. She smiled back.

"No, I don't," Patrick answered honestly.

Anna doesn't say anything. She shook her head and turned back around.

Amanda stood up from her chair and paced towards Patrick.

"Well I'm sure she does like you Patrick, I mean we love having you here."

Patrick smiled politely as Amanda wanted to convey her message even more. "No I mean it Patrick; you do a lot for these kids. More than you realize. They love when you come in. It makes this whole place happier when you're here. So thank you." Amanda said as she looked at Patrick intensely, trying to add more meaning to her words.

"Thank you, Amanda," Patrick said, looking back and smiling at her trying to match her level of sincerity. "And you're welcome…. these kids… deserve it"

Patrick smiled again and excused himself back downstairs to see the fort.

Once downstairs, he found Conner and Zane outside the fort. They both were yelling at Christopher, trying to get him to stop wrecking their fort. The kids saw Patrick walking over.

"Mr. Patrick, tell Christopher to stop breaking our fort!" Zane said frantically while trying to rebuild the broken areas. Patrick stayed calm and looked for Christopher, who was under the fort rummaging around.

"I'm not wrecking it! I just want to help" Patrick heard Christopher say from under the cushions.

"Oh, you hear that guys? He just wants to help you guys make this the biggest blanket fort ever" Patrick said.

"But he's ruining it!" Conner yelled again.

"I'm helping!" Christopher said in a more frustrated tone.

Patrick lowered himself down by Zane and Conner. "How about this, if you guys let him help and let him stay in here, Christopher will promise to protect you guys and the fort, right Christopher? Patrick said loud enough for Christopher to hear.

"Right" Christopher agreed from under the blankets.

"And I'll even go grab the big blankets from the upstairs closet, don't tell Amanda," Patrick told them.

They both look at him with eyes wide open. "The big blankets?" They said in unison.

Patrick nodded his head slowly before Zane ran over to Christopher to tell him the good news. Patrick wanted these kids to like each other, he tried hard to bond with them, and help them bond with each other. All they have is each other at the moment. Patrick smiled, knowing he re-directed the situation and started walking back upstairs to get the big blankets. Patrick was a few steps away from the closet when he felt his fist getting warmer. He knew what that meant and scoped out a safe place.

Patrick slipped into one of the bedrooms and shut the door. Checking that no one is around or hiding, he decided it to be clear. Halo appeared in his hand with prompt.

"You can't just appear whenever you want," Patrick said, scolding Halo.

"We didn't. We waited until you were ready"

Patrick looked around the room and realized Halo was right.

"I was giving you a warning so we could talk," Halo said.

"Okay, what's up?" Patrick asked.

"Something *hateful* has arrived"

"Here? Here like Building Blocks? It's here now?" Patrick asked and pointed at the floor, insinuating the whole building.

"No, not here, In the woods, where we train," Halo mentioned.

"It's there now, uhh can it wait? Patrick asked.

"No, this needs your attention now"

"Is someone in danger?" Patrick asked.

"Not yet, but soon" Halo replied.

Patrick took a deep breath; he could feel the anxiousness coming from Halo. He knew he had to go. Halo disappeared into his hand as he walked to Amanda's office to tell her. She was alone now reading some paperwork. He knocked twice to get her attention. She looked up at him, surprised, as he started talking.

"Hey, Amanda so I remember you saying all those nice things about me, how I'm amazing and super dedicated…Uh but I need to leave right now, something came up. Would that be okay?"

"Yeah that's fine, we should be covered. Is… everything…okay?" Amanda asked, starting to get worried.

"Yeah it should be, just need to make sure," Patrick said trying to sound confident. "Thank you, I will see you Wednesday," Patrick said while rushing out the door.

He stopped at the top of the stairs before he turned around back toward Amanda's office. He quickly rushed over to the closet and opened the door. He grabbed a bunch of blankets before heading downstairs. Patrick reached the living room where Conner, Zane, and Christopher are, and threw the blankets down beside the boys.

"Here you go guys," he said.

The kids rush to the blankets and grab as many as they can.

"Thanks, Mr. Patrick!" Conner yelled.

"You're welcome, play nice okay," Patrick said before sneaking out of the room. He knew saying goodbye would take too long and be messy, so he had to sneak away.

He hopped down the steps of Building Blocks and crossed the street to his car. He opened the door but hesitated to enter. He turned back to Building Blocks to take it in. *It's a special building,* he thought.

Patrick stayed admiring the building when he noticed a voyeur. From one of the windows upstairs, Patrick saw Laney, the new girl who talked about superheroes. She stared stone-faced, as their eyes met. Her face remained emotionless as they looked at each other. Laney, after a tense moment, broke and waved shyly out the window. Patrick smiled back and waved before turning to his car to get in.

I should get to know her more, he thought.

Chapter 8

Patrick arrived at the woods and parked in his usual spot, seeing no other cars. He stepped out of car and looks around to make sure. Feeling anxious and afraid about what lies in the woods, he knew he has to hurry as the sun was close to going down.

"Oh, shoot" Patrick exclaimed.

"You won't need them" Halo responded.

"So I'm going in there without my gear?" Patrick asked.

"I have gear for you,"

"You do? Like how?" Patrick asked as he pulled Halo up to his face. He turned the rope looking from all angles. Patrick was joking around but understood Halo probably never got the joke.

"No, I get it" Halo responded.

Patrick looked at Halo and squinted. "Man, you're *really* in my head, aren't you?"

"Yes, I need to be. You'll be getting your suit now." Halo said as if it was about to happen immediately.

"My suit? You have a suit for me?" Patrick asked as he tilted his head down in surprise. His heart began to beat faster. The excitement and worry mix, as he thought about the possibilities of this suit he's about to receive.

"So what if I don't like it though? Patrick asked.

"It's all you get…you'll like it, you always will,"

Patrick wondered what Halo meant by that but moved on. *It's a lost cause anyway*, he thought.

"Okay," Patrick said as he nodded and walked into the forest. He picked a spot and planted his feet in the dirt. "Ready," he said.

"Okay, form the rope into a circle which can cover your whole body and lift it over your head," Halo instructed.

Patrick molded and flattened the rope, stretching it into a car wheel sized circle. He raised it over his head with both arms.

"Now let go," Halo said.

Patrick dropped his arms, and amazingly, the disc stayed suspended in the air.

Halo spoke up. "Now raise your arms and let the disc cover your body"

Patrick stared up at the disc and did what's told of him. He raised his arms and watched the glowing circle slowly lower over his hands. The yellow mold felt warm to the touch as it reached further down, warming his body. He watched as the disc extended to his face and closed his eyes before impact. He planned on keeping them closed until Halo said something. He waited for a couple of moments, feeling the heat reach his knees.

"You can open your eyes now," Halo said.

He did and saw then that he was holding Halo, in its rope form again. He also noticed that his hands were now cloud white. They're not his regular hands though, and they weren't gloves either. He made a fist and wiggled the fingers, feeling every movement. *They are my hands*, he thought.

He looked down at his feet and saw his legs covered in the same white color. He scanned up his body, seeing that his torso and abdomen were white too. Then came the glowing yellow trim around his waist and wrists. He touched his knees and pats down on his thighs.

"Are these sweatpants?," he asked Halo but got no response. He looked at his chest to see the rest of his outfit the same white color. The glowing yellow aura from his suit lit up his area in the twilight forest.

"Ready to go?" Halo interrupted.

"Yeah, just a second" Patrick said before running back over to the car to check himself out in the mirror. He got to the driver's seat window and admired himself, seeing his face covered in a white mask.

"Whoa, look at my eyes, they're so dark" Patrick squinted to see better, and as he did the eyes of the suit squinted with him. "And they move with my regular eyes? That's so cool!" Patrick said in excitement. "And I have a hood? That's cool too," he said as he flipped it up over his head. He looked at his chest to check for a symbol or a logo but saw nothing.

"You're disappointed?" Halo asked.

"I thought there'd be a logo or something...but no, this suit is awesome, definitely not disappointed" Patrick confirmed.

"We should get going," Halo mentioned, still sounding anxious.

"Okay, where is this thing?" Patrick asked.

"Near the cave, you destroyed"

Patrick headed over, proceeding with caution trying not to be too loud as they approached.

"Does this thing know we're coming?" Patrick asked.

"No"

"Okay good, let's surprise it," Patrick said, then waited for Halo to respond, but he didn't. *I'll have to make the plan*, he thought.

Patrick knew a spot where he could see the cave and hopefully whatever is out there lurking. The sun was getting lower by the minute, so he had to hurry. He got to his spot on top of the hill overlooking the cave then began looking for something he considered hateful and found it. He then understood what Halo meant by that. He stared in amazement at this creature the size of a cow, but with the fur and body of a grizzly bear, a strong large grizzly bear.

He squinted his eyes to see better and caught a better view. *That's no bear,* he thought. B*ears don't look like...that.*

He snuck in closer and hid behind a tree to get a better view. The creature was digging through the dirt, clawing at the earth with its large and foreboding paws. The bear-creature grunted and moaned out, making the ground under Patrick's feet rumble. The bear creature lifted its oversized head and sniffed the air. Its head turned to where Patrick could see its face. Patrick scanned its dark, hairy head and melted looking face before hiding behind the tree once more. He brought Halo up to his face.

"So, I'm supposed to kill that thing?" Patrick asked.

"Yes," Halo said quickly.

Patrick took a breath and looked back around the tree at the creature, getting a glimpse of its smoke-filled eyes.

"Patrick, you have to kill it, or it will do hateful things to your world," Halo said, feeling that hesitance in his mind.

Patrick thought for a moment and realized that the creature did look vicious and could kill someone if they came out here, or worse, went into the city.

"Ready?" Halo asked.

"Yeah, but you have to fill me in more about this...okay," Patrick said to Halo, feeling more frustrated than ever with Halo.

The lack of mutual understanding was beginning to bother him. *Now I have to kill for it?* He thought.

Patrick scoped out the creature from behind the tree and inspected it to be close to four-hundred pounds of strength.

"Screw it, no plan," Patrick said as he walked into the open, confronting the large and powerful creature standing forty yards away.

"Hey! Bear!" Patrick yelled, trying to get the creature's attention.

It turned to locate Patrick. As it did, Patrick noticed that the creature's eyes went from their uneasy, smoke-filled gloss to a dark and menacing red.

His eyes turned red when he saw me, Patrick recognized.

In a violent rage, the bear growled and abruptly stomped toward him. Patrick froze as he watched the creature head straight for him.

That thing flipped out when he saw me, Patrick thought again. W*hy?*

Patrick regained his composure and whipped Halo at the creature's front leg and wrapped it up. Patrick yanked hard, trying to knock the bear off balance, but it did nothing but move himself out of place. The creature powerfully stampeded forward, unfazed, and slammed into his hip, sending Patrick back those forty yards. Patrick collided with a tree before tumbling to the ground. Patrick came to a stop then rolled over to his back and looked up at the slowly creeping night sky.

"Ohhhhhhh, that sucked," Patrick moaned as he started getting back to his feet.

His body felt all the collisions, but it felt fine now. *I have a super-suit, I can take the hits,* he thought.

Taking that first hit gave him a reckless sort of confidence as he faced up to the bear again. "Round 2," Patrick said, clapping his hands together once.

"Ding ding."

The creature located Patrick and charged again with a rage that really worried Patrick. This time Patrick had a plan. Patrick charged back at the ferocious creature, planning to meet him in the middle for another collision. They get within attack range of each other as Patrick jumps-slid away from the creature's charge. He quickly formed a sword with Halo and slashed at the creature's front leg. He cut deep through its dense, muscular leg, getting in a good attack. The bear creature took the slash, but its momentum caused it to slam into Patrick on its way. It barreled into him, knocking him back, as the bear collapsed to the side. They both lay still after the collision before

Patrick rolled over and stood up. He rolled his shoulders, having felt that hit.

"Good plan, though," Halo said in encouragement.

"I just have to get used to this suit. It's different in here. I'll be good...and I just cut that thing's leg off so..." Patrick said, trying to save face.

Patrick turned to the creature, which was back standing on its three good legs. It charged again with monstrous intensity, fuming from its snout. It moved with a steady balance, even on three legs as it barreled toward him.

That thing can still run that fast? Patrick wondered. "New plan," Patrick said as he got into a stance.

He whipped Halo around a tree high above and leapt away safely out of the creature's path. It let out a loud grunt as it missed its target. Patrick landed on the ground and waited for another strike from the creature. It growled and turned to Patrick, about to smash into him again as Patrick swung his rope toward a tree and flew in the air. He turned at the apex of his leap and pointed his palm at the creature, and summoned as much energy he could into his palm. Patrick couldn't see the flames, but the energy was tremendous. Patrick felt the pressure filling fast, as he quickly fired off a yellow blast at the creature's body. He landed on a tree branch and watched the explosion unfold. The blast's explosion was quiet yet powerful and aggressive. He watched as dirt and grass expanded like fireworks through the forest ground. Dust and smoke filled the area in the aftermath. Patrick looked on as the smoke cleared, supplying him with a clear sight of the beast.

"It's dead," Halo assured him.

"Good," Patrick said, letting out a sigh of relief.

"Yes...good" Halo repeats coldly, getting Patrick's attention. The way Halo agreed seemed odd, but Patrick knew already not to dissect things like that with Halo.

She's dead, remember?

Patrick jumped down to the creature to study it. He poked at its dark, dirty face to make sure. As Patrick pressed his finger into the creature's forehead, its body began to melt and dissolve into the earth, like flour through a sifter. Shocked by the strange event, Patrick wondered if he should ask what that was about, but he was tired and wanted to go home. Patrick knelt and waved his hand through the area the creature disappeared feeling nothing, then hustled back to his car.

He hopped, buckled up, then started the engine. Pausing for a moment, Patrick took a deep breath and looked in his window reflection then tugged at his chest.

"Okay, now how do I get this off?"

Chapter 9

Patrick awoke the next morning drained of his energy, very much not looking forward to work. He wondered if he should be calling in sick, and knew he had every right to take a few days, yet the thought quickly disappeared as he realized it would be just him and his mind, alone together. Patrick opted not to call in, thinking his tiredness would wear off later in the day or him needing to eat something. He showered, shaved, and dressed, feeling like a zombie shuffling from room to room getting ready. Patrick paused for a moment in his living room and gazed at the picture of his mother and him at Christmas, the year she was diagnosed. *That was just two years ago,* he thought.

His life changed so dramatically. One minute he was a popular college student, and the next, he transferred and took care of her every day, trying to be a good son. Maria did so much for him, as a mother. Patrick knew he had to be there for her too. Both of them held hope that she would somehow pull through and fight the disease away. Science proved hope was meaningless, yet the way his mother acted around him made him truly believe.

Patrick picked the photo up, remembering the times he would come home and lay in her bed as she watched a movie or TV show. He remembered her watching Game of Thrones, asking him so many questions about the show. She had trouble remembering the plot and details of the characters, but she loved the show. It would have driven anyone else insane, but Patrick was so happy to talk with her. He didn't want to take any part of her for granted. *She's dead, remember?*

He set the photo down and took a deep breath. *Time to move forward,* he thought.

He drove to work, no music, no radio, just the thoughts in his head. He made it through lunch unscathed by any negativity and arrived back to finish the day. Patrick walked back to his office space, getting close as his fist started getting warmer. *I'm getting a call*, he thought. He scanned around the office for a place to go in private, choosing to sneak into an open meeting room. He closed some blinds, as Halo appeared in Patrick's hand.

"Patrick, everything okay?"

"Yeah, everything's...good" Patrick replied, confused.

"Your emotions are...wavering," Halo said.

"Yeah, I've been low energy all day. That might be the reason," Patrick instructed.

"That's not it, your emotions are dark, you are sad. Remember I am inside you. I can feel your emotions" Halo reiterated.

"Ew...don't...say that," Patrick said, shaking his head.

"It's not about last night, it's about your mother," Halo mentioned.

Patrick doesn't reply immediately. He knew that Halo knew anything he did or to be more precise, felt anything he felt.

"Yeah, I've been thinking of her a lot. I wish she was here. You can feel that, can't you? That grief, that guilt, that sadness?" Patrick said feeling emotional.

Halo didn't respond.

"You can feel my emotions but do you understand them, *Do* you? Patrick asked, making his voice echo throughout his head.

Halo didn't respond.

"No, you don't care. You just want to use me for...I don't even know what, you won't tell me, I'm going to need some time t—" Patrick got cut off by someone coming into the meeting room. He quickly hid Halo behind his back as they walked in. It happened to be his crush, Summer.

"Hey," Patrick said quickly.

"Hey...what do you have behind your back?" Summer asked, eyeing Patrick's arms tucked behind his back.

"Uhhh nothing, this is just how I stand now," Patrick said coyly, trying to be believable.

Summer smiled and looked at Patrick curiously. "No I saw something, what was it?"

Patrick realized he'd been caught and released his grip. He pulled his hands up front and opened his palms, revealing nothing.

Summer, confused, stared at his hands. "You really weren't holding anything?" she asked.

"Nope...just standing," Patrick said, shrugging his shoulders.

"Okay, well, I need to prepare this room for our meeting. Do you want to help?" Summer asked.

"Yeah! Wait, we have a meeting?" He asked as he grabbed a table.

They set up the breakroom for the meeting, chatted with each other and laughed. They finished the job and Summer went back to her office. His mood increased, and his energy heightened dramatically as he returned to his office space to close out the day. Not having any plans for the evening, he went back to his apartment and hung out by himself. He made dinner and started rewatching Game of Thrones, feeling the nostalgia of a once deeper life.

He continued to think all night. He thought about his Mom and about his time spent with Summer during the day. He thought about his future and the children at Building Blocks.

Yet in all his time thinking at night, not one minute was spent thinking about Halo or his other life. He chose not to hit the streets for bad guys and decided not to go to the woods to hunt monsters. He thought and he wished for a better life, before falling into a blissful and comforting drowsiness.

Chapter 10

T

he clock on Patrick's phone struck six forty-five as his alarm rang him awake. Patrick opened his eyes and stared at his white pillow, then began to ruminate in his sad, sad head.

She's dead, remember?
You're alone, remember?

This is your life, remember?

Patrick sighed, and remembered why he hated waking up. He got out of bed and went about his day, basically on auto-pilot. Meetings, event planning, and budget reform, all tasks hollow in meaning, slightly took his mind off his life. He was begging to get used to the work world. Patrick has always been a team player, leader, or follower; it never mattered to him and was always situational. He would get his job done and some, if that's what it took. The day ran longer for him than his mood should have allowed, with every minute seeming to be longer than the next. His energy and feelings were affected the same way, like yesterday all over again, but this time he never ran into a friendly face, the friendly face he wanted.

He clocked out and drove over to Building Blocks, knowing that going over there would usually improve his mood. He got out of his head that way. And it was always an interesting day there, with mood swings that ranged from vicious hatred to pure joy. He loved that about Building Blocks and relished his time there. It's become a different type of family for him. *One I hope I don't let down*, he thought.

The day at Building Blocks started as most do. He strode up to Mrs. Pierce to get the game plan for the day and went to work. That day his job was to paint the garden shed. He was happy to get the job, being outside usually helped his mood. Plus it was the start of spring, and the weather in the city was getting nice again. His favorite time. When life returned from the dead, so did his mood.

He went out to the shed where Building Blocks kept their lawn supplies and equipment and unlatched the swinging door.

Patrick swung the door open with force then located the paint. As he did, he heard approaching voices and turned to see three boys walking out toward him. They saw Patrick in the shed and hustled right over.

"Hey, Mr. Patrick!" The boys took turns saying.

"Hey, guys" He returned.

"What are you doing?" one of the boys asked.

It's Evan, Patrick quickly recalled.

"I'm going to paint and clean the shed, Evan," Patrick replied with a smile.

"Can we help?" Evan asked eagerly.

"Of course! That would be great" Patrick said as he grabbed his equipment.

He passed out small brushes to the kids and taught them the basics of painting. The kids listened intently and practiced on the wall without paint. Patrick dipped his brush into the can and brushed the paint onto the side of the shed.

"Back and forth, just like this" Patrick instructed the group.

The kids watched his instructions, determined to learn, then began getting noticeably excited. Patrick couldn't help but notice the bright colored mist over top of their heads. The site of their excitement gave him a new appreciation for the story he has been given.

"These aren't toys though, okay? I don't want to see you painting each other red" Patrick said to the kids sternly.

They agreed and started their painting session. More kids came outside to help, and Patrick taught them too. He barely did any painting himself because of the group that came to help. Amanda even came outside to see what all the commotion was about. She walked over to Patrick who was looking at his team of happy painters.

"See, this is what I was talking about. I sent you out here to paint the thing"

"Yeah, I know, I'm better at delegating," Patrick said jokingly. "I couldn't say no to the help"

"These kids love you, they just want to be around you," Amanda reinforced.

Patrick smiled and looked back to the kids, seeing them all working so hard for something they have in common. He focused on the kids to see their emotions once more. Overhead he saw more forming clouds above the kids, mostly orange and bright yellows and pinks. During that moment the kids weren't dragged down by life or their futures, they were in this moment wholly and emotionally.

There is a lesson in there for you, his mind called out.

Watching their emotions, he abruptly remembered another kid who has been absent today. He turned to Amanda.

"Hey, Amanda, where is Laney?"

"She's inside drawing, I think," Amanda said, still watching the other kids.

"Okay...I'm going to see if she wants to help too" He said, walking past Amanda. He paused and looked back over his shoulder to Amanda.

'Uh...Amanda, what 's her story? If I can ask?"

Amanda's eyes met Patrick's then drifted away.

She's trying to remember, Patrick noticed in her reaction.

Her face contorted into a befuddled expression, as she smiled at Patrick and shook her head.

"I'm not exactly sure, I think...a man dropped her off? I can't recall. I just know she's in our system" Amanda said.

"Was it her father?" Patrick asked.

"Not sure. No other information was provided. We called Social Services, but nothing ever surfaced on their end. Her name is Laney, that's all we know. She's such a sweet girl."

Patrick nodded in agreement and walked inside to find her. He located her in the large open living room, sitting on the ground drawing another picture. Patrick took a moment before walking over to study her emotions.

What is that, a dark green? Patrick thought and sighed. *That probably isn't good.*

"Hey Laney, do you remember me?." Patrick asked from the sidewall in the living room.

Laney turned. "Of course I do," she said in her pure, innocent voice, almost contradictory to her colors and emotions.

"Yeah, we talked about superheroes, and you showed me your picture," Patrick said, helping her connect the pieces she never needed.

Her face stayed unchanged as she recalled her drawing. Patrick walked over and plopped down into the soft cushioned couch. He looked down at her, seeing the picture she was drawing, and recognized a flower, one with patterns and lots of pedals with different but matching colors. It seemed familiar to him.

"Hey Laney, that's a beautiful flower. I learned to draw one just like that. Who taught you?" Patrick asked.

"My dad," Laney answered.

"Wow, that's a lot of colors, it's like a rainbow," Patrick mentioned, trying to get her to loosen up. "That's actually the only flower I know how to draw," He finished with a laugh.

Laney looked up at Patrick, who smiled in return. She looked at him with an expression of skepticism and squinted her eyes slightly. She looked away and colored in another pedal. Patrick watched as the emotions misting over top Laney began to roll and turn. *She's so sad,* Patrick could see in her. Yet her colors were scattered, some blue, some faint red, some yellow slivers on the edges.

Strange, but warm, Patrick thought as shivers rolled over his neck and down his back.

"Laney, is everything okay?" he asked.

Silence fell over the two in the living room when Laney did not respond. Patrick decided to push a little further. He took a deep breath.

"You know I get really sad too, Laney, everyone does. It's okay to be sad" Patrick said, testing out his future fatherly advice.

Her head tilted sideways a bit, but she kept drawing, half trying to ignore Patrick.

Patrick made one last attempt. "Okay, I'll go away…but if you want, everyone is outside painting the shed. We could use a superhero or two to help"

Laney stopped drawing and froze at his words then looked at Patrick. After another odd, tense moment, her face contorted to a smile. She stood up, and raced outside to the shed, with Patrick right behind. The rest of the afternoon, they finished their job and cleaned their mess, ate dinner and finished any school work they had. Patrick said his goodbyes to everyone and drove home after a day well spent. Yet, as soon as he got home, inside his quiet, dark apartment, his mood changed.

He thought about his life, and where it was heading. He thought about his mom. *She's dead, remember?*

He wondered if he was a good person. He always tried to be for the ones around. *But am I? What did I do to deserve this?*

He thought about the kids at the orphanage and wondered if he was good, even before them. He thought about Laney and her emotions being scattered all over the place, from one end of the spectrum to the next. *Why was that?*

He got back to his apartment and immediately laid on his cold kitchen floor. *It's all so quiet…and it's…so dark.*

Patrick was alone again. He closed his eyes, trying not to think at all. A thought would float into his mind and Patrick would usher it away, continuing with a clear mind. He imagined himself sitting in a rocking chair outside his family home, feeling the warm air hug his body and the breeze sliding off his fingertips. He'd watch his thoughts cross his path and help them leave, friendly and calm. After a pleasant ten minutes or so, he opened his eyes and stood up. He looked at his fist and summoned Halo.

"Hello, Patrick"

"Hey" Patrick replied.

"Ready to talk?"

Patrick smirked, then smiled. "How'd you know?"

Chapter 11

"**W**here should we start?" Patrick asked Halo.

"I'll tell you what I can," Halo said in response, repeating his same claim from the past.

"Right, of course...okay, let's start with the bear creature monster thing. What was that?"

"The reason you have these gifts," Halo said. "They're here to spread death. You're here to preserve and restore life. When winter decays in nature, spring follows with restoring life.

"So I'm spring? And the monster was winter?" Patrick asked slowly, trying to get his wording right. *Would that even matter?* He wondered.

"Yes, you understand" Halo replied.

"It can't be that simple though, nothing is ever that simple"

"It's not, we knew that using spring and winter would help you gain a base knowledge. The monsters are ever-growing manifestations that, when untamed, can become reality." Halo ended his lesson ominously.

Patrick nodded his head in understanding but had a different thought. *We?* Patrick recalled hearing what Halo referred to itself as.

Halo halted Patrick's thought. "You and I are now what's called a Deva. A spiritual force behind nature, a separate evolution of humanity. You are to protect and preserve this world's ecology from those growing manifestations"

"So basically...I'm a lawnmower, If the grass gets too long... I cut it" Patrick chimed in, understanding his true purpose in this world now. *A lawnmower,* he thought.

"We knew you'd understand quickly," Halo said again.

Patrick cocked his head back and brought Halo up close. "Okay, so who is *WE?*".

Halo stayed silent, which didn't surprise Patrick. He knew that if Halo didn't answer immediately, *they, apparently, never will,* he thought. *This must be something they can't answer.*

Patrick spoke back up. "Are *we...the* power behind the Devas? Just a simple guess?"

Again, Halo doesn't respond and Patrick decided to move or was rather forced to, without persistence.

"So can people...real people, normal people, see the monsters? And is there a different name for the monsters? Cause monsters are just boring" Patrick said, waiting for a reply, and to his surprise, Halo decided not to answer. *He may be done answering for a while.*

"Did I offend you? Okay, well then, should we hit the streets?... I don't want to stay here" Patrick said, looking around at all of his stuff.

"Good idea, I will locate some crime." Halo said energetically.

Patrick rolled his eyes. *What a quick change in attitude,* he noticed.

Patrick transformed into his white and yellow suit and swung to the roof, up through the fire escape. He wanted to be able to see all of the colors in the city and to see where he is needed. It's a large city to Patrick, but to the rest of the world, maybe not. Over one million people lived in those partially happy and mostly sad streets. He peered out through the city before getting distracted by his flashy suit.

"Man this suit is so cool, I feel invincible in this thing" Patrick jumped up, floating higher than he thought he would as his stomach turned upon his descent. His toes lightly met the ground, as his excitement ratcheted up.

"It's like gravity doesn't affect me as much," he said, as another important thought came to mind.

"Yes, you are bulletproof when you wear that suit" Halo answered.

"You sure? I don't want to be talking trash to some crook and then get shot in the face" Patrick said almost chuckling at the thought.

"Yes, that would be...bad for business, you would say," Halo said, coming closer to landing a joke.

"And I don't lie to you," Halo corrected, sounding sterner.

"Yeah, you just don't tell me things" Patrick replied.

"That's not lying," Halo quipped.

"Well then tell me a lie then," Patrick urged the mystical entity.

"That girl you like from work...doesn't feel the same," Halo said.

"Oh, good one" Patrick retroted then found himself silent for a moment, thinking hard about what Halo just said.

That's a lie though, so does she like me? But does Halo know the—.

"Shall we go?" Halo interrupted.

Patrick snapped too.

"Yep," he sparked, before heading through the city, jumping from rooftop to rooftop with graceful ease. He paused to scope out the area.

"Okay, so what do you have for me?" He asked Halo.

"There are more instances of trafficking and abductions twelve blocks east,"

"Seriously?" Patrick replied, surprised at the update. "That's so horrible, why do people do such horrible things to each other?"

Patrick sighed in frustration. "Let's get to the bottom of that operation then," He said as he continued east as fast as he could. *This is east, right?* He thought as he continued his trek.

He arrived at the location Halo provided and hustled over to the edge of the building to get a glimpse of people being loaded into large, stationary delivery trucks. They are out by the docks of the city, which is where Patrick always thought human trafficking would go down. He's eager to help but scanned the area first.

It's a team of five guys. Two keeping watch with...assault rifles from behind, the other three, loading the people in, fifty yards away.

"Okay Halo, I don't want the other three guys going after the hostages when they see me take out the lookouts. That's not a gamble"

Patrick thought up a plan that he hoped would work out well. *I took down the bear monster, I can do this*, he thought confidently.

He set off into the action and maneuvered his way into position down the building and across the street behind the lookouts. He quietly climbed up the half wall and stalked his prey. *Neither one is looking,* he noticed.

Patrick snapped Halo in two and lassoed both guards around their necks from behind. He yanked hard and reeled them in, by twisting Halo around his arms. He quickly knocked them each out with a swat to the side of their heads and drugged them away.

Well, fantastic! He said to himself as he ragdolled the crook's body behind a dumpster.

He walked over the edge of the wall and peeked at the other men. *Oh, they do have guns, wow I missed that,* he thought to himself, disappointed in his perceptiveness.

Without hesitation, Patrick attacked, he lept and glided through the air toward one of the criminals, and connected with a knee to the back of the middle man, driving him down into the concrete. The other two guards turned from shock, then saw their fallen workmate and realized their situation. Patrick could see it in their expressions, like a magazine, each moment of their processed thought was like reading for Patrick. One shift in expression, one page turned.

Patrick slid quickly and gracefully around to the side of a guard and grabbed their shoulders tightly.

It's a woman, he noticed as he tossed her into the other guard. He jumped over to the hostages and formed Halo into a wide shield in front of him and the hostages. They huddle together, hugging each other for safety, as they look on in shock and awe at Patrick in his glowing suit, as he spreads out his glowing rope to cover their area. The two remaining gunmen must have gotten up because gunfire rang through the air. They fired their weapons into the glowing wall as Patrick and the others heard the shots and braced for impact. Patrick looked around for any sign the bullets went through but it appeared nothing happened when they hit. *They just disappeared? Guess you don't lie, Halo*

Patrick looked up to the hostages. "Okay you guys stay behind this okay," he said as he nodded, trying to get them to nod back in agreement.

They eventually nodded before he jumped straight over the seven-foot glowing yellow wall and landed as the lookouts were reloading their guns. Patrick noticed one of the gunmen he knocked out earlier came too already. He got to his feet, ready to fight. Patrick then notices the man's emotions as he is raised. *Solid grey?* He pondered.

Patrick stood confident and unmoved as the gunmen scanned him over. Patrick looked back at them with his shade black eyes, trying to instill a little intimidation. He squinted his eyes, empowering the effect he hoped to deliver. One of the gunmen dropped the rifle and whipped out a second firearm, a backup handgun, and without warning fired right at Patrick who had no time to react. He closed his eyes, waiting for a sudden rush of pain to rip through his body. He opened his eyes when the firing stopped, hoping to not be on the verge of death. He looked down and as promised the bullets disappeared on impact, leaving him unharmed. A loud sigh of relief escaped Patrick as he returned attention to the gunmen.

"Oh good, that was me testing something out. Cool right?" He asked each gunman while he gave them a thumbs up.

He got no response and decided to attack. He leapt forward as they fired at him again, but to no effect and swung his leg, lifting one gunman into the air, and followed with a kick to the stomach, knocking the man back fifteen yards. *That felt good,* Patrick thought, wanting to fight more.

The newly awakened gunman moved in to fight Patrick alongside his fellow associate. They both charged in, firing punches and knife slashes as fast as they could. Patrick blocked and dodged each attempt. He swiped and guided each attack away, leaving them frustrated. After he felt the energy leaving their bodies from their outburst, he went on the offensive. He blocked a punch and kicked one gunman's knee out and caught their shirt before they crumbled to the ground. He karate chopped the gunmen's neck with force, knocking them out as the other swung at Patrick's cheek, catching him off guard. Patrick felt the slight pressure from the crook's punch, then squared back up to the gunmen. *It's the woman,* Patrick noticed.

Patrick paused for a moment and stepped away from the woman crook. "You know I never thought a woman would be involved in something like this...you know trafficking" Patrick's head turned in sudden remembrance. "Wait, is that sexist?... Noo, it shouldn't be...right?" He asked the woman who turned to run away, knowing her freedom is coming to an end. She didn't get far before Patrick jumped her and pinned her to the ground. He needed answers.

"What is this? Why do you do this?" Patrick asked firmly, hearing his voice echo throughout his head.

"For the money, for my boss," the woman said in a panic.

"Money huh? There are other ways to make money, you know? Ever heard of unemployment?"

"You'd be surprised what you become numb to, I'm not evil," The woman said, sounding almost remorseful. But not enough for Patrick to believe her.

"Yeah alright, who's your boss? Where do I find him?" Patrick asked.

"I don't know, I just do the job, the main hang out is the club, Club Canines I think," she answered.

Patrick paused for a moment, reading her emotions above, trying to tell if she was speaking truthfully.

"What's your boss's name? What does he look like?" He demanded.

"His name is Sal Porruci. He usually wears nice colored suits" He looks like a boss, I don't know, I've never seen him" she said, which to Patrick felt more forthright.

The way her words sounded and the expression in her eyes told Patrick she was telling the truth.

"You just have all the answers huh? You just instantly folded. You weren't even like; *they'll kill me If I tell you"* Patrick said, impersonating a distressed character.

"They probably will if they find out, but *you*...whatever *you* are...they can't stop you, consider me smart," the self-proclaimed, smart crook said.

Patrick nodded slowly "You are caught though."

"Can you just let me go for the in—"

Patrick halted her and knocked the woman out. He stood up and looked at his surroundings, seeing all of the men and the one woman, unconscious. *A little messier than I hoped, but nice,* Patrick thought, as he high fived himself.

As his hands connected, Patrick heard a faint humming. Without thought, his head quickly turned to a few stalled semis. The semis sat motionless and quiet, as Patrick lowered himself down and glanced under the semis and into the darkness that seemed to be lifting the heavy trucks. To Patrick's curiosity, in the dark shadows, he saw two or three faint green colorations. He took a slow step forward for a better view, and with a slow and steady wave, the green objects moved sideways. Along with their movements came the low humming once again.

But that's not humming, that sounds like...piano chords. Patrick questioned.

Patrick stopped moving when the chords stopped too. *I heard at least four chords,* he thought. Patrick tried searching his short-term memory of the chords, but the more he tried the more he could feel it sinking away.

"Halo, was that real?" He asked, assuming he wouldn't get an answer. After a few seconds, he gave up.

"Yeah okay," he said as he walked over to the hostages. He had Halo shrink back into a rope and it flew over to his hand, as he did the hostages revealed themselves from the truck.

There's a lot of them, he thought. *Around twenty.*

Patrick walked over carefully, trying to keep everyone calm and comfortable. They all seemed too far shocked by him to be scared, they stared in awe as he approached.

"Everybody okay?" Patrick asked.

The group murmured, but Patrick heard a few yeses'. One woman spoke up from the middle.

"Are you a superhero?" she asked straightforwardly.

Patrick paused to think for a moment. "Yeah I guess I am now"

"You're so cool," a younger boy stated with an enthusiasm that Patrick thought impossible for a kidnapping victim.

"Thank you," Patrick said, winking at the boy.

"What's your name?" The boy asked eagerly, as the others listened.

"Oh, umm...I guess I haven't thought about that yet, I've been kind of busy"

Patrick thought back to previous conversations with Halo, he didn't want to be called Halo, and he isn't sold on Deva yet.

"Have any ideas? Patrick wondered aloud to the group.

"You like an Angel with all of the white and yellow," one of the group members said, Patrick couldn't tell who.

Patrick nodded his head slowly. "Hmm, I'm no angel though"

"You are to us," someone from the group mentioned, which is quickly followed by the others wishing their same feelings.

"Yeah, you're amazing!" You saved all of us! You must have been watching from the heavens!

The group settled down, as they continued to drink in Patrick's aura and presence. He looked over everyone's emotions to make sure no one was in really bad shape, emotionally speaking, and to his pleasure no one seemed to be too dark or cloudy. He has seen enough nasty emotions to know that dark and cloudy formations are always a sign of internal struggle. Yet everyone in the group seemed to be clearing up.

"Yeah maybe," Patrick said to the group. "But for now, we need to get you guys more help. I'll call this in, you all wait here, stay together."

He walked a few feet towards the road, ready to sling himself up to the rooftop. Before he did, he turned to give his audience one last impression.

"Thanks for the ideas, I'll be around," he said, as he ran and lassoed the roof, he jumped, and was propelled atop the building, out of view.

He called the police and watched as they arrived to make sure they did. He saw a news van show up fairly quickly as well. *This is how people are going to find out about me,* he thought. *I just need a name now.*

He left and scavenged back throughout the city, watching and protecting, like the guardian angel those people wanted him to be.

Chapter 12

The next day was flooded with mentions of what Patrick accomplished the night before. It was a human trafficking case that the police were never going to crack and they knew it, yet they took the credit anyways. It was big news. That big news was, however, overshadowed by another newsworthy mystery. Articles online and on the front page of the paper recounted the event, told by the hostages that saw Patrick do what he did. The angel lookalike idea took off quickly with the media. One of the hostages called him a 'Fallen angel', and throughout the articles and newscasts Patrick was now being referred to as just that, a 'Fallen angel'.

But it seemed that a simpler name, 'Angel' would catch on even more. Everywhere Patrick went, there were talks of Angel and who or *what* he was. There were skeptics and non-believers of course. Only the hostages and criminals saw him, a very small and untrustworthy population. Everyone at work was talking about the story too, it was hard to avoid a story like that. Patrick stayed quiet throughout the day. He wouldn't know what to say if someone were to ask him. This was all so new to him.

He went out to lunch at a nearby bar, where he heard more talk. One group in particular was a married couple talking about the newspaper headline together.

"Quite the story." The husband said, shaking the paper flat. "You think all these people are lying about the same thing?"

"Do I think they were saved by some angel? Sounds way too crazy for this world," the wife said. "We're all far too basic and rational to believe such a thing exists"

"As crazy as our world is, it's not a magical place" the husband mentioned.

Patrick listened to their words and understood now that a majority wouldn't believe it for a while. *The old man may be right, this world could stay simple,* he thought. He still had time to be normal and stay under the radar. *Would that be better for me?*

He ordered his usual and found a quiet spot to sit. It's a larger bar that was usually busy for lunch, but not at the moment. He planted himself in a booth and checked his phone, trying to look busy. He read through his newsfeed and gained more insight into himself as a headliner. He periodically looked up, scanning at the thin crowd enjoying their lunch. He spotted a familiar face as she began to open the restaurant door. As she walked in his way, his heart jumped.

Do I hide? He thought awkwardly.

"Summer," Patrick blurted out from his side booth, grabbing her attention.

"Hey," she returned with an inquisitive smile, then glanced at the bartender. She walked over to Patrick's table.

"Hey...are you stalking me?" Patrick asked, trying to find a balance between flirty and friendly. It might not have been either; he couldn't be sure.

"Yes, yes I am and I found you, you're under arrest" Summer replied jokingly, which calmed Patrick. "No I wasn't stalking, just looking for a place to eat."

"Oh well...have a seat" Patrick gestured toward the spot across from him.

"Sure, thanks," Summer said, then smiled to herself.

"See that makes me think you are stalking me, because you knew I'd tell you to sit with me," Patrick said, once more pushing the flirty, friendly boundary. He couldn't help it, he was nervous.

Summer only smiled in return before looking away and grabbing a menu.

Patrick cringed in his mind, *oof...not a great start*, he thought.

After some warming up on Summers' part, and some cooling down on Patrick's, they talked about music, and about the food they enjoyed, their past jobs, and hopes for the future. The conversation seemed effortless. This was the first time the two have sat down one on one before, yet it was an easy-going and fun conversation. The food arrived and they finished their meals. At the end they both walked out to the parking lot together continuing their conversation. Patrick could feel Summer being pulled like a magnet to the other side of the lot. *She must have parked over there*, he thought.

After Summer closed out the conversation, she took a few steps away. "So what are you doing this weekend?" she asked.

"Uhh...nothing much really, I was going to go see my aunt and uncle and cousins one day. Not sure though. What about you?"

Patrick has had past experiences with girls in this situation, he knew now would be the time to ask her out. His heart began to beat quicker as he awaited her answer.

Well, I don't have to ask her out, relax, he told himself.

"I don't have any plans, maybe go to the farmer's market or a bike ride, I'm kind of boring" Summer answered.

They both stayed silent for a while before Patrick realized he needed to say something.

"You should grab some tomatoes and peppers and make a salsa," Patrick said, instantly hating himself.

He watched Summer's reaction change, as a slight wave of disappointment floated across her face. Patrick involuntarily saw her emotions above as they began to swirl. Summer corrected herself and her posture then spoke.

"Yeah that could make for a good weekend, I'll have to grab some" Her shoulders shifted away, as her back became visible.

"Don't forget onions," Patrick said weakly to Summer as she stepped away. He felt horrible but was frozen in the moment as he watched her leave.

"You have precious feelings for her," Halo said in Patrick's head.

The words boom through and echo inside. Halo doesn't often speak to Patrick out of the blue like that, it startled him.

"Yeah I know," Patrick said in defeat.

"Whatever you did, or didn't do. I suggest not doing that again then," Halo said, teaching Patrick a lesson. "Her feelings dropped immensely when she turned away"

Patrick realized this. He then experienced a moment of pure courage and started jogging back to her car. She was in the car buckled up, as he knocked on the window and smiled. She lowered her window to talk.

"Hey so I know we talked about trying Indian food in the bar. Would you want to try the place just down the street with me Friday night?" Patrick said as slowly and calmly as possible.

She smiled and looked away straight ahead.

"Yeah sure, sounds exciting" Summer replied, turning back to him.

"Yeah? Okay cool, uh...I'll confirm with you at work later"

"Okay," Summer smiled again as Patrick lightly tapped her car's roof, then turned to walk away.

He got to his car and after a few minutes of pure disbelief and internal conversation, he decided to think later about it and headed back to work. The rest of the day flew by. He finished his work and went out for a run. He had good energy and wanted to do something active.

Is it a date? It has to be, he hoped during his run.

He started to doubt that he was even ready. He couldn't focus on relationships when his mom was sick. Those were two worlds that could not coexist. *Can my two new worlds coexist?* he wondered. *Can I balance everything and make it work?.*

He's been trapped in a loop of guilt and anxiety for so long. He got home, feeling good from his jog. and thought more about his life, probably too much. He finally got too anxious and knew he had to get out of his apartment. He stood up and took a few steps out of boredom into his kitchen. He brought his hand up and looked soothingly at its creases and calluses. He looked on, then made a fist. He tightened it and looked on. *Not tonight,* he thought. He grabbed his coat and his keys and left out the front door.

He made the twenty-five-minute drive out to his hometown and drove to the bordering countryside. Parking across the street, Patrick stepped out of his car and crossed to a cemetery. He walked by a large tree that seemed to be guarding the area, standing tall, with roots that should spread for miles below the ground. Patrick inspected the towering tree's beauty as he walked past. He located a familiar large smooth gravestone. He hasn't been there yet to see her, he knew the area and the stone's model, but to be there finally is all brand new. He arrived just as the sun was going down. Standing over, looking down at the headstone, he took a knee. With emotions swirling inside him, he read her gravestone.

> **Maria Ann Thempa**
> **Wife - Mother - Friend**
> **To call myself beloved, to feel myself, Beloved on the earth**
> **03 - 04 – 1979 — 05 - 04 - 2020**

Patrick sniffled like he's going to cry, but the tears never released. He sat across her gravestone, staring distantly into the stone. He stared for a long, quiet stretch, wanting to talk to her, or more accurately, talk into her gravestone. But that's proving to be hard still. He forced the words out, wanting to hear his voice and to prove to himself he isn't a coward.

"I'm sorry I didn't say anything to you," Patrick said, referring to his mom in her final days. The words were there, but they truly felt empty to him. He continued even so.

"I wanted to but I couldn't" Patrick started to tear up then. The words slowly built into his mind. Saying these things out loud was proving difficult. Every word felt different and real now, as his emotions grew in strength inside him. Tears fell from his eyes as he stared emptily at her engraved name. He put his chin in his arms and huddled his body together, hugging his knees. He looked to his side and imagined her sitting next to him. Trying to remember what she looked like, he looked back and stared at the headstone unable to.

"I miss you," he said as he took a deep breath.

He laid down by the stone with his hands behind his head and looked up to the sky. He closed his eyes to relax. He was in no rush, and after a relaxing twenty minutes or so, he fell asleep next to her. But not for long as he woke up shortly after feeling good and somehow healthier.

That was hard, he thought as he walked away feeling lighter. There was the feeling of closeness to his mom that he felt has been losing for some time.

That quenched the feeling a little, he thought. *Just enough.*

Chapter 13

The next day, Patrick woke up in cloudy calmness. *She's dead, remember?*

He rolled out of bed feeling peaceful, his energy upbeat, but his state of mind was calm and gentle. Crying can be cleansing and work as a pain reliever, a pain reliever that stops the pain signals from reaching the brain. When your brain feels pain, your emotions change, usually for the worse.

Patrick left his apartment for his university job, where nothing noteworthy was sure to happen, and it did turn out to be a real bummer of a day. He never got a chance to see Summer, but he knew he had other days before Friday to confirm their dinner. He finished work and it was over to Building Blocks he went, ready to start his day there. He knew the kids just got out of school and they'll be energized upon their freedom. He's thinking a soccer game is in store this evening. He arrived to find it as crazy as ever.

"Mr. Patrick! Mr. Patrick!" some of the younger kids screamed when they saw him.

"Hey guys! I'll be right back!" He told them as he walked up to visit Amanda and get the plan for the night.

"Hey Amanda," he said, after knocking on her door twice.

She looked up from her paperwork to meet him.

"Hey, how are you?"

"I am good," Patrick replied semi enthusiastically. "So what's going on tonight?"

She paused to think a moment, before locking on Patrick's.

"Well, the kids are all loving that Angel story, that must have been the big school story for the day, so they all want superhero stuff to do…and I don't even know what that would be."

Patrick exhaled and smiled then put a finger in the air, "Capture the Flag? But with superheroes?"

Amanda thought about the idea and nodded slowly. "Yeah that would work."

"Cool, I'll set it up," Patrick said while smiling brightly. He knew that Amanda would have approved of any idea, she just wanted to get the kids active in their excitement.

Patrick turned to the hall and walked downstairs to the dining area. It was snack time and they should be eating and conversing about their school days. He sat with them and mingled trying to be light and fun. He made an effort to always be positive, upbeat, and friendly when he was with the kids. He wanted to be a constant source of light feelings for these kids, and he knew they could use it. He knew the sad, brooding piece of him won't help the kids at all, so he tweaked his outlook on life before he entered the building.

After they put their dishes away Patrick made the 'Capture the Flag' announcement and it turned out to be a popular idea as most of the kids wanted in on the action. They all finished their snacks and screamed outside to the backyard. Patrick grabbed some actual scarves from the closet and scurried outside to meet them. He found the kids outside already chasing each other and jumping around. They all stopped and ran over to him when they noticed. He gave them the rules, assigned teams, and handed the scarves over.

"Okay, remember if you tag your teammate out of the *dungeon* you become a superhero. You need to save them." He made the word dungeon sound frightening and evil trying to get the superhero message understood. All of the kids prepared for battle and touched the fence to begin.

"Ready...set...go!" Patrick yelled as he watched the kids go crazy chasing each other and laughing.

These kids never really fight with each other, which is nice, *and odd,* he thought, as he walked backward, sitting on the porch, watching and yelling encouragement.

"Hey" a voice called out from behind his shoulder.

Patrick jumped a bit then turned around to see Anna.

"Anna, wow, you can't just do that" Patrick said as he turned back to the game.

"I wasn't trying to scare you," she snipped at Patrick. "What are they playing?" she asked then sat down beside him.

"Capture the Flag, but with an emphasis on superheroes,"

"Because of that angel thing from the paper?"

Patrick nodded slowly. "Because of that angel thing from the paper, yes."

"He did sound kind of cool. I've always believed there were angels watching over us. Here they are," Anna said with a certain passion that Patrick has never experienced from her before.

"That's a great attitude Anna...I'm starting to believe too" He told her, trying to grasp his own words himself.

"So you think it's an actual angel?" Anna asked.

Patrick hesitated, not sure what to tell her, he didn't even know what's going on with himself. *Am I an angel?*

He is a Deva supposedly. *But is that an angel? Is it something way different?* He thought then looked over to Anna, preparing his words.

"Uh... I don't know if it's an actual angel, but it's definitely something strange... if it's real" Patrick answered, trying to stay neutral.

"It's definitely real, the victims saw it and I believe them. And by the way, I think it's a woman angel" Anna said with the same matching enthusiasm from before.

"Really, why?"

"I don't know, I just do okay," She said in that familiar teenage tone Patrick has been so accustomed to.

There was a moment of silence as they watched the kids play. Patrick wanted to hear more from Anna about the angel, finding and feeling comfort from her reassurances to his actions.

"So what do you think *she* wants then? Why is she here? What should she do?" Patrick asks.

"My grandmother always said that angels are sent to protect people and deliver messages of good will and intent. Angels act as guides and intercessors to the living"

Patrick's eyes widened, "Intercessors?"

"Yeah, like a mediator between two sides." Anna answered maturly.

"Forces like good and evil?"

"Yeah, good and evil, good and bad, light and dark, all of that."

"Winter and Spring?" Patrick asked.

She pondered the idea. "Yeah that's a weird one, but it works."

"It's not that weird," Patrick quiped.

Anna shrugged.

"Huh, okay, you know your stuff Anna," Patrick said sincerely.

She gave him a slight smile, but Patrick could feel the weight of the words and see the look on her face to know they were coming from a painful memory. He didn't need to be an empath to see the change.

Probably her grandmother then, he wondered.

"Well these kids definitely believe in angels and superheroes now," Anna gestured towards the kids, who were chasing and tripping over one another, screaming and laughing the way kids should.

"I want to be an angel!" one kid yelled from the game.

Patrick watched the kids run and play, but his mind was somewhere else. The weight of his future and the guilt of his past kept him in a mindset limbo. He saw what this angel has done for these kids, they loved him, and they all want to be this force of good in the world, just like Patrick. Not the Patrick that turned into a white-suited angel and beat up criminals and slayed monsters, but the Patrick that showed up to the orphanage every day he should, with a respect for these kids and humanity in general. The kids wanted to be actual superheroes and fly and lift heavy cars at the moment. That may not be realistic but the thought of it growing up with these kids will make them into amazing people. *I can do both*, he thought. He could be a positive role model to people, while also being a source of light in the world as an angel. *That's what I'll do*, he thought.

He'll make everyone believe in angels and the good in the world. He meditated on the subject while watching the kids, becoming happier, becoming lighter. He smiled up at the sky and thought about his mom. *You're alive, remember?*

Chapter 14

After a fun night with the kids at the orphanage, Patrick was energized. having talked with Anna and experiencing the kids being enamored with the angel put what he could do in perspective. Patrick didn't want this responsibility at first, no matter how awesome. Who wouldn't want to be extraordinary and have a story like no other and to be a superhero? Every one of the kids at Building Blocks would, they'd give anything to change their lives for greater reasons. All of the staff would, hell, everyone he walked past on the street would. He just didn't want it to happen when it did, and so fast. He had so much going on in his life, so many separate strings pulling at his emotions, ripping him apart. Life pulled him towards sadness, towards grief, towards living a life his own. That's what his mom wanted, to keep living and search for happiness during the hard times, during the quiet times. Now he felt more ready, ready to be that light and inspiration. *I can inspire*, he thought, checking the clock, seeing **6:30 AM.**

That's enough time to do some inspiring work before work, he thought I'm the early morning.

Patrick suited up as the city's angel. He got a rush of emotions every time he changed, feeling that weird feeling, like putting on all of humanity's metaphorical *shoes,* feeling the world's life and positivity around him. It's a warm feeling, one he's enjoyed greatly.

"Ready Halo?" Patrick asked as upbeat and friendly as he could, hoping to start on good terms.

"Ready!" Halo responded with the same energy, possibly just for Patrick's sake, he wasn't sure.

Patrick left out for the city. With Halo leading him to all the bad things, Patrick wanted to take over and do his thing. He wanted to make his presence known and show this city he was real, and that he was there for them. And it didn't take long to do so. During his short morning run through the city, he covered as many areas as he could. No matter how big or how small, from burglaries to assaults, he was there saving the day. Whenever he would save a victim, they would respond the same way, with stunned eyes and dropped jaws. Sometimes in certain situations some would even drop and pray.

Before, Patrick wouldn't want people getting pictures of him, not wanting the spotlight. Now, he's changed his mind. He made sure to let someone snap a quick picture for proof now and then, while he also changed the way he interacted with victims and criminals, choosing not to talk as much. He thought himself being talkative would delude what he was trying to accomplish as a holy persona. He wanted to instill fear into the criminals and have them feel they have sinned or have done too many wrongs and are now receiving their repentance.

Patrick got through as many instances of evil as he could in forty-five minutes, deciding he should turn back home. But he never found what he truly wanted. He wanted to stop someone serious. He wanted to stop Sal Porruci, the boss of the human trafficking ring that seemed to be a booming business opportunity in the city.

I get Sal and that's a good first win...well...the bear monster was pretty big too, hmm.

Patrick stopped his run back to his apartment after that sudden thought.

"Hey Halo. Any more monsters around yet?" Patrick asked eagerly.

"No, I will alert you first thing when one does" Halo responded.

"How often does one pop up?"

"It depends,"

"On what?"

"Some monsters need less evil to form, some need more. The ones that take longer to form are the bigger threat" Halo answered.

"Was that bear...a dangerous one?"

Halo didn't respond, which worried Patrick.

"Oh you tease," Patrick said with a light laugh. "What's next? Anything out there, before I head home?

"I'm searching"

Patrick sat on a rooftop edge looking over the city, waiting for Halo's diagnosis of the city. His pride in the city has grown exponentially. He hasn't cared much for the city in the past, for many reasons. But he had a different way to help people now, so he cared again. *Is that right?* He wondered.

"There's a restaurant uptown that's heavy and polluted," Halo interrupted.

"How far?"

"It's quite a distance, may take a while, but I do believe it could be Sal Porruci"

"Sal Porruci, huh?" Patrick looked back toward his apartment's direction and debated on returning now for work, or going for Sal.

I have to choose quickly, being indecisive is the worst thing right now, he told himself.

"Okay, time-me." He said, before he quickly bursted from his spot, heading uptown, leaping across rooftops, and swinging off of anything he could to gain a boost. He got the hang of swinging after a while, and after he placed a lot more trust into Halo to assist him.

He arrived at a restaurant named *Bari and* he scanned the area, waiting for Halo to inform him of any disturbances. The restaurant was very busy at the moment, with deliveries being sent off and the wait staff bustling around. It would be a bad look to go crashing in. He decided to wait and watched eagerly, listening for activity and changes in emotions. He looked at the people on the street, seeing them happy and laughing with each other. Their colors were pure and light. He saw two men holding hands, walking together smiling, their colors were a soft red, pink almost. He looked to a bus stop and saw another pair of people moving their arms in an animated way, yelling about their relationship; presumably, Patrick overheard the words selfish...lying, and vindictive, so he assumed. Patrick looked at their colors and saw a dark flashing red, fading into a maroon shade for them both.

Out of the back alley behind *Bari,* Patrick then noticed three men walk out through the door. With them was another male being ushered forward, almost pushed. Patrick jumped over to the building, leaping it in a single bound. He looked down at the men, who were then loading the man into the parked blue escalade. Patrick dropped onto the other rooftop slightly above them unnoticed, getting a closer eye. *Now's the time*, Patrick thought as he jumped down off the roof and landed directly in front of the escalade. All of the men instantly stop and look, no-one moved or talked for a moment, and after a tense, almost awkward pause, Patrick stepped over to the two men on the left side of the large escalade. The first guy was nervous but took a swing anyway. Patrick dodged easily and swept the man's leg out from under him. He then slid the man under the car, getting trapped, which caused Patrick to chuckle. The other two men came around the escalade and went for Patrick straight on. They simultaneously swung for him, but Patrick blocked both punches, one after the other. Patrick countered and jabbed the man on the right in the nose, then yanked on the other man's arm, ripping him to the ground. Patrick kicked the other man in the chest, sending him into the escalade door. Patrick's attention was quickly drawn to the man they were pushing. He opened the escalade door, and sprinted off. Patrick watched the man run into the street, then out of sight.

He turned back to the fight to see the first man he put under the car trying to shimmy his way out from under the dirty undercarriage.

Behind, one of the men stood up and went for Patrick.

"Behind you," Halo said, causing Patrick to take notice. He decided to play dumb anyway.

The man approached quickly but quietly, gaining speed and momentum. He coiled his arm back while driving forward with his body. His fist flew for Patrick's head and in almost slow motion from the man's eyes, he watched as Patrick's head lowered and his fist flew towards the escalade window. He connected with the window with a contained thump, yet the glass didn't break. The man grabbed at his hand as Patrick gripped him by the shoulders, but his mind drifted off elsewhere.

It felt like I could...see that moment from his point of view. He thought.

"Let me try," Patrick said, returning his attention to the man.

He threw the man into the car window, waiting for the crash and shatter. The man connected, then fell to the ground unconscious. Patrick stepped to the escalade in confusion and looked at the window. *It still didn't break, huh?*

He tapped the window, feeling its density, and as he did, the man from under the car got up and out. Patrick saw him struggle free and walked over. He grabbed him and threw him into the escalade, pinning him against it with his elbow forced into the man's neck.

"You work for Sal Porruci?" Patrick asked.

The man didn't answer and put on a defiant face. Patrick wasn't sure what to do then, he wouldn't be torturing people, he knew that.

He thought for a moment before having an *ah-ha* moment. He grabbed the man and used Halo to swing onto a tall nearby building. He put the man by a wall and tied Halo around the man's legs so he couldn't run and walked out of hearing distance.

"Halo, what should I do here. I don't want to torture the guy but I need answers"

"If you get him to talk, we can tell if he's lying or not"

"Right, okay yeah,"

Patrick mused for a moment on how to proceed. He walked to the man and grabbed him, taking him to the edge and held him over. The man turned noticeably nervous, Patrick could see his colors shifting and moving rapidly, like atoms heating up.

"Sal Porruci, where is he?" Patrick asked, then shook the man.

"You won't drop me, I'll die. You're an angel right? You don't kill" the man said frantically, trying to stay strong.

Just as he said that Patrick stepped off the edge with the man into a free fall. The man screamed and yelled out in terror. They continued to fall until Patrick landed on the fire escape. The man continued to scream upon landing but stopped after he realized. He looked up to Patrick, breathing heavily.

"This height won't kill you. I don't have an issue with breaking every bone in your body," he shook him again, causing the man to moan out. "And I'm no angel...Sal Porruci, where is he?"

"I don't know!" The man screamed out.

Patrick could feel it, he was lying.

"Yes you do!" Patrick yelled then stopped in frustration as Halo's idea came back to him. He took a deep breath.

"Will he be back soon?"

"I don't know!"

...*He's lying*

"Will he be back this weekend?

"I don't know anything! You moron!"

...*He's lying, he will be.*

Patrick felt the man's emotions. He was nervous, anxious and most of all, he was trying to be deceitful.

He will be back this weekend, Patrick thought, feeling the lie through the man's words, knowing he just needed to siphon them out slowly to get the truth.

"Saturday or Sunday?" Patrick asked.

The man didn't answer. Patrick looked at him and studied his face, watching the tweaks and twitches, feeling each change of emotion. He listened and felt for the lie. It's hard but the answer seemed to come eventually.

"Saturday? or Sunday?" Patrick asked again and looked at the man's reaction to each option.

"Saturday,"

"No!"

...*Yes*

"Where will he be? Here? Canines?" He asked feeling giddy and waited for the lie and emotions to show themselves.

"Canines?" Patrick answered confidently and nodded. "Thank you"

"I didn't tell you anything!"

"Not consciously, no," Patrick said, then knocked the man out with his patented jab.

He jumped down with the man and threw them all into the escalade. He grabbed the keys and set the car alarm off. He phoned the police about a suspected robbery and left for home in a hurry.

I'll get Sal on Saturday.

Chapter 15

He's a true Superhero now. At least that's what the news was calling him, A superhero. He's a one-of-a-kind entity, shrouded in mystery, and the people of the city were loving him. The news loved covering every one of his pieces of historic heroism, having plastered the pictures of him on the front page of the local paper. The police, however, have mixed opinions about what Patrick was secretly doing. Most of the public was stuck in a captivated fog, of what their city has produced. Patrick's new notoriety has frightened this city's crime and in only two nights. He was already beginning to accomplish what he said he wanted to for this city. All he could think of was getting that next win against crime, *Sal Porruci.* Patrick wondered if he'll even risk coming back to the city. *Either way, I win,* he thought.

Patrick heard throughout the day more talk of his angelic actions. His popularity was growing immensely, kids loved him, parents adored him, many found religion in his workings as proof of god. He was quickly becoming a force from heaven to many, even though many haven't seen him. Truly though, he wanted to keep the two lives separate. His life as Patrick was messy as it was. *She's dead, remember?*

At work, things seemed to be quieter. There still was work to do, after all. He wanted a fast day so he could relax a bit later on. He was anxious about running into Summer to confirm the plans they had together, as Friday was fast approaching and he wanted to make their night concrete, and as luck would have it, he ran into her during lunch again. They sat together and talked throughout, once again having effortless conversations about nothing and everything in particular. Patrick waited till the middle of lunch to confirm Friday night with her, hoping she hasn't gotten engaged or anything crazy since. It never came up naturally, so Patrick had to be brave once more.

"Hey, so we are still on for this weekend? He asked as the conversation broke into a pause.

"Yeah of course!" She replied with good energy.

Patrick's heart skipped when she answered and was relieved to hear her enthusiastic response. That monkey on his back was getting heavy.

How are things going this well? Patrick wondered, as Summer spoke back up.

"Actually though, is it cool if my friend Claire comes too? She's coming from out of town and wanted to meet up"

Patrick could feel his body tense up, but didn't let his reaction change.

"Sure, yeah that's cool" he replied quickly.

He has heard that before and knew that wasn't a good sign. She might not feel comfortable enough yet to meet one on one. Or it could even be something more treacherous, *the friend zone,* he hoped wasn't the case.

"Awesome, thanks I'll tell her...I think you'll really like her" Summer said as she brought out her cell phone from her small bag and proceeded to text.

From that moment until Saturday night, Patrick was as nervous as he could be. He would have been nervous if it were just the two of them.

But now she wants to bring a friend? She doesn't want to be alone with me?... We just had two un-awkward lunches together, like, what?

Saturday night did eventually roll around and the plan was to go bar hopping downtown. Patrick met them at Summer's apartment, where they took a cab from. As expected he was a little nervous at first, but the chemistry and friendship between Summer and Claire made it easy for Patrick to take some pressure off.

Throughout the night there was dancing, drinking, laughing, and some serious tension. He got his alone time with Summer often as Claire was something of a social butterfly, so she was always talking with someone new, never landing too long anywhere. Patrick appreciated that and found some inspiration in it.

Summer seemed a little more nervous than usual when talking to him though, he could tell. She eventually became relaxed after they arrived and settled into the bar's rowdy and loud atmosphere.

The night ended rather abruptly, however, with Claire getting sick.

She was a partier, Patrick thought, knowing that he probably won't ever drink like that.

She was in rough shape and needed help getting home. Patrick knew they would be going separate ways. Claire needed help and Summer was her friend, she needed to get her back. Patrick had a lot of fun though and wanted to tell Summer before she left, but she beat him to the punch after loading Claire in the cab. She turned to Patrick who was waiting on the sidewalk.

"Hey, sorry about the ending debacle, I have to get her out of here. I had a lot of fun tonight though and... I feel really good after talking with you all night, you know I never really go into such depth with people in conversations like that, I probably talked too much"

"No, not at all, I liked listening to you, you are very...opinionated" Patrick said with caution, as Summer smiled back.

"Thanks...is that your way of saying you think I'm crazy? "Summer said with a laugh.

Patrick laughed in return, "Well now it is," he said, getting Summer to laugh along. "Well no, I just mean...I know what you mean, our conversations seem like they could go on forever"

A moment passed, as Summer smiled and nodded.

"Well you better get her back to yours, let's do this again sometime though," Patrick mentioned then looked at Claire in the backseat with her head pillowed into the cab window. "Maybe Claire can hang with us next time."

"You barely drank!" Summer said as she hit Patrick's arm. But yes, definitely"
She turned away and got into the cab. Patrick didn't want to stand there waiting, looking stupid so he turned too. He looked back over his shoulder to make one final look and wave.

"Goodnight Patrick!" Summer yelled from the window.

Patrick waved again awkwardly as the cab drove off. He looked over to the other street bars busy with people laughing and yelling. He watched as people crossed the street, speeding up before they halted the incoming traffic. He looked over to a woman typing in her information at an ATM and heard sirens blaring in the distance.

Now what? he thought. *I'm alone again.*

He looked back up at the tall building, and to the people on the other side of the street.

Maybe, he thought and nodded his head. Just then his hand got warm. *Halo wants to speak,* Patrick thought.

Patrick quickly went into an alley and crouched behind the large garbage container. He checked the area before summoning Halo.

"Hey, what's up?" Patrick asked, kicking a dirty towel out of his way.

"Sal is in town...and he's close by"

Chapter 16

"We are by Canines, aren't we?" Patrick asked, confirming with Halo in a newly refreshed tone.

"Yes we are"

"Excellent, let's get going and get this guy," Patrick said, before changing into his suit and heading north, leaping from rooftop to rooftop and swinging with Halo, feeling giddy and confident, ready to take down his first major bad guy.

After his recent victories taking down the criminals and the bear creature, he felt pretty confident going up against more threats. He's stronger and more resourceful than anyone and everything he has faced before. He's unnaturally strong and agile, he has a magical rope that can stretch and be molded into other creations, a right-hand man in Halo, and the motivation to use them all. He could change the world, one bad thing in life at a time. *Starting with Sal.*

"We're here," Halo stated.

Patrick stopped and perched off the rooftop next to *Canine's,* and stared intently at the building. There was no way of telling how many people were inside. Or where Sal was, and he knew it's not like he could just walk to the front door and knock.

"Wait, no yeah I could," Patrick said aloud.

"You're going to knock on their door"? Halo asked for reassurance.

"Yeah, I have other plans though, in case," Patrick said as he jumped down onto the sidewalk. He got to the crosswalk and pressed the pedestrian walk button. He leaned against the pole waiting for the go-ahead. After a few moments the light said go and he casually crossed the street and approached the front door of the restaurant.

Knock knock...

He waited for a moment patiently, inspecting the wooden door. *Is that cedar?* he pondered, feeling the wood, then knocked again.

Knock knock...

Patrick could feel a presence on the other side of the front door as their body reached for the door, the floor creaked as they stepped to it. He spoke out from the side door window, staying out of sight.

"Who is it?" the guard asked in a raspy, buff tone.

Patrick stepped around the edge of the entrance and located the window the man spoke out from. He rounded the corner and watched the man's expression, as it went from an upset glare to sudden terror. The man slammed the window before turning to run off.

Patrick squinted his eyes and walked back over to the front door. He reached for the handle, trying to open it.

"Oh, it's unlocked!" He said with surprise.

He swung the door open, letting it crash into the wall. Patrick looked into the restaurant and saw two guards standing in the foray on the center floor, pointing their guns at him. Patrick could read the fear and apprehension from the men's faces as they stood their ground.

Patrick raised his hands slowly above his head. "I'm only here for Sal, I just want to speak with him…and then have him arrested"

The two guards shifted their focus between one another, then back to Patrick.

They seem confused, Patrick felt as they were frozen. Patrick could feel their anxiousness, and for a split second, he understood their intentions and realized they were going to fire.

"Just don't guys, it doesn't work" Patrick told the guards.

The guard on the left stumbled back with eyes wide as he fired three rounds into Patrick's chest. The bullets dissipate into nothing, not even hitting the floor. Patrick checks his chest, looking for any bullet holes or missing parts, then looks back to the guards. He began walking toward them and pointed to the guard on the right.

"You can go…he stays," Patrick stated.

The guard ran past, through the front door as Patrick jumped on the other guard, and knocked him out with a quick kick to the chest, sending him into the wall. Patrick then busted through the doors into the dining area, trying to make a big show of it, a grand entrance. He looked around to a bare and somber dining floor. *Must be a slow night,* he thought.

Patrick did see a group sitting in the back corner who had just now taken notice. The group seemed relaxed, even though they had to have heard the gunshots from the other room. Patrick looked for a confident-looking Italian man wearing a bright suit, and landed on the man in the back, surrounded by a few other men dressed in regular suits. His maroon suit really stuck out from the others. The man who was presumably Sal Porruci sat back down after taking Patrick in.

"Looks like he's ready to talk," Patrick whispered to Halo.

Patrick stepped slowly over to the back of the restaurant carefully, knowing he had the upper hand. He wanted to make this bad man wait and sulk in sadness, knowing he was finished. He stopped about ten feet from their table and slowly turned his head to look at them.

"Sal Porruci?" Patrick asked.

The man sitting in the booth, wearing his fancy maroon suit, took a deep breath.

"I'm Sal ...and who are you?" Sal asked in an amused tone, looking up at the art hanging on the restaurant wall.

Patrick smirked but they couldn't see it. He knew they knew who he was but he played along.

"I'm new in town, they call me an angel, but don't worry... I'm not...not for you"

"Angel huh. Yeah I can see why" Sal gestured toward the suit. "So I don't deserve to be protected?"

"It kind of looks like you are already," Patrick said, waving his finger over, referring to the guards between them.

"But you do protect right? There's always room for someone like you, I do pay well" Sal mentioned as he looked on at the painting's beauty.

"The ones that deserve it yeah, they get protected"

"How do you know if they deserve it? What is good? You know, in my experience good and bad are the same thing...you'll understand that too someday.... especially in this line of work you've chosen. Are you here to take me to prison then?

"Probably, but I just want to speak for right now"

Sal finally turned to look at Patrick, intrigued by what he heard.

"You're going to try and change my heart? To become a *good one* is that right? Someone that deserves saving?" Sal said, air quoting the words 'good one'. "Well come have a seat, let's hear it"

Patrick watched Sal's smug wrinkle into the cigar he put into his mouth, he leaned over, having one of his guards light it for him. Patrick watched Sal's emotions mist out from above him. He always lost himself a little when he stared into someone's emotions, this time was no different. There was something so warm, comforting, and soothing about watching the emotions swirl and turn above another person's body. He gazed into Sal's emotions, dark *red and purple,* he noticed. *Why are they flashing like that?* Patrick wondered, seeing the dark colors glow and pulsate from within. *I've never seen that before.*

Patrick snapped too, quickly finding Sal. "No, I can feel you won't stop," he said, "You are not a *good one*" Patrick said and air quoted a good one back, mocking Sal.

"I won't see any time in prison. I guarantee that."

Sal said and relaxed into his booth, seeming confident, he inhaled his cigar and blew the smoke towards Patrick, turning his head to do so.

Patrick wasn't sure he knew what he was doing, as he experienced a loss for words at the moment. He thought Sal might be right. *He'll be out and back to his crime life like nothing happened, he has probably been through this before*, Patrick thought, feeling uneasy.

"Why?" Patrick asked quietly.

Sal leaned over the table and placed his hand to his ear, trying to hear Patrick.

"You're not very good at this dialogue thing yet" Sal laughed briefly, before continuing, "It's because of my expensive lawyers, that's why. It's because of the clout my family has. It's because if I'm ever found guilty...I take everyone with me" Sal mentioned, almost growling at Patrick.

Patrick heard Sal mention his family's clout and got a feeling. Patrick now saw and felt some hesitancy in Sal's attitude. *He's nervous.*

Patrick smirked and nodded his head, looking down to the wood-paneled floor. "No that's not what I meant...there are better things you could do in this world," Patrick said, growing more righteous as he continued. "There are people you could feed, families just like yours, that need help...well, not like your family exactly, but a family in desperate need. Choose to be good Sal"

Sal's expression changed, confused at the moment as no one has ever tried to appeal to his sense of humanity before. He shook his head in disappointment.

"In this life kid, everybody needs something. Maybe it's money, maybe it's love, maybe its validation, maybe it's...a legacy. That end there, that's where I fall. I want that legacy...and all the other ones too. Call me greedy"

"That's why? For a legacy? For remembrance?" Patrick said, feeling frustrated, feeling himself slipping.

"A legacy of being the baddest of the bad in this city!" Sal shouted and slammed on the table. He stood up. "And if you're ready to try and stop that and get in the way, go ahead...but you won't, I can guarantee that, I don't need a reason to be bad"

Patrick shook his head, feeling his hood brush over his ears, and Sal's words flowed into his body. He didn't know what to do. He was unable to think clearly at the moment. *Did Sal's words get to me that much?* he thought. *No, that's not it. Why is my head so foggy? He* wondered, feeling lightheaded and dizzy. He turned and walked toward the exit, feeling now was the time to leave. He stopped and grabbed a railing for support and shut his eyes, trying to get his head back to normal. After a moment he opened them and turned back to look at Sal. All three of the guards' and Sal's eyes were transfixed on the kitchen doors of the restaurant. Sal's eyes turned to locate Patrick who returned the surprised look. Patrick could see in Sal's eyes, a terror that Sal has probably never experienced before. Out of the corner of Patrick's eye, smoke began rolling out from under the kitchen doors, spreading throughout the dining floor.

"Did you leave the stove on?" Patrick asked sarcastically, rubbing his temples.

Patrick looked harder at the smoke. *It's dark...so dark, and it's pulsing, just like Sal's emotions. Why is pulsing?* Patrick asked himself as it began to billow faster and faster out from the kitchen. Patrick stood up straighter feeling clearer, he pushed himself off the railing and stared curiously into the smoke. *Something isn't right here,* he thought.

He peered in deeper, seeing the flashes and cracks of what could be lightning inside the smoke. *Are these emotions?* Patrick wondered nervously.

Sal and the guards all stood up on the open dining room floor looking visibly shaken and concerned.

They can see it too?

Sal glanced at Patrick again waiting for some sort of reaction from him. The smoke continued to spread throughout the restaurant and eventually surrounded Patrick and Sal's group. It inched closer and closer before it was all around them, inescapable. Patrick looked around the room at the emotion-filled smoke, feeling his head starting to fill again, but this time he understood why. He fell to a knee and closed his eyes as tight as he could, trying to shut it all out. As best as he tried, it didn't work. Patrick felt the emotions piling into him, pulling his mind apart, twisting and folding into itself. He thought of and tried to stand, but his body wouldn't move properly. He coughed and gagged, almost into a vomit, and felt the emotions rush into him. Each and every type of them, and it was torture.

She's dead, remember?

Chapter 17

Patrick opened his eyes and slowly fanned away the black emotion-filled smoke. He remembered that feeling, that feeling of helplessness. He remembered it so well. He squinted his eyes to shade them from the little amount of light there was spilling into the restaurant, even a small sliver of light was blinding to see. He shifted onto his hands and knees to right himself, trying to think his way out of this mental paralysis. His head was pounding, and he couldn't think straight, he couldn't even imagine what straight looked like anymore. It's as if his ability to think and make decisions was slowly fading away, or already disappeared. He only felt panic, a panic that seemed to be taking over his thoughts and emotions.

"What the hell!"

Patrick heard someone yelling on the other side of the restaurant. It was faint, coming from somewhere inside the smoke, but he could hear it. Patrick shook his head to try and regain his composure and senses. He squinted once more, trying to see where the scream came from, but after only seeing dark grey smoke and his eyes began to burn, he closed them tightly, and searched for himself.

"Aaahh! Aaaahhhhh!"

Patrick heard someone screaming somewhere else in the smoke as he forced his eyes back open and looked over to where he thought the man was. The screams were strong and blood-curdling but quickly faded as they were losing life. He knew something horrible must be happening to the man, something bad but he couldn't see anything yet. The mix of light and dark was too much for his eyes to handle. He shut them again and listened. He heard quiet shuffling and moaning from somewhere in the dark and slid over to a booth to boost himself up. He brought a knee up and stomped his foot loudly into the floor, he couldn't help the noise as he propped himself up. *Why is this happening?* he thought. *What's going on with me?*

He put a hand on his knee and pushed himself up to stand, using the booth for balance. His eyes were still shut, but his head was spinning out of control. He found the table and stabilized himself. He looked and squinted around the place, but still it was too dark. He saw nothing. He stood taller regaining some sense of himself as he continued to search through the fog. *Where is Sal?* He thought.

He took a step, and then another before getting wobbly, feeling weak in his knees. *I feel drunk,* Patrick thought, wanting to have said out loud, but only could manage the thought. He stepped again.

"You ugly son of bitch!" He heard a voice call out in the smoke.

That's Sal's voice, he recalled. *And he's close by.*

He took another step toward Sal's direction.

"Sal," Patrick managed to say aloud, then waited for a response.

He listened carefully as he took another step forward but then the spinning started again, causing him to fall into the wooden wall to his side. *It's getting bad again.*

He was barely standing and the feelings were getting stronger.

"Hel—" He heard Sal's voice reach out weakly. He could tell Sal was in bad shape.

He pushed off the wall and moved toward Sal's direction.

She's dead, remember?

"Sal, you over here?" He asked, getting closer.

He peered through the smoke and caught a glimpse of movement. He focused on it and could see the top of Sal's head and chest floating in the air. His limp body being held up by something Patrick couldn't quite see. Patrick scanned deeper to see Sal's mouth wide open in terror and his face white and wrinkly, looking like a ghost. Patrick saw a black shaded figure, or an arm clutching at Sal's chest, lifting him. The rest of the figure was buried in the fog as Patrick stepped forward cautiously.

"Sal, what's happening?" he asked nervously, knowing he wouldn't get an answer.

What he did hear was a faint moaning, as if someone was crying very far away. The moaning began to build louder and louder, growing in menace. It began to frighten Patrick as well, it was a terrifying sound to him, as he had heard a similar one before, in the not so distant past. He remembered that day so clearly. It was the same sound his mother made when she was dying. An involuntary groan that she would make on her deathbed. The nurses said that it's not a sound of pain. sadness or fear, but just something the body does when near the end.

But that's not coming from Sal, Patrick thought.

The moaning ceased before it could affect Patrick too much, then things grew quiet. Patrick stared in horror at the dark fog. He watched in frozen anticipation, counting the fleeting moments in his head until the dark, buried figure began in his direction. Sal's lifeless body fell to the ground with a thump, as his eyes rolled back meeting Patrick's. The smoke rolled slowly over the figure, and toward Patrick. The groaning began again, starting as a hum. Patrick couldn't look away from the smoke, he was scared and frozen in place, watching as this figure he could only describe so far as death itself approached for his life. His heart thumped faster and deeper as his breathing became slow. Patrick stepped backward, watching as the smoke began to build taller, moving toward him like it had a mind of its own. It completely covered him again as the light groaning stopped. He waited in the open, feeling nakedly defenseless, hoping for something to happen just to break the tension. He wanted this to be over, he wanted to leave, he wanted to cry, he wanted to throw up, he wanted everything to be over. He fell to his knees and watched the fog rush over to console him. He lifted his head looking towards Sal's direction through the fog and saw something moving through it, like a fish through water, slowly and patiently. Patrick squinted and realized the figure was a dirty bandage, floating through the smoke, with almost lifelike sentience. The bandage swam closer to Patrick's face, moving like a snake toward their prey. Patrick's terror won't be hard to sense. He watched the bandage slither around and over him. He closed his eyes to block it all out. *I want to leave. I want to leave so bad.*

He opened his eyes on instinct and saw more bandages hovering around his space, floating through the air. He felt some bandages wrap around his arms and torso, getting tighter and tighter. He didn't fight, he couldn't, even if he wanted to. He only watched as they grabbed hold of him, continuing to tighten the grip. A bandage slowly constricted around his throat, wrapping itself gently over his hood. Patrick has accepted whatever fate they had for him, as he stared blissfully into the emotion-filled smoke, looking for that comfort, looking for peace. A peace that he hasn't felt for as long as he could remember. *It's nice,* he thought, *Where has this been?*

From inside the dark fog, the figure finally showed itself, the peace that Patrick was feeling vanished into a deeply terrifying fright. He saw the figure's bare feet first, light grey and wrapped in the same bandages that are restricted around his body. Then its torso and its hands appeared. All parts of the body were wrapped in those dirty, grey bandages. The hands began to reach out for him, showing slender fingers and dark stained wraps. Then their eyes met. Patrick saw the figure so clear now as it appeared from the smoke. Where there should be eyes, Patrick only saw more bandages. The whole figure was completely wrapped in bandages like a mummy. It was skinny and weak looking, almost sad in its demeanor, with the way its neck was cranked low, looking down to the ground. Patrick couldn't read any emotions from it, only the emotions that surround it. It stepped toward Patrick, making the groaning sounds as it approached, taking slow, deliberate steps forward. The mummy-looking figure inched toward Patrick, lowering its head to meet him face to face. Patrick stared straight at the figure, trying to find out anything at all about it. Looking for any signs that this could be his last night on this earth.

"Unnnhhh" the bandaged figure moaned again.

Patrick watched as the bandage figure's head started to loosen up, it rose up from Patrick's face, seeming to have lost interest. Patrick began to struggle a little, trying to move away, but still couldn't move his body. He looked up to check on the bandaged figure whose back was now turned, and caught sight of the bandages slowly beginning to fall from its head. Patrick watched with anxiety and anticipation waiting for it to show its face. Before it could turn to reveal itself, the bandages quickly shot up and encased over Patrick's head. He had no time to react, as they covered his mouth before he could scream out. Patrick peeked out through a tiny slot in the bandages as the mummy's head disappeared back into the fog. The bandages wrapped over his eyes, shutting away all hope. And then...blackness.

Chapter 18

Patrick awoke to the sun shining violently into his eyes. It appeared to Patrick to be a warm and sunny day, with the smell of freshly cut grass overloading his senses as he comfortably stretched out in the grass. Looking up to the baby blue sky, Patrick moved his head around and squinted his eyes, trying to adjust to the light of the sun. Eventually, they did adjust and he sat up taking a look around him. He turned to see his childhood home standing menacingly tall and still behind him. He looked at the back porch and all the windows that covered the backside of the house, watching for any signs of movement. He stood up and took the day in. It was a beautiful day outside, comfortably warm with a ton of sunshine. *Just like the day mom died.*

"What...is this?" Patrick asked aloud to himself.

He looked around at all of the other houses in the neighborhood, not seeing anyone else outside their houses, which was strange because the neighbors were always outside if the weather was nice. He walked past the shed where his mom kept her gardening supplies and lawnmower and approached the house cautiously. He walked into the driveway from the backyard looking for a sign of life or clues to why he's back home. *How did I get back here?* He thought, as he slid his hand over the garage doors, looking at the basketball hoop in the driveway. He didn't remember much until he got closer to the front door. That's when it all came back to him.

"This is the day she died," he said, confirming his earlier worry. "Why?"

He stepped up to the front door as his heart began beating faster and faster, he could feel his throat getting tighter, making it hard to breathe. He grabbed the handle and froze, knowing, or at least having a feeling of what might be waiting for him inside. He remembered that day so vividly, the day he had to say goodbye. He couldn't find the words to say to her, let alone speak them out loud. If she could even hear his words at all. That was the hardest thing he ever had to do, and he couldn't, he didn't. Patrick couldn't make it real, he couldn't make it harder on himself, not even for her.

Patrick, feeling the door handle's cold embrace, remembered one night in his mother's final week when he was at home. It was around eight-thirty when the nurses told him that she'd be going to sleep for the night. That it was time to say goodnight. Patrick walked down from his room into the living room where she laid on her bed. He took a seat at the fixed-rocked chair and sat with her. The sounds of the breathing machines and faint country music on T.V in the background filled the room of its silence. He couldn't talk to her like normal, even if the nurses left the room. Patrick looked to his mother, who seemed to be sleeping peacefully already. *This might be the last time I say goodnight to her,* he thought, grabbing her hand. He squeezed as tightly as he thought he should, trying not to hurt her but enough to let her know he was there.

"Hi Mom," he said, as his eyes began to water. "The nurses told me you were going to bed, I wanted to say goodnight"

Each word became harder to say, seeming to build in sadness. Patrick dropped his head down still holding her hand tightly. He wondered what else he should say. *What do I say? Isn't there a script or something?*

"I'll be here in the morning when you wake up," He said, bringing his head back up and then gave a weak smile to her trying to hold back from crying. He looked at her as his eyes got heavier. Maria's eyes slowly cracked open as her eyes turned slightly to look at him. He changed his emotions quickly so she didn't see the tears about to fall. She located him with soft eyes, looking from her bed trying to take in every moment. Patrick looked her in the eyes and smiled, finding it easier to speak now.

"I love you mom," he said, clutching her hand.

His mom squeezed his hand in return, Patrick felt the pressure and looked at her before he lowered himself down and kissed her hand. He set her hand down on top of her stuffed horse, gave her one last smile, and walked out of the room and past the nurses in the kitchen. He walked to his room upstairs, shut the door, and broke down. He slid himself down using the wall as support and put his head in his hands. He cried for so long. He felt so alone that night. Each time he cried was a different kind of heartbreak. A heartbreak that he swore he could feel taking a piece of him each time, ripping him away. He cried until he eventually fell asleep that night. That was a night he knew he'd remember the rest of his life.

Patrick gripped the handle as the same emotions he felt during that day washed over him. He turned the handle and pushed the door open, creaking as it welcomed him inside. Patrick took a step inside but abruptly stopped and stood on the front porch. *What if she's in here again?* He thought.

A large part of him wanted to shut the door and run away to never look back, but another part wanted to see her again, even if it was a nightmare. He placed one foot inside the doorway and stepped in. He knew that when he walked in, she'd be right around the corner inside the living room. He could feel it. He took a breath and leaned inside, and to his surprise, the living room was empty. No bed, no nurses, no dying mother. He looked around and walked to the spot her bed was. Patrick stood confused, he was sure this was the day. He circled the living room looking at the art on the walls and the things on the tables, looking for any clue as to why he's here again. He paced through the library, seeing the bookshelves stuffed with books. *She did love to read,* he remembered. His attention was then grabbed by what was on the corner table. Seeing a plastic container filled with toys, he walked over to further inspect. *They're my toys,* he knew, as he grabbed a few of his G.I Joe action figures from the container to admire them. He dropped them back in with some anger, having realized again that he wasn't actually back at his home. He turned away to see another similar container, but the new one had only one toy, a large panda bear wearing a blue shirt, sitting straight up, watching him. *That's not mine,* Patrick knew, *maybe it's Moms?* He didn't touch it, only walked into the kitchen. The place was so empty and quiet. The house had such a sad feel to it for a long time. If life did keep score, Patrick would be losing by a lot, and this house his casket. He walked to the back door inspecting the backyard. He saw the porch and wood line that separated the neighborhood in two. He's sad and getting sadder, and wondered if he should go back outside.

"Patrick" a voice from the living called out.

Patrick heard his name and froze in panic and continued to look outside, hoping he only imagined that. He knew whose voice it was, it was faint but he knew, he hoped to always remember. He hasn't heard it for some time though. He turned to the living room where the sound came from. He didn't take a moment to comprehend the moment, his body moved unconsciously to the living room. He turned the corner to see the bed, to see the nurses, to see his mom.

"Mom," Patrick said weakly.

The nurses walked away into the other room as his mom sat up to see him.

"Hi Patrick," she said.

Patrick saw her to be healthy, and the look in her eyes was different, she no longer looked confused, she no longer looked scared. She looked like herself again.

"Come over here," she said, almost demanding

Patrick started walking over slowly to her, staring in disbelief and apprehension.

"Sit with me Patrick," she said.

Patrick waited for a moment before answering "Yeah, of course" he responded as he sat down slowly in the chair beside her. "What is this mom?"

"What? Don't you want to say goodnight to me?" She asked, as her face contorted to surprise.

Patrick stumbled for a second. He was so confused with this; his mind was racing. He looked into her eyes. "Of course, Of course I do...but I, I already did...before" he stammered.

"What do you mean?" She asked as her face changed back to the concerned and warm look he was used to, but the words seemed too deliberate and straightforward.

Patrick looked at the ground trying to collect himself, then back to his mom. "I said goodnight to you...before"

"I don't remember," she mentioned quietly, almost whispering.

Patrick started to tear up. These were the moments that were so hard for him.

"I know mom" he said then looked to the ground. "I'm back again...to say goodnight...to see you again"

"Again?" she asked.

Patrick felt the lump growing in his throat and his heart began to beat faster. He could feel the same emotions piling into him as the day she died.

"You died mom...I was there," Patrick told her as his eyes started watering. This time his emotions showed. He didn't want to be strong anymore, so the tears fell.

"You were with me?" she asked from her bed.

Patrick responded in between big breaths and through his tears. "Yeah mom…I was…and I'm so sorry" The tears fell uncontained, as he looked over at her blank expression.

"What are you sorry for?" she asked.

"I couldn't do anything…I couldn't help you," he mumbled.

"Did I suffer?" she asked, as a smile slowly formed over her face.

"No," he responded quickly. "You didn't"

"Good" she answered as she closed her eyes. "How did you handle it?" she asked, smiling again.

"It was hard…it was really hard mom…like…torture "He replied, becoming suspicious of her vibe.

"And you said goodbye, right," she asked as her smile stretched wider.

Patrick's eyes got large and he looked away to the ground. Staring into her eyes felt uncomfortable at that moment.

"No I never did…not to you when you were dying, that's why I'm sorry"

Patrick grabbed her hand and squeezed then buried his head into the bed. He didn't know what else to say. He lifted his head up seeing her eyes closed.

"Mom?"

She didn't respond, she didn't even look alive anymore as the color began leaving her face. Patrick remembered that look. It's horrible. He knew that she was gone again. He looked blankly at her while he sat uncomfortably in the wooden chair. Just as he did the day she died.

"Patty," she said softly which surprised him.

"Mom" he said and reacted by sitting up in his chair.

She opened her eyes to look at Patrick. He saw nothing but sadness and terror in her eyes once more. "Patty," she said, "please don't let me fall."

Those words struck Patrick and moved him into a deeper sadness. Patrick's mom began to slowly turn decayed and grey, she looked like a skeleton with skin dripping off it. Something straight out of a horror film. Patrick stood up quickly, knocking the rocker to the floor. He stumbled back into the middle of the living room, feeling a dangerous situation being formed.

"Don't let…me…fall" she said again with each word getting weaker and weaker.

"Mom…. I ca—."

"Doooont leeet meeee faaaaaall!" she screamed, shrieking like a banshee. She sat up quickly and ravished around in the bed possessed, she lost balance and fell from the hospital bed. She scrambled and began to crawl slowly towards him, reaching out for him with every movement. She cracked up from her crawl, her bones shifting as her almost skeleton frame reached its peak. Patrick watched as her eyes met his. *That's not her!* his mind told him sharply.

She began to crack towards him quickly. Patrick turned and ran up the stairs, almost tripping over each step. He got to his room, shut the door, and locked it. He pushed against it, holding the door shut waiting for something to bash into it. Staring anxiously, Patrick waited to hear her scream again. The door slammed hard, almost shaking the whole room, but Patrick kept it shut.

"Heeeelllllp!" Patrick's mom yells on the other side while the banging continued. *Bang bang bang bang!*

Terrified, Patrick stumbled into the bed and threw the blankets over him. He wrapped the cotton blanket tightly around him, hiding from his nightmarish mother. *Bang bang bang!*

"Heeeeelp!!"

The pounding was getting louder and so were the screams. He shut his eyes tightly, becoming overwhelmed by the noise.

Bang bang bang bang! "Heeeeelp meeee!"

Patrick wrapped tighter, the screamed as the noise reached a level of madness in Patrick's head that he felt might kill him. Inside, his head felt as if it was turning in on itself, folding like dough one way then flipping the other. His mind was spinning, and his thoughts were becoming deep and dark. He heard the door being smashed again, this time followed by a loud crash and more psychotic screams. Patrick felt the growing pressure coming from over the top of him. The blankets began to slide away from Patrick as he was being forced back into the open. The screaming began again.

"Doooont leeeeeet meeee faaaaaaaaal!"

Patrick couldn't take it anymore. The fear, the terror, the guilt, the darkness, it all reached a breaking point inside Patrick as he screamed out.

"Stooooooop!!" he yelled loudly, returning to silence and darkness.

Patrick awoke and found himself leaning up into a half wall at the restaurant. He felt exhausted, his head was dizzy and weak, and the air tasted sour. He sat up straighter and looked at his surroundings, seeing the place trashed and the bodies of the guards gone. Sal's body was still there, lying motionless on the ground. Patrick hauled himself to his feet and stood up too fast as the blood rushed to his head, he shut an eye and steadied himself back against the wall. He paced gingerly over to Sal.

"Sal," he said in a low, weak whisper.

Sal didn't answer and remained motionless. Patrick kicked Sal's foot to get a reaction, then knelt by him and turned his upper body over.

"Oh my god," Patrick yelped as he took his hands off Sal and slid backward. Patrick looked on seeing Sal's face and hands pruned and shriveled up like he's been sitting in a pool for weeks. His body and face look to be deprived of all energy and health. Whatever gave him life before, has been sucked out of him, leaving him as a once-living husk. Patrick scrambled to his feet and scurried for the exit. He clutched his head, nursing it from the pain, as he reached the door.

"Halo...what happened here?" Patrick asked.

Patrick braced his mind for Halo's voice but was left hanging. *Maybe we can't talk because of that nightmare*, he wondered with great effort.

Patrick could feel he was still wearing the white suit, but he wasn't holding Halo. *It's time to go,* he thought. Patrick walked out of the restaurant through the backdoor, not caring if he was seen, he wanted to leave, he wanted to go home. He fell out to the alley and walked slowly and carefully, feeling his whole body aching.

What just happened?

Chapter 19

On Sunday morning, Patrick slept for as long as he could, managing to sleep till noon, and even then he tried to go back to sleep as often as he could. He didn't want to wake up, he didn't want to be awake. Being awake meant your thoughts would be awake too, and that's something Patrick was getting sorely tired of. It was impossible to fall back asleep while his mind raced to a never to be reached finish line. He would wake up and immediately think about his sadness and the way he felt inside it. Eventually, he gave up and rolled himself out of bed. His entire body was sore and his mind was shattered like broken glass. He stumbled to the coffee machine hoping for relief that way. He loaded then started it before having to lean against the counter for balance. He started looking around his apartment and noticed a lack of furniture. He didn't have many expensive items or material things but the place was still a mess. He ignored that and walked to the TV and loaded up Netflix and plopped down on the couch. He didn't feel like doing much today and knew he probably wouldn't. *What's another day of doing nothing?* he thought. *No need for a morning walkthrough.*

He hated weekends, no work, no volunteering, no social commitments of any sort. He was getting better at putting himself out there, he knew that and was proud, but he had some work to do. In the recent past, he rarely had plans for his free days and dreaded the days he would spend alone. *I should be used to that feeling by now,* he thought.

He decided he was going to do nothing with the day. A comfort movie marathon seemed right. That's something that's brought him some relief in the past, he could lose himself in movies if he focused hard enough. It's a temporary fix he knew, but it helped, it kept him colorless, and being colorless could be warm. He loaded the movie and grabbed a blanket and threw it onto the couch. He stood and stumbled to the sink for water, he filled his cup and walked back to the couch. Flashed with a glare of the sun from his window, he stepped over and opened blind, looking over the city. His immediate view was a long street, covered in small businesses and antique shops, it was usually a popular location. He stopped to watch the street for a while, checking out the early shoppers and the everyday walkers. It kept him going, knowing others existed on earth with him. He knew everyone struggled with their ever-changing mental forecasts, but he knew not to compare grief. He had it bad, others had it bad, some had it worse. Just watching the street, he could see it, the array of colors floating in the air. He was sad, but so were many others. His sadness is his own though, it was only real for him. He could see and physically feel the pain and emotion of others. He received emotional double duty, feeling others' emotions and pain along with his own set. He was quite the empath. For Patrick, he felt every emotion he focused on, he looked at someone and felt it, he felt the shock of the emotion and he felt the other person. But for Patrick, no one felt what he was feeling. They could only feel and understand themselves. Some struggled with even that.

He looked to the street, seeing one woman walking briskly down the sidewalk, *she looks like mom*, he thought. He spotted a woman pushing her child in a stroller across the street, *a mother*, he thought to himself. He saw a disabled elderly woman in a stroller of her own, wheeling down the sidewalk with her husband. *Like, mom*, he related. He watched for a few more minutes, fixated on the people, watching emotions and colors come and go. After a while, it was hard to determine which emotion was which. He breathed in. *She's dead, remember. This won't ever go away.* He breathed out and shut his eyes then pushed his forehead against the window. *You were just attacked by a mummy and this is all that I can think about?* He thought.

He wanted it to be over, he wasn't sure what exactly, but he knew something had to end. He opened his eyes and softly gazed at his hand.

"Halo," he said, with tears starting to build.

No answer. He waited a moment and tried again.

"Halo, can we— ." Patrick didn't finish the question but knew Halo understood what he wanted.

Halo didn't appear in hand nor speak, giving nothing but silence. *Maybe he's gone?* He thought, I *don't deserve it anyway.* He stared at his hand a little longer hoping for anything. He grabbed and shut the curtains and turned around just as his phone started to vibrate on the coffee table. *I'm surprised it's not dead*, he thought, as he picked it up to look, seeing Aunt Judy. He wasn't sure if he wanted to answer and talk now, he was tired and didn't have the motivation. But it was his Aunt, someone who cared for him. He sighed briefly because he knew he had to decide quickly. *I should,* he thought. *We don't talk often.*

"Hello" he answered with low enthusiasm. There was a short pause as Judy answered back.

"Hey Patrick it's your Aunt Judy"

"Hey Aunt Judy"

"How are you doing?" she asked, her tone dropping in energy to match his.

"I'm tired...," he said. A few silent seconds passed without words.

"Yeah I know, it's been a hard process," Aunt Judy answered. Patrick could feel her grief over the phone, through her words.

"And it always will be," Patrick responded before walking back over to the window.

"Is there anything you need? Anything I can do for you?" Aunt Judy asked.

"I'm not sure," he replied. "It's all so fresh in my mind, I still don't really know how to cope"

"Do you maybe want to talk to someone?" Judy asked empathetically.

"We're talking now," he replied.

"I know and I'm happy to listen. I'll always be there for you, but I was thinking of, well...someone who may be more equipped to help you cope" she stated.

"Like a therapist?"

"Yeah, I have spoken with one, and I know your mother tried it too.

"I don't know about therapy. How can someone tell me how to cope with these things they may not be able to relate to?"

"They don't give out answers to questions. It's more about providing strategies and techniques to handle the emotions. It can be helpful" Judy corrected.

Patrick took the phone away from his head and sighed deeply before returning it to his ear. "Yeah maybe, have any recommendations?"

"Yeah I do, I'll send you some information," she said. There was a pause in the conversation as Patrick heard her write something down before continuing.

"Also me and your cousin Hannah are grabbing lunch together in your area later today if you want to join us?"

Patrick thought for a moment, feeling it was a tempting offer, but he had no motivation to go. "I'd like to stay in today and get some rest before the week starts. Thank you though Aunt Judy... you know, for everything" he said.

"Yeah of course kiddo and if you ever want to grab some food or just want to talk, just give me a call, Ok? I'll come running," She said, trying to sound reassuring, which she did.

She is a mom, Patrick knew. "Yeah ok, thanks," he said, preparing to end the call.

"Okay, well...take care Patrick, I hope to see you soon," she said, before hanging up the phone leaving Patrick with the dial tone.

He set his phone back down and sat on the couch. The silence around him began to press down into him. He started to remember and think about his mom. *She's never coming back; this is life now.* He sat on the couch and stared at the lower part of the wall for a long while, drifting through thought, sometimes going blank. The rest of the day was spent watching movies and feeling hollow. The sunsets and the moon shined bright, ending a day to begin another. Patrick had no motivation to prepare for the week or to try and speak with Halo again. He felt it would be a lost cause. He was starting to feel like a lost cause. As much as he wanted to, he could never out-run or out-think his pain. He's been chasing the high that a once free mind gave him for so long.

He took a very long hot shower and went to bed early, trying to escape the thoughts and hopefully have a distractingly good dream. He woke up the next morning feeling the same hollowness. Feeling he couldn't get out of bed to go on, he picked up his phone and called in sick to work for the next few days.

Chapter 20

*S**he's dead, remember? You are alone, remember?***
Patrick woke once again to the familiar thoughts. *Every day,* he thought as he became increasingly stressed from his thoughts. He muscled himself up and sat up straight, slowly to the side of his bed. The curtains were shut but he could tell it was early afternoon by the sun peeking through the blinds. He couldn't sleep anymore, he felt that overwhelming need to get up and be productive somehow. He grabbed his phone off the counter to check the time. It's past noon on a Wednesday. He has called in sick the last three days of work, with nothing stopping him from adding a few more. He knew that couldn't continue, but he needed a break, a break from people, a break from responsibility, a break from himself. He was tired of letting people down, or at least feeling like he had.

If I'm not around anyone, I can't let them down and If I don't do anything, I can't let myself down either, he reasoned.

He checked everything else on his phone. No messages, no texts, no updates. It's as if the world moved smoother without him. No one had reached out to him besides his Aunt a few days ago. He tossed his phone to the floor and crashed back down on the couch to comprehend the bad thoughts further, wanting to dive even deeper into the sadness, in hopes of getting it all out. *This isn't healthy,* he thought. He wanted to combat the feelings, he wanted to get it all out in the open, start from the bottom. A glimmer of hope arose from the ashes. *It won't always be like this, just keep going!* His mind told him. Which was then quickly followed up by a more gloom thought.

You've thought that before, but you're still here, the thought rang through his head. Positive thoughts were usually trumped by the negative. *I should try meditating, or that therapy,* he wondered.

He stood up and walked to his bathroom. A nice and long scalding hot shower should help him think straight. Humans replace physical touch and warmth with longer and warmer showers, Patrick knew that and felt the comfort science said was true. He was about to jump in when he heard his ringer going off. His heart started to race, he didn't like phone calls, good thing he didn't get many. There was a time in life when that was a welcomed sound, but now, since his mom was sick, it always seemed like bad news. He checked the contact for identification. *Building Blocks. Must be Mrs. Pierce*, he thought. He hadn't been there for a couple of days either. *I better answer.*

"Hello?"

"Hey Patrick it's Amanda from Building Blocks"

"Hey... Amanda, how are you?"

"I'm good, how are you? We haven't seen you for a while, is everything okay?" she asked, sounding truly worried.

He paused for a moment before responding. "Yeah I'm okay, I've been sick for a while. I didn't want the kids catching anything."

"Oh sure okay, we were all worried about you, it's not the same here without you, the kids miss you"

"Yeah I'm okay...um tell them I'll be back tomorrow night," he said, already regretting that promise.

"Okay I will, we just wanted to check in with you to make sure everything was okay."

"Thanks, yeah...I appreciate that"

"Okay well, get some good rest and we'll see you tomorrow then," she said.

"Will do, thanks Amanda," he said before hanging up.

He sat down on his bed to collect himself. *I can't go tomorrow if I feel this bad. I need help,* He thought as he grabbed his phone and checked the information his Aunt Judy sent him about therapy. He dialed the number and scheduled an appointment. To his benefit, surprise and worry, there was a therapist who had a cancellation, who was willing to see him that day. It was a short drive from his place, which was also to his benefit. He arrived at the office, taking in the smaller than imagined building. It looked more like a bank or a real estate office to him. He checked in at the front desk where they had him fill out some paperwork. It's the normal stuff, why are you here? What is wrong with you? What should we do? That sort of stuff. He understood the process of therapy; he had done his research. He knew he had to talk and understand his problems before he could correct them. There was no fixing him because he was not broken, or at least that's what his internet searches told him. The uneasy feeling of therapy had been quenched by the vastness of the world-wide-web.

After ten minutes or so after finishing the paperwork, the woman at the front desk sent him back into her office. He was nervous about this but was truly hopeful it would help. He entered the office and found himself alone.

"She'll be in, in a moment," said the secretary from behind, startling Patrick.

"Okay, thanks," Patrick responded politely before settling into the doctor's patient chair. With his alone time, Patrick scanned the office, reading the diplomas hanging on the wall. *Dr. Gretchen Watson*, he read. He walked to her bookshelf and scanned all of her psychology and therapy books. One caught his eye immediately. *Neurochemistry in Clinical Application? Sounds intense*, he thought.

Patrick looked at the other books, scanning each title, becoming increasingly confused with each read. He reached the end of the line and decided he should resume his patient, wait for the doctor, safely in the appropriate chair. Before he did, he was struck with a sense of tension. Standing in the doctor's office, Patrick felt a sense of pressure coming from the hallway in which he passed through earlier. In his eerie skepticism, he quietly approached the office door, leading out to the hallway. He stuck his head out into the hallway, hoping not to be seen by any incoming visitors. As he did the pressure built. *It's coming from that office*, Patrick looked at the office at the end of the hallway and understood. He looked left then right as if he was crossing a highway before he stepped out into the hallway. He approached the looming presence of the office. The pressure continued to build as if the office and he were magnets being pulled toward one another, he pressed on and reached the office door, seeing the name to whom it belongs, *Dr. Oswyn David,* he read as he heard voices suddenly from the waiting area. He took one last look at the closed office door, feeling something wrong about it. The word *nefarious* floated through Patrick's mind as he turned and quickly tiptoed back to where he should be. He sat back in the chair and waited, hearing a woman's voice say good-bye to someone before approaching the office. Patrick didn't turn around until the woman entered and greeted him.

"Hello, you must be Patrick," she said, walking over to him decisively. She reached out to shake his hand.

Patrick stood and took her hand. "Yeah I am, nice to meet you," he said with that flat enthusiasm.

She smiled again and rounded her desk with carefully placed steps. "My name is Dr. Gretchen Watson, please have a seat" She took a seat in her large cushioned office chair, correcting her posture and office supplies on her desk.

Patrick has always been good at reading people. Even before his empath powers kicked in, he was good at understanding people. That's what staying out of the spotlight got you. Caring and understanding eyes. Patrick looked at Dr. Watson, seeing a mild-aged woman with dark brown hair that covered her ears, and was tied back into a bun. She also has a wedding ring that she touched three times since she walked in and sat down. And when she first walked in, Patrick felt the weight of the room change. She had problems too; Patrick knew but wasn't sure if that was comforting or not.

"So I read the report my assistant wrote down from your phone conversation. It sounds like you're having a tough time coping with a new situation. Is that correct?" Dr. Watson asked.

"Yeah that's...accurate" he responded, as his brows raised.

"Okay, well before we can start, I want to hear why you decided to call?" Why do you want to talk with someone?"

Patrick thought for a moment before answering, letting the silence almost answer the question for him. He knew speaking his thoughts was what therapy called for, but he never rehearsed or thought about what he would say, he took it slow.

"Well," he said through a sigh. "My life has changed...and suddenly the support I had for myself is no longer a thing. I've been stressed and sad for so long...I need ways to cope and right myself, but I'm afraid the damage has been done. I don't feel like myself anymore"

Patrick stopped for a moment to collect his thoughts, as Dr. Watson wrote in her small notepad.

"I was recommended to therapy...and I thought it was worth trying. I have done some research, you know... on what to expect and how to... you know...make it work for you. I feel broken but I know that no one is broken when they come to therapy. There is no quick fix. It's a process" Patrick looked up at Dr. Watson for her reaction.

She has been writing notes since he started talking, but stopped when Patrick ceased speaking, to share her thoughts.

"That's a great start, therapy can be so daunting for people because they don't know what to expect, just scheduling an appointment can be the hardest part." She smiled and continued. "Tell me about these sudden changes you're going through, the information you gave my assistant was... vague," she said inquisitively.

Patrick thought for a moment about telling her about his new life as a Deva. *Patient-doctor confidentiality and all that,* he knew. However, he decided to keep it safe and simple.

"I've been an introvert my whole life basically, only a few friends growing up really and just a few in college, but not many people I could speak with... about life. I had my mother, but...she died recently and I am struggling to do this all on my own, I can't shake the feeling of being ...exposed, I guess"

"And your mother was sick when you were in school?" Dr. Watson asked.

Patrick nodded his head but didn't verbally answer.

"Tell me about the process of your mother's sickness"

Patrick took a deep breath, knowing this may be hard to speak about once again, he started slow.

"Toward the end of my college experience...she was uh... diagnosed, yeah, with brain cancer. She called me the same day to break the news...which really sucked. I graduated as early as I could and returned home. For months I would be there with her, doing what I could." Patrick took another big breath, looking at Dr. Watson, then back to the ground.

"She uh...contacted Hospice care because she knew we both needed help. She didn't want me to see her like that every day. She wanted me to live a life still. There came a point where... because of the tumors and treatment, she wouldn't always remember who I was." Patrick nodded slowly, forcing himself to press on and speak more.

"I feel I lost her before she even died," He said, feeling the tears building. "There was one bad day... in the beginning...I went home to see her. She was alone and trying to come down the stairs, so I went to help her" Patrick's head dropped lower as he continued. "And I... I lost focus while checking something and I... I dropped her" Patrick said then started pulling at and bending his fingers, causing him some matching physical pain.

"She fell down the stairs," he said sniffling "She...broke some bones and had bruises all over...she was in so much pain"

Patrick started getting teary-eyed and looked away from Dr. Watson. He imagined talking to her to be harder than this, yet the words seem easier than imagined. He continued, practically speaking from the floor, the way his head was lowered.

"After that... she would always say to me or the Hospice workers, Don't let me fall...and every time she would... I would break a little more because I was the one that dropped her, I was the one always letting her down. I know it's not my fault that she got cancer and died. But the one thing I could have done for her...I didn't....and now those words echo, her words, echo in my head nonstop... I see her everywhere I go. I see her in sick people, in women that look like her, in anyone's mother" Patrick stopped and looked up to Dr. Watson with red eyes. "I see her in you even"

Patrick smiled weakly and looked away. Dr. Watson wasn't taking notes just then, she was listening to Patrick, and hearing the sadness in his words. She set her notebook down and exhaled.

"That's a lot to unpack Patrick, you've been living through a tremendous amount of guilt and pain it sounds" she stated.

"And it isn't going away," he replied quickly.

"Maybe... because you won't let it," she instructed, adjusting herself in her chair.

Patrick nodded his head slowly because he knew she was right. Dr. Watson continued.

"With losing a loved one, many people ruminate in the guilt or failure they perceived to have caused...when we are too attached to one idea, one perspective, or one memory, the mind is hindered. You see?"

Again Patrick nodded slowly in agreement, thinking of her words. *The mind is hindered?*

"There is a quote from Buddha that I show all my patients who are or have gone through the same thing," Dr. Watson says as she hands him a letter with the quote typed into it. Patrick reads it.

"You shouldn't chase after the past or place expectations on the future. What is past is left behind. The future is as yet unreached. Whatever quality is present you clearly see right there, right there. Not taken in, unshaken, that's how you develop the heart."—Buddha

Patrick, confused, looked up at Dr. Watson for further elaboration. She saw and understood his look.

"A little confusing I know, I usually have more explaining to do...You see, to overcome bad memories, you must actually see them as part... of the present moment." She says slowing down at the end to make a point. "When we realize that the past, the ideas, the past

110

memories and the past thoughts as now... in the present, we can change them"

"Okay but how?" he asked, still trying to grasp her meaning.

"By staying in the present, by replacing the painful memories of your present with new ones. Try connecting with others and finding new things that bring new memories" Dr. Watson taught.

"How can I replace painful memories with better ones?"

"By doing what I just told you. Stay engaged in the present and find new methods of harboring nice memories" She answered and continued. "It won't be easy, even for Buddha, he had years of mental training and practice through meditation. I've known patients who have tried and succeeded, and I know some who tried and failed. You just need to stay focused and committed"

"I can try that," Patrick said, exhaling.

"And I can help," she responded with a smile.

Patrick nodded and reflected on the moment, remembering another quote from his mother's past.

"Actually I—, I remember another quote that was important once"

"Once?" Dr. Watson inquired.

"It lost its meaning as time went on...or I did" Patrick stated.

Dr. Watson raised her eyebrows and looked up at Patrick. "What is the quote?"

"It's more of a poem actually, well it is a poem for sure" Patrick stated. "It's an Emily Dickinson poem, I don't remember the name, but I read it every morning when I slept back home. It was right across my room in the hallway. It went uh—" Patrick looked behind Dr. Watson at her broad windows, thinking of the poem. "If I could stop one heart from breaking, I shall not live in vain. If I could—" Patrick turned away in thought. "Umm, And I don't remember the rest but—"

"I'm familiar with it. And it is very interesting that that is the poem you recall and were enlightened too at home"

"Well it was right outside my childhood bedroom" Patrick answered.

"Yes, and that is my point. It has been ingrained in you. You might not remember the exact phrasing, but you know the meaning, correct?"

Patrick nodded his head in response, as Dr. Watson continued.

"The two lines of the poem you remember are maybe the most important" She repeated the poem. "If I could stop one heart from breaking, I shall not live in vain. You didn't want your mother to fall, and you don't want others to hurt either. But what about you Patrick?"

The rest of Patrick's session was about the methods he could use to ensure he corrected his mental habits. They finished up and said their goodbyes. Upon his exit from her office, he closed Dr. Watson's door and shot a harsh glance over to Dr. Oswyn David's office, confused by the strange feeling that loomed inside. *Who are you, Dr. Oswyn David?*

Patrick walked out and told the secretary that he'd call to schedule an appointment. He got into his car and took a few deep breaths, thinking about the session and what he got out of it. *It was a success,* he thought, feeling better about being understood. He ran through those same words in his head. *When we realize that the memories and the thoughts of the past are now, we can change them. That's where I'll start.*

Chapter 21
This again

E yes open, Patrick sat up from his bed as his hands cupped his face, he rubbed his face smoothing away at his prickly new forming beard. Another day of his life ready to begin, or waste, it was too early to tell for sure. After a very solid argument from the devil on his shoulder, telling him to stay home another day and try for tomorrow, he shook away and freed himself from those wasteful thoughts. All the work with therapy may be working even after the first session. Saying things out loud for someone else to hear could be easing the tension and stress he felt. He knew he could start going out to society again, and he should, but the devil on his shoulder normally got the last say and made a final pitch to Patrick. *Skip work...but go see the kids at the orphanage.*

It's not too much for a day and it would be nice to see the kids again, he could use a laugh or two and they're sure to supply plenty. *You also promised Amanda,* he remembered.

Spending the early afternoon eating breakfast and preparing for the day, the only way he knew how, to brew some coffee and stretch on the floor. His apartment got lots of light in the mornings and he took advantage of that by sitting in the warm patch that shone through the drapes. He put one of his comfort Netflix series on for background noise, closed his eyes, and prepared to visualize going about his day. It's something he has always enjoyed doing since he was a kid. He could be prepared for his day that way and he always liked seeing himself go through the day before he actually did. It helped him during school especially, remembering where classes were located and what his day looked like, schedule-wise. He was prepared for each day because, in a way, he already imagined himself through it. It may be overkill for life, but he enjoyed the successes of his efforts. It's become a game to correctly or almost correctly guess some events of the day. He sat up cross-legged and closed his eyes, beginning his process.

The orphanage was just a few blocks away. It should not take long.

There's a conveniently placed gas station kitty-corner of his apartment building. Past the gas station was a public library where a lot of people like to sit outside on the patio and drink coffee or read their books. Across the library, a small park with nothing but a fountain and some benches resided.

He took a left and continued down the street for a while, passing a dive bar called *Dirty Ricky's,* and then some local mom and pop shops. Once past the bars and shops, he took a right, crossing the street, and ascended the rainbow style bridge that hovered over the rushing waters of the local dam. He could imagine the roaring of the powerful water, almost too clearly. Patrick imagined small boats tied up down river where the water settled. People liked to fish there; he imagined people fishing at the spot in his head. Now, off the bridge, just a block up ahead and to the right and he has arrived.

To Building Blocks...at Building Blocks, his mind echoed inside.

Sitting on his living floor, with eyes shut, Patrick imagined himself walking to the empty lot that he used as a shortcut to get to Building Blocks.

To Building Blocks...at Building Blocks, his mind echoed once more.

He stepped in the lot over the small fence and saw the alley between the two large neighboring buildings. Even in his dream-like walkthrough the buildings seemed to tower and look down over him, nefarious and cruel.

Nefarious, his mind repeated. It gave him the chills just thinking about it, as did the dark shadow escaping the alley, the same way the darkness escaped a cave.

What the hell? He wondered calmly. *Why is it dark? This is just an open alley.*

He took a few imaginary rounded steps, getting a straight view through the alley. He could see through to the other side, but just barely as the smoke disguised the opposite side. It's dark and smoky but nothing seemed to be inside. The smoke got thicker as Patrick peered through deeper, taking more imaginary steps forward.

Why am I... seeing this? This is just my imagination, Patrick wondered, as the clouds of smoke start whirled faster as if there's a fan blowing through. The black smoke billowed out of the alley completely blocking the site to the other side now. It quickly spilled out toward Patrick who reacted and opened his eyes.

"What!" he yelled out loud in confusion, looking around his apartment. He checked the clock, then took a deep breath, setting his head down on the sofa cushion.

He's never been so lost in one of his morning visualizing sessions before. To him, it seemed he was almost being held from coming back to real life and out of his mind. He took another deep breath before standing to his feet. He walked to the window and looked outside. *A beautiful day,* he thought.

That was freaky strange, he thought, as he turned back to the couch and sat. He looked back to the window from his seat, unsure of what he wanted to do. He sighed.

"Halo," he said aloud.

No answer.

"C'mon man, you there?" Patrick asked, and waited for an answer.

He got nothing.

"Okay so If I go, and jump off a bridge, you're not going to say anything? You'll just let me?" he asked, trying to get Halo talking.

No answer.

Patrick sighed and laid back down on the sun-covered floor.

"Fine," he said defiantly.

"I'll just finish my walkthrough then," he said.

He closed his eyes to try and finish his journey to Building Blocks. His mind raced to catch up, flashes of previous stops filled his head until he got back to the alley. He stepped onto the lot looking at his imaginary alley. It was empty at that time. He stepped up to the alley, walking through and touching each wall on his way by. He approached the end and ran into nothing, inspecting it to be a normal alley that time. He got to the end of the alley and stepped onto the street to cross before turning around to look back at it. He peered through to the other side lot. *Still empty,* he thought. .

Now, just a block down the street and he would be at Building Blocks. *To Building Blocks...at Building Blocks*, his mind echoed out.

He stepped twice on the sidewalk before forcing himself to stop. He got an eerie feeling after taking that last step, like something bad was going to happen. The closer he got to Building Blocks, the worse the feeling it seemed. He put a foot in front as if he was going to stop but didn't put pressure down, he soaked up the feeling. It was a heavy feeling of pressure and nausea that gave him an unsettling feeling. He stepped backward, as the feeling went away. He turned back to the alley, seeing it covered in the same dark smoke from before. It was pushing up higher into the sky, covering over his immediate area by the roofs of the building. He stumbled backward-looking upon the smoke, getting scared now. This is his mind but he didn't seem to be in control of it. The smoke descended and surrounded him before suddenly coming to a complete and silent stop. Patrick waited in silence for a moment, looking through the smoke. Suddenly, that same silence from before turned into a hellish pressure. It began to constrict his head and body, as Patrick began to go into shock. He tried snapping out and waking, back to the real world but he couldn't for some reason. The silence seemed to be attacking him now, pounding on his eyes and his head. His fingertips went numb as he decided to try and scream. He shut his eyes and screamed out, but heard nothing. He opened his eyes while screaming again but received only silence. He focused again, with everything he could manage, hoping to snap himself out. He shut his eyes and slammed his fist into the ground with force. A quick jolt of fear struck through him as he ended back in his living room, with tears on the verge of forming. He shot up from the floor and walked to the kitchen before they could shed any. He splashed himself with water and snapped his fingers repeatedly at his ear, hoping to hear and to know he was back to normal. *What is going on with me?* He wondered.

He jumped in the shower and prepared his clothes at a rapid pace, not trying to think further about what just happened. He feared he may get stuck in thought again. It's a little earlier than when he would normally go over but that didn't matter, he had to leave, he had to move. He grabbed his keys and left out the door, not stopping at all to think about what just happened.

Patrick made a stop at a grocery store to buy the kids some treats, he chose cupcakes thinking everyone would enjoy them. He understood that he has been gone for a while with no explanation and there are sure to be some hard feelings, so the cupcakes may help. The kids at Building Blocks all know and understand too well but he is not going to burden them with more hardship and negative views of the world. He pulled up to Building Blocks and parked his car. He took a moment to peer down the road to the alley, which was part of the reason he drove instead of walking. *It looks normal enough now,* he wondered.

He took the cupcakes out and paced to the front door. The kids had off from school that day and they should all be outside, or at the park with the staff. He planned that, so he could go see and talk with Amanda first. He already knew what he was going to tell her. He was going to tell her that he was sick and didn't want them getting sick either and that he was sorry for the lack of communication throughout the week. *That should settle it,* he thought. He opened the front door, wondering why it wasn't locked, and looked around. It's still the same as he left it, toys scattered, colored pencils everywhere, and the smell of milk overloaded his sense of smell.

It always smells like milk doesn't it? He wondered.

"Hey, thought you died or something," a familiar voice from one of the rooms spoke out. Patrick peeked around the corner of the activity room to see Anna reading a magazine on the couch. He walked into the room holding his box of cupcakes.

"Hey...no I didn't...die...that's dark Anna" he replied as he set the box down. "I've been.... sick for a while, needed some time," He said as he shut the door behind him.

Anna didn't reply and went back to reading her magazine, or pretended to.

"So what's the day been like today?" Patrick asked, walking over to the couch.

"Been like this" she said and gestured toward the floor and all the toys. "I'm supposed to be doing some yard work, but then I saw this lonely magazine here and thought I should keep it company instead" she replied with low-level sarcasm.

"I see...what's the job?" Patrick asked, intrigued.

"They want me to organize the shed and clear space"

"Oh that's a great job, I can help," He excitedly tells her hoping to get her up and excited too. She looked up to him from her magazine, eyebrows raised. Patrick couldn't help but smile back.

"Okay, let me finish this. Gimme ten minutes" she said as she settled back into the couch.

"Deal," he said. His eyes got wide as he realized the cupcakes. "Oh yeah and also, I got you something."

He grabbed the cupcakes and placed them in front of the table so she could grab one.

"Seriously?" she asked, looking down at the two trays of cupcakes.

Patrick cocked his head back and squinted his eyes. "Yeah, what? They're just cupcakes, relax...I'm not a monster. I also baked them myself"

Anna squinted her eyes back at him as she peeled off the price sticker. "And you priced them yourself too? Serious business you seem to run"

"Mmhmm" he grunted, as he nodded his head.

"Kind of expensive, don't you think?" she asked, crumpling up the sticker.

"Nope, not for Building Blocks"

"Thank you," she remarked as she began to grab one.

Patrick nodded his head and walked over to the stairs. "Ten minutes!" he shouted to Anna as he ascended the stairs to Amanda's office. The door was wide open and he could see some movement inside. He reached the doorway and knocked lightly. He saw Amanda lift her head from the messy paperwork scattered across the table.

"Patrick! Hey, how are you?" she said, greeting him.

"Hey Amanda, I'm.... okay" he said with a pause, which got Amanda's attention.

"You okay? Are you feeling better?" Amanda asked, tilting her head.

"Yeah I'm feeling better," he insisted.

This is where I tell her that I'm sorry for being sick and not communicating more, he thought, but now at the moment, things were different, he didn't want to gloss over things anymore. *It's time to heal. It's time to be real,* Patrick knew deep down.

"Actually Amanda....um, I wasn't sick I— " Patrick paused and took a deep breath, he leaned back and rested against her spare table.

"Uh so my mom... had been sick for a while...and uh she, well she died not too long ago, and it's been a confusing and really weird time since. I'm just trying to stay afloat" Patrick said, looking directly into Amanda's eyes.

From Patrick's perspective, Amanda's reaction to the news was one of empathy and sadness, he expected nothing different. She genuinely liked him and has said so on multiple occasions. At the moment Patrick wondered, *Why was I so hesitant to tell her?*

"Patrick I'm so sorry, I had no idea. If there's anything I can do for you, please just ask" she said, as she stood and walked over. Without hesitation or ask, she wrapped him in a hug. Her words seemed genuine to him, so he returned her embrace. They break but Amanda stood a few feet away, looking caringly into Patrick's eyes. From the way her eyes looked, Patrick could feel her heart. *She sees me as a son?*

"I don't want the kids to know, so if you wouldn't mind keeping that secret for me," he asked, assuming she'll agree.

"Of course," she said graciously. "Do you have anyone you can talk to that you trust, it's important and will help, trust me...I know" she said. Patrick saw a twinge of pain in Amanda's face. *She's lost someone too.*

"I have an Aunt that's around, she's been helpful"

"Good. Well if you need more time away, please do what's best for you, I understand and I think the kids would too" she replied, giving him a look of certainty.

"Thanks Amanda...I want to be here though..." He said leaning forward to look down the hallway. "Back with these kids. You know they may be the most understanding of all I think." Patrick reached down nervously and scratched his leg.

"Well they are going to go crazy when they see you, they asked about you a lot, they were really worried," Amanda said. "They didn't have school today so they all went to the park with some of the other staff, you can head over there if you want."

"I'll wait for them here, Anna is downstairs avoiding chores so I'm gonna try to motivate her"

"Ahh yes... the shed," Amanda said, turning back to her desk. She sat down. "I thought she would have enjoyed that."

"Not...as much as a magazine apparently," Patrick answered before heading out of her office towards the stairs. Just as he stepped out of her office, his hand started to get warm.

*Halo is calling...*Patrick knew and furrowed his eyebrows, annoyed at the sudden communication.

"Patrick" Amanda called back from her office.

Patrick, still close to her office, walked over and placed a hand on her door frame,their eyes met upon re-entry.

"I know I say this all the time, so its meaning may become lost sometimes...but these kids are lucky to have you here, you are changing *their* lives for the better, so thank you" Her emphasis on the kids struck Patrick in the right place. He didn't need the recognition to keep doing good things, but it felt nice all the same, knowing someone saw the good in him.

Patrick smiled and nodded slowly. "I know... they are changing mine too" He tapped the door frame lightly, and turned back into the hall. He looked around for anyone, took a deep, calming breath, and scurried to one of the closets. He grabbed and turned the handle and shut the door behind him quietly. It was a maintenance closet filled with mops, brooms, and cleaning supplies. *Not the best spot*, he thought, and without having to even try, Halo appeared in hand, glowing brightly from his hand and unraveled down to the ground.

"Hello Patrick," the mystical voice called out in his mind.

"Who is this? Sorry I just got a brand new glowing magic rope and didn't save any old contacts' ' Patrick responded sarcastically, giving a wry, self gratified smile.

Halo didn't indulge in the joke and moved on. "You are up," Halo said.

"Up?" Patrick replied.

"Your needed, there's something out in the woods"

Patrick didn't answer, preferring to shake his head instead, thinking of what to say. He was about to respond with a joke about being needed when Halo made a surprising announcement.

"I'm sorry for the lack of communication Patrick, you need answers that I can't always provide," Halo said, still deflecting.

Hearing this made Patrick even more frustrated. He realized that that is exactly what he would say. He was even going to tell Amanda the same thing. *Is Halo avoiding me?* Patrick wondered.

"No. I am not. Like I said, there are things I don't know or can't tell you about...yet. I'm your guide, remember? You're not broken...you don't need to be fixed."

Clever, Patrick thought, hearing his own words of therapy used against him. "Yeah and you're great too" Patrick sniped back.

"You know you can't neglect this, just like you can't the kids" Halo mentioned, and he was right. Patrick knew he had a duty now. A duty he still had no clue about, but a duty nonetheless. Patrick still wasn't happy about their current relationship. He felt like a pawn to Halo, some soldier that would be easily replaced. *Or am I being punished?*

"Fine, but it waits until later," Patrick said and meant it.

"Okay," Halo said before evaporating into his hand. Patrick took a deep breath and thought about what could be out there in the woods.

The frightening image of the dark smoke billowing out of the alley came to mind, as did what happened to Sal last week. He hasn't heard any news reports about it, and come to think of it, Patrick hasn't heard many reports about the city's new angel for a while. *Probably because I haven't done anything for a while,* he knew. He quickly shook off that thought and walked toward the closet door. He opened the door and exited the closet quietly, shutting it with the same caution. He turned for the stairs but a voice from behind the corner stopped him in shock.

"I like your color"

Patrick froze up, wide-eyed and turned to see Laney, the little girl he spoke with a while ago about superheroes. She poked her head around the corner still hiding her body.

"Hey Laney," Patrick said, "What did you say?"

She stepped in clear view into the hallway and pointed at Patrick's hand. "Your color, I like the color, it's really bright," she said in her pure, energetic tone.

Patrick paused for a moment. *What could she be referring to?* Patrick wondered. *She can't see Halo, can she? I was alone in the closet. I checked the whole thing.*

"Bright? Uh...what do you mean?" he asked, stalling for time and waiting for more information from her. She took the bait quickly.

"It's yellow and really bright. My father's rope was Violet and it didn't glow as bright as yours does" Laney said, looking at Patrick's hand.

What did she just say? Patrick thought to himself.

"What rope Laney? When did you see me with a bright yellow rope?" He asked, growing increasingly anxious.

Laney smiled and looked at Patrick like he just told her a joke. "In the closet just now, I could see it"

The door was shut, I was alone. Patrick knew. "Laney the door was closed; you weren't in there." He said.

Without missing a beat, Laney answered. "I don't need doors to be open to see, I have eyes."

Patrick cocked his head in confusion, about to ask another standard stall tactic question when Laney made another bomb-shell comment.

"You're the Angel, the one that's out in the city. That's you, isn't it?"

Patrick did not respond, but the answer was written clearly on his face. Patrick could see in Laney's expression that she knew she was right. Patrick stood frozen in confusion, finally realizing this isn't the time or the place to talk about that. He had an idea.

"Come help Anna and me clean the shed. We could use some help" Patrick said, trying to smile, but couldn't manage one for her. He turned and started walking toward the stairs as Laney followed closely behind.

What the hell? He thought as he descended the stairs. *This little girl just learned everything.*

Patrick eyes Laney as she hopped down the steps, two feet at a time. *She seems happy though,* Patrick thought as they reached the bottom step and headed out back to the shed.

"Ten minutes is up Anna! Let's goooo!" Patrick shouted from the kitchen.

They get to the shed with Anna jogging up behind. They all grabbed items and moved them out from the shed so they could clean. Patrick didn't ask Laney anything, and went on as normal. They swept the shed floor and moved all of the items and toys back into the shed. It was a team job and he was glad he had these two helpers. Anna saw that they were almost finished and took off to go get some drinks. Patrick noticed this would be a good time to ask Laney a question or two. He leaned up against the riding-lawn mower watching Laney as she reeled the garden hose up around her tiny arm.

"So Laney, you said your...Dad, had a rope too? Patrick asked, realizing his poor choice of wording.

Laney seemed to understand what Patrick was wondering and spoke truthfully, "Uh huh, Daddy had a rope just like yours and fought monsters just like you do now I'm sure," she said, starting to struggle with the weight of the hose.

Patrick's eyes grew wider as he was finally hearing some details about his new life. These were the things that Halo would never tell him. *Yet this little girl knows?* Patrick wondered.

"What else did he do, Laney?" Patrick asked, pressing on, feeling her comfort in the subject.

Laney shook her head in what seemed to be a frustrating and contradicting move.

She wants answers too, Patrick thought, before Laney spoke back up.

"He never really liked talking about that stuff, only bedtime stories" Her head dropped, "But he did teach me something, something I could teach you if you'd like?" She asked, looking back up with changed energy.

"Like seeing through walls?" asked Patrick.

"Like I said before. I see through my eyes" she answered. Laney was so young but Patrick could see her, she was more confident and self-assured than her age should allow. *Maybe it's because she's the one providing the knowledge,* he wondered.

"Eyes? Like, my eyes?" Patrick asked.

"Yep, anyone's eyes. And, I'll prove it to you" Said Laney, as if Patrick had asked for proof.

"Okay yeah," Patrick said, looking around the shed. He spotted some chalk in an old ice cream container and picked it up. "Okay I'll write a word on the floor in the shed, where you can't see. You walk over there and I will stay here and look at the word, cool?" He asked, then pointed to the house.

Laney smiled and nodded her head, before running over to the side of the yard. Patrick knelt and wrote *Puppies* in pink chalk. He stood up and looked over at Laney who was facing the opposite way.

"Okay Laney, ready!" he shouted.

"Are you looking at the word?" Laney yelled back.

"Yep!" Patrick answered, before quickly looking at his word, *Puppies,* written in pink chalk. He waited for a moment before hearing Laney yell over.

"It says Puppies!"

Oh my god, Patrick thought, as he turned back to her. "Another!" he yelled, as he bent back over and wrote *Spaghetti.*

"Ready!" He shouted and waited for a reply, and sure enough.

"Spaghetti!" she yelled through enjoyable laughter.

"What color is it written in!" Patrick yelled.

"Pink!"

"Oh my god, Laney... you're amazing!" He yelled, still hearing her laughter.

"Okay one more!" He yelled and bent over to write, *teach me how to do this!*

"Okay go!" he yelled.

Laney turned over her shoulder, smiled, and gave Patrick a thumbs up. "I sure can"

Chapter 22

The rest of the day was spent hanging out with the kids and connecting the same way he always tried to. Things were normal for a long time, Patrick even found himself forgetting his other life for a while and was enjoying the time at Building Blocks. He passed out the cupcakes and made more jokes about him making them, but the kids all saw through that. No one seemed angry at him for being gone, they just seemed happy he was back. Around five o'clock Patrick said his goodbyes to all the kids, promised to be back tomorrow, and prepared to leave. He grabbed his phone and walked through the building, making sure the messes they caused were cleaned up. Once satisfied he ran upstairs to ask Amanda if there was anything else he could do. Amanda couldn't think of any more to ask, said her goodbyes, and of course, shared more words of encouragement for him. He got to the stairs just as Laney was ascending.

"Hey Laney, I'm heading out. I will be back to see you tomorrow. I have so many questions" He said as he got to the bottom and smiled at her. Patrick saw her smile in return but was unable to feel her emotions. *I can't even see them*, he thought as gave Laney a salute and opened the door.

"Bye Laney," he said as he turned back before shutting it.

"Bye," she said, "Be careful."

Patrick heard and paused momentarily in thought, he brushed that off and walked out to his car, checking the sky for any signs of danger. Once on the street side he looked over to the strange alley from his walkthrough, but saw nothing off or suspicious. He looked away to the sky. *It's still nice out, at least three more hours of daylight*, he knew.

He hopped in his car, started the engine, and drove off. *Good thing I drove*, he thought, as it was a decent drive out of town and out to the country woods. He arrived on site and parked his car, once again the lot was empty. *This place is spooky*, he thought as he looked around at the tall creaky treetops, and through the thick dark woods. *Good thing I'm a ninja*, Patrick thought proudly.

He got out and began walking into the woods, ever wary of the tall lurching treetops and dark shadows of the forest.

"Okay, I'm here...obviously," Patrick said aloud, looking into the forest.

"Good, now go that way," Halo said abruptly in Patrick's mind.

"Which way?" Patrick, annoyed, asked before looking up to see a large cloud of dark smoke hover over the top of the thickly wooded area straight ahead. "Whoa that was not there before," he said quickly

"It was. It was only being hidden from your perspective," Halo answered.

Patrick raised his eyebrows in surprise, "Why?" he asked. Patrick wasn't really surprised though; he knew secrets were a common thing in his current situation.

"It would be too distracting to see every day," Halo instructed "The less you respond to negativity, the easier peace becomes"

"Aww you're looking out for me? I appreciate that" Patrick said flatly.

Patrick reached the woods and peered through as far as he could. Those dark and dreadful feelings washed over him again as the image of Sal and the mummy creature flashed in his head. He looked further in and felt comfortable enough with what he saw in the woods and proceeded forward, following the guidance of the dark cloud. He noticed that the smoke seemed to rise from the clouds it formed and moved higher into the sky. Patrick surveyed deeper into the woods away from where he parked, getting to where he felt was the center of the dark clouds. He scoped the wooded area out for danger.

"You should prepare" Halo reminded him.

"Yeah, for sure" Patrick remembered and looked at his hand. He summoned the glowing yellow rope and molded it into a large flat disc. He lifted it high over his head and let it slowly descend over his body, changing it to the bright white and yellow as it went. Patrick opened his eyes after feeling the warm wave overlap his body, and saw through his dark eyes. He forgot how great it felt to wear this thing, all that time spent away from the world must have hindered his memory.

Holding Halo, he continued his walk through the forest, looking for any hint of danger, and after searching for a while longer, Patrick came into contact with it head-on.

"Halo is this thing even in the forest?" Patrick asked aloud, looking inside a neighboring bush.

"Yes…and it can see you, It's to your right" Halo answered coolly.

Patrick shuffled over behind a large tree to his right, hiding from view. He looked around it for the danger. "Why hasn't it attacked me, if it can see me?" He asked Halo. "And why haven't you told me sooner?"

"You have not gotten its attention yet" Halo replied. "It won't attack until provoked."

Patrick looked around the forest, feeling relieved at the words, and then spotted a hidden figure stretched up between two trees. He scanned the shadowy, long figure seeing what appeared to be a tall, lanky bat-like creature stretched out between the two trees, with its claws dug deep into the bark. It's a dark part of the trees and it was hard to see clearly, but Patrick could make out the large body of the creature now, and feel the energy emanating from it. He moved backward, hiding behind the tree.

"What's the best way to kill these things again?" Patrick asked, getting nervous.

"You took care of the last one just fine"

"Yeah but it sucked" Patrick replied, remembering the bear creature's raging strength. He waited behind the tree for a few moments to psych himself up. He could feel the thoughts of negativity and darkness rising from the base of his mind, becoming heavier and heavier.

Sensing his hesitation, Halo spoke to him. "Remember, if you don't confront the creature now it may become reality."

Those words were not very reassuring to Patrick but were enough to get him moving as he stood up. Halo continued the pep talk.

"Patrick, at your full strength this challenge would be as easy as a blink of the eye. You're stronger than that…and you're stronger than yourself."

Those words helped more as Patrick nodded in agreement. *He always knows what to say to me*, Patrick thought as he walked around the tree. Staring at the bat creature, Patrick prepared himself a few feet behind. Patrick stepped further into the open ground and with Halo in hand, lassoed it around the trees the creature was sprawled between. Patrick caught the other side of the rope, wrapping them up along with the creature as loose as he could. As the rope fits loosely around the trees and the creature, Patrick readied himself to trap the creature. *Here we go,* Patrick thought and counted down. *Three...Two... One!* He yanked as hard as he could, ripping through both trees. After a still moment, the trees collapsed loudly to the side, leaving only the bat creature tightly wrapped in Halo's burning clutches. Patrick saw the monster more clearly now in the light Halo provided. Seeing what could be a bat, but the face and head were tightly formed, almost set like concrete, it reminded Patrick of the gargoyles above the churches and buildings he'd seen pictures of in Europe. The creature stood alone in the aftermath of Patrick's plan and faced him head-on. Patrick noticed the creature was bigger than it was letting on, hiding in between the trees. It was at least seven feet tall and even then it had a horrible arch in its back forcing it downward. The creature lay still, trapped tightly in Halo. Patrick could see Halo was burning the creature's skin from its touch but there was no reaction from the towering beast. It stayed calm and unmoved as it stared at Patrick. The bat-creature slowly swayed back and forth, moving the rope in a gentle sway. A familiar sensation struck Patrick about the creature causing him to freeze for a moment. Patrick knew he had to finish it off quickly, yet its calm demeanor was unnerving to Patrick, who wished he had the creature's perceived confidence at the moment. He looked down at his hands, wondering his next move, and decided. With one of his hands, he broke off a piece of Halo and molded it into a small flat disc. He held the rope tightly with his left hand and with his right whipped the disc as hard as he could at the creature's neck. The disc flew through the trees, slicing off pieces of bark as it cut swiftly through the quiet woods, about to slice through the creature's neck. The disc missed its target as the creature ducked at the last moment, it flexed and muscled its body, letting out a terrible, beastly roar. Halo tightened up and broke into pieces as the bat creature spread its muscular arms outward. Before it could regain its balance, Patrick willed the missed disc back towards the creature. It couldn't react fast enough as the disc sliced the side of it's foot and returned to Patrick's hand. The creature turned from the disc and located Patrick, then leapt for him. Patrick quickly molded Halo into a large shield and absorbed the creature's long claw attack. The creature slid away, losing its balance from the strike, and Patrick took advantage by leaping over and striking it hard in the neck with a right hook. It was sent flying

127

through the forest ground, barraging into a few trees before it came to a halt.

Whoa, that was something, Patrick thought about that exchange which brought him some confidence. The creature scrambled up to its monstrous grey claws and looked at Patrick with that cold, unnerving stare once more. Patrick moved first this time as he molded and threw two discs at the creature. Patrick quickly jumped and followed behind the two slicing discs, hoping the creature would be distracted. The monster avoided the first disc but the second one caught its abdomen, causing it to lean off balance. The third attack from Patrick came right after the disc sliced through. The creature was focused on Patrick however, as it grabbed him from the air with its long claws digging lightly into his skin. It pulled Patrick away and slammed him into the ground. Patrick felt helpless as the monster dug its claws into his shoulder deeper. Patrick screamed out in pain as the creature twisted and threw him viciously to the ground, sending him scrolling away. Patrick took the fall well enough and bounced up to his feet quickly. He checked his shoulder for damage, which he didn't see fortunately, but it was hurting all the same.

Patrick stood up, suddenly filled with anger. He gracefully molded Halo into a sharp sword-like figure and a shield to match. He felt the warmth of Halo over his fists as he squared up to the creature. Their eyes met as Patrick charged first at the creature, then it charged back. They met in the middle as its long claw took the first swing at Patrick, he blocked it with the shield then swiped at the creature's back leg with the sword, barely making contact. The creature counter swung at Patrick as he met its long, sharp claws with his sword. Patrick heard the simmering of the contact and leaped backward. The creature dove forward with him and swung another low claw at Patrick who read it completely. He jumped over the swing dodging it narrowly and connected with another forceful right hook into the creature's dark, slimey cheek. The punch landed and sent the creature hurling sideways, Patrick grabbed the creature's leg before it could fly off, and swung it around, launching the creature as hard as he could. The creature crashed through the trees, causing a crackling eruption of trees and earth, before it came to a silent pause. Patrick watched eagerly and through heavy breath to see the creature sitting motionless up against some unearthed dirt. Thinking it dead, Patrick began to walk toward it as Halo interrupted.

"It is not dead," he said.

As he heard the words, the bat-creature lunged at Patrick with its claws sprouting for the attack. It got within range and swiped twice. Patrick had ample time to react and evaded both strikes with ease. He jumped up high preparing to finish the fight, yet a third swipe came from the creature slicing at Patrick's hand, sending him sideways. Patrick took the hit and tumbled out of danger. The creature teared through the earth, scrambling towards Patrick, claws drawn, ready for more action. It swiped at Patrick predictably, so Patrick blocked it with a shield and quickly stabbed the creature in the abdomen, causing it to roar out in presumed pain. The creature swiped again, throwing a weak hook. Patrick dodged it and followed up with a kick to the creature's side, sending it into a tree. The creature, stunned for a moment, tried to regain its balance to strike again, but Patrick leapt in and struck before it could ready itself. Leaping over the creature's head, Patrick cut through its neck without any resistance. He landed behind the bat creature to see it topple over onto the woodland ground.

"It's over," Halo said coolly. "Well done"

Patrick nodded and walked over to his enemy. He stopped and crouched, using a nearby tree for support. He stared at his dead foe, feeling the depletion of energy from the fight, feeling tired. It's been a while since he suited up, so he was bound to be rusty. He looked deeper at the creature and got that familiar feeling again, he just couldn't place it.

"Anything else out here Halo?" Patrick asked, from the creature's side.

"Do you really want to know?"

Patrick smirked, "Yeah not tonight," he said as he stood up, still staring at the bat creature. "I need some practice," he said, walking in the direction of his parked car. He turned back to take another look at the giant bat-creature and to embrace that familiar feeling again. He looked at the sky, seeing the dark clouds had vanished, leaving only the evening sky. He continued his walk out of the woods, feeling accomplished, feeling...bad.

Chapter 23

It's time to wake up.

Again, Patrick awoke to the sun beaming violently through at him from his half-closed drapes. *I need to move my bed,* he thought. *Or get better drapes.*

Like every waking morning he has ever experienced before, Patrick came back into his life. He didn't dream at all during his night. Dreaming can be great, having no dreams could be even better. Patrick rolled away from the sunspot onto his shoulder and nestled back into the pillow hoping for a few more minutes of sleep before his alarm clock inevitably went off. *An hour would be great.* He wondered while shutting his eyes. He wondered what his day would bring. He thought and relaxed. *It's going to be a good day today.* He felt excited at his prospective day, a feeling that was new and refreshing. *Go back to work...get through that, go see the kids and train with Laney, maybe get some answers and then go out looking for some trouble. Fantastic,* Patrick's hoped.

He rolled back over, through the sun and grabbed his phone from the charger on his nightstand, and checked the time, *seven-twelve,* he read. Patrick smirked in amusement as he set his alarm clock the night before, for seven-fifteen. *Damn, I could have slept three more minutes.*

Patrick ran through his normal morning routine, opting to skip his morning walkthrough again, unable to go back from the fear of the unknown. He made sure he looked presentable for work, then took off. His normal responsibilities were waiting for him and had to catch up on some major projects. But he was an organized and efficient worker, so he was confident. He worked through the day and said hello to his coworkers that passed by or that he would see in the breakroom, trying to be friendly. Patrick was walking, talking, and thinking, but his mind was truly somewhere else, he opted for an auto-pilot sort of day. Mornings, lunches, dinners, and nights, all blurred together and moved on quickly for Patrick. He lived out the days in his monotone outlook, ready to move to the next. His days were more exciting than they were. *But it— it doesn't feel...*

It was two hours past noon when Patrick was working on his community outreach project, one that had him genuinely excited and present. Getting an opportunity to have the community see what his coworkers and he did for it, and for the school was always an assignment Patrick wanted to lead. Patrick's boss stopped by his desk to welcome him back.

"Patrick, your back, excellent," he said frankly.

Patrick swiveled around in his chair to make eye contact. The truth was Patrick saw him approaching before and turned away, he hoped not to be noticed.

"Hello, Mr. Rant," Patrick returned, forcing a tip-lipped smile.

"How are you feeling? Must have been a *nasty* bug for you to miss almost *two* weeks." Mr. Rant said in a tone that made Patrick want to stand up and smack him in the face. But he had another thought. *I was gone for two weeks? It was only a few days, four, five days max.*

"Yeah, thanks for asking...Sir" Patrick responded.

"Okay…. well I'll let you get back to *all* of this work," Mr. Rant said, smiling and gesturing toward Patrick's desk before turning to walk away.

Patrick sat for a moment staring at the wall to stew in that moment. He regained his focus on work, then lost it again when a beautiful sight appeared, rounding the corner of the hallway. *It's Summer, she looks nice,* Patrick thought.

He knew this would happen. After all of his time away, he regrettably never really thought about Summer. But now she was here, he could see her. Patrick's mother gave him some advice about women when he was growing up. She would say, in her stern motherly voice "If you're unsure about your feelings for a girl, it's best to let her go."

And that's how Patrick saw every relationship in the future. He wanted to be entirely sure he liked the girl before he would pursue anything. It had its benefits and its negatives, but it was ingrained early. But now here, in reality, seeing Summer, it was harder to think about. Summer walked toward him, smiling and pointing over her shoulder to where Mr. Rant passed by.

"He missed you, you know," Summer said as she reached the desk.

"Oh, he did?" Patrick replied and gave a big smile, unable to control it.

131

"Yeah, the other day I saw him crying and drinking whiskey in his office," Summer said and placed a hand on Patrick's desk.

Patrick snickered. "That's just about his normal life I'm sure, not for me"

They shared a laugh. "You actually saw him drinking though?" Patrick asked.

Summer looks over her shoulder to make sure Mr. Rant wasn't around. "Yeah actually, I'm not telling, I don't want to get involved though," she said with a raise of her eyebrows. She took a few steps around his desk.

"Right," Patrick said and nodded. He didn't care about Mr. Rant's drama either. It wasn't worth talking about, even with Summer.

"But, you're back!" Summer said as she pumped her hands in the air, raising the roof.

Patrick smiled and looked away. "Yeah, I'm back," he said before looking back up to Summer. "And I'm happy to be here. Did you miss me as much as Mr. Rant?"

"Of course, even more, you're my favorite work, drinking buddy" Summer replied.

Patrick smiled and looked down at his desk as Summer continued. "But yeah so speaking of...you're not mad at me or anything, right?"

Patrick shot a look up at Summer and raised his eyebrows in visible curiosity and shock. "Uhh no, I'm not. Why?"

"Okay good, I just felt bad about the ending, with my friend getting sick. And then I heard something weird happened at a restaurant downtown, close by, and I just felt really bad about ditching you. So I'm sorry" Summer confessed. "I just thought maybe you were angry"

Patrick waited for Summer to be finished. His heart was beating fast and he was getting a little anxious. *That was nice,* he thought as he replied slowly.

"No, I'm not... angry at all. Your friend was sick; you did the right thing" Patrick said before pausing. He didn't want to bring up the restaurant but he knew he had to say more. "But, hey um, that was really nice, you know, to worry and care, I appreciate it." Patrick said, flashing a smile.

"Okay, good. That's a relief. Well, maybe some weekend we could go for some drinks again? Mr. Rants got me inspired...whenever you're free?" She stated.

"Yes, let's do it. I'll be the one throwing up this time" Patrick said jokingly.

Summer laughed and smiled. "Gross," she said and walked away.

Patrick sat still, letting all of the emotions from the recent exchanges flow in and out. So many conflicting feelings. Patrick checked the time, knowing he should get back to work, and after a few more hours he clocked out for Building Blocks. Having arrived, he entered the orphanage with fresh excitement, wondering what they would be doing today when he arrived. Something entertaining usually, and to his wish, he was not let down. As soon as he walked in he was greeted by Amanda, who was on the phone. She saw him and covered the bottom part of the phone with her hand.

"Hey Patrick, I am glad you're here. Would you like to go with the group to the park?" she asked.

"Yes, for sure!" Patrick exclaimed.

Amanda placed the phone back to her ear and mouthed the word thank you toward Patrick. She walked off to finish what sounded like an important call. Patrick eyed her emotions above to make sure everything was fine. He saw Amanda in decent spirits and walked out back to where they usually met beforehand, to go over the health and safety rules. Patrick saw them through the kitchen hallway all outside listening to Ms. Kathy speak. He noticed Conner, sitting on the steps facing the other way listening. Patrick snuck up behind, knelt and tapped Conner's shoulder to get his attention. Conner turned to see and lit up, he was about to scream something before Patrick put his finger to his own mouth to tell Conner to keep listening. It worked, as Conner settled for a side hug.

"What are you guys doing?" Patrick whispered to Conner.

"Ms. Kathy is taking us to the park to play kickball" he whispered back.

"And she's going over the safety rules again?" Patrick asked.

"Yeah, *again,*" Conner says as his eyes roll.

Patrick chuckled. "They are important,"

Patrick stood up and looked over the crowd to all of the kids. He located Laney in the middle, sitting crisscrossed playing with the grass, completely oblivious to what Ms. Kathy was saying. She eventually finished her speech and permitted the kids to stand. They all one by one, saw Patrick and hustld over to say hello and ask if he could be on their team.

The group eventually congregates out by the front porch fence, leaving through the hallway to get their stuff ready, everyone except Laney, Patrick noticed. Ms. Kathy, who noticed him watching Laney, walked over.

"She got into a little argument earlier today with another kid. She's been moody today, poor girl" she said, then briskly walked off toward the others, yelling directions.

Patrick walked up to Laney and sat down beside her. "Ready for the park, Laney?" he asked softly.

Laney looked up at him and then back down to the grass. "I didn't think you were coming back."

"Of course I would. I live nearby. And I like coming here. But more importantly, you have some teaching to do, remember?" Patrick said those last words, which must have worked because Laney was standing up now.

"You're always coming back?" Laney asked.

The question shocked Patrick a bit, but there was only one answer. "Yes, I'll always come back" he answered.

Laney grabbed Patrick's hand as they walked back inside, following the group to the park. They brought up the end of the group, and as soon as they arrived at the park, all the kids sprinted off in different directions. Like a group of wild dogs, they were gone. Ms. Kathy ran off to try and scramble the kids, while Patrick gathered the ones he could and sat down on the bench, ready to watch the game. It *might be a while*, he thought as he watched the kids sprint around playing and running through the field, except for Laney, who stayed back so she could spend time with Patrick.

"Okay Laney, let's do this," he said, as she turned to him eagerly. "Is it hard to do?" Patrick asked cautiously for more details before his life got a tad weirder.

Laney shook her head. "No it's easy when you get the hang of it, you can do it"

"Yeah but you're like, really smart already" he replied, hoping to encourage her.

Laney smirked and looked at Patrick. "Okay let's start"

As Laney and Patrick sat along the field on the bleachers, occasionally being interrupted by Ms. Kathy, who wanted a break, Laney did her best to teach Patrick her gift.

"Okay, I've been thinking about the best way for me to teach you, because it is hard to explain. I'll do my best" Laney said nervously.

"Okay so, first, it's easier if you can see the person's eyes and their body, that way you can see and feel your way over. You see the person and then you kind of move your focus, like, don't look at them, just float your way over, and then make contact" She said, with more assurance. She looked up to the park. "So pick someone out and try, kids are easier, but adults work too" Laney paused and lightly gripped Patrick's shoulder. "Just make sure you don't take the next step though, it can get scary" She said.

"The next step?" Patrick asked skeptically.

"Yeah, the next step, you'll feel what I'm talking about. It's the feeling of knowing you could go further, knowing you have the power to. I've done it before. Please don't, okay?" Laney asked as terror rose into her eyes.

"What happened? Patrick asked, unable to help himself from the mystery.

"I didn't feel good after. I felt really bad…I felt like I lost something close to me, but I couldn't tell what. Like I left something important somewhere but I couldn't remember what, or where? Like—"

"Like a piece was gone?" Patrick asked, slightly understanding her meaning.

"Yeah…it went away after a few days, the feeling. Then you feel normal again" Laney said, staring at the ground.

Patrick saw her colors floating over her head. *Not good.* He thought. *This feeling shook her up it seemed. I shouldn't press anymore.*

"Laney? You okay?" He asked.

Laney was still staring at the ground, but answered his question "Yeah, I'm okay"

Patrick nodded and gave Laney a concerned look. "Good, okay, well who should I try it out on?" he asked Laney, as they both looked out into the field.

That question perked Laney right up, she sat up straight, looking out over the field scanning the other kids. "Ummmmm," she said as she studied the kids. "How abooouuutt, Eliza! She'll be easy."

"Yeah, she is the catcher," Patrick pointed out.

"She just doesn't want to play, she's boring, that's why I picked her," Laney said.

Patrick smirked and looked over at Eliza. He studied her intensely. Eliza was standing in front of the large cedar tree that was blocking the sun. He could visualize what Eliza was seeing in front of her. He gazed over to her, trying not to focus too hard. He breathed in and out trying to close the distance between him and Eliza without actually moving. He shut his eyes and imagined. *This is hard,* he thought, as he went even farther. He was about to give up and ask Laney for advice before a voice was heard.

"You're on the right track. Just *lose* yourself" Halo mentioned.

Patrick refocused into his mind, He pictured Eliza watching the kids, looking at them swinging and kicking the ball. Watching them swing and miss, kick the ball, and run. He opened his eyes and just as Laney said earlier, he felt himself floating to Eliza. He could feel his own body still, but his eyes, or his soul, or some part of him was floating over to Eliza. The next thing Patrick saw was one of the kids up close to him beginning to run. As the kid ran, his sight moved toward the dirt by his feet, then a quick swivel toward the road looking across the way at the tennis courts. Two people were playing Tennis, a boy and his father. The view swung back over and looked at Anna who seemed to be checking her phone. Patrick was now viewing what Eliza was, like it was his own vision. He was not in control, which was weird, but he could see everything Eliza was seeing. Patrick watched as the view changed again to Ms. Kathy who was pitching now. Patrick suddenly felt nervous and had enough, surely some practice and repetition would get him over that. *Laney never mentioned how to get back,* the thought snapped at Patrick, but with Halo's help again, Patrick figured it out and snapped back to his form. He looked over at Laney with his mouth wide open in shock and wonder.

"Wow, that was insane!" he said, almost yelling.

"Yeah, it's cool huh?"

"Yeah it really was" Patrick sighed, "It was really weird though. I didn't feel in control at all, I didn't like that"

"But, you could have been," Laney said.

Patrick cocked his head slightly. "What?"

"The feeling, you know, taking the step, you were not in control, but you could have been?

"The step you were talking about? Is that it? Gaining some control while inside? Patrick asked, instantly remembering he shouldn't have asked. He sighed.

Laney didn't answer, but shook her head and looked away from Patrick.

"Now that you mention it, there was something," Patrick said.

"Like what?" Laney asked, still looking away.

"I don't know, there was this moment, or feeling that I could have grabbed onto too. It passed by my view, and I had a lot of time to think about grabbing it, or going with it. But I never did. Was that the step?"

"I think so, mine was different, but it felt similar," Laney said.

"So you must have grabbed it then, when it went by," Patrick said as Laney looked back down at the ground. "But, I'm glad you made it out okay" Patrick said to Laney, whose head rose slightly. "Laney, I have another question for you, and then I think we should go play some kickball."

Laney smiled and nodded her head. "Okay"

Patrick pauses for a moment to get his wording right. "Laney, you said your dad had a rope, but no suit, right? Not like mine?"

Laney shook her head. "No, no suit, but I know he had the rope for sure. He would show it to me sometimes, he could do all of these really cool tricks with it"

"Okay, interesting," Patrick acknowledged, slowly unraveling his mystery. "Did he tell you anything else about it? Like, did the rope...talk?" Patrick asked Laney, knowing the question was strange to hear.

"Did it talk? I don't think so...not that he ever told me" she replied, unfazed by Patrick's perceived strangeness.

"Huh, okay"

"Does yours talk to you?" Laney asked.

"It sounds crazy, doesn't it?" Patrick took a deep breath. "Yeah though, it talks...to me, all the time, well, not all the time. I call him Halo, he can be cryptic, and... abrupt"

"What does he talk about?" Laney asked, inching closer to Patrick.

"Me and the powers it gave me mostly, it said it's my guide and that it needs me to learn things, and to contain some bad energy out in the city, real spooky stuff" Patrick replied, looking out into the sky.

"Like monsters?" Laney asked.

"Yeah actually. They are ugly most of the time" Patrick said, chuckling, as Laney laughed along.

"Alright, let's go play." Patrick told her as they both stood up from the bleachers and descended the metal stairs.

"So you know how to do it now then?" Laney asked about her practice. "That was quick."

"Yeah I think I figured it out, Halo helped out a bit, and you were a great teacher," Patrick said as he put his hand up for a high five.

"We should think of a name for it"

Laney thought for a moment. "How about floating?"

"I like it," Patrick said as Laney slapped his hand.

The rest of the day was spent playing kickball and eating dinner back at the Building Blocks cafeteria. Patrick decided to stay for dinner with the kids and the staff. After he managed his goodbyes to Amanda and the rest of the staff and kids, it was Laney at the end who was waiting by the front door. Patrick saw her and smiled.

"Hey, teach," he greeted. "I'm off to go fight some monsters," he said, winking. He high-fived Laney. "I'll be back."

"Maybe, someday you could show me Halo? And what he can do," Laney asked as she watched Patrick open the front door then halted.

"We'll see," he said and smiled. "Good night Laney"

Patrick shut the door behind him and looked over the far away buildings in the distance and took a deep breath. Tired from being out all day, he felt it would be best to head home for the night. He wanted to go home, eat some snack food and watch Netflix. That sounded like a fine enough night to him. He reached his car on the other side of the street and grabbed the handle to open it. He threw his stuff in the passenger seat next to him, and sat down. He stared ahead and saw to the left the opening of the alley he had those weird, eerie feelings about the other day. When too much guilt eventually kicked in, Patrick started the car and drove off, only to park the car a few blocks down. He hopped out and locked the doors. The guilt of making the city safer got to him. *I should do something,* he concluded.

Patrick crossed the street and found an alley. He ducked behind the wall and transformed into his glowing white and yellow suit with Halo in hand. He jumped to the roof and stared back over to the mysterious alley, which seemed to be staring back. He leapt back to the ground and ran over to confront the alley once more. It was getting dark now, but he could still see through the alley to the other side. *Not so scary now*, he thought as he walked through. Suddenly, as Patrick reached the middle, he was confronted and startled by a voice.

"What are you looking for?" Halo asked.

"Nothing, more of a feeling," Patrick answered. *She's dead, remember?* Patrick shook his head.

"Feelings about the alley, when it seemed to grab you? In your mind?"

"Yeah, I guess...exactly" Patrick forgot just how connected Halo was within his mind for a moment. Thoughts, words, dreams, sight, all of it, Halo knew it all.

"That's troubling," Halo said in a soft voice, but without real concern.

"Yeah! I think so too!... What happened that night Halo? Patrick asked again, hoping for the truth, for an answer. He got none.

"C'mon Halo, please!... I saw some pretty horrible things, I felt some horrible things" Patrick waited again for an answer, before growing frustrated. "I don't want to see that thing again, monsters are fine...a giant spider, devil monster...is fine, just not whatever that thing was, I won't, not again"

Patrick crossed his soft, warm arms to comfort himself, waiting in silence for a few moments longer before deciding to give up. He transformed out of the suit and started to walk out of the alley to his car.

"He's not a monster, he's like you, Patrick" Halo echoed through Patrick's head.

Patrick didn't react to what Halo said physically. He was mad and frustrated with Halo and wanted space, but ironically enough, he couldn't. Patrick drove home and did what he originally wanted to, eat snacks and watch mind-numbing television. The more Patrick thought about Halo's words, the more he understood that what Halo said was the perfect thing. It was just what Patrick needed to hear, or wanted to hear. Patrick was still mad, but less afraid.

He...is like... me?

Chapter 24

The next morning Patrick opened his eyes, awakened by guilty thoughts. *She's dead, remember?* He shook his head. *You're alone, remember?*

"Okay, enough," Patrick said to the thoughts that greeted him most mornings. He shot out of the bed and began his morning preparations. The act of moving broke his mind free from the persistent negativity. He finished preparing and left for work. He hasn't been doing his morning walk-throughs since the last time with the alley. He hasn't felt good about doing it lately, his mind hasn't been in a good place.

Later in the day, Patrick finished his work with no outstanding events occurring. His boss stayed away and let him work, and Summer apparently took the day off. He worked hard and was afforded an early departure, he used that time to head to Building Blocks early. He assumed that today would be like the rest of them over there, this time of day, it was probably free time. No trips, or lessons, just the kids hanging out, and to his knowledge, he was right. When he arrived, it was a large group of the kids in the big living room, with video games and art supplies scattered everywhere. Some of the kids noticed Patrick walk in and take his shoes off.

"Hey Patrick!" Conner yelled from his spot on the couch. He was watching some of the other boys his age play Wii tennis on the TV. The others turn around and say hello right after. Patrick watched for a while before going off to see the others. He scoped out the library area where he found Anna, Eliza, and another girl named Sadie, hanging out in silence reading their magazines. Patrick walked in and wasn't greeted by any of the girls. He knew they saw him enter, but they never acknowledged him.

"Wow! That's super nice" Patrick exclaimed.

He saw Anna trying to hide a smile, which made the other girl, Sadie smile, and then Eliza.

"Hello," Patrick said.

The girls started laughing as Anna moved up to speak.

"Sorry, we saw you come in, we planned that"

"Yeah it was a great joke. Well done" Patrick said as he clapped lightly. He looked around the room and back to the girl's magazines. "So what are you girls up too?"

"Nothing at all, this place is so boring," Anna said as Eliza shook her head in agreement.

"We talked about this. This place is great" Patrick raised his arms and looked to the ceiling. "And! Amanda told me you guys are going to a water park tomorrow! That's gotta be cool, right?"

"Yeah it is kind of cool, but there's nothing the rest of the time" Sadie said, winning back the moment.

"And Eliza isn't even going tomorrow," Anna mentioned.

Patrick looked over to Eliza. "Oh, Really?"

Eliza nodded her head and looked down and away. Patrick felt Eliza emitting the emotions of shame and embarrassment, Patrick knew he shouldn't press any farther, maybe even back her up.

"That's alright, I'm coming over tomorrow to fix some things, maybe you could help me?" Patrick asked as he smiled at Eliza. Her eyes perked up and she smiled shyly in agreement. Patrick saw Laney walk into the room from the other door.

"Hey Laney!" Patrick greeted.

"Hey!" she said back, but turned her eyes towards the other girls.

Patrick looked to her right and saw a whiteboard and some markers. He lit up as he got an idea.

"Let's play Pictionary!" he yelled to the room.

"Pictionary?" Anna asked.

"Yes!" Patrick said as he walked over to the board. "Pictionary is awesome, I always have fun. You will too"

"Okay!" Laney agreed as she ran over to help set it up. The girls had not responded yet, which Patrick knew wasn't a good thing.

"Cmon, it'll be fun," Patrick mentioned again.

"Okay fine, I'll play," Anna said.

"Yeah me too" went Eliza, and then Sadie.

Anna looked over to Patrick and Laney. "Okay you guys set it up, we'll go get some snacks." The girls stood up and left out the door towards the kitchen.

Patrick placed the board in the middle of the couches as Laney put the markers on the table. They both look around the room.

"Not much to set up really," Patrick said as he sat on the couch. Laney sat down on the other end of the couch and eyed Patrick. "Hey," she said, which caught Patrick's attention. "I was wondering if you could show me Halo, and what you can do with it? Just like my dad."

This caught Patrick off guard a bit. She has asked him this before, but not as directl. He pondered the question for a second before he answered. "Laney I—" He began talking but saw in her eyes she wanted to see it again, the rope, as a reminder of her absent father. He couldn't say no to that.

"I'll skip the trip tomorrow and you can show me. It'll work, Ms. Kathy will fall asleep" Laney sayai before Patrick could finish the rest of his words. He looked at her and smiled. He still couldn't say no.

"Okay," he said as Laney squeaked in excitement. "After I do some chores here thought"

"Okay," she yelped and nodded in agreement.

"But not for long okay?" He looked at Laney sternly. "This isn't a secret I want to tell anyone"

"Right" she agreed again.

"Okay, then we can," Patrick said to Laney before turning back to the board. "But first I'm going to crush you in Pictionary"

"I don't even know how to play," Laney revealed to Patrick.

"What! It's easy, just guess what the picture is, you can be on my team" He said back. "I may even *float* during this game, I need a little more practice."

Laney smiled and agreed just as the girls came back with popcorn, some sodas.

"Okay you guys, versus us," Patrick said to the girls while pointing to himself and Laney.

"Easy," Anna mentioned as they all sat down. Patrick got his phone out and opened a Pictionary generator app.

"Okay, you guys know the rules?" Patrick asked the girls. They all nod. "Okay you guys first then"

They spent the next fifteen minutes playing before Patrick decided to *float*. It was Anna's turn next and he decided he was going to try it again. He sat and watched Anna, who was walking over to the board. He lost his focus and could feel himself floating over to Anna. It worked again quickly, he was now seeing the world from Anna's eyes, feeling his presence from over on the couch. He watched as she picked up the phone, looked at the random picture generator button, and

142

clicked it, causing a word to pop up, its *cheese-grater.* Patrick watched as the phone dropped down to her side. He snapped back to himself and watched as Anna drew a very bad version of a cheese-grater, the girls ran out of time before they could guess it and Patrick let them know.

"Time!" he yelled loudly. "We can steal Laney!"

"There's no way you get that!" Sadie yelled back.

"Yeah, it was impossible to draw" Anna agreed.

Patrick smiled and looked over to Laney. "It's a cheese-grater," he said confidently, looking at Laney.

"What, no way!" Anna screamed.

"Was that right?" Eliza asked.

"Yeah. How could you have gotten that? Anna asked Patrick, who was still smiling.

"I'm really good at Pictionary, I told you"

"That's so bogus, no you aren't," Anna said.

"It's one point, you're fine," Patrick told her as he looked over to Laney and winked.

They finished the game and played more for a while as Patrick checked on some of the other kids before asking Amanda about anything she needed. She went over what needed to be done tomorrow in her absence and Patrick agreed. He said goodbye to the kids and told them to have fun tomorrow on the trip. He left Building Blocks with quite a bit of sunlight left. He scurried home, changed his clothes, and ate before hopping up to the roof. He summoned Halo and transformed into his suit. He wouldn't be bringing up any touchy subjects with Halo tonight. He was just excited for the upcoming night.

"Shall we get started?" Patrick asked.

"We shall" Halo responded.

Patrick looked around and saw a few dark clouds all over the city in little spots. In the daytime, he could see them very clearly. Then something occurred to him.

"Halo, can you show me all of the clouds? You said you were holding back before. Show me them all" Patrick said confidently.

"Are you sure? It's a lot of emotions to experience" Halo said in response.

"Yes, do it. I'm sure" Patrick said, and with that Halo seemingly flipped a switch from day to night. Patrick couldn't believe his eyes as he saw the dark clouds stretching all over the city, further than he could even see. It's like there was a factory chimney, letting all of the pollutants into the air. The sight was a lot to take in but the feeling that came after was worse. He could feel the emotions in the atmosphere billowing into him, it was too much. It was the same feeling he had from that night at Canine's, with Sal and the mummy creature. After a few more seconds Patrick pleaded to Halo.

"Okay, enough," he said. "You were right, it's too much." With that Halo flipped the switch back to the first set of clouds. "I'll stick with these for now" Patrick looked back up to the sky.

"Would you like to learn to teleport?" Halo asked out of the blue.

"You can teleport? Or I can teleport?" Patrick questioned.

"Yes, it's rather easy"

"Well then yeah, definitely," Patrick answered.

"First, pick a spot you wish to go to," Halo guided. Patrick looked around the neighboring buildings and chose one in the distance with a large billboard of a dog and its owner, sitting atop.

"Next, just as you mold the rope to transform. Mold it into a door or a big enough portion" Halo said. Patrick did just that, taking his time to make a big enough door to fit through comfortably. "Now walk through it"

"Just walk through?" Patrick asked for confirmation.

"Yes, imagine your destination and we'll take care of the rest," Halo said.

"Naturally," Patrick said, taking a jab at Halo.

He walked up to his created door and looked over to the billboard for clarity, then walked through. As he did, the sight of the billboard unfolded before him. It was larger than he imagined from far away, as he looked up at the billboard. He looked back over to where he started and molded Halo again. He made this version smaller but still was able to fit himself through. He leapt and dove headfirst through the portal, falling back onto his building's roof.

"What, this is awesome! Now I don't have to run everywhere" Patrick was excited but was quickly hit with some concerns. "So should I be concerned with this, what are my limitations?"

"None, you just need to know where you're going"

"So I could go to Egypt?" Patrick asked.

"Yes, if you can imagine it in your mind," Halo said.

"Cool, well let's use this," Patrick said before heading off into the city, where he had jobs to do.

Patrick did just what he said, and used his new teleporting ability to bounce around the city, going from one bad crime to the next. Over an hour he stopped a few muggings and a robbery. Wherever there were clouds of evil, he would rush over and erase it. Around nine o'clock, after hours of being a superhero, Patrick decided he should retire to his home. *One more*, his mind called out to him as he looked around the city for a cloud to erase. He caught sight of one that seemed to be moving over by the bank, he teleported over to a roof and peeked over the edge. He arrived in time to catch sight of a police officer chasing a man running away with what looked like a handbag. *Must have robbed someone,* Patrick thought. He watched as the man slowly lost ground on the officer on the long street. Patrick noticed the officer was a woman. The female officer looked to have it covered and was gaining on the man but Patrick decided to help out anyway. From atop the roof across the street, Patrick whipped Halo toward the man. The rope extended down the building and across the street, and snapped the man in the ankle, causing him to trip over. The bag flew out of his hands as he reached for his injured knee. The officer caught up to the man and slammed her knee into his back, causing him to scream out. The female officer turned and watched as Halo was recalled back to Patrick on top of the building. Patrick watched the officer turn back and start cuffing the guy as Halo reached his hand. He saluted the officer as she yanked the man to his feet. He turned around out of sight and walked back toward the other end of the roof. *That was a tough officer,* he thought as he started to mold a door. Before he did, he caught a glimpse of a familiar roof over the edge. He walked to the edge to get a better look. *It's Canine's,* Patrick knew as he stared over at the building, feeling fear and uncertainty. The restaurant sign was on and the building seemed to be in good shape. Patrick thought with Sal dying the place would be vacated. No one was going in or out. He jumped down to the street and ran over to the back door. He opened the alleyway door and quietly walked in, closing the door behind him. He tiptoed through the dark kitchen into the ballroom area, seeing no one. The place was empty and all of the lights were off, but weirdly, the place was clean. Patrick walked over to the table Sal sat at and looked around the rest of the ballroom.

"We hoped you'd be back," A voice from behind Patrick said aloud. Patrick, on edge, turned quickly, looking for the source of the voice through the dark shadows. He didn't see anything but recognized the voice must have been from the kitchen. He watched intently as the door slowly opened, giving him flashes of the last time he was here.

"You just have to know," the voice said again but deeper than before. The figure walked through the doors, holding its palms out, grinning like a demon.

"Sal? Y—" Patrick managed before being interrupted.

"Maybe...maybe I did. It definitely changed me" Sal said, chuckling. "Right?" he asked, looking over at the wall. To Patrick, it didn't feel like Sal was talking to him just then.

"Sal, what happened?" Patrick asked, which elicited a startling response from Sal.

Sal suddenly snapped to attention, almost re-awakening from Patrick's voice. Their eyes met with an intensity that felt threatening on its own. Patrick looked into Sal's eyes and felt something was missing from them.

"Yeah yeah yeah yeah yeah yeah yeah yeah, that happened," Sal said, clenching his fists and raising them to his face. He grinned once more. "It sucked everything out of me, and replaced it!" he said as he pounded his chest.

"With what?" Patrick asked.

Sal shook his head and muttered something Patrick couldn't understand. Sal turned away from Patrick and stepped forward. "My past life feels... so far away now," he mentioned, reaching out to nothing. "But I don't care about any of that anymore. Being feared, being respected, all of it. Now there's just...the voice"

"What? What voice?" Patrick asked, stepping toward Sal lightly.

Sal suddenly began pacing back and forth and started wagging his finger at Patrick. "You know...that thing had you too, just like me" Sal laughed hysterically. "Yeah yeah yeah yeah, it touched you" Sal stopped to look at Patrick and leaned in. "So what do ya think? He asked, giving a wink.

Patrick tried ignoring Sal's craziness, but he was slightly off. His heart beat faster, as he thought of Sal's words. "Sal, what voice?"

Sal wagged his finger at Patrick again. "They knew you'd be pushy...the voices did, they know you're not getting answers but me...yeah yeah yeah, they love talking to me, can't stop actually" Sal rambled on. "But the thing is, I agree…. with all their saying, it makes sense, they have... vision, direction," he said as his eyes widened and placed a finger to his lip. He stared off.

"You have a guide, like me? Is that what you're saying?" Patrick waited for an answer but Sal seemed too focused with something in his head. *Maybe the voices?* Patrick concerned himself.

"Did that creature give you the voice?" Patrick asked Sal, trying to sound sympathetic.

"Clearly, your idiot!" Sal yelled, looking away still. His eyes met Patrick's again as he crouched down and hugged himself. "They said you really didn't know anything, frustrating, isn't it?" Sal said and smiled. "They said you would understand that"

Patrick turned away and walked from Sal. *Halo doesn't tell me anything! And now Sal is mocking me about it?* He thought and turned back around, now facing Sal who was still crouched down.

"So you, the voices… and that creature are all on the same side?" Patrick asked Sal.

Sal laughed and shook his head. Patrick expected Sal to yell again but was surprisingly even. "No actually, that *creature*, that *thing...* is on its own. I have no idea what it wants. Think of it as a loose cannon, it has a cool name though" Sal said and stood up. "You're not ready for this," He said smiling. He slowly walked to the kitchen doors, turning back before he exited. "Risvegliare la vita," Sal said, then disappeared into the dark kitchen, as the doors swung closed behind him.

Patrick didn't watch, he stayed standing in the ballroom staring into space, racking his brain for answers before he gave up. He left the restaurant and got a few blocks away before teleporting home, falling back into his apartment's living room. Halo didn't say anything, just faded away back into Patrick's hand at some point in the night.

Patrick laid down on his couch and lost himself in thought. *This is all so overwhelming.* He took a deep breath, wrapped his hands together, set his head down, and began to tear up.

She's dead, remember?

Chapter 25

On Saturday morning, Patrick slept in as long as he could before the inevitable morning depression reared its relentless head. They bullied their way into his thoughts and refused to let Patrick's mind free from ache. He tumbled through his bed but didn't get out. He sat on the edge, looking through his window and the bright blue sky. He had no plans for the day besides going to Building Blocks, so the beautiful day only helped his mood slightly. He reached for his phone and checked for anything, messages, calls, downloads, updates, the works. His Aunt texted him but other than that, nothing new. He hopped up, grabbed a coffee cup, and filled it from his pre-started coffee pot. He turned to the window and sat down at the table. Alone with his thoughts, he replayed the events of his recent past. There was a lot to unpack, he was stressed about it, but also felt free. The stress feeling was drowned out by another feeling, a feeling of indifference. Bad things were going to happen to him, there was nothing he could do, he was used to being helpless. He looked out the window and watched the people around him battle through life the same way he did. He encouraged and wished for the well of others, and was always looking to save someone in need, but it was different when it came to his own life, his own being. He imagined himself sinking to the bottom of the ocean, watching himself sink lower and lower, feeling nothing. *How do you save yourself?* He questioned.

Patrick brooded for a while longer before having to get active. *Exercise the body and the mind will follow,* he thought.

He put in a home workout in his living room for an hour, after having to tidy the place up. He showered, changed, and headed over to Building Blocks in the late afternoon. He knew most of the kids would be gone, with the water park field trip happening, so he could really focus on the work. *And Laney,* his mind reminded him. He drove over, parked his car and strolled inside through the front door. He walked inside through the living room and the kitchen area, seeing no one in sight. He went to the backyard and found Ms. Kathy asleep on one of the lawn chairs. Patrick chose not to wake her, but he did adjust the umbrella above her to cover her from the sun that's beating down on her. He went back inside to the maintenance closet, looking for the tools he needed. Patrick came over to Building Blocks to fix some of their creaky and off-kilter doors, a window or two, and then paint the smaller shed for the garden tools. He was hoping for some help but no one seemed to be around. He decided to get to work anyway, knowing one of the three who stayed behind would eventually come down and he was right. To Patrick's surprise, Conner was the first one who came down when Patrick started hammering on the door hinges. He accepted Patrick's request for assistance and gladly helped screw in some new hinges. Patrick never really grew up using tools much but spending time at Building Blocks has helped him learn some skills, since there was a lot needed to be done.

Laney came by next and wanted to help. She greeted Patrick with a large bright grin, clearly trying to remind Patrick about their deal from yesterday. Patrick remembered their pact and smiled back.

"Hey Laney"

"Hey" Laney said as she walked over to Patrick and hit him on the arm. "You remember what we're doing today?"

"We're doing something? I don't… remember" Patrick said and wrinkled his face pretending to search his mind for answers.

Laney hit Patrick's arm again and put on a mean face. "Yes, you promised. I know you remember!" She said, her voice growing louder.

"Okay okay, jeez I remember, don't yell," Patrick said.

Laney looked away from Patrick, still mad. "Well don't be mean then."

Patrick waited for a moment to see if Laney was joking too. She didn't seem to be so Patrick spoke up.

"I promised, so we can, but remember this is important, okay?" Laney nodded slowly and turned around. "We need to paint a little and then fix windows, then we can go"

"Okay, but how do we get to the woods and then back in twenty minutes?" Laney asked smartly.

Patrick nodded and smiled, having realized how sharp Laney was. "I have that covered, let's get started on the paint," he said.

Conner, Laney, and Patrick all got started on the projects. Patrick had Conner and Laney start painting the doors, while he fixed the windows. They were both capable kids and really good helpers.

Patrick felt confident enough to leave them to paint, knowing well they may fight and argue eventually. From the second floor, Patrick fixed the window looking down over the backyard. Patrick could see that Eliza was down there now too, helping the other two. Patrick used a block and hammer to open the stuck window and applied some wax and lubricant to the window. He read the wax thing works so he tried it out. He gave the window a few test runs and after a few minutes the window worked like new.

"Boom" Patrick said aloud before heading down to the yard.

"Hey Eliza, thanks for helping," Patrick said upon seeing her.

"You're welcome," Eliza said lightly. "Ms. Kathy told me to come get you guys for lunch too"

"Oh okay," Patrick said. "You guys about done?" Conner and Laney looked up from their brushes.

"Yeah almost," Laney said, while Conner stayed focused on the brush. Patrick wondered how much they fought over the course of the job. They also have a history of arguments, being the same age. Patrick knew they were close friends, but at that age, they were going to argue. Patrick inspected their work and congratulated them on a job well done. He stayed to eat with the kids and Ms. Kathy after their duties were fulfilled. They all sat and talked about the day, enjoying the time at the table before Patrick mentioned having to leave soon. Upon his request to leave, Ms. Kathy, the kids, and Patrick all cleaned the kitchen together before Ms. Kathy eventually lost herself in another nap. Eliza and Conner both went upstairs while Laney hung back in anticipation. She tugged on Patrick's arm as he washed his hands, letting him know now would be a perfect time for their deal.

"The field trip group will be back later; we should go now while Ms. Kathy is sleeping"

Patrick dried his hands and turned to Laney. "Okay sure. Head out to the garage"

Laney did what she was instructed to do and went through the backyard and into the detached garage. She shut the door behind her and walked to the center of the pavement. She looked around and waited for Patrick at the door. She walked over and peeked out the window back towards the house, getting antsy. Laney started to wonder if she had gotten played. *Was Patrick coming out here? Did he lie?* She wondered as she watched the house intensely. From behind her, she heard a faint humming noise. Laney looked down and started falling uncontrollably through the floor. She closed her eyes tightly. Before she hit the ground, something caught her, then set her down on the ground. She opened her eyes seeing leaves and grass, and the bright canopy of tree tops above She looked around completely confused, turning in a three-sixty circle. She does a double-take and finally lands on the figure that caught her mid-air. First, she saw the dark blue eyes of the figure, then the white hood and white mask.

"Wow," Laney said, still a bit shook, but slowly starting to realize where she was and who she was with.

"Hey Laney," the white hooded figure said back.

"Patrick? … that's you?" Laney asked, walking closer to him.

"Yeah it's me, cool right?"

"So cool," Laney said while touching Patrick's suit.

"So your dad didn't have a suit like this?" He asked.

Laney looked up at Patrick's dark eyes. "No... he didn't, just the rope" Laney looked down, seeing the rope tied around Patrick's waist. She reached for it with child-like wonderment.

"They say I look like an Angel but—" Laney grabbed the rope, cutting Patrick off mid-sentence. She screamed in shock as she quickly let go.

"Whoa, you okay?" Patrick asked.

"Yeah, it burned me. Why is it so hot?" she asked Patrick before looking down at her hand.

"Oh sorry, I don't know, it's like that sometimes. Are you okay?"

Laney saw her hand wasn't burnt but was now on edge from the sudden sensation. "Yeah I'm okay" she replied.

"Good, I wouldn't touch it again then okay?"

"I won't" she agreed and nodded, looking frightened.

"Well alright, what do you want to see first? Besides the teleporting"

Laney's eyes got bright as she realized what he said. "You can teleport! That's how you got me here?" she asked as the realization slowly came across her face.

Patrick nodded and loosened Halo around his waist. "What did your dad show you already?"

"Umm…. he showed how the rope can stretch really far" Laney answered.

"Oh like this?" Patrick said and whipped Halo over at a tree, extending it in an instant before slashing into it.

"Whoa" Laney said as the loud crack echoed in the forest.

"What else?" Patrick asked.

Laney shrugged "That was it really…. and he turned it into a silly putty too."

"Oh, just like molding it," Patrick said before molding Halo into a large shield and then down into a slim spear, and then back into a rope.

"Is it always a rope though?" Laney asked.

"It usually starts as a rope, yeah, that must be the default setting" Patrick showed off again and whipped the rope at another nearby tree. Laney stared in amazement as the rope flew back toPatrick's hand.

"I really like your suit too! Yellow is my favorite color"

Patrick looked down to his feet and checked out his body. "I wish I could change my eyes though…. seeing myself in mirrors is freaky"

"They are a little scary… they should be yellow or bright blue…."

"Yeah, maybe" Patrick looked down at the rope in his hand. "Halo, can the eyes change colors?"

"Oh, that's the voice in your head? What did he say? Has he talked yet?" Laney bombarded Patrick with questions, but Halo didn't answer.

"Halo? What am I thinking?" Patrick asked, and waited for a response. Patrick and Laney shared a look.

Patrick shook his head. "Nothing," he said.

"Awe" Laney moaned.

"He does this a lot; I don't get much from him these days. He told jokes at the beginning, but not anymore" Patrick shook his head and looked back to Laney.

Laney started to jump a little, clearly excited about something. "Okay okay I have an idea"

"Oh boy this must be good" Patrick looked at Laney and started to bob up and down with her.

"Okay, can you fly?" Laney asked.

Patrick's shoulders slump down and his hands fall to his knees. He looked up to Laney.

"No, I can't, c'mon… but I can teleport, that's pretty special"

"Yeah it is... how about a bow and arrow?" Laney asked as her eyes got bright. She urged Patrick to try. "That would be pretty cool, right?"

Patrick nodded his head and smiled at Laney. "I can try"

Patrick broke two pieces off from the rope. He molded one into a long curved bow, the other into a connecting string. He molded the arrow and showed it to Laney. Laney watched in amazement the whole time, seeing the rope mold and change on its own, within Patrick's grasp. She watched Patrick's hands as they smoothed out the rope quickly, twisting and turning it into the shape he needed.

"The rope is moving on its own" Laney said in amazement, pointing to the longbow in Patrick's hand.

Patrick looked down at his hand and thought about what Laney was saying. It finally clicked in his mind. "Oh yeah, I think since the rope and the voice are connected to my mind, just thinking about things I want kind of … gets me through things"

Laney stared at the glowing rope and seemed to be in a trance as she watched it glow. The emotions slowly started to get to her as the tears built. She was trying her best not to let it start and to let Patrick see. Patrick didn't notice, he was wrapped up in an idea that Laney just incepted. Laney looked longingly at the rope, finally coming out of it when Patrick began talking.

"I may be able to fly," he said with a finger pointing up. "You're a genius Laney"

Laney forced a smile and wondered what Patrick was talking about.

Patrick paced back and forth for a moment before stopping back at Laney. "Okay, what if I mold Halo around my feet and then just...think...really hard...about flying" Patrick finished the sentence with each word sounding more ridiculous than the last. His hand slapped the back of his head. "Okay, that sounded stupid but it makes sense"

"Are you going to try now? Laney asked promptly.

"Yeah, why not? I could use the practice" Patrick relented.

Laney walked over to Patrick and pointed at him "Well first, you haven't even shot the arrow yet" Patrick looked down at the bow and arrow resting in his hands in front of Laney and then back to her as she continued.

"Second, it's already been like half an hour, you said only twenty minutes"

Patrick waved his head back and forth in guilt. "Yeah I did…. crap," he said as he glanced at Laney. "After I try flying?"

Laney smirked, happily accepted and seemed to be more elated now than at the beginning.

"First, though," Patrick said as he knocked his molded arrow. He pulled the arrow back with ease and held it in place.

"You ready?" Patrick asked Laney before picking a good target to shoot at, then finally landed on a large tree flat on its side on the ground. Patrick took a deep breath and released his grip, letting go of the glowing arrow as it pierced through the air silently before it exploded into the tree with a flash. The tree cracked and flew backward as Patrick ran over to see the damage with Laney. They both gaze down where the arrow made contact.

"Wow, that may come in handy" Patrick said.

"Time to fly!" Laney exclaimed, seeming to be over the arrow gig already.

"You're not impressed with that? That could take down an airplane" Patrick told her.

"Yeah yeah, it's cool but I want to see you fly! It's going to be awesome!" Laney shouted and pumped her fist in the air.

"Yes, it will," Patrick said as he looked up and walked over to an open area.

With Laney watching close by safely, Patrick molded Halo by breaking it into three pieces. With one piece left in his hand, he tossed the other two onto the ground. He stepped on one piece, but nothing happened. Laney watched on intensely as Patrick bent down and molded the piece around his foot. He did the same with the other foot and stood up straight to test out his new kicks. He looked down to his feet in admiration. "Dang, these things look sick, better than Jordan's if you ask me"

"How do they feel?" Laney asked.

"Warm.... they feel warm and tingly. Like I should be able to fly"

"Try then"

How do I just try to fly Laney? It doesn't make sense." Patrick said sarcastically back to Laney.

"Idunnaknow" she mumbled and shrugged.

"Yeah, me neither" Patrick agreed.

"Try just thinking really hard about it and then take a step up," Laney instructed.

"Like a fake staircase?"

"Yeah, try closing your eyes too" Laney mentioned.

"Sure," Patrick agreed as he closed his eyes. He knew Laney had been right about his powers before, so she might be again. He imagined his body floating up, reaching the treetops, climbing over into the clouds. He focused on his balance and he felt his entire body, he shifted focus to his warm feet and slowly started raising his foot until his knee was above his waist, ready to take a step. "Here I go," he said, as he slowly lowered his foot back to the ground, expecting to finally step onto something solid, the anticipation stressed him out. He lowered his foot until it finally reached solid footing but he knew it wasn't the ground, his knee was still raised. He put more pressure down to test the strength and safety of this imaginary step.

"Oh my god, it's working, this is so weird!" Patrick exclaimed, putting more strength into his leg, he lifted himself higher, onto one leg. "Ha-ha!.....how does it look?" he asked.

"It looks crazy!" Laney shouted from right beside Patrick.

"I'm going up another one"

"Okay keep your eyes closed!" Laney shouted out.

"Let's go," Patrick said, syncing himself up, he lifted his other foot in the air and slowly brought it down for the step. His foot never made contact with anything as it came back to his body. "It didn't work that time," Patrick said to Laney, but she didn't reply. "Okay, I'm going to open my eyes to try it out," Patrick said before opening his eyes. He looked down at his floating foot slowly, hoping to not scare himself down. He looked carefully down to see he was standing atop a large orange bucket. "What the f—" Patrick said but stopped himself and looked down to Laney who was rolling on the ground, beginning to laugh. As she did, Patrick hopped off the bucket and walked to Laney. "Okay, that's hilarious.... where did you get a bucket?

Laney did not respond, she couldn't through her pure enjoyment and laughter. After a minute she finally came back down. "The bucket was lying over there, it worked out perfectly," Laney said through heavy breathing before starting to laugh again. Her laughter was infectious, even Patrick started to laugh with her that time. Seeing her smile and hearing her laugh brought joy to Patrick, he was enjoying his new friendship with her. He decided to razz her back. "If I ever learn how to fly, I won't be telling you now, that's for sure"

"Oh please c'mon....it was a joke" she said through a smile that wanted to explode.

Patrick smiled and looked at Laney, watching as the curls at the end of her bangs bob up and down as she moved. He looked to the forest, then back to her. "Jokes are only for glowing yellow ropes, Laney. Isn't that right, Halo?" Patrick asked, then looked up at his eyebrows hoping for a response from inside his head. No voice right away.

"Ah, nothing, he must be sleepi—" Patrick suddenly got cut off by the voice in his head.

Lookout.

Patrick tightened up as he caught a glimpse of something above him coming down quickly. Without thinking, Patrick slung Halo over to Laney. The rope molded mid-air into a large egg-like shield that encased around Laney. Patrick saw a glimpse of the shield over Laney before being impaled in the shoulder with a few long claws. Luckily he was able to catch the end of the creature's arm before it went through his entire shoulder. The weight of the creature's attack was too much to bear, however, as it sent Patrick flat into the ground. Patrick screamed out in fright but made out the face of his attacker, seeing it to be the same large bat-like creature that he fought in the woods a few days ago. The creature's eyes darted at Patrick as it lifted back its long slender claws for another stab at Patrick. The creature moved back slow enough for Patrick to react as he molded a shield from Halo quickly and blocked the creature's trajectory. The creature yanked its claw from Patrick's shoulder and struck down hard again. Blow after blow, Patrick's shield absorbed the frantic slashes. When able, Patrick kicked off the creature's knee and rolled backward. But the danger was quick. Before Patrick could steady himself, he was blind-sided again by a second bat creature coming from behind his shoulder. Patrick caught a late glimpse of the incoming attack and deflected the attack sideways, the monster swung with its other claw and caught Patrick in the chest. The blow sent him tumbling backward towards Laney, who was still inside the protective dome Halo made. He checked his chest for damage, it hurt, he could feel that, but it looked fine. Patrick stood up to face the two bat creatures.

"Two of you now huh?" Patrick said to the lanky, ugly creatures. He looked down to Laney, he couldn't see her through the yellow but he knew she was safe inside. He looked back up to the creatures, seeing one move slowly left, one to the right. *They're planning on flanking me*, Patrick could tell. Patrick broke the rope in two and with one in each hand charged straight at the one to his right, trying to single one out. He felt the pressure of the other creature following behind, tearing through the woodland ground catching up quickly. Patrick reached the other creature first and dodged a strike, leaping up behind its back. He grabbed the creature's head just before the second incoming creature slashed and missed. Its momentum took it out of the fight and Patrick took advantage and kicked the creature's head, sending it crashing through the ground. The other creature barreled back toward Patrick as he landed. It leapt off the ground and prepared to slice. Patrick started molding Halo but dodged the creature's strike first, the creature flew by and Patrick instinctively dodged another slice coming for his legs and followed up with a chop to the creature's arm. The creature's long muscular arm fell to the ground as it let out a quick roar, it swiped again and got deflected by Patrick's shield. Patrick goes to chop the other arm when the other creature flew up, teeth drawn, and lunged for Patrick's throat. Patrick snagged the creature in an instant and speared it up through its head, stopping it abruptly, without life. Patrick pulled the sword out of the creature's head and leapt backward, leaving it to fall to the ground. The other creature stayed still and watched Patrick stare right back. Their eyes stayed glued to each other as Patrick walked over to Laney. He knelt beside her with the yellow shield helping to lower himself.

"Hey, everything's okay," he said to Laney.

Laney looked up to Patrick and then over to the creatures. "What happened?"

"Those things attacked us," Patrick said and gestured over to the creature that was still staring menacingly at the pair.

"That one is looking at us, he's ugly" Laney said.

"Yeah it is. He stopped attacking for the moment, I have to finish him. I'm going to send you back, okay?"

Before Laney could answer, a familiar voice spoke out from the forest behind the creature. Patrick scanned the area intently. He had an idea of who it may be.

"It's great to see you again" the voice sounded from behind the trees. Patrick squinted through the area before the figure showed itself. "Funny, how we keep meeting like this. deve essere destino" Sal Porruci said with the last bit in Italian which confused Patrick.

"Sal," Patrick said aloud. "What are you doing here?"

Sal's head and eyes dart quickly at Patrick, his glare showing intense anger. "I'm here because of you...because of what you've done...for what you've been doing," He said.

"What have I been doing?" Patrick asked.

Sal didn't answer, he walked over to the creature and slapped its rough, leathery skin.

157

"Brutta cagna...sorry that means ugly bitch in Italian" Sal pulled his hand back and looked at Patrick. "They are team players though.... willing to die.

Patrick grasped the moment and realized what was going on. "You guys are with each other? You and them"

"Another side effect from our night at Nine's.... remember?" Sal asked and walked around the creature, looking down at the dead one on the ground beside them. He shook his head and looked back to the other one who rose to a towering stand. "Bring in the others," Sal told it.

The creature's head cocked up to the sky as its mouth opened slowly, stretching further and further. Patrick waited for it to screech out a terrible scream, but nothing came out. He looked down to Laney, who he figured would be terrified, but Patrick only saw a brave face. She was nervous, but looking, and feeling brave.

"Ready to go?" he said to her.

Sal overheard Patrick's words and yelled out. "She's not going anywhere! They need her!" Sal looked back at the creature aggressively. "Hurry up!" he screamed.

In the distance, Patrick heard trees being torn down and terrible high-pitched screeches approaching quickly. He looked back down to Laney. "Bye bye Laney," he said as he threw another protective shield over her. He looked back up at Sal and carefully listened to what was coming. He glared at Sal. "Sal, why do you want her?"

"Her name is Laney," Sal said back, correcting Patrick.

"Why do they need her?" Patrick asked, tightening his fists.

The sounds of snapping trees and screeching bats ceased as they doubtlessly approached closer. Sal filled the silence. "She's special, you know that. She could be the missing piece for this world...this puzzle to be finished......a new puzzle.... a different type of puzzle" Sal finished, looking off into the distance.

Patrick shook his head. "No way, never going to happen Sal" he looked over to the creature as the other ones got closer. "Tell that to them too!" he said, pointing to the incoming creatures.

In anger, Patrick molded a sword. He has had enough of Sal. *And of these creatures*, he thought as two creatures lunged for him. He jumped in the air avoiding the creatures but left Laney. Patrick landed away safely as one of the creatures began pounding on the shield furiously, trying to break in. Luckily the shield seemed to be holding

158

firm, but Patrick didn't know how long it would. Patrick molded a disc and flung it straight for the creature that was slamming on the shield. He watched the disc fly right by as the creature continued to hammer away. Patrick with a shield and sword in hand ran toward the two creatures. From far away, Patrick swiped quickly with the Halo sword, its length extended during the swing, and caught one of the creatures on the arm. The same creature leapt to Patrick and pounded down with its claws, Patrick avoided the claws but with a follow-up swing of its arm, the creature slammed into Patrick's head knocking him off balance. Before he could gather himself the other creature rushed through and tackled Patrick, sending him to the ground. The creature grabbed his chest and launched Patrick through the forest, colliding with a few tightly packed trees. Both creatures stomped over to the yellow shield and started hammering down on it. Smoke began rising from their claws with every slam as the shield started to crack. Patrick stood up peering over to the creatures and Sal who had joined their position.

"Let us take her.... you can become a piece in our new puzzle. Sal said, sounding almost reasonable and sympathetic.

Patrick shook his head. "No.... a world with monsters like you...and them in charge cannot be good" He said pointing at the bat creatures.

"One way or another kid. These things are ruthless, they get what they want," Sal replied, slapping the creature's back as it slammed into the dome, trying for Laney.

"Yeah we'll see," Patrick said proudly before leaping over towards Sal.

The creatures see him coming and stop smashing. Patrick cocked his arm back and unloaded a punch into Sal's block, sending him backward toward the creatures. One of them reached and clawed at Patrick, who dodged and unloaded another powerful right hook, that time connecting into the creature's face. The other creature swiped for Patrick as the other one hit the ground. Its swipe missed as Patrick leapt in the air, and landed behind it. Before the creature could turn to find him, Patrick molded a disc, raised his arm, pointing at the creature with the disc in his palm. He focused as much as he could into his palm, gathering energy from across his body, and once his palm felt ready to blow, Patrick punched his flat fist at the creature, causing a beaming explosion of yellow energy, blasting powerfully at the creature. It could only turn slightly and watch as the blast flooded over it, vaporizing its long body. There was no explosion, the creature simply vanished along with the blast of energy. The other creature abruptly leapt back toward Patrick and slashed out at his arms. Patrick moved in and caught the creature's arm below its claws before it could finish the swipe. From his hip, Patrick unloaded another blast from his palm, destroying the creature's lower half completely. Patrick threw the creature's top half away from him and watched it crash onto the ground. He watched to make sure it was dead, before turning to Sal.

"I like watching you fight, kid, it's really something," Sal said first to Patrick. "But I will say..." he said as two more creatures came galloping from behind, joining him where he stood. Sal raised his arms to stretch,"You look like you've worn yourself out"

Patrick looked to the creatures and then back to Sal. "Sal, I'll take any of the ugly things you got" He looked to Sal for some smart comment but Sal never spoke back. "But yeah, I am tired, you're right," Patrick said as he started to sit down on the ground. He crossed his legs and looked at Sal. "Can we just talk like old friends instead? You love to talk about old times. C'mon let's do it!" Patrick slapped the ground next to him signaling he wanted Sal to sit down with him. Sal looked at Patrick without expression for a few moments. "You okay?" Patrick asked, amused.

Sal stared at Patrick and then down to the ground. "You did this kid" Sal shook his head and looked at the creatures. "Do it," he said, as they both began hammering on the shield protecting Laney, to finish the job. It began to crack more and more as Patrick stood up, realizing it was going to break, and got into position. He watched as the creatures slammed on it, leaving fewer and fewer pieces, it finally shattered, causing a flash of yellow light. Patrick readied himself. The yellow shards fade away into the air revealing a space where Laney was, Sal walked over confused, staring at the space. He turned back to Patrick.

"Ohhhhh, that was awesome!... you're so confused! Boom!" Patrick said through light laughter.

"Where is she?" Sal asked angrily, almost barking.

"Somewhere safe," Patrick answered evenly, trying to enjoy the fun moment, which was ruined terribly.

"Back at the orphanage?" Sal asked coldly.

Does he know where she lives? Patrick thought.

Sal shook his head. "Of course I know where she lives…. I'm better at this, kid"

Patrick looked over to Sal and smiled through his mask. Sal couldn't see the smile through the mask but that didn't matter to him, he just realized something about Sal. "I don't think you can get her there? Can you? If you knew where she was, these creatures would be tearing through the place.

Sal smiled and pointed to Patrick. "That's exactly right! They can't roam the city... yet, but as you can see" Sal pointed over to the creatures. "They *are* getting closer"

"So why do you want Laney if they are getting closer?" Patrick asked.

"Ahhhh, stop asking questions now, we're done with that" Sal said and walked over to Patrick, who was standing still.

Sal seemed even-tempered, Patrick knew he wouldn't attack. He came to a stop a few feet in front of Patrick.

"Are you giving us the girl? Or are we waging war?" Sal asked confidently.

"War, one hundred percent," Patrick said, nodding his head.

Sal exhaled loudly and stared at Patrick. "War then," he said, before making another shocking revelation. "You know who else visits that orphanage quite a bit?" Sal said as Patrick raised his head to meet Sal His heart began beating quicker.

Sal looked down at Patrick as a slow grin unrolled over his face. His teeth shined in the new evening. His grin reached the end as his eyes twinkle.

"Nice to meet you Patrick," Sal said as the creatures picked him up and took off running into the woods, leaving Patrick out alone with only his thoughts.

Oh no, that's not good, Patrick worried. He sat alone for a few minutes before standing to leave. He looked around the woodland ground at the damage he caused in the fight and brought Halo to his face. "Is that why I'm here? For her?" He asked Halo.

Patrick, knowing he probably wouldn't get an answer, readied himself to teleport back and set his mind for Building Blocks. *I better check on Laney,* he thought as he walked through Halo appearing on a rooftop near Building Blocks. *What do I tell Laney? Do I tell her anything? If Sal knows who I am…what does that mean?* Patrick asked himself all of these questions, trying to find the answers within, but truly hoping Halo would for him. Before he could manage any rational answers, he spotted red and blue flashing lights coming from the street below. He sprinted over to the edge and looked down seeing Building Blocks covered in police cars and ambulances. Patrick watched as officers were running around, asking people questions, consoling someone Patrick couldn't make out. He anxiously scanned deeper at the person sitting on the back of the police car, covered in a stress blanket and finally noticed that it was Eliza. *What happened?* He wondered nervously.

Patrick scanned the area more and caught sight of an officer heading to their squad car, Patrick recognized the officer. *It's the woman cop from the other night,* he remembered. Patrick watched as the officer entered the driver's side door and shut it behind herself. Patrick scanned the area for safety, knowing he needed answers and molded a doorway and focused on the officer's car. He fell through and was then instantly sitting in the back of the patrol car, touching its smooth black leather seats. Behind the metal gate, Patrick watched the officer speak over her radio and listened to the other officers on the radio bark out police jargon. The officer didn't notice Patrick sitting in the back. Patrick waited for the right moment before speaking softly to the officer.

"Officer" he said lightly.

The officer whipped her head around shockingly quickly and looked directly at Patrick.

"What the hell! How did you get in here?"

Patrick didn't answer, he only wanted answers. He waited a moment for the officer to comprehend who he was. "It's okay," Patrick said, assuring her safety. "I just want to know what happened here?"

The officer looked at Patrick with worried eyes. "You tell me, you're the superhero"

"Officer please" Patrick pleaded.

She took a deep, unsure breath. "There's been an assault and an abduction," she said. "The eye witness said she heard a loud crash and then loud screams from the child who was taken. The story checks out, the woman who was there at the time was knocked unconscious, then whoever it was came and took the child"

"Who was the child?"

"I shouldn't disclose that, not even to…. whatever you are" She said, acknowledging how weird Patrick looked.

162

Patrick grew restless from the officer and decided to get out of there. Before he did, a weird feeling washed over him when he looked back at the officer. It was a feeling of familiarity and warmth that gave Patrick the tingles. His eyes began to blur as he shook his head. He looked at the officer who seemed to be affected also, she rubbed her eyes as it finally came to a stop. She stared at Patrick through her rearview mirror.

"What the hell did you do? The officer yelled.

Patrick looked up at the officer's emotions, studying her aura. *My question exactly,* he wondered. *I'll find you later,* he thought as he teleported into the seat and out of the car. He changed out of his suit and ran over to Building Blocks. He was stopped by police tape but ran around it over to where Eliza was sitting. She was gone now but Patrick spotted her and Laney standing beside one another by the ambulance. They saw him as he walked over.

"You guys okay?" he asked.

Eliza nodded her head and looked down.

"Eliza, what happened?" Patrick asked, looking at Eliza waiting for a response. She shook her head as Patrick looked over to Laney. Eliza looked back up to Patrick with tears in her eyes.

"They took Conner," she said. "He's gone"

Chapter 26

66"How could this have happened?" Amanda asked the room in a panic as Patrick watched the detectives and the uniformed officers shift their gazes from side to side. Amanda looked at each one, hoping they had the answers she wanted to hear. **A child has been taken from Building Blocks.**

Last night, after Patrick talked with Eliza and Laney, he waited around for Amanda and the others to return. He stayed with the kids out in the backyard, while Amanda talked with the police and detectives that showed up on the scene. Patrick and the kids all sat in silence; they couldn't bear to play any games or take their minds off Conner. Patrick knew he should try and distract the kids from this crisis, but was unable to act. *How confusing a time this must be for them?* he wondered. *This is a confusing time for me.*

This is all my fault, he thought as he stared off into the wooden fence. He couldn't bear to even look at the kids. *It could have been any one of them that was taken*. Patrick, starting to get fidgety and distant, was brought back by the sight of Amanda, walking with the police. She looked sad, and in that sadness, she was anxious and deflated. She walked over to Patrick, after breaking from the officers. She knelt beside some of the younger kids.

"Okay......I'm sure you guys are wondering why the police are here?" Amanda sighed and looked at each kid. "Something happened to Ms. Kathy here today at Building Blocks, I will tell you guys all about it tomorrow. It's important tonight that we all get some sleep. I promise I will tell you guys everything tomorrow, okay?"

Patrick watched as Amanda stood up and turned from the kids and wiped away a few tears. She stepped away quickly. After Amanda left, the kids slowly followed her inside and went upstairs. After the police and CSI's were done with the house and things were quiet, Patrick left through the back fence without saying goodbye. He went home to be alone.

Now, in the present moment in Amanda's office, Patrick watched and listened as the Detectives filled her in on the investigation. Patrick remembered meeting the detectives last night. Their names were Detective Brandt and Lindsay. Seniority went to Detective Brandt, who Patrick guessed, had about thirty years of experience on the other, but it was Detective Lindsay who spoke first.

"Well... Ma'am, we've put out search parameters around the city. We've notified multiple counties in the area of the Amber Alert for the missing child"

"Okay, but why take him? Why come here?" Amanda asked, growing upset.

Detective Brandt spoke up to help. "Orphanages can sometimes be seen as an easy place to commit such a crime. Very little security...and targets they believe to be..." Detective Brandt looked over to Detective Lindsay and back to Amanda. "Unwanted" he finished.

"Who's going to want to help a poor orphan?" Amanda said quietly but loud enough for everyone to hear. Patrick wanted to speak up and tell Amanda that all of this was his fault. He wanted to tell the detectives they should be looking for Sal and to go look into the woods, just after they put him in cuffs too. The detectives spoke back up before he could..

"We're doing everything we can to find him, as soon as we have any more details, we'll be in contact. For now, we will have a patrolman positioned here for a few days." Amanda nodded and thanked them. Both detectives look over simultaneously in inspection at Patrick, before turning for the door. They never really questioned him, Amanda must have told them something that eliminated him as a suspect. Patrick sheepishly looked over to Amanda who sat down and combed her hand through her hair.

"We have one field trip, and this happens," she said. Patrick did not respond, unable to at the moment. Amanda's tone seemed rhetorical. Plus, what was there to say? Amanda sat silently looking at her computer screen. Patrick watched her, the expression on her face was crushing him, he knew he messed up big.

"I'm sorry Amanda," he said as he stood up. "This shouldn't be happening" he looked at her, then walked out of the office. He went down the stairs for the front door, grabbed the handle in anger and flung it open. Before he could close it behind himself, Laney scurried through and met him outside on the porch.

"Patrick," she said, looking up to him. He returned the look, trying to smile. "Are you going to get him back?" She asked.

Patrick heard and felt the weight of her question. *That's a lot of pressure, but this is my fault.* He smiled. "Of course I am. I just need to be brave"

Laney nodded and put on a serious face. "Okay, I'll help find him too!"

Patrick admired her will, but got caught by surprise when he realized the truth. "No way, you have to stay here. No one else is getting taken"

"What c'mon" Laney pleaded with Patrick.

"Yes Laney, this is the safest place for you, and besides what would you tell Amanda?"

Laney didn't answer, she looked out across the road and sighed. Patrick dropped to a knee and looked out with Laney. "I have to find him alone okay? But I'm going to need your help later, you are still my coach right?"

Laney's concentration returned as she turned back to Patrick. "Yeah, I'm your coach," she said as she hugged Patrick around the neck, then took off back inside.

Patrick arrived back home and went into his apartment. He sat for a while and thought of what he should do next. He abruptly stood and transformed into his suit. Patrick teleported over to Canine's in broad daylight, hoping to find Conner or Sal. He knew the odds were almost zero of Conner being there, but it was a start. He arrived at Canines and entered the restaurant through the backdoor. The place was vacant again and eerily quiet, with no sign of Conner anywhere. Patrick sat down in a booth. "Where is he Halo? Can you help?"

"No," Halo replied quickly.

"No? That's all you're going to say?" Patrick said as he stood up.

"I can't find him. There's interference blocking me. I can't trace the boy. I can't do anything for you" Halo instructed.

Patrick sighed. That wasn't what he wanted to hear. "There out in the woods somewhere, I guarantee it" Halo didn't answer and Patrick got ready to leave. "We're going there next," Patrick said as he teleported through Halo. He stepped through the yellow portal onto the solid woodland ground. He looked out into the woods.

"Can you pick up a signal here?" Patrick asked.

"No" Halo retorted.

Patrick sighed. "Okay...damn," he said as he started walking further into the woods. The walking quickly turned into a run, as desperation kicked in. Patrick searched the woods for hours, leaping through trees and running along open fields looking for any sign of life or foul play. There was nothing that caught his attention and Halo never said anything that helped. After a long day of searching, Patrick decided it's no use for that day and teleported home. Once there, Patrick showered and prepared to make something to eat, but paused at the site of the newspaper that he brought in and threw on the side-table. He walked over and picked up the paper, unfolding it out, and flipped through the pages. He paused when he got to the one he didn't want to see. It was a small box section in the lower right that read.

Local Boy Kidnapped from Orphanage: Boy,11, taken late last night.

Patrick quickly closed the paper and threw it back on the table. *She's dead, remember?*

Monday morning Patrick woke up just like he used to when his mom was sick. The worrying feeling hit him right when he opened his eyes up, making it feel like home again. He couldn't do anything about his mother dying, but he could do something about Conner. Patrick left for work, having planned on leaving early to go look for Conner. He showed up on time and worked hard through lunch so he could get approval to head out early. After he finished his work and packed his things up, he ran into Summer in the break room. She was there first microwaving a plastic dish and was wiping up a spill when she noticed Patrick walk in.

"Hey, Patrick," She said, turning to him.

"Hey, how are ya?" Patrick said as he opened the fridge. He felt a little awkward now with Summer there.

"I'm okay... yeah," Summer said with each word growing quieter, matching Patrick's lack of energy.

Patrick smiled and shut the fridge door. He turned and walked back towards the exit. Summer caught him before he left.

"Hey Patrick, so I saw on the news that...a boy was taken from an orphanage around here. I remember hearing that you hang out at one sometimes. He wasn't taken from the one you work at? Was he?" She said, looking caringly at Patrick.

Patrick broke eye contact. "Uh..." Patrick sighed and nodded his head slowly. "Yeah I know him"

"You know the boy that was taken?" she asked.

"Yeah," Patrick said.

Summer walked over to Patrick but stopped midway. "That's so horrible. I'm so sorry. Are you ok?"

Patrick inhaled, then exhaled. "I'm fine, yeah. Just worried about Conner"

'Yeah," Summer agreed and looked to the ground, letting the conversation lose some steam. She looked back up to Patrick. "I'm sure you don't want to talk about it, but I'm thinking of you guys...and I'm praying for Conner"

"Thanks, yeah.... We're gonna get him back" Patrick nodded. " I'm actually going over there now," Patrick said to Summer.

"Okay......hey do you need anything over there? I could make a bunch of dishes and bring them over" Summer said, trying to be helpful.

Patrick nodded and smiled a little. "Uh yeah...... I'll ask the boss. I'm sure she'd love the help"

"Okay nice. I can make like four different types of casseroles, so we should be good there"

Patrick smiled again and turned for the door. "Okay...I'll text you about it. Thank you Summer" Patrick headed out back to his desk, and grabbed his things before heading to his car. He sat for a quiet moment to think about a new idea that popped into the forefront of his head. Hearing Summer offer to help was refreshing. He can't have Summer help him with finding Conner, but having her help sounded nice. His mind was quickly taken to the night Conner was taken. Meeting that officer in her patrol car, and feeling that intense connection. *There was something different about her.* Patrick thought. "Halo, that cop from the other night. You know the one I'm thinking of. Was she? I mean...who is she?" Patrick asked.

"I don't understand your question" Halo responded.

Patrick sighed and tried again. "There was a feeling we both got in the car. It was spooky"

"Was it love?" Halo asked.

"No... it wasn't love Halo," Patrick said as he sighed again. "Can you at least track her down? I mean I remember her feelings; I can feel them. Like right now"

"Yes, of course," Halo said. "You better leave this area first"

"Why? Are we in danger?" Patrick asked.

"No, but there has been a person watching you talk to yourself" Halo jolted Patrick's attention.

"What?" Patrick asked, looking around the lot, finally noticing a person sitting at the picnic table eating and trying not to make it noticeable that they've been watching Patrick.

He saw the man and dismissed him as just a stranger. "Alright, yeah let's go. Take me to her" Patrick said as he drove out of the lot and downtown following Halo's directions. After a quiet drive through the downtown area, Halo told Patrick to park and walk into a Cafe. Patrick hopped out and faced the building, reading the sign. *Sunflower Cafe.*

"So, that officer is in there?" Patrick asked as he reached the door.

Halo didn't respond as Patrick headed inside anyway. At first sight, Patrick saw the huge wine rack along the wall, filled with different bottles of wine, then he saw the pastries inside the glass case. He looked to his left to see a bunch of open tables sitting out in the sunlight. He checked his right but didn't see the officer. Finally, all the way in the back he saw a familiar woman sitting in front of the fire, book in hand. As Patrick approached, he noticed she wasn't reading but peering into the fire distantly. Patrick stopped at the counter and ordered a coffee. He grabbed his order and slowly walked over to the woman. Her drink of choice was a white wine glass filled almost halfway up with a matching white liquid. He arrived without her notice and sat down across, looking into the fire with her.

"I hope this is your off day," Patrick said jokingly, slowly getting her attention. He crossed his leg over the other and settled into the soft lounge chair. The woman noticed but didn't react much. She watched Patrick as he returned her icy stare with a smile. "Hi, Officer," he said.

"Do you know me?" she asked as her face tightened.

Patrick squinted his face and shook his head a little. "No... I don't, but for some reason I—... I wanted to meet you," Patrick said.

The woman raised her eyebrows. "Was that a line?" she asked.

"A line?" Patrick asked.

"A pick up line...You know I'm a cop and you're still hitting on me? That's gutsy"

"Oh no, sorry, yeah... that sounded like it, didn't it?"

The woman squinted and mouthed the word, *yeah.*

"Um okay," Patrick exhaled. "I… need help with something, And I think you're worried about it too." Patrick pointed to her wine glass and looked above the woman's head, seeing her swirling dark emotions.

"What do you mean?" Asked the woman, who adjusted straighter in her seat.

"That boy that was taken last night from the orphanage. We need to find him and get him back. I saw you their last night and knew somehow that you could help"

"You were there last night?" the woman asked, as a slow realization started to blossom.

"I was," Patrick answered. "I work for the orphanage part-time...and I was there last night with the kids"

The building realization went away as the woman relaxed back into her seat. "Okay, I know I'm a police officer, but there are more qualified officers and detectives on the case already. There is a citywide, and countryside search happening. We're doing everything we can do to find the kid"

"Yeah okay, of course. But I was also hoping we could maybe work together on this?" Patrick asked the officer, understanding the weird moment.

"I'm sorry, police officials aren't allowed to discuss details of an ongoing case with the public. Not even to someone who knows the kid. I know you understand the law" she said, taking a big sip of her wine.

"I do but—" Patrick paused to think about Sal and his creatures and that somewhere out there, the mummy lurked, waiting, and then the fact that they needed Laney for something. He couldn't do this alone anymore, he couldn't keep screwing things up on his own, he needed someone in his corner. *I need help.* Patrick took a deep breath and looked back at the woman.

"Officer, my name is Patrick. I wasn't just with the kids last night...I was also with you, in your patrol car" The woman's eyes grew larger as her head turned to Patrick, she shifted her seating position again as Patrick continued. "I asked you what happened because…because I caused it, I'm the reason Conner was taken. It's all my fault" Patrick said as he looked at the officer, feeling more and more emotional as he watched the woman lean into him.

170

"So…you're saying that, that was you who I saw on the rooftops, and then again last night? You're the angel that's been going around the city? What are you?" the woman asked.

Patrick flinched at the word angel, starting to dislike that nickname. "Yes, I am, but I'm no angel and I need help. You're help, officer"

The woman smiled as if to say she wasn't buying it. "Why me? Why do you need my help? There's other officers out there you could have chosen."

"Yeah, that's true, there are, but I chose you, and I'm starting to learn that things are all happening for a reason now... you're the one I saw, you're the one I decided to come talk to. And besides, that feeling I got from you in the car, you felt it too... I think we were meant to meet"

That last bit resonated with the woman. Her body relaxed as she sank back into the chair, lips smoothing along with her clear thinning glass.

"That was a line," Patrick said, smiling.

The woman looked at Patrick but didn't return the smile "So you really are that thing?" she asked for confirmation.

"I'm not a thing, but yeah, I am. So will you help me save Conner?" Patrick asked the woman.

She gazed up to the ceiling and then slammed her head back against the couch cushion. She grumbled something inaudible and shook her head before looking at Patrick. "I will help you, but only on a few conditions"

"Okay sure," Patrick said back.

"You have to listen to everything I say, if someone finds out about this, I'll be screwed," she said.

"I can keep a secret," Patrick responded quickly.

She continued. "Second, you share with me everything you know, that way I can coordinate a search," she said, which caused Patrick to nod.

"Third…" she said before pausing. "You have to prove you are who you say you are"

"Fine" Patrick nodded.

"Okay then. My name is Alex. Alex Shade" she said, reaching a hand out to Patrick.

"Hmm," Patrick grumbled. "Officer Shade? That's pretty cool" He said, shaking her hand.

"You can call me Alex; do you have any conditions?" She asked.

Patrick put a finger into his palm. "Don't tell anyone who I am," he pointed down second, "Don't tell anyone about the things I tell you"

Alex cut him off. "Anything else?"

Patrick stopped for a moment and sat forward in his seat, staring into the fire. He turned to look at Alex, then up to her cloud of emotions. "Yeah, what powers do you have? What can you do?" he asked.

Alex visibly tensed up. "What do you mean?" she asked.

"Part of my powers are being able to sense things. ...That moment we had in the car. I've only ever felt that with one other person, and that person has powers too. What can you do?" Patrick asked.

Alex looked away from Patrick and then stood up. She dug in her pockets and grabbed her phone before handing it to Patrick. "Here, put your number in and we can meet tomorrow night. I'll send you an address of where to meet."

Patrick did what she said and handed the phone back. She packed up her things and left without saying goodbye or looking back. Patrick watched her go and wondered, *Am I doing the right thing?*

Chapter 27
Shshshsh shshshsh shshshsh

Patrick woke up to the sound of maracas rattling on his side table. He rolled over to look at the message and the time. It was Officer Shade, she must be up and out on her shift already. Patrick looked at her message.

Meet me at 7 tonight, 522 Goodwin St. Don't be late or I'm leaving: Sent at 6:24 a.m.

He rolled back over and closed his eyes knowing he could get a little more sleep before his alarm went off. After a few moments of trying, Patrick realized it was no use, as his body awoke, so did his mind. *Should I have told her? Should I have met with her? She knows my secret. Was that the right thing to do?* He gave up and got his day started, taking the extra time to write out what he was going to tell Officer Shade tonight and then walk through what he planned to encounter in his day. He remembered that he forgot to ask Amanda if Summer could come by with food one night. He'll have to break that news to Summer today. He was going to work an extra-long day to get ahead of his deadlines and take up as much time as he could waiting to meet with Officer Shade. He packed his lunch and headed out to his day job. He proved himself brave the first thing he did and walked over to Summer's desk to tell her, but she wasn't there, he wrote a note and placed it on her desk. Around five o'clock, the time that Patrick normally left, she stopped by. Patrick heard her footsteps and looked up to greet her.

"Hey, I came by your desk earlier to talk," Patrick said as she approached.

"Yeah I got your note, I must have been off somewhere else." Summer answered.

Patrick spoke up quickly to avoid the awkward pause. "So hey I'm sorry, I haven't gotten around to asking if you could come by the orphanage yet, Amanda's been tied up lately" Patrick said, breaking the news.

"Yeah it's fine, you guys have a lot to worry about right now," Summer mentioned as she nodded her head in understanding. "I just want to help anyway I can."

"And that's amazing of you...I really think the kids could use somebody besides the staff and me around, even for a bit"

Summer smiled and nodded her head. "Let me know, okay?" she said then locked eyes with Patrick. He nodded silently and looked back at her. After a moment, Summer walked off.

For the next two hours, Patrick pushed through his assignments before readying to meet with Officer Shade. Working surprisingly quickly and diligently, he left and drove over to the address Officer Shade sent him. He pulled up right at seven to see that it was a bar named, *The Mourning Pub.* Patrick walked up to the front door staring at the large neon sign hanging above. Before he could reach the door Officer Shade caught his attention from the side.

"You're punctual," she said.

He nodded. "Yeah it's the one thing I can usually get right,"

Officer Shade didn't smile or reply, she walked straight for the door and pulled it open. "Let's go, I need a drink," she said as she walked inside first and sat immediately down at the nearest bar stool. He inched his barstool over for more space and sat next to her.

Officer Shade was wearing her usual police-issued pants but had changed out of her police polo top into a large sweatshirt. He checked out the bar, seeing the place was busy but the bar area was empty. The bartender saw the two of them and came over to greet them and then grabbed their ordered beers along with Officer Shade's shot of cheap vodka. Patrick sipped his beer as he watched Officer Shade down the shot and chased it down with her beer. He felt hesitant to speak at the moment. Feelings from this morning came raging back up. *Should I be here?*

Officer Shade set her glass down, sighed then looked at the bar counter. Patrick felt she had forgotten his presence, but she didn't. "Okay, let's start from the beginning...from wherever your story begins," she said, turning to him to scan his vibe.

Patrick did not respond, but his expression told the story, Officer Shade noticed. "I get it kid. You have a secret...a secret you never wanted to tell anyone. You understand that this secret comes with danger, not only to yourself but others around you. What's happening right now is the last thing you want to be happening, I do get it...but youre going to have to go all in with trusting me here, otherwise…we fail, and Conner dies…We lose. I know that sounds harsh but… it's the truth"

Patrick looked away. *She's right,* he knew.

He turned back to Officer Shade. "You're right…that was all…spot on," he said, smirking.

"So you understand?" Officer Shade asked as she took a big swig of her beer.

Patrick waited for a moment to think as she set her glass down. "I just always feel like bad things will happen, no matter what I do."

She nodded her head in two big motions and laughed lightly. "I understand and I genuinely don't have any advice for you on that, I think a lot of people feel the same way. There…. there's my advice" She said before taking another drink.

Patrick thought for a moment to process the moment. " From the beginning then, you're going to have to believe me too" he said as he took a big drink of his beer.

"Are you going to need another?" Officer Shade asked.

"Yes please, officer" Patrick responded pleasantly.

"It's Alex, remember?" she said without showing emotion. She waved the bartender over and ordered another round before Patrick began his story from the beginning.

"Okay, I'm going to summarize the story to save time—" Patrick said.

Alex responded quickly. "But you share everything. Everything that's happened"

"Okay yeah," Patrick said before getting started with his story. "So, around four months ago, I was back at my…childhood home, when I found a glowing yellow rope."

"That's the rope you have when you're that thing?" Alex asked.

"Stop, I'm not a thing" Patrick shot back.

"You're an angel then?" She said, without energy.

Patrick wondered for a moment. "I've never thought that but, I don't know…maybe. That would explain some things, but anyway I found the rope and then...a few months later and...it talked to me"

"The rope talked to you?" Alex asked.

"Yeah or maybe it's not the rope, maybe it's just in my head but... yeah there's a voice," Patrick said, starting to hope that the more he shared the more these two may have in common.

"What does it say?"

Patrick sighed before answering. "It said once that it's my guide of some sort, and it has been teaching me things, you know about my powers... but it's in my head, like...really in my head" Patrick gestured towards the back of his head. "I call him Halo. Halo showed me the suit and all of the things I could do." Patrick's finger began tapping on the table unconsciously. "With what he gave me I—, I had to do something to help, you know? To help people. Anyone would make the same choice."

Alex didn't respond and kept listening carefully to Patrick's story, taking mental notes.

"And this is the part you're not going to believe" Patrick paused to exhale before starting up again. "A few nights in... when I got the voice, I was out in the city and went to a restaurant downtown, named Canines. Halo...can help me focus and zone in on danger and evil... throughout the city, like a bad guy detection system...and there at the restaurant I met a man who probably was the leader of the Italian mob or something. His name's Sal Porruci. He's the man that took Conner.

"And Halo probably can't track Conner or something stupid like that at the moment?" Alex asked.

Patrick paused for a second. "Uh...nope"

Alex nodded and mouthed something underneath her breath. "Okay continue," she said, sounding annoyed.

"Okay so...at Canines while me and Sal were talking, something attacked us, it was this mummy creature with these creepy floating bandages. It paralyzed me somehow and I watched it suck the life out of a few of Sal's men. He picked Sal up and did the same...I thought he died" Patrick exhaled, and took a deep breath. He's not used to talking so much. He continued, as the emotions began to roll in. "It got me too...I thought I was going to die, but then it just...dropped me, like I was nothing and disappeared. The next week or two I felt horrible"

"Have you seen this thing since?" Alex asked quickly.

"No not since but I do have more to tell," Patrick said as he took a big drink. He exhaled and began again. "So, apparently the reason I'm this special being, according to Halo, is that I am to balance the scales of good and evil, or good and bad I don't remember exactly," Patrick gestured confusion with his hand and continued. "So there are these other...creatures, out in the woods that supposedly form from emotionally neglected hazardous areas, or something like that"

Alex's head cocked to the side in confusion. Patrick jumped back in.

"I know, it's strange. But I'm the one that needs to go out there and monster hunt those things to keep balance" Patrick shrugged his shoulders.

"What kind of monsters?"

"Crazy, scary ones, that I definitely don't want to see around the city" Patrick looked to Alex with raised eyebrows, meaning what he said. "They haven't been able to reach the city for a long time, but, apparently they're moving in"

"Yikes," Alex said in a relaxed way.

"Yeah, I know," Patrick said with a laugh, but then seriousness befell him. "And that's where Conner comes in"

"The boy? Why?" Alex asked.

Patrick paused for a moment to run through his words. "When the mummy thing picked up Sal in his restaurant it didn't kill him, it changed him somehow. And now he's working with the creatures from the woods."

Alex's eyebrows furrow in question. "Why take Conner though?" she asked.

"Because they—" Patrick sighed and felt the stress roll in. "They want another kid...from Building Blocks, a girl named Laney. She's special to them, for some reason. The creatures can't come into the city for her, so they tagged in with a human who has connections" He shook his head, pushing his beer glass away. "I should have saw that coming"

"Connections that can kidnap a kid?" Alex said, understanding the circumstances. "Why do they need her? Did he say?.."

Patrick shook his head. "They want to create a new world, Sal used the word puzzle"

Alex turned her body to face Patrick. "So they're hoping to trade the kids. Or just put enough pressure on you to give her up" She turned away. "That's a tough spot"

"They also know who I am. The real me, under the suit."

"They were probably watching Building Blocks," Alex answered, making Patrick feel stupid. Having listened to her talk and come to conclusions has eased Patrick's mind about enlisting her help. She's proving to be very sharp. *And a little intimidating*, Patrick thought. Alex continued. "So we have no way to track them down, and we can't trade one kid for the other. They took Conner to get leverage, so they're going to be in contact with you soon. Our only options right now are to wait for him to contact you, or we find them somehow first and extract the boy" Patrick did not respond, he wouldn't even know what to say to that. She kept talking through the plan. "I'll contact the detectives on the case and point them towards Sal Porruci. We'll comb through the Sandhill Woods looking for signs. If they're out there we'll find them. You should look out on your own too. Maybe Sal will find you"

Patrick agreed as he grew even more confident in his choice to bring Alex on his team. *I mean, I didn't even know they were called the Sandhill Woods.* He thought as he took another drink, finishing his beer.

"This girl Laney though, I want to meet her," Alex said.

Patrick and Alex make plans for her to come to visit the orphanage in uniform tomorrow night. They closed out their tabs and said their goodbyes. Patrick left for home and felt the weight of the situation not completely lifted, but lighter. Finally having a semi-eased conscience, he arrived home to be alone. *This feeling won't last long;* he thought, before calling it a night.

The next day Patrick did the same thing. He worked, made more progress with his assignments, and made an appearance at Building Blocks, and upon arriving, Patrick noticed a police vehicle parked street side. He went through the front door and was greeted by the sight of all of the kids in the living room working on a project together. He took his shoes off and walked in towards them. He looked down, and saw all of the inspirational words and writings on a large poster.

"Is this for Ms. Kathy?" he asked as the kids turned to see him.

"Yeah," Laney answered, having seen him first, her voice boomed through the quiet house. *The kids must feel horrible right now,* Patrick thought as he knelt down to grab a marker. He paused for a moment to think of something to write. He thought for a while but couldn't even gather the words. He put the cap back on the pen and stood up. He walked over to the couch and sat down. Amanda walked into the living room seeing the group and Patrick.

"Hey, Patrick. How are you?

Patrick jumps to attention upon hearing her. "Hey Amanda, I'm...yeah. How are you?"

Amanda smiled a weak smile and looked out over the kids. "We're all sad Patrick."

I know, I can feel it, It's all my fault, Amanda, Patrick thought.

"Yeah me too," he agreed just before the doorbell rang. "I'll get it," Patrick said as he shot up off the couch. He opened the door to find Alex dressed in uniform, carrying a few large pizzas. She noticed the look on Patrick's face after he opened the door.

"You okay?" she asked.

"Hey, yeah I'm okay, it's just…kind of sad in here"

Alex nodded. "These should help" she gestured towards the pizzas. "Mind helping?"

Patrick reached for and grabbed the pizzas from her hands and brought her inside. Amanda walked over to greet them.

After explaining to Amanda that the police force wanted to check in and bring pizzas over, Amanda told the kids to head to the backyard to eat. Patrick motioned to Laney and halted Alex in her place. He looked over to Anna who was just passing.

"Hey Anna, do you mind taking these for us?" he asked her. Anna looked over and stopped. Without complaint, she grabbed the boxes from Patrick's hands and paced off. He thanked her and waited till she was gone before looking at Laney.

"Laney, this is Officer Shade," Patrick said, waving to Alex. "And this is Laney. Laney is good friends with Conner." Laney stared up at Alex who then looked over to Patrick.

"I told you to call me Alex"

"Oh I know, and I will. But, Officer Shade" Patrick said and waved his hands like a showman. "Is SO good"

Alex didn't respond to Patrick; she looked down at Laney. "Call me Alex, it's nice to meet you Laney"

"Hi, it's nice to meet you too, are you guys friends?" Laney asked her.

Alex responded before Patrick could. "We are. I want to help find Conner too."

Laney smiled shyly and looked over to Patrick.

"We should go grab some pizza before it's all gone," Alex said as she watched Laney turn and run off, they followed her through the hall as Alex turned her head to say something.

"That's her huh? She's adorable. You made her out as some scary demon"

179

"What? No—" Patrick replied as he laughed nervously.

They both walked outside without another comment. Patrick sat outside and watched the kids take turns playing around with Alex's radio, and her badge. They all seemed to forget about their situations for a moment as they enjoyed the pizza and Alex's attention. Patrick wanted to sit on the sidelines for a while, it felt like his body was filling up with guilt with every passing moment, which seemed to be weighing him down. Watching Alex interact with the kids, Patrick could see a little hesitation and uncertainty in Alex's interactions with the.. She stayed around for a few hours before gathering her things to go. She made her goodbyes and walked to the door accompanied by Patrick. Laney cut her and Patrick off before they got to the door and asked if they were both leaving. Patrick told her that Alex was and that she'd come back another time. Alex said goodbye to Laney as she and Patrick stepped outside to the front porch. Alex turned to Patrick as he closed the door.

"So what now?" Alex asked.

Patrick's expression quickly turned urgent, as he looked around before answering. "I'm going out to the woods soon to look. I should have a few hours of daylight left and still I'll—...I'll sleep out there if I have to."

Alex looked calmly at Patrick. "I've finally got the lead detectives to check on Sal. They know a guy like him is capable of human trafficking, so they agreed" Alex looked away before starting up again. "The bad news is... they won't go searching through the forest. They have no cause to"

"Well, what if I tell them? They should believe me; you did" Patrick said assuredly.

"I was different. You even said. But, they may believe you. You're sure Conner's out in the forest?"

"Yes, absolutely"

Alex paced around for a second before stopping to answer. "Okay...okay, then we should plan on that. I'll try and set up a meeting with the detectives...are you sure you want to really out yourself like that?

"What do you mean?" Patrick responded.

"I mean that's a lot of notoriety, if the city still doesn't believe you exist, they definitely will then," Alex mentioned.

"Yes of course, I have too" he responded without hesitation.

Alex bobbed her head in agreement. "Okay, if you have no other options, that's the play. Because Laney is way too adorable to trade away."

As she finished those words, the front door swung open. Out through the doorway stepped Laney, looking upset. She walked past them both and down the stairs, she got to the sidewalk before turning back around. Patrick and Alex stare in confusion and before Laney could explain, Patrick realized what just happened. "Oh no," he said aloud. Alex turned her head sideways to look at Laney.

"You can trade me? For Conner?" Laney asked, patiently awaiting their answer.

Alex looked over to Patrick in confusion and mild horror. Patrick stepped forward to speak to Laney. "Laney we would never do that," he said.

"How did she?" Alex asked, still confused.

Patrick turned back to Alex. "It's her thing, it's called floating. She can see and experience through people's eyes, she must have with one of us."

Alex didn't respond, she looked back at Laney.

"Is that an option?" Laney asked Patrick.

Patrick looked over to Alex, who had begun slowly pacing the porch. "Alex, I think we should be honest," Patrick said, wondering about the consequences.

Alex paced away. "Go ahead then," she said as she walked back towards the house.

Patrick walked down the stairs towards Laney and sat down on the bottom. "Okay so the other night when we were in the woods and got attacked, the man with them said that they wanted you for some reason. Do you know why Laney?" he asked.

Laney shook her head as Patrick continued.

"So since they couldn't have you...they took Conner instead"

"But if they had me, they wouldn't need Conner right? He could come back here?"

"Laney, we are not going to do that," Patrick said, shaking his head. "We will find him some other way. I promise"

Laney took a moment to think before answering. "You don't know where he is?."

"No we don't. He's in the woods somewhere, but I can't pinpoint exactly where, even with Halo's help."

"I can find him," Laney said abruptly, drawing heavy attention from Alex and Patrick.

"What? How?" Alex asked, stepping down to Laney.

"I tagged him," Laney said.

"What, like a tracking device?" Patrick asked.

"Yeah, I got a good look at him in the woods. I'm tracking his heaviest emotions. I could walk you right to him" Laney answered.

Patrick looked over to Alex hoping that she would take this one. Luckily for him, she moved down to Laney and began talking.

"Laney, we can't take you with us. It's too dangerous. There's already too many innocent people involved" Alex said as Patrick felt the sting of his guilt kick in again as Laney fought back.

"I can't describe my feelings to you. There's no way you could find them without me. We could all go safely, and if things go bad, you can always teleport me out of there, so I'm safe" Laney argued as she looked at Patrick. Everyone was quiet for a moment letting Laney's words hover over the scene. Laney broke the silence again, hoping to seize the moment. "Conner needs help, and I can help. Just like you Patrick, you both want to help people, so do I…. I'm going." Laney said with some finality, lightly stomping down to the ground to make a point.

Patrick looked over to Alex and then closed his eyes. He rolled his head back on the stair above and covered his face with his arm. "I don't know" he muttered. He heard Alex exhale loudly and start pacing once more.

"How sure is your teleporting thing?" Alex asked.

Patrick knew that question was for him as he uncovered his mouth. "I mean it always works, so unless they somehow stop me, it will work"

"I don't know," Alex said, still pacing the front porch. Feeling her emotions, Patrick could sense that her soul was filled with intense stress. He knew he was about to burden someone else, but he didn't let his mind go there.

"Please" Laney pleaded from the bottom step, still pressing her case.

Alex stopped walking and Patrick uncovered his face.

"If we do this, we plan for it. I'm going to recruit some help. As soon as we find Conner, you get them out of there and back here okay?" Alex asked Patrick who just nodded in agreement. "Okay then, that's our plan," Alex said with confidence. Patrick looked over to Alex and nodded. Suddenly a thought popped into his head, that he wanted to ask out loud.

"Hey what's Laney's excuse to leave? She can't just walk out of Building Blocks. Not now at least."

"When school starts I can!" Laney said in the excitement that suggested she forgot herself at the moment.

Patrick and Laney both looked over to Alex, who seemed to have a plan for everything. She noticed them and stopped pacing then squared up and looked back with a solemn expression. "I may be able to do something," she said, before closing her eyes. Patrick watched the colors above her and let in the feelings.

There's that pain of hers again.

Chapter 28

"Like... what?" Patrick questioned from the bottom step, looking to break through Alex's defenses. She shrugged off his question and quickly changed the topic.

"So Laney, how exactly are you able to find them? You said something about tracking his emotions. Have you done it before?" Alex asked, descending the stairs.

Laney gave a thumbs up, presumably about the last part of the question. "I can get you to him, I can feel him now. It's.... sort of like that game, you know, hotter and colder."

Alex nodded as she reached the bottom step by Patrick. "Okay, so what if Sal isn't with Conner. It's not a guarantee that they'll be with each other" she continued to pace along the sidewalk. Patrick considered she may be going down the rabbit hole on this one. He decided to speak up.

"Okay, the truth is.... Laney doesn't need to find Sal. Sal will find her. If Laney is outside of the city, Sal and whatever else wants her can track her" Patrick stopped to let it sink into Alex. He continued to drive his idea home. "So my idea is simple. We go out into the woods looking for Sal...who will probably find us first, you and the force arrest Sal, I'll take care of any creatures out there and then we make Sal take us too Conner"

"And you think he's just going to tell us where to look?" Alex interjected.

"I can get the truth out of him...one way or another" Patrick responded ominously.

Alex stopped pacing and sat on a porch chair. In her mind, these plans were sporadic and sloppy. There are plenty of possibilities here for disaster, she knew that. But she's outside of her normal policing element. She wanted to trust Patrick and Laney.

"So as soon as we find Conner, you get both him and Laney out of there"

"Yes, of course. Always" Patrick said.

Alex thought for a moment on the sidewalk, nodding slowly. "Okay, I am going to go fill in the SAC and the Precinct Captain. Hopefully, they see it our way and send some additional units. It's doubtful but…"

"So what kind of information…are you going to fill them in with," Patrick asked inquisitively .

Alex realized what Patrick was asking and cut to the chase like always. "I won't tell them about you. If they agree and send some units out there, you can meet us out there"

Patrick nodded. "Cool…cool"

Alex walked towards the steps and kicked off the bottom stair. She turned to make one last order. "I'll meet you back here tomorrow so we can talk to Amanda and refresh." She turned away and walked toward her car before heading off down the street, leaving Patrick and Laney still on the porch. Patrick looked to Laney.

"Are you sure about this? There's always another way Laney"

"Yeah, I have to," she said with a bravery that inspired Patrick once more. He smiled proudly.

The next day, after taking a vacation day from work he prepared himself for the night's upcoming rescue mission. Patrick ventured over late afternoon to Building Blocks to meet with Amanda and Alex. Patrick arrived but never went inside. He sat in his car to have a moment to himself. No thoughts or worries revealed themselves. He closed his eyes and focused on his breathing. *In…and out…In…and out.* Clearing his mind, he started the process anew. *In…and out…In…and out.* He took another small moment before opening his eyes. There was no light switch moment there as he hoped, as the unrelenting tension filled his head immediately. Instead though, of worrying about Conner and Laney, and whatever Sal was up to he worried about himself. He worried about his own life. It's been exhausting. He's tired. *Shouldn't the world be tired too?* Now guilt crept in. *Shouldn't I be more worried? I feel…indifferent.* Patrick grabbed the door handle to try and physically move away from his thoughts. It was no use though, as his mind was stronger than his body, he came to another conclusion about himself as he relaxed back into his seat. *I'm not happy,* he knew while the beginning of Gymnopedie No. 1, played over his mind.

Without any more thought Patrick opened the door, stepped out, and walked over to the building only ever glancing up when he crossed the road. He got to the porch before he stopped suddenly, wondering if he should wait for Alex or just go up. He decided to wait and take another moment there alone. He sat down on the stairs and stared straight ahead looking towards the bridge a few blocks away. His eyes wander out toward the sky and the clouds. It was a nice day, he should be happy, he should be out with friends or with his far-away family. *She's dead, remember?*

Just as that thought made another comeback. Alex pulled up in her police car and hopped out quickly, then paced towards the building. Patrick saw that she was in uniform, and could feel that she's laser-focused, yet frustrated. She got to the steps as her eyes located Patrick's.

"Hey"

"Hey"

She climbed the steps as Patrick got up.

"You okay?" Alex asked.

"Yeah I'm good, you?"

Alex scanned Patrick over, as a detective would, and sat at the step. Patrick rejoined her and sat down.

"So the SAC and the lead detectives didn't believe Conner would be out in the woods. They won't be helping. I figured they wouldn't" she said.

"So it's just us then? Patrick asked, referring to the three of them.

"No, I was able to recruit some other officers to help. I didn't tell them much besides I had an idea of where Conner may be. They all agreed to help. It's not the full force but with you we should be fine"

"Yeah, speaking of, you definitely didn't tell them about me, so how is that going to end up?"

"They all know about you," Alex said. "I was freaked at first but I'm over that, they'll get over it too. You'll have to just meet us out there"

"Nice, I'll make a grand entrance," Patrick said and smiled weakly.

"Yeah you do that, I'll bring Laney out there," Alex said standing up, she walked the steps with Patrick behind and grabbed the door handle. "Oh," Alex said, stopping at the door. "For Amanda, all you need to do is tell her that Laney will be safer in police custody for the night. I'll take care of the rest"

"That doesn't make any sense. Why would she believe that? And then allow it?"

"Jesus, just trust me," Alex said as she flung the door open and marched inside. Patrick confusingly followed her up the stairs toward Amanda's office. They reached the top floor and peered over to the office, seeing her door open. Alex shot Patrick a glance before they reached the office. Patrick could hear Amanda and Anna's voices inside talking about something he couldn't make out. Alex approached and knocked on the door then awaited recognition. Amanda and Anna looked over to the door. After greeting each other and Amanda's thank you to Alex for the meal, Alex shot Patrick a glance and a head nod towards Anna. Patrick understood and looked at Anna.

"Hey Anna, can we have a minute with Amanda?"

"Sure," she said, without a fight as she sauntered off through the door. Patrick watched her go then closed it behind her and turned over to Amanda who seemed a little confused.

"So... Amanda" Patrick said as he shot another glance at Alex, who was standing patiently nearby. He continued, "We were talking earlier...uh downstairs, and we think that it would be a good idea to have Laney stay with Officer Shade and the rest of the police tonight in uh...protective custody," He said, finishing his statement through squinted eyes, awaiting a full rebuttal of questions and worried thoughts from her, but to his surprise that never came any. Amanda paused in thought, almost as if she was a frozen computer. She snapped back and looked at Patrick. "Yeah, that sounds like a good idea. I trust you"

Patrick loosened up and looked to Alex who was still standing patiently by the desk. "Okay...yeah," Patrick said looking at Alex. "Great, okay then," he agreed, smiling at Amanda.

Alex walked around to the front of the desk. "Thank you, ma'am. We'll keep her safe and bring Conner back" She turned and walked back out the door. Patrick didn't follow, he stayed with Amanda surprised at her sudden agreeableness. He sat down on the couch. *What just happened?*

Amanda seemed just as unnerved as she sat back into her chair. There was a moment again where Patrick wanted to tell her everything. He's one-hundred percent sure he could trust her. Telling her everything may make him feel better and it may make the future easier, because right now he could see and feel the toll it was taking on her. Emotions can come and go, but when strong enough could leave a lasting impact. Telling her may unburden her, but it will rack up his guilt to an even greater height. Anna snuck back in before anything came about, she sat down on the couch looking at Amanda and Patrick. There's a weird tension in the room that she immediately picked upon.

"What did you guys talk about?"

"It was just about the investigation. There's a lead" Patrick told her.

Anna perked up and leaned towards Amanda. "That's great!"

Amanda looked up to Anna and smiled. "Yes it is!"

False confidence in a situation can be a good thing, Patrick understood. But that wasn't what Amanda was projecting. *She truly believes that,* Patrick wondered.

Amanda looked over to Patrick and smiled. "So what's new with you?

Patrick shifted positions as the eyes fell on him.

"Yeah you asked that girl out yet?" Anna asked with sharp straightforwardness.

"Whoa whoa. That's personal" Patrick said with a wry smile, as his energy picked up. "Oh but that does remind me. I have a..." Patrick stopped and side-eyed Anna. ."..friend who wants to make some food to bring over here. She wants to help out"

"A friend?" Anna asked curiously.

"Yeah, a friend?" Amanda chimed in.

"Yeah…a friend" Patrick stated.

"No, you wouldn't have looked at me like that if it wasn't the girl you like," Anna understood.

Patrick broke and confessed that it's her, but reasserts that they were just friends. He made them agree not to say anything as Amanda said she would love some extra help and that she was excited to meet her. He stayed for a few more minutes before getting up to go clean the kitchen for Amanda. After finishing, he packed his things and went to find Laney. He found her in the backyard drawing on the sidewalk with some chalk. He bent down to look at her drawing. He could tell it's a flower but wanted to mess with her.

"Whoa, is that dolphin?" He asked.

Laney shot over a mean-looking glance and confronted Patrick. "No, it's a flower"

"Well, it looks like a dolphin," he said and smiled.

Laney shook her head and continued drawing "No it doesn't"

"Yeah it does, see you have the fins here," Patrick said as he pointed at the pedals on the flower.

"Those are pedals!" she answered, as she swatted Patrick's arm. Patrick grinned, knowing his job of messing with Laney was complete.

"So did Alex talk to you?" he asked.

"Yeah. She's picking me up at five. Then we are driving into the woods" Laney responded.

"Good, okay"

"You'll be there too, right?" She asked looking up to Patrick with her soft eyes.

"Yeah, of course," Patrick said, smiling back. "I think you get to fight the monsters this time though"

"Fine, but that makes you the sidekick then" She answered then looked away.

"I'll be your sidekick any day," Patrick said proudly, messing her hair up before he stood up. "See you soon captain," He said as he walked into the house and out through the front. Laney ran up to the front door window and watched him drive away.

Five o'clock rolled around and so did Alex in her patrol car. She hopped out and met Laney on the front porch. Behind the porch pillars, Anna popped her head out and walked over next to Laney. Alex made it to the stairs to greet them.

"Hey Laney, hey Anna"

Without reply or hesitation, Anna confronted Alex. "So Laney says she's staying with you at the station"

Alex looked back at Anna and smiled politely. "We think she'll be safer with us tonight" Alex's eyes scanned over to Laney. "And... she's our expert detective" she gave Laney a wink. Laney smiled and grabbed her backpack. Before Laney could walk off, Anna got one last word in.

"Is she in danger? Are WE in danger?"

Alex's expression went from relaxed to empathetic and worried. "No, absolutely not, you all..." Alex looked down to Laney who reached the sidewalk. ."..are completely safe. There are officers stationed here overnight to make sure that happens. You can trust us" Alex assured them before asking Laney if she was ready

"Bye Laney!" Anna shouted out then retreated into nervousness.

Alex and Laney drove off towards the woods. The area they planned on meeting at was a forty-minute trip. After a few quiet minutes in the car, Alex knew she had to say something to Laney, anything. She racked her brain for an appropriate question to ask.

"So are you enjoying school?"

"Yeah I am"

"Good, it ends for summer soon right?" Alex asked.

"I think so," Laney said while shrugging her shoulders.

After another ten minutes, Alex guessed, of silence, she couldn't take it anymore. She's so bad with kids and knew why, but wasn't going to visit those memories. She looked over to Laney who was staring out the passenger window.

"So Laney, what's it like having powers?"

Laney slowly turned her head around to Alex. *That question intrigued her*, Alex knew. Her eyes land on Alex's coolly. "You know what it's like," she stated.

Alex tensed up. *How could Laney know that? Did Patrick tell her?* She wondered. Laney spoke back up to save Alex from herself.

"It's okay though…I understand how you feel about them, and it's okay. The powers I have…they're a great gift to me. They make me feel more—" Laney halted her sentence in thought before continuing. "What's the opposite of alone?"

Alex stared straight ahead towards the road while answering. "Connected…. you feel more connected with them" she answered, starting to feel emotional.

"Yeah, I feel more connected, like…I have something," Laney said while she looked back through the window.

Alex realized the moment they have and wanted to share more. "I do have powers…but I don't feel connected to anyone when I use them. It's the opposite even"

Laney turned back to Alex. "Well then change that. You're the only one with the power to change yourself"

"Whoa….so inspirational," Alex said, impressed.

"My dad used to say that to me"

"Your dad knew you had powers?"

Laney nodded. "He taught me"

"So your dad had powers too?"

"Yeah he did, and he had a rope like Patrick does," Laney mentioned.

"Just like Patrick? Was your dad a superhero too?"

"No, I don't think so. He only showed me the rope"

"Hmm, so what makes Patrick different then?" Alex asked Laney in a serious tone.

Laney shrugged again. "I don't know. There just is…something weird about the voice in his head though"

"What do you mean?"

"My dad never had a voice or a suit, but he was able to do things with the rope that Patrick can. I don't know…I just feel weird about it"

"But you trust him? Patrick?" Alex asked.

Laney gazed back out the window before he answered quietly. "He's the only one I trust"

Laney's words ease Alex's mind. She has been so uncertain about everything happening lately and never felt right trusting Patrick, even though he has never proven himself untrustworthy. They continued their drive out to the forest with little more conversation, and eventually pulled into the natural resources lot. Laney saw two other police cars already parked, with officers standing nearby at the ready. Laney counted three others then looked over to Alex for some sort of confirmation. Alex looked back and obliged.

"It's okay, we might need some backup. I haven't told them about you or Patrick. You can trust them too" Alex said, then parked the car. She jumped out quickly and jogged to the passenger's side and opened the door for Laney. Alex brought Laney around the car to introduce her to the other officers. Alex parked Laney by one of the cruisers and started the quick introductions.

"Okay Laney, this is Officer Sabrina Jeffers. We attended academy together, and joined the force at the same time a few years ago. I call her Sabby, you can too." Laney looked up at the officer. Her probably long brown hair was tied into a tight ponytail. She smiled at Laney, which made her nervous. Alex continued with the next introduction.

"Over here we have…regrettably a high school friend of mine a—"

"And present day friend…so" the officer cut in, then backed down.

"Yes, and present day…friend. He's a good officer, but he is bad at basically everything else. Don't ever ask him to water your plants" Alex said, shaking her head.

"I…got…thirsty!" the new officer yelled.

"What does that even mean?"

"You know, conserve water, save the animals"

"Oh my god. Moving on" Alex said, starting to walk over to the last officer.

"Wait! You never said my name!" the previous officer yelled back.

Alex stopped and turned around then began to chuckle. "Oh, I did forget...sorry"

"That was on purpose!" the slender officer yelled.

"No it wasn't, stop...Okay Laney, this is Officer. Kenny Stix. Kenny, this is Laney" Alex said then walked off. Officer Stix saluted Laney who inspected him back, seeing not much character besides his shaved blonde hair and blue eyes. She turned and followed Alex, and reached the last officer. Laney saw the muscular officer standing tall, holding his waist belt.

"Laney, this is Officer. Gabe Jackson. Officer Jackson is actually in the Special Child Abduction Unit set up by the FBI. We're lucky to have him on board" Laney saw Alex smile over to him and nod, he returned her nod and greeted Laney. Alex gathered the officers around her and Laney. Laney looked up to all of the officers and listened to their plan.

"So Shade, why are we out here really? You said it was about the missing boy" Officer Jeffers asked.

"It is. I have plenty of information that says he and his abductors are stationed out in the woods" Alex answered.

"Then where is our back up? We should have tactical units out here. Not just us" Officer Jackson responded.

"Yeah, not just us and... a little girl," Officer Stix said looking down to Laney" She returned his look with a fiery-eyed glare.

Alex started to pace again, which did not make the situation anymore relaxing.

"Alex, seriously, please tell us," Officer Jeffers pleaded as Alex stepped away.

Alex stopped pacing and looked at Officer Stix. "Hey, what time is it?"

"What? uh its—" Officer Stix unzipped his pouch to check his phone. "Five fifty-eight"

"Jeez, hurry up" she mumbled under her breath. "Okay, guys...all of this is to find Conner, okay? I'm sorry to deceive you guys, but we need help" Alex said.

"You and the little girl need help? You've partnered with a little girl?" Officer Stix asked.

"Not quite," Alex said under her breath but loud enough for them to hear.

Officer Jackson walked over to Alex who turned to face him. "Alex, we all appreciate your braveness and commitment to finding a missing kid, but we can't do this alone, we have to wait for another moment, otherwise something bad could happen"

Alex turned away from him, trying not to let the words hit her. *It's gotta be six,* she wondered, as she turned back slowly to Officer. Jackson, to defend herself. "I just want to help the boy, that's been my only motivation"

Officer Jackson sighed and looked over to the other officers. "We'll be there for him when the full force is." The officers began walking toward their cars as Alex tried to get them to stay.

Officer Jeffers looked back to Alex with her hand on the door handle ready to open it. "Alex…we need help"

Just as her words rang through the air, the sound of light humming filled the void. In-between Alex, Laney, and the officers appeared a standing glowing yellow circle. The officers stared at the circle in shock as Officer Jackson placed his hand on his weapon. Just as he unclipped it, a figure in a white and yellow suit, with a holstered yellow rope stepped through onto the forest ground. Patrick's dark blue eyes met the officer's as he walked completely through the portal. The circle behind him faded away, as Patrick looked over to Laney who was smiling as wide as possible and gave a wave. He looked to the other officers who all had their guns drawn. In a tense moment of silence, Patrick spoke.

"Officers. Thanks for coming"

Chapter 29

Upon seeing Patrick step through the portal and greet the officers, Alex rolled her eyes and scanned the officers standing behind the patrol cruisers. She looked at each one's reaction to Patrick's arrival, trying to understand what they were feeling. Officer Jeffers seemed a little shaken and worried. She looked over to Officer Stix, who was alternating between a dropped jaw and a crazy smile. She then looked over to Officer Jackson, whose reaction she was almost afraid to see, yet it was stoic and calm. Alex couldn't decipher if he was mad, scared, happy, or sad. She started getting worried, *how could I deceive them all like this?* she wondered. She walked towards Patrick and the other officers. "Guys" she started, trying to reason with them first. Officer Stix cut her off.

"You're the Angel? You're real" He said as he pointed both fingers at Patrick, who nodded in return.

"So you're working with him Alex?*"* Officer Jeffers asked.

Alex turned her head towards Patrick without answering her question.

"That's why she didn't want to tell us," Officer Jackson added on.

"He came to me about finding Conner. He has a way to track him down" Alex said, hoping that was the end of it.

Officer Stix shook off the nerves and slowly walked towards Patrick and his glowing persona, staring in amazement and wonder. Officer Jackson shut his car door and walked over to Alex. He looked into her eyes, seeking out any worry or franticness. "Is everything okay Alex? Did he do something to you?"

She squinted and shook her head. "What? No. I'm fine. Look, he has a way to find Conner. I want to do everything I can to help, and if that means working with—" Alex looked over to Patrick who returned her look, upon hearing her stop. "Well I don't know what he is, but he wants to get Conner back, just as much as we do, if not more, and…you guys said we needed back up, and trust me…he's plenty backup"

Officer Jackson eased up a little as Officer Stix reached out to poke Halo, who was tied up on Patrick's waist. "This is cool, it's so bright. It's like a piece of the sun. Is it hot?" he asked Patrick, seeing his reflection in Patrick's dark eyes.

"It's been known to burn things," Patrick answered.

"Can I touch it?" Officer Stix asked.

Patrick didn't answer, he watched as Officer Stix reached over and poked the rope a few times. Patrick was waiting for a yelp or a squeal, but Officer Stix placed his hand around the rope and nothing happened.

"Yeah it's a little warm," he said before removing his hand and looking up to Patrick. "So what do we call you? What's your comic book name?"

Patrick waited for a moment to think. He knew he didn't want to be called Angel but it's not the worst name ever. He racked his brain quickly for a spur-of-the-moment name but got nothing good. Before he could reply with anything, Alex spoke up.

"Okay guys, it doesn't matter, right now finding Conner matters, and we only have a few hours of sunlight left. We have...him, so we should be good to go. If you don't want to help us, that's fine. You can head back to the precinct. But I'm helping him find the kid tonight" Alex finished her pregame speech as Patrick began to clap lightly. The clapping didn't catch on but the officers started to move. Officer Jackson shuffled in place uncomfortably, while Officer Jeffers walked around the car and over to Alex, Laney, and Patrick. Her eyes fixed on Patrick the entire time.

"I'll help. I'll always have your back Lex" she said, turning to Alex.

"Thank you"

Officer Stix was still standing next to Patrick, admiring his suit and general magical aura. "Oh yeah, I'm in for sure. Ready to see this guy in action!" he said excitedly, and almost slapped Patrick on the back before realizing it was a bad idea.

"Awesome, don't forget your gun" Alex retorted.

"Yeah, thanks mom" he replied.

Patrick watched and listened as Alex and Officer Stix banter. Hearing Officer Stix say that struck an emotional cord again for Patrick. She's dead, remember? He looked over to Laney, who had been waiting patiently for the extremely professional policemen to finish their meeting. He shuffled over and crouched down to Laney, as

Officer Jeffers and Jackson took notice and watched. Patrick looked at Laney and put up his fist.

"You ready for this boss?"

Laney bumped his fist and grinned. "I'm ready"

Patrick nodded his head and smiled. Once finally having realized that his smile doesn't show, he stood back up and eyed the officers.

"You're just a person under that, aren't you?" Officer Jackson asked.

Patrick looked at Officer Jackson and nodded.

This moment took Officer Jackson off his guard as he opened up. "I can't do this"

"What?" Alex asks.

"I can't do this; I can't help.... This isn't right."

"What do you mean?"

"I mean, it's not natural. What he just did getting here, whatever else he can do. I'm sorry, but it really has me worried. I mean everything the human race has ever learned is being challenged by this guy…with everything he can do"

"Are you serious Jackson?" Officer Jeffers asked from beside him.

"Yes, I can't. If the police force is going after the kid, I'm there. But if it's him…" Officer Jackson looked to Patrick. "no, I can't…. I won't." He quickly walked off and hopped into his car. Without going after him, the rest of the officers let him go without even a word. He drove off, leaving the five of them on their own. Patrick watched the other two officers for any hint of apprehension or nervousness. He didn't see or feel any but figured he should speak up anyway.

"I only want to help. That's all I've ever wanted…I'm not your enemy. Those enemies took an innocent kid. It may be dangerous and it may go bad…it definitely won't be what you signed up for as a police officer, and the things you may see and experience won't be any good. So if you do want to leave and have no part of this, that's your right. We'll accept it either way" Patrick said as he looked over to Alex, giving her a nod. They waited in silence for a moment for anyone to speak or walk off, but no one did. Alex stepped up and was about to run through the plan before being cut off again by Officer Stix.

"Hold up though. What did you mean by 'the things we may see and experience?"

Patrick didn't answer, he looked over to Alex and gave her another nod, telling her to continue.

"I'll get to that Kenny," Alex said before motioning the group to come closer together. "First, Angel guy here will take Laney, they're going to track down Conner's kidnapper. His name is Sal. Once they locate Sal, our mission is to find Conner and extract him out as fast as possible. Once we have the boy, we can all teleport out of there and back to the station," she finished, as everyone shared a look.

"Oh that's so cool!" Officer Stix blabbed.

"Okay, and will there be any opposing resistance?" Officer Jeffers asked.

"Good question" Patrick remarked as he nodded his head.

Alex inhaled deeply before exhaling out loudly. "Yes, there will be, more than likely" she sighed again. "Sal Porruci works for the Italian Mob here in the city, so he will probably have some security around with him"

"Alright, alright...nothing you can't handle, right?" Officer Stix asked and looked at Patrick. Patrick never reacted, he stared, continuing to watch Alex.

"That shouldn't be the problem though. So I haven't seen or heard about these before, but, our friend here" Alex gestured toward Patrick "says that there are monsters roaming the woods that protect Sal. So we may have to deal with them too"

"Excuse me, monsters?" Officer Stix asked.

"Yeah what?" Officer Jeffers chimed in looking for clarification.

Alex looked over to Patrick who returned her stare. "Hey man, this is your world, you explain that"

The officers turned to look at Patrick, as did Laney, who waited for his answer.

"Yes, there are... monsters, but you won't have to deal with them. I will" he assured, adding a hint of toughness.

"Why are their monsters in the first place? What are they?" Officer Jeffers asked.

Patrick looked away, thinking through his words carefully. He wanted to be honest, but not forthright about his life. He looked back at the officers.

"The monsters... they come from a different world or existence, I don't have all of the facts, but I know they need Conner for something" Patrick stopped to look at Laney before continuing. "If we fail, there's no telling what happens to us, and the world. Because, like I said, I have no idea what's happening"

"The world is at stake? Oh my god!" Officer Stix shouted and fell back onto the patrol car.

"Jackson was right, this is crazy, no sane person would go fight actual monsters...luckily, I'm crazy" Officer Jeffers said before smiling over to Alex, Patrick watched the emotions above Officer Jeffers shift and flow over one another. *She's in a good place right now, she means it*, Patrick could tell.

"That's my girl," Alex told her, returning the smile. Officer Stix shot up from the car hood looking shocked.

"Are you kidding me?" He stood up and walked over to Patrick and began bombarding him with questions and concerns. "Well, what do they look like? Are they scary? Will they eat me? Do they even eat humans? Will they like the way I taste? Oh god!" Officer Stix stopped and looked up to Patrick for answers and reassurance. Patrick waited a moment thinking the questions were rhetorical. He could see the officer's emotions swirling around and collapsing into themselves. Patrick stared into his distressed emotions, losing focus, he felt a warm rush as the soothing waves flowed over themselves. He shook himself present.

"Yes, to all of those, are you ready?" he replied quickly.

"Jesus," Officer Stix said before walking over to Alex. "Are you sure about this?"

"Kenny you don't have to come, if you don't want to. I always thought you were a coward anyway, nothing changes" Alex said with a grin.

Officer Stix turned his head back to Patrick and began to walk back over again.

Laney watched the officer freak out and decided to intervene. "They're not that scary, you'll be fine"

Officer Stix swung his head and looked at Laney. He scrambled to her and bent down to her level. "You've seen them? What are they like?" he asked, with bulging eyes.

"They look like bats, but way bigger"

"Oh that sounds scary," he said quietly.

"If you get attacked, he'll put up a shield for you, so no matter how hard the monsters hit, you'll be safe" Laney said, referring to Patrick.

"A shield?" Officer Stix repeated as he turned to look at Patrick. His eyes go straight to Patrick's rope. "It's the rope, it can make a shield? that's cool too"

"So you're in then? Good let's get going" Alex said as Officer Stix turned quickly to confront her statement.

"Whoa! Wait, I don't know yet"

"Kenny, we need to go now, this is happening so get on board or go home," Alex urged and began to walk to the wood line. Everyone turned and followed, the sudden slow movement of his peers got Officer Stix to rush his decision. Officer Stix rolled his head back and started moving too, walking up behind the group.

"I'm coming but I—, I declare a shield!" he said loudly.

"You what?" Alex asked.

"You declare a shield?" Officer Jeffers confirmed.

"Yes, you know what I mean" He looked over to Patrick. "Is that okay? Sir"

Patrick smirked from under his mask, starting to enjoy Officer Stix's goofiness and his ability to make light of any situation. He nodded in acceptance to Officer Stix and patted him on the shoulder. "I'll be around," he said as he walked off.

"Okay, one more thing!" Officer Stix exclaimed.

"Oh my god KENNY!" Both Officers Shade and Jeffers yell out simultaneously.

"Well we do need to clarify what we call him. I mean I can't just yell out, heyI'moverherecomerescuemeahhhhhhhimdying" Officer Stix said, getting Patrick to laugh. Patrick wondered if he was right as a name clicked in his mind. He turned back to the rest of the crew.

"How about.... Deva?"

"Deva? What's that?" Laney asked.

"It's just something I was told once"

"Well I like it!" Officer Stix yelled out.

"So do I!" Laney agreed.

"Okay then. Kenny, if you're ever about to be clawed to death, just yell out Deva, and he'll come running" Alex said sarcastically, looking at the newly christened Deva.

"Got it!" Officer Stix said not picking up any of the sarcasm. Alex looked over to Deva as soon as they reached the forest line.

"Here," Alex said as she stopped the group.

Patrick grabbed Halo and in one smooth motion, whipped out Halo and created a large teleportation circle. It stayed floating as Patrick looked over the officers.

"Okay, you three go through here," Patrick said, referring to the officers. "It's near where Laney said to go. Alex knows the area…you guys just stay out of sight. I'll send a signal for you guys to go in"

Alex and Jeffers nodded their heads and moved toward the yellow portal, with Officer Stix following behind, still visibly nervous. Patrick looked back into Officer Stix's cloud of emotions as he walked, watching the swirling movements and the ever-changing patterns come and go. He watched Alex help Officer Jeffers through the portal first. She needed some encouragement to go through but ultimately did bravely. Alex needed to physically push Officer Stix through the portal, even Laney had to help knock him through, but he too eventually made it. Alex was about to walk through before Patrick subconsciously yelled out.

"Alex!"

Alex stopped moving and turned around to face him and Laney. He felt guilty again and wanted to tell her how sorry he was for having chosen to involve her in the first place. He took a moment before saying anything. Alex looked back waiting.

"I—…Thank you, Alex," he said and nodded lightly as she smiled weakly and turned around, moving through the portal.

Patrick looked over to Laney who was already staring at him. Patrick could see his reflection in Laney's bright brown eyes. *I have to protect her*, he thought as he closed his eyes. He took in all of the air and the life around him. He inhaled, in…and out and gazed at Laney again who was copying him, matching his breath as best she could. She opened her eyes too and looked at Patrick.

"Ready Deva?" she asked.

"Lead the way, teach"

Chapter 30

Laney and Deva stepped through the other side of the portal and waited quietly before moving along. There's plenty of sunlight, yet the countless number of trees, branches, and leaves made it feel like dusk. It was an eerily quiet night as sounds of the leaves rustle in the wind, mixed with their footsteps and quiet exhales, only added to the tension. Deva kept a close eye on Laney as they walked through the woods. He checked the tree branches above them expecting the trees themselves to attack. He knew the creatures liked attacking from above and knew he had to be ready and on top of his game. *This night is too important,* he knew. Deva ushered Laney to the right but Laney stopped and pushed back.

"No, it's this way," she said, dragging him by the arm.

They continued walking to the rendezvous point. With no monsters, and basically, no life at all Deva began to worry. He followed Laney closely, feeling her determination and willpower. *She won't ever stop looking,* Deva thought as he sensed something else, not with Laney but with the forest, it seemed different now, the air was heavier, it's as if the elevation changed. Deva scanned the area seeing the same forest. A few minutes passed before Laney came to a stop and crouched by a tree. She gestured for Deva to kneel too.

"He's close...but something feels bad." Laney said.

"I feel it too. What's changed?"

"I'm not sure...it feels...sour"

Deva looked to Laney and saw the first sign of apprehension he had seen from her all night. *Has she felt this before?* he thought. She's spooked and distracted but managed to raise herself.

"Laney? You alright?" Deva asked, growing concerned.

She shook herself present, glanced at Deva, and then her desired destination. "I'm okay." she said before starting to walk. "He's just ahead, at the end of the woods"

Deva followed closely behind and heard an opportunity. "So if he's just up ahead. I'm sending you back"

Laney turned around sharply and stared at Deva. "No, I'm staying, we haven't even found them yet"

"I'll handle the rest...you said he's just up ahead. I'll swoop in and grab him"

"No, I have to be here.….. I know it" Laney said sternly, looking off toward the ground.

"What does that mean? Why?" Deva asked.

Laney ignored the question and trotted off, causing Deva to close the distance. He watched as she stepped between a pair of thick bushes, and ducked under the tree branches. He couldn't help but empathize with her, he imagined the world around her and what she's gone through and lost. He felt for her and could feel her pain. He tapped her shoulder. He wasn't sure what to say, he had nothing planned or written down, he didn't think he had the answers. When Laney turned, and he saw the painful look in her eyes, then he understood what to do.

"We're going to find Conner," He said before sighing. "Then we're going to find out what happened to your dad. I promise" He took a moment waiting for Laney to soak that in before he stood up. "Let's get going"

The two walked closer to the edge of the woods through the remaining trees where they saw the opening. It went downhill from there but they could see the drop in the forest ground. They approached slowly towards the edge of the woods. Deva could see a decent-sized cabin at the bottom of the hill leading into a field. In paranoia, he checked behind them for danger. He glanced over to Laney before she stopped and tugged his arm.

"There he is" she instructed.

Deva circled back around the tree to scope out the area with Laney. He noticed Sal rounding the corner of a small wooden cabin, heading to the porch. He stopped at the top and dug through his pockets before pulling out a cigar. Deva shuffled to the other side of the tree, locating Sal again. *Why is he wearing that dirty grey suit still?* Deva wondered, wanting to charge over to rough it up more. He peered through the windows for any sign of movement. Unable to see much, Deva began to stress. *Where are you, Conner?* Sal sat down and lit up his cigar as he looked out into the forest. Deva felt something amiss. *He seems relaxed, is he stalling? Or does he know we're here?* Laney swatted Patrick's knee to get his attention.

"We should get him," she said.

Deva watched Sal closely and wondered what the play should be. *Sal is in the open, with no guards or defenses of any kind. This could be the time to strike.*

"Yeah maybe," Deva said without moving, his mind quickly changed as he stepped out in front of Laney. "I know what he's doing. It's definitely a trap, those creatures are hiding somewhere"

Laney looked over to Deva and then the area for the creatures. Deva did too, and scanned the cabin again, his peripheral vision caught movement to his left, he noticed Alex and the officers approaching the wood line.

"He knows we're here," Deva said as he crouched down to Laney. "Are you ready?"

Laney put on a mean face and nodded.

"Good, Alex and the others are close by. We'll keep you safe" Deva grabbed Laney's hand and walked out into the open. They made it to the wood line as Sal took notice. Deva watched Sal's face for his expressions, and noticed they kept changing form, smiling one second, frowning the next. From fear and terror to surprise and excitement. Sal stood calmly as he took a puff of his cigar, which seemed to relax his twitch. Deva walked with Laney up to the cabin, stopping thirty yards away as they waited for him to speak. Sal blew out his smoke and shot a glare right over to Laney which slowly contorted into a grin.

"Ciao, Laney," Sal greeted.

Laney stared straight at him, not giving any ground. Sal conceded the staring contest and turned to Deva.

"I'm surprised Patrick," Sal said, still grinning. "And relieved really...I mean things could have gotten messy. Does this also mean you're joining our cause then? Things would be a lot more scripted with you on board"

Deva looked down at Laney and gave another worthless smile to her. Her eyes stayed glued to Sal though as he turned back. "You're wrong," he said.

"Wrong about what, Patrick?"

"I didn't bring her here *for* you, I brought her here to *stop* you,"

Sal shook his head and placed his hands over his ears. He began pressing his head in as if he had a terrible headache. He stopped and released his grip and looked to Deva. "She doesn't have that kind of power. She exists for them! Not you!... Not me! Them!" Sal yelled.

He rounded the porch chair quickly and walked to the front door of the cabin. He grabbed the handle and angrily shoved the door open, causing it to smash against the wall inside. Sal stepped away in front of the cabin so they could see inside.

"You want him! You give her up... or you and the boy both die"

Deva shuffled over to get a better view. Finally, able to make out his face, he saw Conner lying on the ground tied up, unconscious, but in good condition. Deva tensed up fueled with anger that Sal was stoking. He clenched his fist before taking a step toward Sal. Sal shut the door leaving Conner inside and stepped out further on the porch.

"So... what'll it be Patrick?" Sal asked, looking away into the forest.

Deva stared at Sal, hoping just by glaring hard enough Sal would disappear forever. He wanted to rush over there and smack him as hard as he could. *And I'm going to,* he thought as he looked down at Laney.

"Bye Laney," he said as he started to form a portal next to her, he nudged her over to it.

"Don't do this!" Sal shouted.

Laney reached for the portal as her tiny hands pressed in on the yellow substance as she steps forward. Her hand hit the portal and stopped. She pushed harder, trying to force her way through, but was unable. Her face turned to Deva, who was staring bewildered by the yellow portal.

I felt that would happen, Deva thought before hearing Sal yell something else. He abruptly caught sight of incoming danger, wherefrom around the other side of the cabin, a familiar long bat creature barreled towards them. Luckily, Deva had time to react, and picked Laney up and leapt sideways away from the creature. As they landed, Deva watched two more bat creatures stride up alongside the other one. Sal stepped out in front of the creatures and raised his palms. "We're not letting that happen again," he said before grinning wide.

Officers Shade, Stix, and Jeffers watched from a safe enough distance as Deva and Laney were confronted by the creatures and Sal. Officer Stix peeked out in fear around the tree he hid behind, and caught a glimpse of the creatures. He quickly returned to his safe position.

"Oh my god," He whispered. "Those things are terrifying…those claws were like…two feet long. Oh my god"

Alex noticed but didn't console him, she peered over to where Deva and the creatures were, trying to formulate a new plan. She looked over to Officer Jeffers, who had a steady attitude at the moment.

"Okay, Conner must be in the house. Deva wouldn't start fighting unless he saw him" Alex told her.

"But why is the girl still here?" Officer Jeffers asked.

"I'm not sure, she should be gone already, that was the plan"

"Maybe his powers aren't working, oh my god" Officer Stix whispered sharply to them both.

"Kenny, shut up," Alex said as she scanned back to the cabin. "As soon as we can, let's get to the cabin and grab the kids. He can take care of the rest"

"What if we—" Officer Stix started to say before Alex cut him off.

"Kenny enough, we won't even have to deal with the monsters, maybe just the man," Alex mentioned and looked over to Sal, wondering what's going to happen next. She watched Deva, waiting for him to make a move. *C'mon Patrick, get her out of here.* Alex thought as she circled her tree to talk with the group. "Okay, new plan. I'm assuming Deva can't teleport Laney right now. We'll have to wait for him to distract them so we can go and grab Conner and Laney and go"

"Got it," Officer Jeffers said in response.

Alex looked over to Officer Stix for confirmation, but he was staring straight ahead towards Deva and the creatures. She asked him again if he understood, to which he said yes quietly, before he watched two of the creatures take off towards Deva and Laney. One jumped high in the air, while the other stayed on the ground charging straight for them. Deva whipped out Halo and covered Laney again with a shield, just in time as the creatures reached him. He did his best to defend himself, but the bat creatures were too coordinated and flanked him from two angles. He whipped Halo towards the creature in the air, cracking it in the chest, but the other creature took advantage and swatted Deva away with his claw, leading him to be knocked down away from Laney. The creature slammed on the shield once before Patrick came right back at it. He leapt over to the creature, molded, and threw a disc hard at the creature, but it missed badly. *That was the plan?* Deva thought as he reached the creature. He dodged another wicked slash, then connected with a powerful right hook as the other creature appeared behind to strike. Before it could, the disc Deva threw earlier came back like a boomerang and sliced through the creature's arm before it could swipe. Deva dodged a slash from the creature in front as he leapt up and tied Halo around its neck, yanking hard. Deva could feel the burning on the creature's neck, and with a vigorous shake, the creature freed itself from Deva's strangle. Deva landed by Laney who was still safe inside her shield. Deva tried once again to get her out of there and back to Building Blocks but it didn't work. He looked over to Sal.

"These things can't beat me Sal"

"Then more *things*...should join the party" Sal replied as the two bat creatures next to him started vibrating and contorting their bodies. Deva looked on as the creatures began growing and expanding, inflating like balloons. The creatures continued to grow, looking as if they were going to pop until they broke off completely into two more creatures. Deva looked on seeing four creatures standing around Sal, growling, showing their sharp teeth, but hiding their claws. Sal stepped out in front. "They have an army Patrick... you have a rope"

"Yeah? Where are they?" Deva said to Sal who backed down a bit. "Without Laney, there is no army, only you and some... scouts," Deva acknowledged and pointed at the bat creatures. He watched as Sal's reaction turned to anger.

Sal looked over to the creature on his left, staring up at its large black eyes and terrifying snout. "Go," he said as all four creatures raced towards Deva.

In anticipation, Deva broke off Halo and formed two medium-sized swords. He held them firmly in hand and charged straight ahead at the group of creatures.

Alex, hiding behind a tree, realized this might be their moment. *Patrick is sure to cause a big distraction,* she knew as she looked over to the other officers, giving them a nod. They started moving closer to the cabin using the wood line as cover.

Deva and the creatures collided out in front of the cabin. Deva dodged three consecutive strikes from the creatures and retreated to open space. He wasn't able to attack with them coordinating and watching each other's backs. As he landed away, two of the creatures leapt to him as well, ready for an attack. Deva blocked one of the attacks with his sword, then jumped away from another incoming stab. He landed behind a creature, catching it unguarded. Patrick thought of attacking, but as he did, another creature came from behind and slashed out. Deva turned in time and blocked with both of his swords, but a second swipe was unguardable, as he was sliced on his elbow. He took the cut, then leapt away towards Laney, clutching his arm. *They aren't allowing me to attack,* he worried.

"They are connected through sight. Nothing you do will go unnoticed" Halo said inside Deva's head, guiding him.

"Yeah that makes sense," Deva said aloud. *Well, what can I do?* Deva wondered, then waited for an answer from Halo. It took a moment longer than Deva thought it should but Halo guided him justly.

"Take away their sight" Halo instructed.

Immediately understanding what that meant, Deva turned around to peek at Alex and the rest of the officers, trying to let them know it was time. Looking at the creatures, Deva molded and stabbed a large piece of Halo into the ground like a spear. Still watching the creatures and Sal, Deva noticed the top of the spear began to light up, getting brighter and brighter. The creatures put up their arms to shield themselves from the attacking light, as did Sal.

When Deva was completely covered behind the light, he cracked off two pieces and formed two medium sized swords. He folded them behind his back, hiding them from sight and gathered his energy into his legs. He jumped as high as he could, leaping over the bright lights looking down to the cabin and his enemies. They still haven't moved or noticed him jump as he reached his apex and began to fall quickly. Deva prepared himself for the fall, and what's to follow. *This has to be perfect,* he understood as he plunged down and landed right in front of the two creatures on the right. They took notice quickly but it was too late. Deva reached up and punched the two Halo swords right through both creatures' heads, catching them cleanly. The creatures fell back and Deva gathered himself while landed, then slung Halo around both creatures to his left. They were slow to react and both got tethered inside the rope. While it burnt their skin, Deva tightened his grip and pulled them, swinging them through the air. They crashed away on the ground before Deva looked back towards Alex and the others.

"Go now! Get them both!" Deva yelled before leaping off towards the creatures.

Alex and the others sprinted towards the cabin, drawing their weapons as they reached Sal. Alex was the first to run up on Laney, who was now out from inside the shield. She knelt beside Laney and inspected her for injury. "You okay?" she asked.

Laney nodded as Officers Jeffers and Stix ran up to Sal pointing their weapons.

"Down on the ground! Now!" Officer Jeffers yelled.

"Now!" Officer Stix screamed while looking over to Deva and the creatures in the distance.

Sal didn't respond or move. He slowly brought his hands up as if he was giving up. He watched the officers then glanced at Laney.

"Go get the boy Kenny, I'll watch him," Officer Jeffers said.

Officer Stix shook off the nerves and began to take orders. He walked over to the porch stairs. Officer Jeffers pointed her pistol attentively at Sal, who was calm and unnerved. Her attention momentarily slipped as a big explosion rocked the field where Deva was. Sal took advantage and unleashed a new dangerous power of his own.

"You get down on the ground" Sal ordered as he turned his palms to the ground.

Officer Jeffers dropped her gun and fell to her knees as Officer Stix slowly fell on the stairs and then descended, crashing to the ground. Alex saw this and rushed over and raised her gun. Sal noticed and put her under pressure too. She fell abruptly to the ground, on all fours. She could see behind her that Laney was being affected too. It's as if Sal was changing the gravity on earth. Alex watched slowly flattening out to the ground, as the others laid stuck to the ground. Sal started moving closer to Laney, his grin and persona became increasingly deranged as he stomped over. Alex struggled her hardest to free herself from the weight by pushing against the ground, but Sal noticed and looked down at her emotionless. He bent down to speak with her.

"You know officer...he only brought you into this because he wanted someone else to take the blame... when things go... very...badly," Sal finished as he turned to Laney. Walking over he reached Laney and knelt to her. "And you, you have no idea what's in that subconscious of yours," Sal said as he rubbed Laney's head. He lowered himself down to her ear and whispered. "Do you want to find out?"

Laney cried out, unable to move, frozen from panic and the weight that was pressing down on her. Sal looked up to the sky and located the moon as he turned back to Laney.

"Bella notte per questo" He said, exhaling.

Sal grabbed Laney and stood. She's turned into a backpack as Sal threw her over his shoulder and walked towards the cabin. Officer Jeffers and Stix could barely open their eyes from the weight and Alex could only watch as Sal reached the bottom steps. She couldn't move or talk, but she was not helpless. Alex shut her eyes and took a breath, she opened them and shot her attention at Sal. Sal precipitously stopped on the middle step and he staggered a little before dropping Laney down on the last step. She hit the bottom and rolled off then stood up and ran over to Alex as she got back to a knee. They grabbed each other's hands and ran over to the others before Alex turned back to Sal. She raised her gun and opened fire. Just as she did, the gravity of Jupiter was one again pressed down upon them. They hit the ground hard as their upper bodies folded over whatever limb was in the way. Alex squinted at Sal who was clutching the side railing of the porch, she could see blood on his hands and the railing. He slowly stumbled toward them. Alex thought again for a solution. *Okay, I'll just try again.* She looked at Sal and prepared. Before she could start a white blur came from above landing on top of Sal. Alex looked through squinted eyes, and caught a glimpse of Deva connecting with a kick into Sal's chest, sending him backward. The weight lifted as they all worked to stand up. Deva turned to them all.

"What are you doing? Get them out of here!" He said as he helped Alex to her feet.

"That guy has powers too, it's paralyzing," Alex retorted, getting fully to her feet.

Deva didn't give Sal a second thought, he looked off to the distance from where he came from, then back to the group.

"Those things keep coming, no matter how many I take out. Get Laney out of here. I'll get Conner and catch up… we have to make it out…of the woods" Deva said through a heavy breath.

"Okay," Alex said, grabbing Laney by the hand and running off.

The other two officers followed closely behind. Officer Stix tripped over his foot and tumbled to the ground. He scrambled to his feet quickly and bolted off. As he did, he looked up to catch sight of a creature to his left, coming straight for him. The creature took a great wide stride and leapt for Officer Stix. It drew its claws back and stabbed forward with furious precision. Officer Stix had no time to scream or move, only able to close his eyes. Expecting to be slashed in the face or body, he prepared himself to die. He awaited his fate but only heard a loud buzzing, and the faint sound of a struggle. After an excruciating five seconds, he opened his eyes to inspect his life. He saw no injuries and scanned for the reason why and saw Deva struggling with a creature on the ground. He looked around and saw nothing else, only the others running away. His eyes returned to Deva who was on his feet. Deva spun to Officer Stix.

"Run Kenny!"

Officer Stix snapped to the ready and took off towards the others at a life-saving speed. Deva focused back to the creature that laid on the ground as it slowly got to its feet. Gathering its long gangly limbs, it leapt towards Deva. Deva readied himself for the creature in front, not realizing another one was ready to strike at the same time. The creatures were too quick and caught Deva helpless. He attempted to block both but instead opened himself up better for both attacks. The creature from head-on slashed through Deva's shield and pierced his torso as the other creature connected with a kick to Deva's other side, sending him barreling through the field. As he slid backward, and before Deva could gather himself, the creatures were already on top of him. Deva formed a small shield in time but got sent soaring backward even more from the sheer force behind the creature's swings. He rolled back from the momentum, and was finally able to land on his feet, he placed a hand on the ground to stay upright. *These things are relentless,* he thought, before pushing off the ground and looking over to the cabin. *I have to hurry,* he thought.

He stood up fully. *It's time to get loud,* he thought as he formed two discs and placed them in his palms. He took a deep breath and looked to the sky quickly before returning to the bat creatures. He charged them both and jumped high in the air. Midway up his ascension, he fired down two beams from his Halo-powered palms. The blasts landed and caused a loud and destructive explosion. Deva landed on the ground still watching the impact, he looked through the chaos of smoke, dust, and dirt and waited for movement. *I hit one square in the chest, I know it. And the explosion must have gotten the other one,* Deva worked out.

Deva started jogging toward the cabin, still watching the cloud of dust. From behind him, he heard the rustling of movement and turned around to one of the creatures lunging at him from out of the smoke. It's in bad shape, yet it still looked menacing. Deva raised his palm towards the incoming creature and with one push of energy, Deva's hand cocked back and sent another blast right into the creature's chest, leaving only a hollow circle. The creature fell back dead as Deva looked on for clarification that it was dead, before he turned towards the cabin. *It won't be the last one,* he knew.

He jogged over to and reached the steps, stopping to look over to where he kicked Sal. *Where did you go, Sal?* Deva wondered.

Upon entering the cabin Deva saw Conner laying on the wood floor. Deva reached Conner and inspected him for any damage.

"Conner?... Conner hey? you ok?" Deva pleaded as he shook Conner a little to get him awake. "C'mon, hey wake up. You're going to be fine , okay," Deva said as he lifted Conner.

Conner seems fine physically but he wasn't waking. Deva walked with him in his arms outside and started running in the group's direction, moving quickly through the woods. *This is going well,* his mind told him, but inside, in his head, he felt different. Something just felt wrong, he couldn't shake the feeling. He reached the wood line and continued striding through the forest ground towards Laney and the others.

I hope they're okay. I hope...she's okay.

Chapter 31

Deva glided through the forest ground, and wondered what was to come. The feeling of emptiness and apathy clouded his mind, as he tried to plan for the worst. Holding Conner on his shoulder, he continued through the forest, hoping it was in the right direction. He stopped running and scanned the twilight forest for any sign of his comrades. Spinning in circles, Deva saw only duplicates of everything from the dizziness, and nothing else. Panic-stricken, he burst off in the direction he thought was right, through the forest he went, worrying more and more with every step. *Where are they?* He thought.

Deva picked up the pace, having hoped to cover as much ground looking as possible. With still no sight of anything, he paused to collect himself and think. He focused on his breath and closed his eyes to listen. After a few silent moments, he heard something moving. Above him in the trees, were sounds of branches moving and breaking. He opened his eyes to find the source and located it high above. Deva made out a smaller bat creature traveling high in the tree, as it slung from branch to branch. *Must be going to Laney,* Deva figured. He followed closely, staying a safe distance away to not alert the small creature high above. He quickly picked up the pace upon hearing gunshots way ahead. Deva moved full speed along the ground, holding Conner tightly over his back. He kept an eye out for the creature above for any sudden moves. He heard more gunshots before finally locating Officer Jeffers, who was leaning against a tree. Deva bolted over to her, grabbing her attention, she raised and pointed her gun at him, almost firing a few bullets into his chest. Luckily, she restrained herself when she saw him and lowered her weapon. Officer Jeffers slid further down the tree onto the ground. Deva could see blood running down her head over her eye. She's a little banged up, but could still move. Deva set Conner down next to her.

"Officer Jeffers, where are the others?" He asked.

"They're around here somewhere" She responded, clutching her elbow.

"What happened?"

Officer Jeffers winced and sighed out. "We got ambushed by one of those monsters, god I hope Kenny is okay"

"Can you stand up? We have to go find them" Deva asked as he circled around to help her up.

Officer Jeffers slammed her palm into the tree to force herself up, Deva lended a stable hand to help. She walked gingerly around the tree, as Deva grabbed Conner holding him at his chest. Deva and Officer Jeffers walked through the open area, where she said they were ambushed in the dark area of the woods.

"Are they okay though? What happened?" Deva asked.

"It...came from above. It was heading straight for me and the girl" Jeffers' shook her head before continuing. "Kenny stepped out in front, and pushed us away, he got hit pretty bad. I got pushed away, Alex and the girl must have run off with Kenny. They shouldn't be far" Jeffers answered before starting to pick up her pace through the forest.

After a few minutes of no sight, they heard gunfire and scrambled up the hill. As they ascended, Halo gave another warning of incoming danger as the smaller bat creature waited to strike from the treetops. Deva heeded the warning, and knew the attack would likely come from above. His eyes searched the treetops when he saw the target hanging from the tree branches. Deva caught up to Jeffers and handed Conner off to her.

"Keep going, I'll keep that thing away" Deva instructed.

Officer Jeffers lifted Conner over her back and trudged up the hill, determined to make it out of the woods alive.

Deva turned and saw the creature in a better light now, as a sliver of light landed onto its body. Smaller in mass, stature, and having shorter limbs, Deva knew it would probably move quickly. Deva recognized its climbing speed in the trees. A speed that he had trouble keeping up with earlier. The creature swung off the branch, propelling it into another before it sprang off down towards Deva. Deva quickly formed two discs from Halo and hurled them up at the creature, which quickly changed its course as it slammed into a tree and leapt off like a grasshopper. The discs sliced through the treetops high above, but Deva reversed them, bringing the glowing discs right back at the creature. It continued evading Deva's discs, leaping off trees and branches, as it continued evading. *That's right, keep moving,* Deva planned.

Deva turned away and watched Officer Jeffers reach the top of the hill, she paused and looked for any sign of the others. She apparently did as Deva heard her yell something from up on the hill. Deva rid himself of the discs and turned back to run up the hill. As he did, the creature scorched down and slammed into a tree near Deva. The creature moved smoothly and struck Deva before he could prepare himself, and sliced him on the leg, before it sprung off to another tree. Deva clutched his leg and watched the creature for a second before turning again to ascend the hill. He could feel the creature's pressure and presence, and even the small claws swiping at his heels as he lunged up the hill. Deva got cut once more and finally snapped from the constant annoyance and pain. Once at the top of the hill, the creature cut his back thigh and jumped away. Deva formed another disc and placed it into his palm. Deva turned up to locate the creature, getting a tiny look he fired a beam right up into the treetops cutting through at least two trees in its path. Deva couldn't see if he hit the small creature but presumed he didn't. He turned around and jogged up to Officer Jeffers and Conner, looking over both their shoulders as he arrived.

"Why did you scream? Are you okay?" Deva asked.

"I saw Alex up here a little way," Jeffers replied.

"Okay let's go," Deva said as he ushered Officer Jeffers forward. He checked his back often looking for that small creature to appear. He hoped it would because that thing has got him fuming.

They continued on and with no sight of the creature, Deva began to relax a little. Officer Jeffers caught sight of some human movement up ahead. "Look, there, behind the tree," she pointed out.

Deva scanned over to the tree and saw a pair of boots. With her weapon drawn and Conner on her back, Officer Jeffers rounded the tree with Deva to see who it was. Deva looked on and saw Officer Stix bleeding through the rag he was holding against his chest.

"Kenny, oh my god," Officer Jeffers said as she set Conner down softly. She began digging through her supply pack around her waist and applied more rags.

Officer Stix groaned lightly before he spoke through the pain. "It looks bad, but it's just...uhh a few...deep cuts" He said as he looked down at the dried blood on his hands. "I might just… bleed out... though"

Officer Jeffers lifted the blood-soaked rags off of his chest, and inspected the cuts. "You're still bleeding but if we keep pressure on it, it should stop"

"Oh good" Officer Stix mumbled.

"Where are Alex and Laney?" Deva asked him, who waited for the appropriate time to ask. His answer was quickly answered as they heard more gunfire nearby.

Without a word, Deva streaked off towards the gunshots. He began to jump from tree to tree using Halo and his momentum to propel him quickly. He landed on the ground from a big leap and caught sight of the small creature from earlier just up ahead. He looked ahead further to see Alex with her gun raised up at the creature. She cracked off a loud shot but missed as the creature leapt closer. Deva ran over. *No way,* he thought, as he launched another disc at the creature, followed by a lasso towards Alex. The disc nearly hit the creature, whose momentum was hurtling straight for Alex. The creature cocked its claw backward and sliced toward her as she cracked off another shot. The lasso wrapped around Alex, as Deva yanked her away from the creature just in time. She hit the ground while Deva leapt over to her defense. The creature retreated up high to a tree and glared down as Deva knelt down by Alex. Deva inspected her, seeing she was exhausted and dirty, but overall in a healthy condition. Her weary, adrenaline-filled eyes found Deva.

"What took you so long?"

"It's a big forest," Deva said, before shaking his head. "My powers are being affected here, I can't teleport or—" Deva mentioned before stopping to look above Alex's head, where her emotions usually showed but mysteriously were gone.

"Or what?" Alex asked.

Deva shook his head. "Never mind," he answered as scanned the trees and looked around. "Where is Laney? Is she okay?" He asked urgently.

Alex didn't answer, she only pointed forward, behind Deva. He turned around quickly and noticed Laney leaning up against a tree, unconscious. He sprinted over to her and fell to his knees, and inspected her face. He turned back to Alex.

"What happened to her?" He asked. "Is she okay?"

Alex sat up and pushed off the ground to get to her feet. She gingerly walked over to Laney and Deva. "She saved me somehow... I didn't see what happened but... I don't know," Alex said looking down at her.

"Alright," Deva said, staring down at Laney, feeling worried. "She seems okay for now... but we have to get out of here, Kenny over there needs help too"

"You really can't teleport us out of here?"

Deva shook his head again. "I can try again, but everything is... off"

"That's shitty news. At least we have everyone together though" Alex optimized.

Yeah, I guess we do, Deva thought as he looked around for any danger, peering over towards the almost set sun. He guessed another hour of visibility, probably less. Deva looked over to Alex.

"Let's go over to Kenny and Jeffers and get them moving. I'll carry Laney" Deva picked Laney up and followed Alex, as she limped back over to the others while watching for the small creature to show its ugly face. After no sight of the danger, they reached the other two, still by the tree. Alex lowered down to her knee to be by Officer Stix.

"Kenny...hey, you ready to get out of here?."

Deva couldn't see or feel her emotional state, but he could tell Alex felt guilty about Kenny's situation. Luckily for her, and unlikely for Deva, Officer Stix turned his emotions onto Deva. He looked up at Deva as he got to his feet with new energy.

"Great, we're all together...now can you please do something and get us out of here?"

Deva didn't answer, he watched as Alex and Officer Jeffers helped Kenny up from the base of the tree.

"Are you able to walk?" Officer Jeffers asked.

Kenny grimaced and clutched his chest as he got to his feet. He took a practice step as he put some weight down. His face showed pain but he gave a slight thumb up. "It hurts, but I can"

Officer Jeffers clutched Kenny and supported him as the group continued to walk through the forest.

"If we make it to that field up ahead, we should be in clear space," Alex told the group as they slowly moved forward. Deva hung in the back, watching and keeping guard. He knew he had to do the heavy lifting from here on out if they wanted to make it out safely. Deva looked over each one's bodies for any sign of emotions or worries, but still couldn't see anything. It began to worry him as he asked for guidance. *Halo, why can't I see their emotions anymore?*

He waited for an answer, but as usual, Halo stayed silent.

They continue forward, almost reaching the wood line that began a decent-sized grass field ahead. As a group, they reached the border of the field. Deva looked across, then turned around to check their backs. Everything was quiet, he knew enough about movies and TV, that when things seemed quietest, they were also the most dangerous. *I hope that's not true this time*, he thought as he looked out further. Halo confirmed his suspicions as he finally spoke up.

"They're making their stand here. You must fight Patrick"

He was about to reply to Halo when he noticed movement up ahead at the other end of the field. Walking towards them were Sal and three tall bat creatures. Deva could see that one of the creatures was already injured. *It must be one from before, then they aren't infinite after all,* he thought, as he slowly lowered Laney onto the ground behind a tree.

"Watch her, I'll be back soon," Deva said as he stood and walked out of the woods, into the field. With Alex and the others watching, Deva reached the middle of the field and squared up to Sal and his lanky goon creatures. Sal looked over to Deva with menace and anger in his eyes. His mouth opened.

"New plan, we're killing you first. Then we're going to finish him off" Sal said, referring to Officer Stix. "I'm taking the women cops to our own prison... then the girl," Sal said as his expression turned to a blank stare. "All the things you fear *amico mio*"

Deva shuffled his stance, letting Halo's glowing yellow rope unravel lightly to the ground. "Well bring it then!" Deva shouted.

Back over to the edge of the woods, Alex, Office Jeffers, and Officer Stix all watched with anticipation as both sides stayed passive before the inevitable crash.

"Do you think he's going to win?" Officer Jeffers asked Alex, never breaking eye contact from the upcoming battle ahead.

"I hope so" Alex responded quietly. Just as she spoke, her attention was caught by the movement below her. Laney started to blink and twist as if waking from an afternoon nap.

"Laney? hey wake up," Alex said, as she touched Laney's shoulders gently.

Laney twisted on the ground before her eyes began to open, she looked up over her surroundings in confusion before seeing Alex above her.

"Hey Laney...you're okay now," Alex said as she and Officer Jeffers helped her sit up.

"What happened?" Laney asked groggily.

"I was going to ask you the same thing. You saved me earlier" Alex responded.

Laney's expression went from confusion to concern rather quickly, as she looked away from Alex without answering. Her gaze shifted over to the field where she caught sight of Deva and the creatures. "What's happening?"

"We're almost out. We have Conner. We just need him to take these guys down so we're home free" Alex said, pointing over to Deva.

"We have to help him," Laney said in a panic while trying to stand up. She lost her balance and fell backward, Alex caught her before she could fall.

"Easy Rocky, he can take care of the rest...hopefully," Alex repeated, as she looked over the field. *Don't let us down kid*, she thought.

They all watched closely as both parties started to move. The creatures spread out slowly as they stared over at Deva. Sal took a couple of steps towards Deva too, seeming to be joining the fight this time. Deva cracked off some pieces of Halo on his waist and molded them into his palms. Holding a sword in each hand Deva walked towards Sal, keeping an eye on the separating creatures. Their coordination has proven difficult to defend in the past, so he must stay vigilant. Getting closer and closer Sal broke the silence.

"Arrivederci Patrick"

"That means goodbye!" Deva shouted. "I know that one"

Sal started running as the creatures all converged towards Deva. One by one the bat creatures took slices for Deva's head, but one by one they missed as Deva flipped through and above their strikes. Deva landed in a safe spot and struck back, whipping Halo at one of the creatures and snapped it in the face. It stumbled back as another one leapt for Deva, slicing down for his legs. Deva evaded the slice, and pushed the claws down into the earth. Deva slammed his fist down on the creature's head before jumping off it backward, landing in the grass. Deva hurled his sword right for the creature stuck in the ground, but before it could reach and punch through the creature's head, another creature took the sword right through it's own arm, shielding its terrifying comrade. From Devas left came another vicious swipe. Deva dodged most of it but was caught slightly on the elbow. He swung his sword for the creature but his momentum took him away as he came up short. The same creature landed and dove again with claws ready. Deva molded a shield quickly, blocking the attack. While he was busy holding off one, the other two blitzed over for the kill. The attacks were coming unnoticed as Deva held his ground about to be blind-sided.

"Behind you!" someone shouted.

Deva heard the warning and without looking or thinking, broke contact and leapt up high out of danger. He peered down as he ascended into the sky, seeing the two creatures airborne, jumping for him. He molded a disc into his palm and sent a powerful beam down at them. He connected with one, sending it crashing back down. The other reached its apex as Deva began falling. It grabbed hold of Deva as they started grappling. The creature gripped tightly, not letting go. Deva tried to free himself, but couldnt as they slammed back into the ground, causing a cloud of dirt and dust to consume the area.

"Patri—!" Laney managed to scream out before Alex covered her mouth, trying to keep her silent and safe. She put her finger to her lips, telling Laney to be quiet, as they both looked back through the disappearing dust. They heard crashing and a struggle behind the dust, and could finally make out Deva jostling claws and hands with a creature. It swung Deva off his feet and launched him backward. Deva slid on balance, before looking over his shoulder to Laney and the others. His moment was quickly interrupted by a quick slash on his thigh. He fell to a knee and looked for any sign of that little creature from earlier, knowing that was it. *Five on one? That's not good.* He thought as he scoped out the little creature landing far away in the field. He stood up and scanned the field. All of the creatures were staying still for the moment, keeping spread out so they could continuously attack Deva and defend each other. He knew blinding them won't work now, since they have such a wide field of vision. He planted his feet and attacked again. He picked one of the creatures out and charged. Two other creatures moved with him as they converged closer and closer. Deva rushed straight at the one in front, as two others came in sideways. Deva whipped the creature in front hard in the snout before turning to the others. Before they were able to reach, Deva fired off two bursts from his palms, connecting with one's upper arm. It crashed into the dirt, motionless, as the other creature avoided the blast and regained its balance on the ground. It leapt back at Deva, who turned, ready to swing his glowing sword. He pulled his arm back but was abruptly smacked hard in the side of his upper body, the attack completely caught him off guard. He felt the incredible force growing stronger and stronger over his body, as he was violently sent slamming into the ground, tumbling back across the field. He finally crashed to an end, and could feel the lack of strength and soreness in his body. Lying on his stomach he placed a palm into the ground and pushed his body over slightly before rolling over. He sat up and rubbed the dirt off his eyes and white soft pants. He glanced up, looking across the field. Seeing nothing, he started to worry. *Where did they go?*

"You're facing the wrong way, there behind you" Halo answered his worry.

Patrick flipped around seeing his enemies. "Oh okay, thank you so much for your help," Patrick said sarcastically, as he located the incoming danger.

One of the creature's approached Deva and kicked straight for his chest. Deva instinctively swiped the large claw-foot sideways and unloaded a vicious right hook through the creature's chest. The creature flipped backward and crashed to the ground behind Deva. He turned around to look but something tremendously heavy slammed down on him. He collapsed to his hands and knees, and looked up trying to see what was happening. He peaked up and saw Sal pointing his arm right toward him. *Alex did say he had powers now,* he thought as he tried his hardest to move. He flexed his muscles and slowly moved his arms up, swinging a leg up with. He squared up to a stand, fighting off Sal's gravity. Sal noticed that he was in trouble and slammed more weight onto Deva. It was no use as Deva held strong and began to stomp towards Sal. After a few steps, the weight suddenly vanished. Before Deva could leap off towards Sal, two creatures struck. Devas body wasn't prepared for the creature's attack as the two strikes landed perfectly.

Deva looked down, seeing at least four long claws buried into his shoulder and leg. One of the creatures pulled its claws out as the other pulled him in the air. Using its sunk claw to lift Deva, it prepared to launch him. Deva screamed on the inside as the bat creature flung his body off, tossing him onto the ground.

After a few tense seconds, the group back in the woods began to worry. Alex held Laney tighter as they watched the creatures slowly converge toward the helpless Deva.

"Should we help him?" Officer Jeffers asked.

Alex sighed, unsure of what to say. She couldn't take a risk like that. The kids and her friends were already in tremendous danger; they had to prepare to run. She held Laney back as she looked for a way around.

"We're going to run for it," Alex said.

"Whhharhah!" Laney mumbled out from Alex's hand muzzle. Alex nodded at Officer Jeffers, who nodded back. Officer Jeffers hauled Conner over her shoulder, and helped Officer Stix up.

"On my signal," Alex said as she grabbed hold of Laney. She watched Deva, to see what fate had in store for him, ready to move.

Lying face down in the dirt, Deva regained his mental balance. He rolled over and looked to the sky. He knew he was in bad shape, but couldn't bear to inspect the damage. Deva watched the sky seeing a mix of orange and blue, with slight hints of purple and pink. *Must be sunset,* he wondered peacefully. Looking into the sky Deva saw the moving of the clouds above. They reminded him of emotions, the way they floated and swirled above people's heads. It's soothing, the way it could relax his mind, and ease any worries. *This isn't a bad way to die,* he thought.

Lying on the field, watching the clouds, Deva heard Sal barking out orders. The sound of his voice and intentions jolted Deva back within himself. Just as he did, another familiar voice called out.

"Destiny… is not in your favor," Halo predicted.

I am going to die, Patrick thought as he slowly began to relax into the idea.

"Grant me an opportunity to change that," Halo echoed though his mind.

Patrick closed his eyes. "What do you mean?"

"Give up and die… or find me" Halo offered.

Patrick relaxed into the idea. It's been a long couple of months, he was tired, tired of living, or tired of something else perhaps. He couldn't put it into words, but he feels depleted, depleted of the energy that fueled him each day. He's felt it slipping for a while. He imagined his emotions escaping his body, never to return the same way. *What would you do mom? Should I give up? ... Do I want to die?* He wondered.

He rested lifeless on the ground, sinking into his thoughts and his mind, being submerged without fighting back. He awaited his fate. "I'm sorry everyone" he whispered as he shut his eyes tightly, hoping to forget his troubles behind. Everything fell to black.

...But.

He opened his eyes, standing in a cold, dark, echoed area. Patrick rubbed his eyes making sure they were still there and working. He took a step and heard a slight splash of water, then the echo of drops that followed. He stopped a second, hearing the light splash before taking another one and heard another tiny drip. He leaned down to touch his knee. *It's there,* he felt. He took another step, then another, then another. He thought about running, but the sound of a familiar voice stopped him in his tracks.

"A gift"

Patrick spun around for any sight of Halo.

"Let me help you"

"What gift?" Patrick asked, still searching for anything besides darkness. He made another full turn before meeting himself as Deva, face to face. He looked into those familiar dark blue eyes, scanning the rest of the face, seeing what the outside world must-see in him.

"What is this?" Patrick asked.

"A gift" Halo's voice answered.

Patrick watched as Deva raised his arm, holding up his palm as if asking for a high five. A closed-mouth smile appeared across Deva's face, which should have been unsettling, but Patrick couldn't help but smile too, as he reached up towards Deva's hand. Lightly, Patrick pressed his hand into Deva's and with a sudden snap of fingers, he woke up.

"That wasn't so hard," Halo said.

Deva's eyes unfolded wide, as he heard incoming footsteps. His mind raced to catch up as he remembered everything from before. He slowly began to roll over as one of the creatures rampaged over, clawing out, to make the final strike. It leapt over and made a deadly stab at Deva's chest. But before Deva could even blink, he suddenly appeared mid-air, right behind the attacking creature. He watched as the creature swung at the dirt and dust, Deva left behind. *What is this?*

Deva thought as he slowly floated through the air, landing on the ground.

A gift, Deva answered within himself.

Deva looked angrily at the creature, and with barely a notion in his head, was already punching through the creature's back. He landed as the creature went tumbling across the field and crashed to a lifeless halt. Deva watched for movement but knew it was dead. *This is crazy.* Deva thought as he looked over to Laney and the others. Each of them is frozen with a mix of shock and surprise. His eyesight was caught by a glowing light coming from his chest and the rest of his body, which was now trimmed with the yellow glow. It glowed brightly in a stream of yellow up his legs and down his arms like veins. *A gift huh?* He thought.

He turned around to find Sal standing back with the two remaining bat creatures. Deva looked in between them, and again, before even he could follow his own movements, he smashed one of the creatures in the chest with his knee. Before he and the bat could land on the ground, Deva glanced at the other and appeared right behind it. He quickly impaled the creature straight down through its back with two long glowing spears. The spears cut through with ease as they pierced into the ground, leaving the creature still standing. Deva landed and glanced over to Sal, who was now visibly unnerved.

"Gesù Cristo," Sal murmured, starting to trip backward.

Deva watched as Sal decided to blink. In his blink, Deva disappeared.

Stumbling backward, Sal felt a hand press into his back, and without turning around, Sal challenged Deva.

"You certainly are special…but destiny is strange. It's the one… and… the only"

Deva stared at the back of Sal's head, resisting the urge to smash it into the ground. Before deciding what to do with Sal, Deva caught a quick glimpse of the small creature that was terrorizing him on the hill. Deva smiled with delight and with his full might and focus, burst straight for the creature, who was mid-air and helpless when Deva arrived with a quick slice of his own. The creature smacked the trees in two separate pieces as Deva quickly appeared back behind Sal. Deva lifted him and threw him high into the air. Sal screamed as he free fell to the ground, crash landing into the dirt. *That should get my point across,* Deva thought as he looked at Sal rolling around on the ground.

Deva turned and walked back towards the others, who all came out from the woods to meet him. Laney ran up and jumped on Deva's leg. Deva bent down and gave her a hug in return.

"We thought you were uh…K-I-A," Alex mentioned.

Deva stayed silent and nodded.

"What is…and was…all of that?" Alex asked, waving her hand over Deva's glowing trim.

Deva looked over to her hand, hovering over his arm. "A gift," he answered, as he visualized reaching out for his own hand for guidance.

"We barely saw you move, that was incredible," Officer Jeffers said.

"Yeah nice work" Officer Stix said, as he held a thumb up.

Laney tugged down on Devas leg, drawing his attention.

"Are they all gone?"

Deva looked up to scan the area, seeing the creatures lying on the ground lifeless, but Sal wasn't where he landed anymore. Deva figured he must be crawling away like the cockroach he was. Deva looked back to the group. *They all look so tired.* Deva knew as he looked to Conner who was leaning up against a tree behind them.

"Yeah… they're all gone… it's over, we won," Deva answered. "Let's go home"

"Can you teleport now?" Alex asked.

Deva reached for Halo and molded a large flat portal in front of the group. Alex slowly reached for the portal. She looked at Deva before pressing her hand through, but once again the portal was solid.

"Damn it!" Alex said. "Now we have to walk"

"Owwwhhhhh!" Officer Stix moaned.

"Kenny," Alex said sharply, ready to make fun of him before realizing the shape he was in. "It won't be that long, we'll get you out of here"

"Okay," Kenny groaned.

Alex looked over to Officer Jeffers. "Okay, Jeffers you get Conner…I'll help Kenny," Alex said as she began walking over. Officer Jeffers walked away as Laney followed to help, Alex paused to look at Deva.

"Are you sure you're okay?"

Deva froze for a moment before mumbling back that he was okay. Alex nodded and stared intently.

"You should get Sal, we don't want him getting away…break his legs or something" Alex walked away, leaving Deva alone.

Deva turned around but didn't leap, jump, glide or move. He was frozen in thought again. *Am I okay?* He wondered as he looked at his white-clothed palms. He began walking over to where Sal probably crawled off too and after seeing no sign of Sal, the walk turned into a jog, as he began to get anxious. Deva finally saw a figure lying down on the ground thirty yards ahead. Deva got closer and looked over, knowing it was Sal for sure. Deva walked up drawing Sal's attention.

"You got me good" Sal said through obvious back pain as the words barely made it out.

"It's over Sal. You'll be going to prison now, just like we talked about…probably have to stop at the hospital first" Deva knelt by his side to look at him closer. "You won't be causing any more trouble, and you won't be touching Laney"

"A…fortuitous night" Sal managed to say before coughing. He caught his breath as Deva began to tie him up with pieces of Halo. "There…are no accidents," Sal said weakly.

Deva flipped Sal around and picked him up by the back, hauling him like a briefcase as he began to walk back towards the others. He got a few feet before his body froze up again. He could feel it, the tingling in his spine, the weight of something urging and pushing him forward. He planted his feet to balance himself. *I've felt this before*, he thought. The uneasy feeling overflowed and consumed his entire essence, mind, body, and soul. He took a few stumbling steps backward, hoping to get away from the feeling. Sal must feel it too, as he spoke out again.

"What a strange development, ragazzino"

Deva heard him, and let go of his grip, letting Sal slam into the ground face first.

"Is this?" Deva asked rhetorically.

"Yes it is!" Sal responded quickly and loudly. "Call it a… contingency"

"What? you planned this? You planned on that thing coming?"

Sal chuckled. "Better get your girl"

Deva picked Sal up and jogged back over to the others. On his run, he noticed the dark emotions slowly fogging over the forest ground, moving and creeping towards the others, he looked over to see the

225

others prepared for departure. They all seemed anxious as well as if they could also feel what he's feeling. Only Laney seemed calm.

"Laney, hey you alright?" Deva asked as he lowered her level. The others took notice and surrounded her.

"How do you guys feel?" Deva asked the group.

One by one they say they feel weird, leading Deva to worry even more. He turned back to Laney.

"Okay, let's get moving" He picked her up and began walking towards Sal. He walked back towards the way they came in as the others followed closely.

"Alex, how long until we're out of the woods?" Deva asked, sounding worried.

"I would say forty minutes, give or take"

Deva nodded, as he continued walking.

"What's going on? Are we not clear out of danger yet?"

"No...not yet" Deva answered as he looked over his shoulder.

"What is it?" Alex asked.

"Let's just keep going so you never have to find out."

After thirty minutes of Deva and the others walking through the forest on pins and needles, and the growing worriedness of Deva spilling over, they realized they were close to the edge. Deva hurried the group through, before dropping Sal and trying for a portal again. After a failed attempt Deva looked to Sal.

"Sal what did you do? Let my powers work"

"We never did anything," Sal answered.

"Well then why can't I get it to work"

Sal rested his head on the ground. "I think you know why"

Deva snapped too, realizing he did understand. He understood and knew that they had to get out of there. The feeling was stronger now, it was right on top of him, he could feel it, and Laney could feel it too. She nestled her head into Deva's shoulder, trying to hide. He held her tight as he forced himself to walk forward. He put his head down and gingerly walked towards the others. "We have to hurry up," Deva said, strolling upon them.

"Yeah yeah...we're close," Alex said in return, not enjoying Deva's sudden secrecy. "I really wish you'd share what kind of danger we're in."

Deva looked around before answering. "Trust me, you don't." He said, sensing the beginnings of something sinister.

The colors and landscapes around him began to change. An unconsciously colorful world has turned into a solemn and dreary atmosphere. Deva looked around seeing colors, yet he couldn't truly feel and consume them. Holding Laney, he trudged forward, hoping to god that they would make it out. The heavy dark fog began to float over the forest ground, building up to a point where Deva could barely see the others. Alex and the others were quiet, but they were there, staying close. Their terrified silence started getting to Deva too. He couldn't see a foot in front of him and has lost all sense of direction. They were sitting ducks in the middle of an open space, waiting to be attacked. Deva pulled out Halo and tried to lighten the area up to see. The light did not help much, only illuminating the fog, like a blizzard. Deva's knees began to feel weak, as his lips quivered. *This is all my fault;* he thought as he looked at the others. Though they couldn't tell, Patrick's expression was one of terror, he was completely helpless. Deva felt Laney squeeze tighter, bringing Patrick out of his mind. He felt a tug on his arm.

"C'mon...we're moving this way." He heard Alex say quietly as she pulled his arm with. Deva followed the group, unable to see, or even feel, and after a few minutes, the group stopped.

"Uhh what is that?" Officer Jeffers asked quietly.

"It's a person I think," Officer Stix replied.

Deva walked closer and closer to their voices until he saw them. He walked around the ground to the end with Laney tucked into his chest. Ahead of them he saw that the fog had spread out and cleared ahead before them. Deva focused at the end of the parted fog, a figure standing like Moses himself, parting the red sea. Patrick immediately lost himself at the sight of the familiar figure, the one who caused him so much pain and rue in the recent past. Deva hoeld Laney and stared at the skinny lean dark figure, waiting for it to move. The dark figure didn't seem to be looking at them, Patrick could see its head turned sideways, looking motionlessly at the ground. It almost seemed to be sleeping. *Or waiting,* Deva thought.

"Who is that guy?" Alex asked, only seeing a tall, dark figure through the fog.

Deva stepped over to where he heard Alex's voice. He touched her shoulder, getting her attention. "Watch her again, okay?" he instructed, as he set Laney down on her feet in between Alex and Officer Jeffers. He stepped through them and walked ahead, staring straight at the looming dark mummy.

"What are you doing?" Alex asked.

Deva didn't answer. He continued to move away.

"It's the mummy," Laney whispered.

Alex looked over to Laney in surprise, then looked back to Deva.

Deva watched, as he planned his attack. *He's human,* Deva heard Halo's words echo in his voice. The words quickly popped into his head, as he slowly stepped towards the mummy.

"I don't care, I won't go back," Deva said out loud as he brought up Halo. He snapped off a piece and moulded Halo into a disc. He held the disc tightly as he stared at the creature. *Should be an easy target,* he thought.

He flipped the disc in the air before flinging it hard, square at the mummies head. Deva decided to go for the kill with the first shot. The disc screamed through the fog quickly as it approached the unflinching mummy. Deva watched as the disc was set to decapitate it. The mummy didn't look or move much, it tilted its head down, causing the disc to narrowly miss. The disc flew away as Deva focused and summoned the disc back, sending it back at the mummy, but again without leaving its feet, or even trying, it bent away from the sharp disc. Deva caught the disc as it returned to him. He cracked off another piece, before molding and launching two discs this time, spinning through for its head. The mummy slowly turned its face towards the discs as they spun straight for it. Through the bandages on its face, a mouth appeared. Before the discs could slice through, the mummy let out a high-pitched, throat-ripping scream. The discs disappeared into the mummies mouth, as it slowly turned and faced the group. Its mouth disappeared back into the bandages, as its seemingly full attention was now put on the group. Deva, sensing the mummy about to strike back, molded another disc into his palm. He brought his hand up pointing towards the mummy and started building up the energy into his fist. His progress was quickly suppressed, as he felt his leg being wound up by something. Before he could bring his leg up to see and free himself, he was yanked off his feet. He fell to the ground, being covered in the thick fog. The pressure on his leg yanked him again, then launched him across the woods slamming through a few trees.

Alex watched Deva get tossed as she stepped in front of Laney.

"Step back," Alex said

The group listened and began to move backward. Alex stepped forward and drew her gun, pointing it at the mummy firmly. She fired off six shots at the mummy creature, yet it felt like she was shooting blanks. The mummy did not move or flinch as she began to step back towards the others to get them to run. Keeping her eyes glued on the mummy, she got by the others. The mummy expanded outward, it's bandages shot out from behind its body, heading straight for Alex. The explosion of movement startled her as she tripped and fell to the ground. She scrambled up and turned to the others. It was too late though as the bandages wrapped around her body, immobilizing her. She's raised off her feet and screamed for help as the bandages cover her mouth and head. Through the bandages, she managed to see out, and caught a glimpse of the others lying on the ground unconscious. As she wondered what happened to them, she was pulled high across the forest towards the mummy. It brought her face up to its own, inspecting her ominously. Alex screamed again as she caught sight of the mummy's features up close. She saw the bandages wrapped around his head and shoulders were filthy as if they've never been washed. Its lean, muscle less body hung in the air, barely holding itself together. It silently stared back as its head slowly rolled back and away. Alex stared terrified at what's to come. It snapped forward, startling Alex. It opened its mouth and let out another agonizing screech. Alex screamed with it, as she slowly lost consciousness. The mummy halted its scream and unravelled its bandages from around Alex's body. It set her on the ground to her knees and released its hold on her and moved away. Kneeling lifeless on the ground, with her eyes open and a blank dead stare, Alex re-lived her most troubling memory. Images of a small town's water tower and a church haunt her psyche. Her mind was as paralyzed as her body. She ruminated in her past and began to lose the pieces of herself that might never return.

Away from the group, Deva muscled himself up. There's less fog where he was at, so he figured the mummy has some sort of range. Following the fog, he jogged back towards the others, hoping they're all still alive. He arrived to catch sight of the mummy creature, with floating bandages around it. He watched the long, creepy mummy in horror, as it approached something. *Is it Laney?* he wondered. *Is this the moment I was feeling?*

He caught sight of Alex kneeling over, as his breathing became unsteady. He watched the mummy inch closer and closer to Laney, not knowing what to do. Anxiety and a lack of a plan caused Deva to yell out to act on instinct.

"HEY!" he screamed.

The mummy stopped, its skeleton-like body cracked and contorted to face Deva.

It worked! Deva thought.

The mummy stood with its back hunched over, remaining motionless, as its attention became fixed onto Deva. Its legs cracked and snapped as it began to lurk forward slightly. Taking a few very menacing steps forward, Deva instinctively stepped back. The mummy is in his head, figuratively and literally. *Shit.... What now?* He thought as he looked around to see all of his fallen friends. He saw behind the mummy creature that Laney had started to roll around, surely regaining consciousness. It was a bittersweet sight for Deva, now he knew he had to do something. A notion suddenly popped into Deva's head. *The gift...How could I forget?*

Deva stared at the mummy through hazy eyes as he focused his anger and his strength, building it up to strike. At first, nothing happened, but with a little more force, the trim on Devas suit lit up once more. The glowing yellow light illuminated the area around him, lighting it up like an industrial lamp. Along with clearer vision in the forest, his mind felt sharper as well. The cloudiness began to fade away as he started to visualize smacking that thing as hard as he could. As he readied his stance and focused on his charge against the mummy, Deva caught sight of Laney crawling over to Alex. The mummy stayed fixed on Deva as it continued to ease closer and closer. Deva took one last look before he decided to attack. He imagined zooming across the field, and as he did, he just as quickly appeared next to the mummy ready to strike. The mummy had not noticed any movement, as its head was completely unguarded. With his entire heart and soul, Deva cocked his arm back and unleashed a punch toward the dark creature's head. Completely blindsided, the creature slid backward a few feet, dodging the blow. Deva landed and quickly went at it again, appearing behind the mummy with his hands clasped, he drew back and slammed his fist down on the creature, making contact. Deva put his full might into the blow, yet the mummy barely moved. The mummies head lifted slightly, coming to Deva's level who fell to the ground. An eerie feeling came to Deva as he disengaged and leapt back. *Jesus, what now?* He thought, worried.

Deva looked around for Laney but didn't see her. He snapped back to focus on the mummy. He formulated a plan that mixed all of his other attempts, hoping this time will be a charm. He molded a disc quickly into his palm and built up his energy. He stared over, waiting for his opening. The mummies head cracked, as it quickly snapped sideways. It began to stagger forward weakly, looking like a deer fawn learning to walk. Deva moved. *Now!* he thought, as he beamed over to the mummy, appearing above. As he did, he instantly noticed the horrible sight of the bandages floating around him. *Was it a trap?* He thought, and before he could fire his palm blast straight through the mummies head, its bandages circled over his arms and legs. Deva struggled to free himself, tugging and jostling with the bandages, but it was no use, the bandages had him completely immobilized. He watched as the mummies head cracked and tilted sideways. With the bandages beginning to loosen upon its face, they slowly began to fall off its head and down its chest and shoulders. Before Deva could accept his fate once more, or beat himself mentally about failing again, the bandages covered his head. Once again sending him into that familiar, warm, kind darkness.

Chapter 32

Patrick arrived on a warm and sunny day, feeling like himself. The smell of freshly cut grass overloaded his sense of smell, as he laid comfortably stretched out in warm, thick grass. Looking up to the baby blue sky, Patrick moved his head and squinted his eyes, trying to adjust to the light. He sat up and took a look at what was around him. Seeing his childhood backyard and then the back porch, he looked at all the windows that covered the backside of the house, and the plants hanging from the railings. He stood up to take it all in. *It's a beautiful day today*, he thought.

Just like the day mom died...

Just leave her alone... let her rest, he wanted as he stared up to the large window covering the left side of the house, knowing well that terrors await inside. He felt his heart begin to beat faster and heavier from his chest, with one step at a time he began to walk. His bare feet were hugged from the hot grass with each step, as he walked around to the front door. He stopped to look at the landscape of rocks, hastas, pots, and tiny trinkets that covered the front porch area. He stayed and reminisced about how good she was at landscaping. Their yard was immaculate, with no weeds or bare spots, and her gardens were overflowing with beautiful floral arrangements. *She was good*, Patrick remembered warmly.

He walked to the front steps and ascended the stairs with no second thoughts. Only when he reached the front door did he hesitate. This last step was the hardest. He closed his eyes to sulk in his sadness, before moving forward up the stairs. Beginning to water, Patrick's eyes found the door handle. He pulled the handle down and opened the door with a slight push. With fearful eyes and an aching body, he stepped through the threshold and side-eyed the living room, looking nervously for the hospice bed. His side-eyeing of the living room quickly snapped to his full attention, as he saw something else entirely.

Patrick stood in the foray looking into the eyes of his mother, Maria, who was sitting in the corner rocking chair. Patrick stared over stunned, not because it was her, but because of the way she looked. *She looks good, she looks...like herself.* Over the last twenty-some months, Patrick must have forgotten what she looked like before she was diagnosed, and began treatment. Because here and now, she looked like the version he had always remembered, and it was warmley jarring. Patrick walked around the half-wall into the living room as Maria sat un-rocking in her rocking chair, smiling lovingly up to Patrick as he stepped closer. He stopped a few feet in front of her and looked down skeptically with his red puffy eyes.

"So what's this then?... another opportunity for torture?"

Patrick watched Maria's face change appropriately into a look of concern.

"No... that won't ever happen to you again. I promise" she said.

Patrick lost his wind. *That's her voice,* he remembered. "So what then?"

Maria smiled brightly and through forming tears answered her son. "A gift Patrick"

Patrick melted at the sound of his name. All of the doubt and fear he has felt was on the verge of floating away.

"This is a gift" she repeated quietly.

Shaking on his feet from the influx of emotions, Patrick began to feel uneasy. "It's really you?" he asked before beginning to lean off balance.

Maria shot up from her chair and caught him before he leaned over to the ground, and pulled him up into a hug.

"Yeah it's really me sweetheart," she said before they both collapsed into their serene and thankful emotions, letting their tears and gratitude flow. Patrick shut his eyes tightly, trying to trap the feeling in his mind, forever ingrained.. For whenever he thinks of her, he'll have this moment to cherish. *What a gift,* he thought, as he squeezed tighter.

Maria eased up and cupped her hands around Patrick's wet, teary face. She smiled at him brightly as she scanned his face, trying to remember every tiny detail.

"I think you need to buy a razor," she said as she put her hand over his cheek.

Patrick smiled back. "It's kind of been the last thing on my mind lately"

She pulled her hand back from his face. "I know" she said with a sorry face. "And I'm so sorry you had to go through that."

"Me?... no mom... you were the sick one, you were the one fighting for their life... I was just—" Patrick said, stepping away to shake his head.

"And it meant the world to me that you were there... knowing you were with me, my whole world"

Patrick looked away and began to pace the living room floor, before turning back to her.

"Mom...the look in your eyes, you were so scared... you were so scared to die and I—... I couldn't—" Patrick said and began to shake his head lightly as the emotions started to escape through his breath. "I couldn't do it... and it broke my heart watching you like that"

Maria quickly paced back over to Patrick and wrapped her arms around him, holding his head in her shoulder as she comforted him. "I know sweetheart... it hurt me too, that's why I'm so sorry you had to go through that" She brought his head back around to look at him. "And I was scared of dying... it was scary, I won't shield you from that, but I was only scared to leave you... I was only ever thinking of you..."

Patrick's tears ceased as he heard his mother's words. She continued.

"I enjoyed every second I spent with you Patrick. Even the times you'd step on the plants in my garden with your clumsy feet"

Patrick laughed softly. "Yeah I guess I get a chance to apologize about that now"

Maria smiled as Patrick continued to remember. "Or that time I accidentally shot a firecracker while you were trying to saddle that horse"

"Accidently?" Maria asked.

"It was," Patrick laughed. "I was just as surprised as you were...but not as much as the horse," Patrick said as he began to grin.

Maria lightly punched his shoulder. "You jerk," she said with a smile.

Patrick's smile faded away as the thought of having to say goodbye again popped into conscious thought. Though a precious gift, it was one of fleeting nature.

"I have so many great memories with your mom... and I've missed you... so much. Life is so...lonely and bleak now. Honestly, it doesn't feel worth it sometimes" He said, as he closed his eyes, remembering what real life was like without having her alive. He knew he had that to look forward to.

"Patrick. I'm so sorry… and I've missed you so much too. But you need to be stronger than that… what happened to you… what happened to me… it shouldn't destroy two lives, Patrick. Please don't let it… promise me" Maria pleaded, visibly beginning to tear up too, as she put her hands on Patrick's shoulders.

Patrick stared back at his mom with shock and remorse. "I promise," he said before truly understanding her wish.

"Those memories that you and I cherish, Patrick. They are the light of my life. You were… and always will be, an *angel* to me" Maria said smiling through her happy tears. She reached up to comb through Patrick's hair.

"But there is room in this big head of yours for new memories…memories that you can look back on and cherish the way I do with you"

Hearing his mom rattled something loose in his head as he remembered his life. His life at Building Blocks, with the kids. His life at work, with Summer, maybe. The big dreams he once had for himself but lost. His life as Deva, as a superhero. He looked at his mom, taking in her beauty, still unable to believe she's here with him.

"There are some people I care about—" Patrick said and was going to continue before his mom cut him off.

"Then grab on to them and don't ever let go. Dive head first into what you love and make those memories that you'll hold forever. And then, and only then, can you rest. Be grateful for what we had together, Patrick, and be thankful for what you have…"

Patrick nodded to his mother as her words started filling him with inspiration and meaning. His spirit felt electric and his body tingled with energy. He raised his chin, in a show of strength, knowing it's what his mom wanted to see. She smiled in approval.

"That's exactly what I'd expect from a superhero," Maria said, poking him in the side.

Patrick's eyes got wide in disbelief. "What? No I'm not a—"

"Patrick, it's okay. I'm not upset" Maria replied with a smile.

"Really?"

Maria smirked happily at Patrick. "Really...I'm not. I am actually very proud. You always did have a kind heart. The world got lucky... you'll make a fantastic hero"

"Thanks mom," He said, smiling back. His facial expression turned to discomfort as he thought harder about his life as Deva. "It's hard though, I feel like every decision I make ends up bad" Patrick said, while slightly laughing at himself. "The people you want me to love and cherish, they've been the ones in danger"

Patrick paced over and sat down on the rocking chair. He folded his arms over his knees and hunched over in sadness.

"You put your life in danger too...don't ever forget that," Maria said as she walked back over to Patrick. She placed her hand on his head and ran her fingers through his hair.

"You have to be as kind to yourself as you are to other people, that's the meaning of your life sweetie...to love yourself the way you do others...with or without superpowers. And you know what babe" Maria said, as she tilted his head up. "You're the only one out there with the superpower to change yourself" Maria gave him a strong look of motherly love, which then turned into a smile. "And I believe in you. I think you'll find happiness...I think you'll continue to be a hero" Maria said as she placed her hand over his cheek. "My boy," she said, starting to tear up again. "And I think you'll save yourself too."

Patrick stood up and wrapped his arms around her. He closed his eyes to cherish the moment and melted into her arms, feeling like a kid again. Those words she said really hit the spot. They were the right amount of heart and inspiration. Exactly what he needed to hear. Maria was always good at the heart-to-heart moments, she never ceased supporting his wellbeing. She was his angel and an even better mother. Patrick opened his eyes. The moment grew in more beauty as Patrick watched the flight and flutter of a gang of butterflies above. He watched in complete bliss and peace, as the butterflies danced through the air around them. He slowly released his hug around his mother.

"Butterflies," Patrick acknowledged, drawing her attention to them.

Maria looked over to the dancing winged angels, and then back over to Patrick. With a loving smile, she gazed at him. "I think that means the gift has been received"

Maria walked back over to Patrick and wrapped him in another hug, she took a few deep breaths to prepare to say goodbye. With her arms enfolded around him, she did just that. "I love you so much, sweetie.

You're going to make the world a better place, no matter what you choose. And have faith that we'll see each other again."

Maria lightly punched his shoulder. "But until then...please love yourself too...okay?

"Okay," Patrick agreed, as nodded. He wanted to send her off in a strong way, a way they both could be proud of. He smiled at her as she slowly walked back towards the butterflies. She got to them as they scattered and flew out through the front door. Maria stopped before the front of the door and looked back to Patrick one last time.

"Mom," Patrick said. "I couldn't remember what the last thing you said to me was"

Maria smiled both with her face, and also her eyes. "It was always...I love you'"

Patrick smiled back. "I love you too"

Maria turned away and grabbed the door handle and pushed it open. She took a step-through, then stopped. She turned back to Patrick. "Take care of her too Patrick... I love you both"

Maria said as she stepped out the front door. Patrick watched her go the same way he did the first time, but this time it was different. This time he felt different, he felt lighter. The feeling of relief washed over him as he believed he had finally come to peace with himself. *I said goodbye,* he thought warmly.

He took one last look out through the door, seeing nothing but shrubs and the empty yard, and marched outside. He walked around the house, picked a spot in the grass, and tumbled down, stretching out his arms and legs through the thick warm grass. He folded his arms behind his head and stared up to the clouds, taking a deep breath. He stared up to the sky, knowing that his mom was looking back down at him. He shut his eyes and returned home.

She loves us both?

Chapter 33

"This is looking like your last night alive, kid!" Sal yelled out to Deva from the ground where he was anchored, "Exhaustion can make a coward out of a man" He said looking down at his own legs, which were more than likely broken. From where Deva tossed him, there was no way Sal was getting out of the woods by himself. "God damn kid messed with my life too much already...kill him!"

Sal watched as the mummy figure lifted its arm and the giant cocoon of dirty, dark bandages. Inside somewhere, Sal knew Deva was struggling for his life. Sal knew he wouldn't be walking out of the woods either, and was taking immense pleasure in that. He looked around at the others who were close by, and saw a female in dark blue leaning and staring lifelessly on her knees. He saw the other two officer's unconscious on the ground as well. *Where is the girl?* He thought, digging through his pockets to retrieve his cell phone. He inspected the screen and the back for damage. It seemed to be in good condition as he flipped open the phone, still hoping it wasn't broken. He scrolled through his contacts and made a call.

Deep inside the nest of dirty bandages, Deva struggled for freedom and movement, kicking and pulling, trying to dig and rip himself free. He struggled and muscled as hard as he could but seemed to get nowhere. Deva could feel the bandages wrapping tighter against him, clutching his wrists and ankles tightly. He stopped fighting to catch his mental breath and focused. He thought he could hear voices outside, someone yelling beyond his cocoon. He tugged on the nearby and unseen bandages and focused as hard as he could about blasting out of there. He swiped and kicked hard, trying to swim his way out. Every time he pulled a handful away, more filled its place. The frustration built up inside as Patrick began to clash with his thoughts. *This can't be it. Mom just said I was...* He remembered, as his breathing began to accelerate as the pressure of the bandages smothered against his cheeks and forehead. Chills ran through his spine and his fingertips as a wave of hopefulness eased his mind. He closed his eyes to take the feeling in, knowing he'll need it. He steadied his breathing, living in a few deep breaths and took one last mental moment. Following the last breath, Patrick screamed out and built the energy from within himself, trying for one last all or nothing grasp for life. He felt the bandages fighting for a hold, but releasing their pressure, slowly falling away. He continued fighting as the bandages began to clear his body cleanly. Without hesitation, Deva glowed brightly and jumped up, punching through the bandage cocoon. His fist and arm flew through the other side as his head and shoulders followed to fresh air. He gave out one last scream for life as he ripped his legs free from the mummy's clutches.

Deva slid back to the ground and instantly located the mummy creature. Deva ran straight for it, dodging and leaping away from the bandages that closed in again. He still couldn't get near the creature without having to avoid the protective bandages. *Let's get loud then,* Deva thought as he molded Halo into his palm and blasted a few loud yellow beams towards the mummy. One of them connected into the ground causing a loud crack, while the other collided into the mummies bandage defense. The bandages smothered the blast energy, making it disappear, and shot straight back at Deva, trying to tie up his ankles. Deva rolled away to the side and dove to the ground, evading their grasp. He knew the mummy was controlling them, but the way they were turning and reaching out made him think they were acting on their own.

He came to a rest when he knew he was far enough away. He checked his surroundings for any sign of the bandages or any other danger, but all he could see was the thick fog that covered the forest ground, rising to knee level and the treetops. It was getting darker too, which did not help his sight or his confidence. He stared back at Mummy waiting for it to strike once more. To Deva's relief, the mummy didn't move or attack. It waited patiently in the looming dark fog.

What do I do? Deva asked himself for ideas, hoping that Halo would answer his prayer.

Halo didn't respond to Deva's call for help, but Deva did come to a definitive conclusion himself. One that brought him a sour and bittersweet relief. *I can't beat this thing. It's time to leave,* He knew.

With all of the power Deva has and all of the things he could do, Patrick's mind inside has caved from the pressure and failure as the realization set in. His fight or flight response and bravery have been tethering back and forth since the mummy has shown back up. There was some fight response earlier, yet now the flight was too prevalent to ignore. He looked around the forest. *Where is she?*

Deva looked around and jogged through the forest ground looking for Laney, while also keeping a close and focused eye on the mummy and its bandages. He yelled out. "Laney! Laney! Where are you?"

He waited for an answer but never heard her reply. *She must have passed out,* he thought as he continued searching. He stayed low, trying to keep out of view from the mummy, and tiptoed around some trees and through some brush. He peeked his head up above the fog, occasionally checking to see if the mummy had moved. It could strike at any moment. He stayed on high alert as he paced back over to where he thought he last saw the others. Deva squinted and fanned away the fog to check the area. He couldn't find anyone at first but then spotted a pair of black boots on the forest ground. He squatted down and over to the officer, wiping away the fog to see who it was. Before he could tell who it was, he spotted another pair of boots nearby, then saw Conner's face lying in the grass. He quickly checked on Conner and then the first officer. Seeing it to be Officer Stix, Deva stepped over to the other and confirmed it to be Officer Jeffers. He dragged them both over and behind a large tree for cover and safety. Officer Jeffers was unharmed for the most part but was unconscious, presumably from the emotional fog that overwhelmed her. Officer Stix was a different story, his chest was bleeding from the nasty slash he took earlier, as he too was unconscious. Deva could feel Officer Stix's health and life moving away. If Deva didn't do something soon, he may die tonight. Deva rested Officer Stix's head and body down softly on the tree's base. As he did he heard movement nearby. It was faint, but he could hear some dirt and leaves being scraped. Deva turned back from the officers and cautiously stepped towards the movement.

Please be Laney, he hoped.

As he approached he fanned away the fog and peered through for any sign of Laney. He stepped closer and closer until he got a visual. He looked down to see the same black boots as the other officers. *Damn it!* Deva thought, as he crouched down to Alex, who was on her hands and knees. Deva saw she was awake, but distant as he put a hand on her shoulder to stabilize her.

"Alex hey, it's me… it's Patrick"

Alex looked up to him slowly with her mouth agape from exhaustion, then back down to the ground. "What the hell...was that?" she said with fatigue.

Deva looked down at her and felt the guilt once again. "I'm sorry Alex… I know how it feels. You're going to feel really bad for a while, but it will end, I promise."

Deva lifted her arms over his shoulder and hoisted her up to her feet. "For now though, I'm going to put you over here with the others."

"They were hit too?" Alex asked.

"Yeah not like you though, those bandages are... different." Deva said as he set her down with the others. He looked over the group of his unconscious comrades. *This has gotten out of hand again,* he thought.

"What are you going to do?" Alex asked.

Deva could tell she was starting to regain her mental health by the way her eyes looked up to him. Deva sighed. "I have to find Laney, she's out there somewhere"

"Do you think that thing has her?" Alex asked.

Deva looked over to it and saw it still standing docile in the thick fog, he shook his head. "If it did... I think we would know. Things would be getting weird"

"Weirder than this?" Alex said jokingly.

Deva didn't catch the joke and was once again consumed with grief and remorse. Alex must have felt his mood change because she offered up her inspiration. "Hey I'm joking; I knew the risks" She said as she looked over to the others. "We all did… this isn't your fault" She turned back to Deva. "Now go find Laney...and get her back to the orphanage, I'll watch over Conner"

Deva nodded. "If I find her and run, that thing will probably follow. Then I'll be back for you guys… I promise"

Alex smiled weakly. "Go," she instructed, as she stood up and walked over to Conner.

Deva turned and continued through the fog, waving away and blowing it aside. Ugh, *what was she wearing, again?* Deva wondered and crouched through the fog. From the corner of his eye he caught sight of something moving, before he could truly see what it was, it

241

darted straight for him. Quickly, Deva realized it was the bandages zeroing in on him. Deva molded a short sword and sliced at the incoming cloth. He tore through it as another reached out for him, then another, then another. With an intense ferocity, Deva cut through each and every one that came close. He leapt away, looking around for any more. He could see the mummy standing far and away, but the bandages seemed to camouflage into the fog, which made the task of locating Laney more difficult. Up from his feet struck another bandage, it quickly wrapped around his ankle and pulled. Deva kept his balance and cut himself free, then jumped into the air. He jumped high enough to be clear from the fog and also to see the entire field. As he was airborne, he scanned for Laney, but his vision was cut short as more bandages flew up to entangle. Deva molded his sword into a disc and launched it down at the incoming bandage missiles. The disc flew and cut down through the bandages, stopping their progress for him. He fell back to the ground safely and felt the frustration and anger building as each minute passed. He contemplated an idea before realizing the only course of action was to continue walking in search of her.

Deva molded two swords and held each one in hand, ready to slice at any incoming threat. He stepped quietly through the fog, pacing through and listening for any sign of movement. Deva listened carefully, but couldn't hear anything. He listened for anything, crickets, birds, leaves, and even the wind, but he heard nothing. The silence turned deafening, as Deva tried to tune it out with a laser-like focus for Laney. He brushed away more fog. *Or are they emotions?* He wondered. Stepping through the fog, his nerves began to rack up as his breathing became more unsteady. He checked through brushes and combed through the forest ground, trying not to miss any spots.

"Patrick" A voice from nearby called out.

"Laney?" Deva said as he recognized her voice.

Without a second thought, Deva stood up and ran over to where he heard the voice. He got to where he thought it came from and looked around. He didn't see her, but he spotted a shoe. He bent down to examine it, picking it up to see a small purple shoe. *These are Laney's,* he remembered as he looked around again for her.

"Laney," he said halfway between a whisper and normal volume and waited.

"Patrick" Laney's voice whispered back from behind a tree nearby.

Deva heard it and crouched over, getting to the tree, he peeked around for Laney. To his surprise, she wasn't there. Deva walked around the tree looking for Laney and as soon as he dropped his guard, he was slammed face-first into the tree. He felt a tightly wrapped bandage on his back pinning him to the tree, as he pushed off for freedom.

It was a trap? He thought.

Deva muscled off from the tree, trying to loosen the hold. As he was making progress, another bandage slammed around him, immobilizing him on the tree. He felt the pressure building on his back, and it continued to build as Deva thought pictured himself snapping in half. Tighter and tighter the bandages got. Before Deva could scream out, the pressure from the bandages snapped through the tree, cutting it in half. There was a loud snap as the tree collapsed down to the ground. Deva got pulled away from the falling tree, but he was completely tied up again. Slowly, he was lifted through the air, and back towards the mummy. Deva could see it starting to move now as he approached. Closer and closer Deva got, as the mummy began to slowly open its mouth. Deva fought and struggled to get loose once again, seeing the creature's large black mouth expand. He was lifted over to the mummy's face as the bandages around Deva's throat began to tense up. Deva felt this time was different.

No visions this time, Halo's mind echoed in Patrick's mind.

The bandages began to get tighter as his airways closed up and his lungs fought for air. His arms and legs thrashed out, as his body fought for life. *I can't give up,* He thought as he continued to shake and choke, his eyes began to wince as his head pounded on itself. His lungs filled with fire as he watched the mummy's face staring ominously at him. Patrick's eyes inside the suit began to wink and his vision slowly began to fade. Before Deva could close his eyes for good, his body fell to the ground. Deva gasped for air and coughed out. Half-awake, Deva watched as the mummy staggered backward. It reached for its head with its bandaged hands and let out a terrible wail. At first, it was a high-pitched screech, but it changed into what Deva related to a whale call. Its low-pitched hum boomed through the forest. Deva looked on seeing the mummy scratching at its head.

What's happening? Deva wondered.

The fog slowly began to fade from the forest ground as Deva watched the mummy creature stumble. It let out another echoed boom from its mouth as it slowly began to float into the air. Deva watched in shock, preparing himself for another attack, yet the mummy continued to slam and scratch at its head, as it rose and rose until it reached the treetops. The fog followed it into the air, leaving the ground visible. Deva looked around for any sight of Laney and was pleased to see her standing nearly ten feet behind where he laid.

"Laney," he said urgently, as he slid over to her.

Her eyes were open, as she stared up at the mummy high in the sky. Deva looked at her emotionless face, as her skin turned pale and blue.

"Laney," he said again, weaker, as he looked into her glazed, unmoving eyes.

Deva touched her shoulders gently to get a reaction. *Her skin is so cold*, he thought as he shook her slightly. Laney's body began to lean off base and toppled lifelessly towards the ground. Deva caught her as she fell, and set her down on the ground. He placed her head slowly on the ground and looked at her, waiting for her to move or even blink. Deva heard the mummy high above the trees moaning as Alex jogged over to join them. Without speaking, she knelt beside Deva and immediately inspected Laney and began CPR. In between compression sets, Alex questioned Deva.

"What happened?"

Before he could answer, the mummy wailed again. It howled out in seeming agony as it started emitting a thick fog from its body. Deva and Alex briefly looked up to see the outpouring of fog and smoke spread through the sky. They both returned to Laney as Alex questioned Deva again.

"Patrick, what happened to her? She has no heartbeat!"

Deva looked down at Laney as he slowly realized that he failed her. He couldn't find her and he couldn't save her. *You let her die.*

"Patrick!" Alex said louder, snapping him to attention. He met her stare. "What happened to her?" she asked again urgently.

"I don't kn—" Deva began to say then stopped mid-sentence. He lifted his head and looked up to the sky at mummy. He rotated to look back at Alex and then down to Laney's body. "I think I know," he said, looking down sadly at her precious face as his heart began breaking to pieces.

High above the forest, the mummy continued to spill out its emotional fog. It completely covered the sky above the forest causing waves of darkness to roll over the trees. It continued to float farther away and farther out, spreading like a thunderstorm over the city. After a few minutes, the clouds of emotion reached the city and covered it in a storm high above. The people of the city watched as the clouds began to flash like lightning and build up so thick that the sky turned chalk black. Loud cracks and booms came from within the high above the fog, scaring patrons below as they scrambled indoors.

On the other side of the city, in the neighboring ocean of hills and forest, a burly chested, bearded man with a chain wrapped around his waist slammed an ax through a log, splitting it in half with ease. He stopped to look up to the sky, seeing the powerful and menacing-looking storm wash over the sky. His eyes flared with anger and purpose as he turned to his younger travel partner, a thin, dark-haired boy of about fifteen years old, who stepped up closer. They shared a concerned look before they jumped into action, heading towards the city.

"Patrick, what do you know? Is she...gone?" Alex asked. "She's breathing, but—" Alex paused, either from adrenaline or fear, Deva couldn't tell. "But she has no heartbeat and she's so cold and pale"

Deva looked down to Alex, who was caressing Laney's face. Deva couldn't see her face but he knew she was tearing up. *She paused for fear,* Deva thought, as he stared into Alex's emotions above her head, swirling and fanning above. Staring into her emotions, he lost himself as he let his mind go. He understood now that by looking into other people's emotions, he could piece together his own.

"I don't know," he said quietly.

"What?"

"I don't know if she's gone or not, but... I know where I can look," Deva said, as he looked up to the mummy high in the sky, lashing and flailing around.

"Where?" Alex asked, staring into his mystical dark blue eyes.

Deva, without answering, continued to look up at the mummy, and pointed softly to the sky.

Chapter 34

It's a special type of torture, watching someone you've loved and cared for a fight a battle that cannot and will not be won. Patrick knew that, he's felt and experienced that torture before. He looked down at Laney in disbelief and hopeful optimism. He refused to accept that she was gone. Although her body had gone cold and soulless, he knew her mind was stranded, and that it was ready to return to life.

She saved my life, I have to do the same.

He turned back to the sky looking up to the epicenter of the thick, billowing fog, locating the mummy scratch and claw at its head in agony, trying to shake free of Laney's mental clutches. The fog was spreading quickly and the sky began to shade to black and maroon. Under the thick clouds, Patrick and Alex's vision was blurred and dark. He could still make out objects and people but it's as if they're in a dim red lamp shining through the clouds. He looked at Alex, seeing her face is a third of the way covered by shadow, with a slice of dark red over her right eye. Although his vision was impaired he could still see and feel the fear and anxiety through her eyes. Deva turned away knowing his eyes are easy to see and didn't want Alex to see them. As he does, Alex knelt back down to Laney looking over her face the best she can through the darkness.

"So... this went horribly" A voice from out in front of them said through the darkness. Deva looked over and lit the area up a bit with Halo. Over the illuminated area, they see its Officers, Stix and Jeffers. As they approached, Deva looked at Officer. Stix, noting a healthier-looking walk and Officer. Jeffers was carrying Conner on her back as she approached.

"Hey guys," Alex said, as enthusiastically as she could manage at this moment. She looks at Officer Stix.

"Kenny, are you okay?"

"Yeah I'm good," He said, sounding strong.

"You really looked like shit earlier" Alex remarked.

Kenny's face shifted to a look of burlesque. Alex noticed the switch and tried to save herself. "But I am really glad you're okay"

He lightened back up, not trying to make a big deal of it. "Yeah though, honestly, I got super tired earlier and was just like, falling asleep..." He sighed heavily before continuing. ."..I really thought I was dying...but then I just woke up! And I feel—" he chuckled. "I feel amazing" He gave Alex and Deva a thumbs up and said. "Two thumbs up for you guys"

Alex shot a glance at Deva then looked away. Deva neither turned nor walked away. He stayed looking at Officer. Stix, but wasn't focused on him. He was frozen in thought, worrying about Laney.

"But what's happening?" Officer Stix asked, looking back to Deva.

Officer. Jeffers shook her head and walked closer to Alex. She saw Laney lying flat on the ground. "What happened to her?" She asked as she leaned down beside Alex.

Looking at Laney's pale face, Alex saw a strand of Laney's dark brown hair over her face. She brushed the hair off and tucked it behind her ear. Officer Jeffers put a hand on Alex's shoulder as she looked down with her. Officer. Stix noticed Laney on the ground too and realized he should tame down the enthusiasm. He sank away and retreated into the shadows of the group, not wanting to draw any more attention. Deva looked to the sky as the group sat in the following silence from Officer Jeffers's question. Deva was completely content with the silence, and the stewing tension, but he decided he should tell them. They need to know what happened to her, and they need to know what he's going to do about it. He closed his eyes to take another moment to himself. Taking a deep breath, he turned to the others, to where Laney lay and prepared his words. He watched over the group and looked them all in the eyes. First, he looked at Alex, she stared back with hope in her eyes. He looked over to Officer. Stix and give him a nod. Although Officer. Stix has proven to be goofy and borderline incompetent, he showed up, and that's all that mattered. He looks over to Officer. Jeffers. Throughout the night Deva has noticed the bond they all share. They don't just work together. They weren't just thrown into this ragtag team. These weren't just cops that came to save a child, they were friends. *Alex brought her friends,* Patrick understood.

Deva scanned the group again, then away to the ground after. Before he could start his speech, a quick thought flew across his mind. *Did I just see another set of eyes?*

Deva looked behind the group and saw Conner rubbing at his left eye.

"Conner!" Deva said with enthusiasm as he jogged over. The others turned in confusion behind them, as Deva got to him and lowered himself down. "Hey Conner, are you alright? Do you feel okay?" he asked, but then quickly noticed the change in Connors's facial expression. Conner leaned away a little, looking to the Police officers around him for safety. Patrick stood back up and backed off, taking a step away. Alex noticed and knelt to Conner.

"Hey Conner, you're okay now. My name is Alex, and we're with the police" she said as she gestured to the others next to him. She looked at Conner and then swiveled her head around to Deva. "And this," she said while standing up, "this is Deva, he came to help us find you."

Conner gazed up to Deva as his eyes grew wider and wider. "Are you the angel superhero? From the city?"

Deva paused for a second before answering. *What do I tell him?* he wondered.

Deva nodded solemnly to Conner as an answer.

Alex shot Deva a look before returning her attention to Conner. "You are okay though, right? I mean you look good...physically" she said as she inspected the back of Conner's head. He didn't flinch, keeping his full attention draped over Deva, he looked on in amazement.

"Yeah I feel fine," he said in a trance-like state. He stared deep into Deva's large blue eyes, and they stared back.

Should I tell him?

Deva turned away, and paced back towards the wood line, illuminating his circled area. Conner's eyes followed as he took in the suit in more detail. The glowing of the rope and the light coming from his suit made Conner feel a warmth he has never felt. His entire body heated up and hugged him softly. Goosebumps ran across his spine, reaching to the top of his head. A warm, happy smile came across his face as he looked at Deva's aura. The feelings were too strong; he couldn't help it and looked away. As he looked away from Deva's direction he spotted a pair of familiar pink shoes. He blinked his eyes quickly, trying to regain his vision. He rubbed them lightly before standing to his feet. Before anyone in the group realized, Conner began to walk over. With each step he took, he got a clearer and more depressing sight. Just as he saw her face, Deva noticed him, looking down in shock at Laney lying on the ground. Deva watched as Conner's already monotone emotions swirled and stirred over his head, becoming a darker mix. *That's not good*, Deva thought as he approached Conner slowly. Conner has taken a knee to be closer to Laney and Deva knelt beside him. After a silent moment of watching Conner look at Laney, he knew he must console him. Before he had the chance, Conner turned to him.

"Why is she here?"

Deva slowly turned from Conner's stare, looking to Laney. "She wanted to rescue you"

Conner stared into Deva's large blue eyes, but upon hearing Deva's words, he looked back to Laney's still, pale face. "Is she dead?" asked Conner, with a maturity that surprised him. Conner didn't turn to look at Deva, keeping his eyes fixed on Laney, awaiting an answer.

"No," Deva said. "No she isn't."

Conner's eyes shifted to Deva. "Then why isn't she waking up?"

Deva felt the tension and anxiety coming from Conner. His emotions quickly seeped through into Deva's head. He could feel everyone's emotions. He was a sponge, letting everyone's emotions wash into his own, and it was becoming stronger now, his empathy. He was proud of the way he could feel and understand people without ever speaking with them. Even before his mom died, he could always relate and empathize with people. It wasn't a hard thing to learn, understand or deliver. But now, things were different, now things felt different. He stepped away from the group, looking up into thick emotions high overhead.

"I'm so sorry, Conner," Deva said, watching the mummy. "I will get her back"

"How?" Alex asked.

"It's a long, weird story, Alex," He said as he turned his attention to her and the other officers. "But I do want to say, thank you, thank you to you all. You risked your life tonight to save Conner...and for that I—" Deva nodded. "I am so grateful for that" Deva looked down to Conner, who still looked spooked. "And thank you, Conner. You don't know it but, you saved my life tonight too, so thank you"

Deva turned away, grateful for the fact he hid behind a mask. *I almost told him*, he thought as he closed his eyes. He built up his energy, feeling the warm, glowing veins spread out across his body. He felt it reach to his fingers tips and down to his toes. He imagined levitation, and felt his body surging slowly into the air. He opened his eyes and ascended into the sky, reaching higher and higher, up over the treetops. He levitated closer to the mummy who seemed to be done with its outbursts. Deva reached the mummy, watching it spasm and jerk as the bandages swim around it. Deva stared at the fowl mummy creature, taking in its presence and lack of feelings. *Loneliness can be warm sometimes*, he thought as he shut his eyes and floated over. His mind arrived at the mummy creatures as he prepared to float into its presence. Before he did, Deva's feelings saw the mummy for what it is. Out of the bandages, Deva sees an eye peeking out, looking for help.

He's like you, remember?

Patrick teared up, knowing what he was about to do, which could be the last thing he ever remembered. He embarked into the mummy creature's mind, shutting his own, hoping that will make it easier. He felt the mummy's presence all around him, as he grabbed onto the passing moment and he took the step.

Alex, Conner and the officers watched as Deva and the mummy creature collided in the air. There was an explosion of light, but before it could erupt, it folded and vacuumed back into itself. A sudden crack and boom occured before dust and smoke filled the area high above. Alex didn't take her eyes away until something fell from the black dust. She caught a slight of something very small, falling very quickly toward the earth. *That's not Deva*, she recognized as she checked the sky for him. She never saw anything but ran over to check on her group. Conner coughed, then looked to the officers.

"Where did they go?"

Please help me…

Patrick came aware, once more staring into dark and cold nothing. He heard his breath and felt his heartbeat, so he knew he was awake. He took a step forward and heard the soft ripple of water underneath his shoe. He took another, knowing he was inside the mummy creature's mind. *This is what mine was like, before. But this isn't mine now, it shouldn't be*, he remembered.

A loud crack of thunder snapped from behind him, causing him to turn and suddenly see whose mind he was inhabiting. In front of him, sitting on a wooden bench, sat a young boy, with fiery red hair, staring off into the black nothing. The two shared a long, intimate look as Patrick approached from behind. A thought, notion and some guidance raced through Patrick's mind as he spoke softly to the boy.

"If I could stop one heart from breaking, I shall not live in vain"

"If I can ease one life the aching, or cool one pain" The boy continued the poem softly as he continued to stare into the ocean of darkness.

Patrick continued the poem as the words found themselves without searching. "Or help one fainting robin, unto his nest again...I shall not live in vain"

Patrick finished and slowly lowered himself down and sat beside the boy on the bench. Patrick took a deep breath, looked at the boy, and placed his hand on the boy's shoulder. They both sat in silence, taking the moment in until the boy spoke to Patrick.

"Why are you here?"

To be continued...

CPSIA information can be obtained
at www.ICGtesting.com
Printed in the USA
LVHW031257101121
702937LV00003B/241